PIERCE ME

A CONSPIRACY OF RAVENS BOOK ONE

SHELBY LEE

table of contents

author's note

Pierce Me is a dark, romantic suspense novel that contains triggering situations. It is a why choose novel, meaning our heroine does not ever have to choose between our three heroes. This book is intended for mature audiences 18+ and contains the word 'fuck' probably far too many times.

For a full content warning list, please visit:
https://linktr.ee/authorshelbylee

Quick but important note about Chapter 9: It involves a full non-con scene between three of our main characters. This chapter was hard enough to write, edit, and publish, and *will* be hard for some to read. Note that you CAN skip over it, and I have also provided a full page break beforehand as an extra warning. Please take care of yourselves out there.

Shout out to all of the misogynists, narcissists, bigots. To the patriarchy, the cheaters, the abusers.

I self-edited, self-published, and self-promoted this work of absolute amazing art...

IN SPITE OF YOU ALL.

So fuck you, and thank you for the inspirational fodder I've used you for.

If the above shoes do not fit you, welcome to this wonderful world I've created. It's going to be a great fucking time from here on out.

FIVE MONTHS AGO

About a month ago, my mother died. Barely minutes after, the last words out of my mouth were "Goodbye Mom".

I haven't spoken since.

No one can explain the onset of the mutism, only that the events leading up to it caused my brain to short circuit.

I allowed the doctors to pull the plug on my dying mother while also telling her I'd continue on. That still feels like a lie to this day.

Told Pierce Jackson I don't love him; also a lie.

My words became toxic little weapons and my brain decided we wouldn't use them anymore.

Unfortunately, everyone is still unsure why I'm unable to make sounds in general.

Now, a month later, I'm cleaning out my mother's home, set to stay at a mental health facility where some stranger can potentially diagnose and attempt to "fix" me. Unsure if it'll work, but hey, I've got nothing better to do now that I'm alone.

"But in the end," Henry's saying as I tune back in to him, "whatever you want to do with all of this paperwork is up to you, Miss Hill. As your mother's attorney, I'd advise you to keep them for at least seven years."

I nod as I rub my throat, continuing to sift through the paperwork with my free hand. It's not as if my throat hurts, it's just so strange to feel what's there and know it doesn't work right anymore.

"Miss Hill?" Henry places his hand on my arm, scaring me and I jump a little. I watch as the pieces of paper I was holding fall to the floor and scatter everywhere. "I'm sorry. I didn't mean to startle you," he says. "Do you need to take a seat?"

Shaking my head, I squat to clean up the scattered pages, blinking back tears as I note my mother's name over all of them. Nothing was ever truly sent to me. Not in the traditional sense.

My childhood best friend and I would send letters back and forth, one each per summer, but those were never mailed. No stamps in the corners. No addresses. Just our names written on the outside.

I blow out a breath, grabbing for a piece of paper that had slid underneath my mother's bed. What I pulled out would have brought me to the floor if I wasn't already on it. As it is, I fell to my butt and gripped the envelope tightly as I read the outside.

To: Miss Raven Hill
From: the Scholarship and Admissions Office of
**   Cobalt University**

No fucking way would I open this with the lawyer present. I stand up with the other papers in my hand, and place the letter addressed to me off to the side, quickly sliding it underneath my purse.

Looking toward Henry again, I tilted my head and shrugged, hoping he'd get the silent communication. I had not a fucking clue what he was talking about. He looked peeved, to be honest, but I couldn't quite care at this moment. I wanted to look at the letter, and afterward I wanted to sleep in my bed for what would be the last time for three months.

"As I said," he snapped, taking a deep breath before continuing. *Good choice, dude.* "I will be going through most of this paperwork and filing it away properly with my offices. Otherwise, any personal documentation not concerning finances will be boxed up for you and left here. There is a key available to you for the safety deposit box the late Miss Hill had bought many years ago."

I continue to nod along as he speaks, placing the personal documents in one box and financial in another. Bills, shut-off notices, and such went to Henry. They would figure out what to do with the life insurance money I'd be receiving upon my high school graduation in May. I already had a trust fund from when my father died when I was five. It opened up when I turned 18 last July.

Orphaned at 18. What a time to be alive.

Note the sarcasm.

"Alright then," Henry said, clearly impatient with me at this point.

Pick a number, dickhead.

"Drop those off on your way out of town tomorrow morning. Miss Hill," he spoke softly.

I nod again in reply, flinching slightly when he places his hand on my arm. He tries to comfort me with eye contact. Not likely. "I truly am sorry for your loss, and I hope you're able to find some semblance of healing in therapy."

He leaves swiftly, leaving me alone with the remnants of my mother's life, all of the paperwork staring back at me like they could sense my external and internal panic. A task like this, although large, should be easy to compartmentalize, but I truly could not figure out how neurotypical people did that.

So instead of doing the task I need to do, I pull out the envelope from Cobalt University, give myself a paper cut by opening it so damn fast, and plop myself on my bed with my legs crossed. I feel like a kid with candy, but I'm filled with both dread and elation to have it, because, hey, *finally I got to have some*!

After opening the papers inside, I unfolded them and held them out in front of me, scanning the pages with more excitement than I thought I should have after losing my last living relative.

> ***Dear Raven,***
>
> ***We are pleased to announce to you that you have been accepted into the Arts program at Cobalt University. Please find attached news of a scholarship that has also been awarded to you, should you accept the conditions.***

I quickly blinked back the tears falling from my eyes. Surely, my luck wasn't good enough to be accepted into CU, much less with a scholarship offer. Wiping the tears from my eyes with the sleeve of my black hoodie, I quickly turned the page and took in the scholarship conditions. It offered a full ride; books, room, and board. It would cover all four years at CU so long as I fulfilled one year of the terms laid out on the final page. Flipping to said page, I took in a deep breath as I continued to read.

TERMS AND CONDITIONS:
1. Serve for one year as the Alpha Mu Secretary.
2. This includes building up their reputation and keeping it in good standing with the Board of Education at Cobalt University.
3. Outside of serving as Alpha Mu Secretary, report to the current Alpha Mu President for volunteer work on an as needed basis.
4. Obtain and maintain grades at or above a 3.5 GPA.
5. Maintain attendance at or above 75%.
6. Remain in good legal standing.

I blink furiously, staring at the paper with my head cocked to the side. This would have made me nearly pass out in excitement before I lost everything.

I exhale loudly, flopping back on the bed, staring at the ceiling.

There's no way I could fulfill the terms of this scholarship now...

Right?

raven

"Welcome to Cobalt University!" A young looking blonde screams.

Not saying I'm not young, I simply feel like I'm far older thanks to *trauma*.

The girl looks at me expectantly, and I smile at her, nodding toward the office behind her, the one I'm supposed to be entering to begin this journey of being a 'Fraternity Secretary'.

It seems sexist. It probably will be, honestly, but whatever gets me a free ride at this point. My mother's life insurance policy has been held up for some reason, and while the attorneys are hard at work on it, it's still not in my pockets right now.

"Okay then," the girl says, clearly uncomfortable that I haven't responded to her. I'm too tired to explain the traumatic mutism to her, so I don't. "Well, Mr. Langston is inside and he will walk you toward the apartment building after a short tour. You're expected to be at the Alpha Mu summer party tonight."

She stops speaking, looking at me expectantly. She shrugs

before leaning in and whispering to me. "Just so you're aware, they are on their fourth warning right now. If they mess up one more time, well, they're out permanently. Mr. Langston can tell you more about that, however." She opens the door, smiles far too brightly and waves me in with a high-pitched "Good Luck!"

Rolling my eyes, I plaster a bright fake smile on my face as I enter the room, patting down my black pencil skirt and adjusting the sleeves on my cream-colored blouse. Immediately I'm on guard. The man sitting behind the desk looks far too excited to see me.

He shoots up from his chair behind the desk, grinning wildly and reaching his hand over the top. My hand clasps with his, and I inwardly cringe at how clammy his hand is as it runs across mine. The handshake goes on for way too long, but I allow my eyes to meet his deep blue ones, maintaining eye contact until he finally releases my hand and sits back down, gesturing for me to do the same.

"Miss Hill, I am so incredibly pleased to meet you," he says joyfully. Loudly, too.

Wiping my hands on my skirt to dry them off, I sit down, crossing one leg over the other and keeping my eyes on his face. I try not to meet his eyes again, as eye contact makes me so incredibly nervous.

He clears his throat after waiting for me to respond, clearly forgetting the letter I wrote to him while in therapy explaining my sudden condition. "Ah, sorry, it will take some getting used to you not being able to speak to me. I'll give you my phone number so you can text me often, keeping me up to date on your status and the work you do for Alpha Mu. And with that," he opens up the large folder laying on his desk, "let's get the last of your paperwork done. Afterwards, we can introduce you to the President and the two Vice Presidents. They're impatiently waiting to meet the person who is going to help turn their reputation around."

His grin is creepy, but I nod in reply as I lean forward to read the paperwork as he presents it to me. It's as if centuries pass when I finally sign the last of the documents and he closes it up. I am so incredibly relieved when we stand and leave his stuffy little office.

"Alright, so you have the map in your hands, your key to your apartment, and some of the fraternity will help unload your car as soon as you're introduced. So, off we go," he says, waving his hand out of the front door, and I exit ahead of him.

It's only a ten minute walk from the admin building to Greek Row, but in these heels? By the time we walk up the stairs of the Alpha Mu building, I'm in an immeasurable amount of pain.

The house is made up of old bricks and basic white accents, much like a typical frat house you'd see in the movies. There's an actual hoard of lawn flamingos in the front yard, and I have to hide a snicker behind a cough. I'm supposed to be here to help the boys. I say boys because it's clear they aren't men. I'm not here to encourage their childish behavior. I can hear the voices inside of the building, but they quiet when Mr. Langston enters with me behind him.

"Boys," he greets them, shifting to the side to show my nearly shaking frame. I'm a complete introvert, and I hate social situations, so this is a terrifying moment for me. "Meet your new Secretary, Miss Raven Hill. At this point, you answer to her. Clean yourselves up. I will not allow Alpha Mu to go down under your screw ups."

A chorus of 'yes sir's' echoes around the room, before Mr. Langston turns toward me with a smile on his face. "The president will be down in a moment. I believe he is in a meeting. You have my number, so please let me know of anything you need. Anything, Miss Hill," he implores. I nod once more, and chew on my lip, wringing my hands together in front of myself. He pats me on the shoulder before walking out of the door without another glance.

And I'm left in what could be classed as a wolf's den. I'm here for slaughter, not for work. I may be better off just...not doing this, right?

Those thoughts are broken when a set of footsteps–three sets–descend the stairs.

Boots–that's the first thing I notice. All three are wearing slightly altered styles of combat boots on their feet, all leather. Two of them are tied up tight, but one has them half undone, which is curious but I shrug it off as I trail my eyes higher. One set of black jeans with holes in them, another wearing black jeans–sans holes–and the third is wearing faded blue jeans. That guy is the one with his shoes half undone. I notice all three of them are wearing black leather jackets, open and showing their attire underneath.

The first guy, wearing the blue jeans and blue shirt, has a shit eating grin on his face. His hair is dirty blonde and a mix of long and short, with the long portion of his hair falling over his right eye and cascading down half of his face. His eyes are gray, almost like the sky before a storm. He's absolutely gorgeous, and his smile grows when he sees me.

The second guy, wearing the black button down, looks serious, almost like he's deep in concentration, and his jaw is ticking in anger. There's what looks like an angel on his throat, at least the wings of an angel. I can't see much more from here. His hair is in a knot at the top of his head, and the deep shade of black offsets his brown eyes. Those eyes are so warm, and

I'm struggling to breathe. I recognize him from the mental health facility that I spent three months in from January to April. His eyes don't show a hint of surprise at seeing me here.

Did he know about the job offer when we were in therapy? Is that why he encouraged it in our group sessions?

The third and final guy stops me in my tracks. I find myself slack jawed as I look at him, taking in his curly black hair and familiar forest green eyes. His square jaw covered in stubble, those kissable lips. Lips I've kissed many times.

Pierce Jackson, my childhood best friend turned lover only to implode when shit got hard.

In this moment...I do not want to be here anymore.

I refuse to be under any sort of contract where my ex best friend is in charge of me. I broke his fucking heart, and I have the smallest of inklings he might break my soul in return.

Turning on my heel, I try to leave but run into the broad chest of one of the other frat boys. I panic, trying to slide under his arm to escape this shitty situation. He doesn't allow my escape, however. I hear Pierce Jackson's voice clear as day when he says "Restrain her. We have a lot to talk about, and I need her to shut her fucking mouth for this conversation."

I'm turned around and am forced to look up into the eyes of my childhood sweetheart. Pierce Jackson looks down at me as he enters my personal space, the look he is giving me so full of hate. I'd fall down if not for the guy behind me. He holds me close to his chest, wraps one arm around my torso, and brings a hand to cover my mouth.

If I was curious about whether or not Mr. Langston told them about my mutism, I'm certain now that he, in fact, did not divulge that information.

Fucking great, now they're going to think I'm being a cold-hearted bitch.

Pierce's hand comes out and wraps around my throat, the toes of his boots touching the toes of my heels. I'm breathing heavily at this point, the panic obvious in my stance, sweat building on my brow. I'm struggling to hold eye contact with him, but that doesn't bother him. He squeezes lightly around my throat and brings his nose to mine and forces me to meet his gaze.

Now call me crazy, but with the precarious situation I've found myself in, I don't want to test the hands that bind me right now, so I don't attempt to free myself.

"Listen here, little bird." I flinch at the nickname, one he gave me so long ago out of love and nothing more. "Not a single soul answers to you. In fact," he snarls, and I try to back away, only to panic more when I can't move an inch. "You answer to every single person in Alpha Mu, until further notice. You do as they ask, when they ask, and you don't speak a goddamn word to anyone. Do you understand?"

He lets my throat go, backing away to take me in. I nod, letting out a breath when the guy behind me releases my mouth. Pierce holds his hand up as if to stop me from speaking, which is absolutely frustrating at this point. He wouldn't listen even if I could let him know I'm mute. He's on some high horse he refuses to get off of.

"Boys," his voice rises, "everything except sexual favors is on the table. Those," his lips curve up into a wicked grin, "are saved for the VPs and me. Got it?" He looks around, waiting for the affirmatives to echo around the room. "Good. River?"

The second guy, the one in blue jeans, comes up, nearly tripping on his undone laces and cursing as he lifts them to look at the traitorous objects. "Yeah, PJ?" He grins when Pierce raises a brow dangerously at him.

"Take Miss Hill to her apartment and grab whatever you

think is necessary. We've got a cage for the little bird set up and ready to go, after all." His cruel grin slides to me and I must look a sight, because he cracks a laugh before waving his blonde friend toward me.

Turning around Pierce grabs the third guy, the one I recognize from therapy, by the arm. Those chocolate eyes hold mine captive for a moment before he turns in the direction that they eventually disappear into. Surely he knows what I've been through at this point, and he won't allow this to stand.

But as the blonde guy pulls me under his arm and walks us out of the frat house, I realize for the first time in forever...I am utterly alone in my own misery.

HOURS LATER, half of my stuff has been loaded out of my car and into some random guy's truck, and unloaded again into a room at the frat house. I had no choice in where it went. I was kept busy, forced to clean up the kitchen and make a meal for the entire frat house.

That's around 30 guys, by the way.

So I made a huge batch of spaghetti and meatballs, thankful they had the materials to make it in the first place. Someone stocked up, and I'd like to thank them.

It's been quiet around me, aside from random jeers and catcalls. Like these boys haven't seen a woman ever before. I roll my eyes when another guy comes and leans against the counter. He's cute, but the cocky demeanor makes him instantly ugly. A nice personality goes a long ass way, and I'm disappointed in ninety percent of the men here.

The other ten percent revolves around acceptance of River. He may be under Pierce, but he's been nothing but kind to me.

He cracks dumb jokes, and he may have made a few cracks about my ass, but he's not super disrespectful about it. He held the doors open for me wherever we went, and showed me to the kitchen, showcasing where everything was put away so that I wasn't left alone in a long search for necessary items.

The dumb ass sitting against the counter leans forward and tilts my chin up, grinning wide after I glare at him. I go to slap his hand away, but someone else beats me to it, removing him entirely from my personal space. The other Vice President, the one with black hair wearing the black button down, is the one helping me. I don't understand who it is until I'm staring at the way he has the douchebag pinned to the wall next to the fridge.

"Don't fucking touch her," he says, his voice so low and husky making my body shiver involuntarily. I bite my lip and look around the room, noticing random eyes peering inside the kitchen with various levels of amusement. When I look back at the men, I see those chocolate eyes are boring into the guy. "The Prez said to keep your filthy fucking paws to yourself. Now you get to take bathroom cleaning duty from Miss Hill for the next 24 hours."

He releases the guy, who promptly falls to the floor and curses in embarrassment, "Yes, VP. Got it."

Pointing, the VP glares at the guy until he takes off out of the kitchen. Those chocolate eyes are on me and they soften a smidgen as he crosses the room toward me, his fingers brushing over my chin where the other guy touched me. "Sorry about his behavior, Red," he says.

I met this guy when I was an inpatient at the hospital a town over from here. His story is as traumatic, if not more, than mine. I'd wanted to hug him countless times in group, but we were so discouraged from interacting with the opposite sex that I tried not to interact with anyone not presenting as female.

My mouth is open wide as I take him and the scene in. He nudges it closed with a simple nudge of his index finger.

He's grinning when I manage to look at him long enough to notice. "Phoenix West," he says, introducing himself. "We've met. I'm so sorry for your loss. However, I am incredibly glad that you took the leap to come here after all." He brushes a finger across my lower lip, and I blink a few times. Am I in some sort of alternate universe?

My little daydream is broken, however, when Phoenix's eyes harden at something over my shoulder. He lets me go and backs away a few steps, his eyes meeting mine. He's angry now, but for what reason?

"Like I was saying, hopefully those noodles aren't under *or* overcooked, or there will be consequences, Red." Phoenix's voice is low and dangerous, though loud enough for whoever is behind me to hear it. Regret shines in his gaze before he turns and walks out of the kitchen.

"I see you've made friends already, little bird," Pierce says from behind me, his fingers trailing up my arm and to the back of my neck. He brushes my hair aside and grips me in one hand, his head coming near mine as he growls in my ear. "Don't get too friendly with anyone here. Those closest to me know how the bitch from my small town absolutely shredded me, and they'll be out for vengeance on my behalf."

He shoves me forward, forcing me to catch myself on the fridge, and my wrists twist painfully in response. I sniffle, trying to keep any tears at bay. This new version of him is my fault, and I refuse to cry over the monster that I created with my lies.

It's only fair now that I am here and facing his wrath.

"Dinner looks like it's almost done, so I'll have the boys come get some. Your cone of silence remains, little bird, and you best fucking keep it up." His forest green eyes meet my deep blue ones, and I swallow hard as I watch him tap the door frame before he walks out of the room.

The tears still try to fall, but fail. Unlike my shattered heart which turns to dust in the moment.

pierce

"Boys, dinner is ready. Eat the fuck up and leave the mess for the little bird," I announce as I walk into the den, looking for signs of Phoenix and River. One is on my shit list, and the other created said list with his stupid ass jokes a long time ago.

Don't get me wrong, I love the boys, for some reason, but they're trying to be nice to Raven and I refuse to allow it. There will be no way they treat her with any kindness. They, of all people, know she doesn't deserve it.

"Yo, PJ," River yells, coming up to me and patting me on the back. He's grinning wide, his eyes filled with mirth.

"Don't fuckin' call me that, Riv or I'll cut your nuts off and feed them to Jimmy." I push him off of me, grab him by the bicep, and drag him toward the corner of the room where Phoenix is sitting. Pushing River down onto the love seat near Phoenix, I stand in front of them with crossed arms and raise a brow.

"One, don't threaten my jingle jangles. Two," River swallows hard, looking panicked, "Can you at least feed one to

Jared and the other to Melissa? Jimmy's probably eaten enough nuts in his life with how far up Maxwell's ass he is." He bellows out a loud laugh, slapping his knee as tears shine in his eyes.

"Riv," Phoenix says, looking toward our unhinged friend.

"Yeah, Nixy boy?" River manages to choke out.

Phoenix glares, grips him by the ear, and leans in to whisper-growl, "Shut the fuck up."

River falls out of Phoenix's grip, rubbing at his ear and glaring between us. "Fuckin' spoil sports. Y'all need to get laid, honestly." He grumbles a little more but I tune him out as I begin to tap my foot while waiting to grab both of my Vice Presidents' attention.

"Alright listen the hell up, both of you," I snap impatiently. "Both of you are showing kindness toward the little bird and I'm not fucking having it. Our job," I point between the three of us, "is to use her like the piece of trash she is. She doesn't deserve kindness–"

"Dude, you have no idea what the fuck–" Phoenix tries to interrupt me, but I hold a hand up and glare hard at him.

"I," I growl, "do not give a fuck. Her mom died, that sucks, but she didn't need anyone by her side, she made it clear as fucking day. So she doesn't need a support team. Back the fuck off her Nix, or I'll bash your head in." I spin on my heels and make my way toward the crowded kitchen, biting back a grin when I hear the heckling Raven is receiving from my Alpha Mu boys.

I didn't set out to be head of this frat, but their previous president and VP got arrested on felony charges, hence the reason our frat is now on its fourth warning from the board.

I'm not a legacy, and I'm sure as shit not president material, but the fact that I have been Maxwell Langston's little bitch for the past four years means I'm important enough to come in here and do his bidding. He's had me by the balls since the moment he could, and my mother let it happen. I sometimes wonder if she even knows what's been going on.

As is tradition, I wait until the last guy gets food before I trudge forward and grab myself a plate. It's a big mistake to let Raven cook. Her cooking has always been a comfort for me. Whatever. I'll take advantage of good food in order for her to keep her scholarship. Among other things. This manipulation isn't like me, truly, but the day that Raven Hill told me she didn't love me something inside of me broke. I don't know if it was my soul or my heart, but whatever it was shattered entirely.

"Hey pretty girl, you gonna lick my plate clean with that tongue of yours after I'm done eating?" One of the frat brothers says.

I should ignore it. And I try to, honestly.

Phoenix beats me to whatever I had planned to do, reaching forward and gripping the dumb ass by the back of the neck and proceeds to toss him out of line. He places himself in the guy's spot in line and glares at the offender until he walks out of the kitchen.

Raven's eyes, when I meet them, are glossed over as if she's been fighting the tears welling up in them for a while now. I take a deep breath and place meatballs on top of my spaghetti, drenching it all in the last of the sauce. I have to hold back my laugh when River throws a tantrum over it.

My misplaced glee is ruined, however, when Raven takes a deep breath and reaches behind her, producing a brand spanking new jar of sauce and walking it over toward River. She holds it up and gives him a soft smile. My blood boils hot enough to cook another pot of noodles. I lean in their direction, pretending to grab something before bumping into both of them. The jar of sauce falls and breaks open on the white linoleum floor.

"Oh no," I say in monotone, "the pasta sauce. It's broken."

River, unable to contain himself, busts out laughing. Suddenly, he goes quiet and is trying his hardest to hold it back when Raven's eyes dart between both of us. I bite back a grin, tilting my head, curious what she'll do or say next. I have a few punishment ideas for when she doesn't obey my silence rule, so I'm all for her breaking it this early.

What I don't expect her to do, however, is to spin around and rush out of the kitchen toward the cleaning supplies. I meet Phoenix's angry glare and raise a brow in challenge. Instead of responding to me, he turns around and walks out of the kitchen, probably to his cave of solitude.

River is still laughing as he pats me on the back and chokes out, "Good one. Should have done that when the trend was viral, though, bro. Coulda recorded it and made BANK!" He grabs his plate—sans pasta sauce—and walks toward the movie room. Most of the guys tend to eat dinner there while they watch whatever is decided on that day.

Sniffling precedes Raven as she walks in with a bucket and a mop. She kneels down on the floor so graciously in front of me, and I broaden my stance, folding my arms as I watch her. Her beautiful blue eyes meet mine in anger before she looks back down at the red mess on the floor, the red nearly matching her hair color.

I wish I could say that I get a sick sense of happiness from watching her be at my mercy, but I stand there and take in the beauty of my best friend for the first time in what seems like an eternity.

You saw her at her graduation, Pierce.

Yeah, we won't mention the fact I managed to sneak into

my old high school to watch her walk across that stage, hardly anyone there to cheer her on. I wanted to yell for her so badly. I wanted to go to her, hug her, hold her, kiss her, make her mine all over again. But then I remembered her cruel lie and simply walked back out after the tassels were moved and the hats were tossed.

She felt alone that day.

I felt my heart grow colder. She was the one who created her own loneliness.

I shake my head to rid it of all of the sappy ass thoughts, and find that Raven has nearly cleaned up all of the pasta sauce and is mopping the floor in front of me. When she goes to walk away with the mop and put it away, I grab one of my meatballs, take a bite and try not to groan at the magnificent taste. I toss it on the floor and smirk when her eyes flare wide. *Yell at me, little bird, I dare you.* "Oops?" I say.

She inhales this long, deep breath in a way I've only seen her do when she's angry and ready to fight. I'm almost ready for her to throw hands at me. I'd deserve it, probably. For something. But instead of breaking those hands out, she shoves forward with the mop and leans down to grab the meatball. Throwing the food away, she mops up the red mess it makes. Once finished, she simply leans against the counter and stares at me as if she's waiting for me to try her again.

My firecracker is still in there.

I want to tell her how fucking beautiful she is in this moment, standing up for herself and being so strong willed.

Instead, I lean forward and meet her gaze. I snark out a "Good girl," before grabbing my plate and walking toward the dining room. It's empty, of course, but I sit my happy ass at the end of the table anyway and enjoy the taste of home Raven has given me, in more ways than one.

A FEW HOURS LATER, half of the Alpha Mu boys are either out at a party, or doing work for me somewhere else. I've intentionally made it so they are all out of the house right now. I have plans for my little bird, and I know she's going to throw a fit about it.

With probably the biggest shit eating grin on my face, I go toward the tiny closet we have dubbed Raven's room. It's meant for a maid, which made it a fitting place for her. It's the only room in this entire building that doesn't have an en suite. It's also directly across the hall from my room, which makes my bathroom the most convenient for her to use. This is something I plan to take advantage of many times while she's being whipped into submission behind closed doors.

Maxwell expects me to train Raven up in the drug business he has going, but I don't want her to get mixed up in any of this. So instead of doing what he wants me to, I've thought up a brand-new set of conditions. I'll report back the good things to him, and they'll all be lies. Lying to a piece of shit like him is easy. Proving a boost in production without extra rap sheets? That'll be the hardest.

I walk up to Raven's door and knock on it, pausing for a moment when I hear panicked shuffling behind the wood. Dunno what she was doing, but it's fun to make up stories in my head. I knock once more and announce "I'll come in there with the key if you don't get your ass out here soon, little birdie. Fly, girl, fly!' I shout the last bit and grin to myself.

I think I'm funny, at least.

River comes up beside me and pushes his shoulder against me. "What're we doin' with your girl?"

I chance a look at him, raising a brow. "Say what now?"

"Yeah bro," he bounces on his feet, rubbing his hands together. "We're a team, right? You said Nixy and I are part of the *sexual favors* bit of this deal. I want in!"

I groan and roll my eyes, running a hand across my jaw as I listen intently to what's going on behind the door. Her footsteps are padding closer, so I press myself closer to the door, my nose nearly touching the wood. I place my finger to my lips to indicate that River should indeed, for the first time ever, shut his damn mouth. He grins, but does as I ask. Just in time too. The door opens and a scared, but fresh faced looking Raven appears.

I don't remember the last time I saw her without makeup, so I'm thrown off, so much so that I don't even deck River for his whistle of shock when he sees her.

Raven tilts her head, raising a notepad up in the air. I cock my brow high and she holds it up in front of her face. I read the words she wrote on the page.

What do you want, Gre-Pierce?

I try not to notice she almost wrote down the nickname she gave me all those years ago. Instead, I grit my teeth at the fact that she's taking this silence far too seriously. Someone dumber than her might have asked, but nope. If nothing else, my gir–*not my girl*–Raven is dedicated to rules.

"Good one. Smart, really," I snark, reaching out to grab the notepad and shove it in my back pocket. Her nostrils flare in anger and I bite back a grin at her frustration. "Come with me. I need to get off, and I'm not up for finding a dirty college bunny right now."

I back up toward my room and nudge the door open,

waving an arm in indication for her to enter. Her eyes are wide, and she looks panicked. I truly, at this moment, do not give a fuck about her feelings.

In her hesitation, I step forward angrily and snarl, "If you do not hold up this end of the deal, I'll send you back to Maxwell so fucking fast. You'll be tossed out on your ass. Something I know you cannot afford, Raven. So get your ass in my room and get on your knees like a good little whore." The last of those words are nearly spat out at her. As it is, some spittle does fly and nearly hits her in the face.

Again, I couldn't care less.

"C'mon, RaeRae," River croons, placing his hand on Raven's shoulder and pulling her across the hallway. He's being a fucking gentleman about it, and he grins when I glare at him. My eyes would burn his soul if they could, but they can't, so he makes his way into my room and I'm forced to follow them both.

"Take your shirt off," I bark, shutting my door and turning the lock.

"Bro, I didn't know you liked me like that?!" River snarks, a grin on his face. He's on my ever-loving last nerve. Especially when he takes his shirt off, and my eyes follow his every movement.

My dick jumps, realizing how damn firm and defined his abdominal muscles are. I glance at the silver barbells going through his nipples, like beacons calling my tongue to them. I have to hide my groan when I see that his pupils are blown with lust. Looking away swiftly, I look toward Raven, praying she didn't see our silent exchange.

She definitely did, though. Although she didn't ask to be here, she's surely curious about a little guy on guy action happening. I see the way her nipples are beaded in her shirt, and I rub my thumb along my lower lip to hide my grin as I raise a brow at her. "Shirt, little bird. Now."

She blinks out of the lust daze she found herself in, and I head toward the desk in the corner of the room, nearly jumping out of my skin when I see Phoenix standing in the corner with his ankles crossed and his arms crossed over his chest.

"Holy fucking shit, Nix!" I yell, nearly tripping as I pull the chair away from the desk and toward the middle of the room where River is currently helping Raven out of the hoodie she had on. "Next time warn a guy, will you?" I tell Phoenix, glaring in his direction as I sit my ass down in the chair in front of a now half naked Raven.

"Don't think I will. I don't like this, Pierce, and I don't want you to hurt her. She's been through far too fu–"

I whip my head toward Phoenix and growl low in my throat, "I do not answer to you, Phoenix. You answer to me. So either you stay back and watch like a good boy, or you piss off. Now shut up. River, show me her tits." I widen my legs, unbuttoning my jeans and sliding them and my boxers down just enough to free my aching dick from its confines.

I don't remove my shirt. I actually can't, but that's a story for another day.

River leans forward and whispers something sweet in Raven's ear, and her cheeks get pinker, but she nods as she meets my gaze. Riv leans in a tad more and gives her a soft kiss on her cheek, a grin on his face.

I roll my eyes, but I do notice the way her body lights up in goosebumps when his hands trail up her thighs, her hips, her sides, before moving toward the front clasp of her basic white bra. It's hotter than I want it to be when he frees her breasts and tosses the bra at me. Both because it showcases the exquisite nature of Raven in nearly all of her glory, but also because the wink River throws my way has my dick aching more. I fist my cock in my hand, slowly stroking it as I watch with hooded eyes.

River leans in and runs a tongue along one of Raven's nipples, and her eyes roll to the back of her head at the contact. Makes me wonder how long it's been since she's allowed someone to touch her. Surely she wasn't out being a slut since her mother died.

"Oh fuck yeah, she tastes like strawberry soda, boys!" River barks out, a groan escaping him as he begins to knead Raven's flesh. His thumbs on her nipples rubbing in rhythmic circles. I'm stroking my dick harder at this point, faster, hoping for release. But I stop, remembering I brought her in here to take care of this inconvenience for me.

"Come here, little bird," I snap, bringing up my free hand and crooking a finger at her.

I nearly come from the surprise at her doing as I ask. The way her lids are hooded tells me she's currently lust drunk, or maybe she's simply lost in her head to avoid the sickness of the situation I've thrown her into.

She licks her lips as she begins to stand, but I wave a hand and point at the ground. "Fucking crawl to me, slut. I didn't give you permission to walk."

Halting her movements, I see the hesitation and the promise for retribution. All I can think is bring it, baby, before all thought leaves me when she does as she's asked, again. Her ass looks delicious in the black sleep shorts she's wearing, and I see the hint of bright purple underwear underneath the waistband. I want so bad to lean forward and–

Smack!

Raven nearly jumps ten feet in the air when River lands the

blow to her ass. In the next second she's biting her lip, and her eyes grow heavy again as she continues her trek toward me on hands and knees.

This whole scene is going in the spank bank for life.

Once between my legs, Raven leans back on her haunches and trails her hands from my ankles all the way up until they land on my thighs, bracketing where I'm stroking my pulsing cock. I'm ready to blow the moment she puts her mouth on me.

"Give me your hand," I grit out. When she does, I spit on it, and place her hand on my dick, tossing my head back on a loud groan. I notice River has his dick out, and I watch from the corner of my eye as he strokes it, my hips bucking in time with his in response.

I look back down when I sense Raven's attention slowing on me, placing my hand over hers to keep it moving. I meet her gaze, our eyes telling a million secrets in seconds. To avoid spilling mine so easily, I grunt, pulling her hand off of my dick. My free hand goes to the back of her head and I grip her hair, pulling her closer to me. "Spit," I tell her. She does. "Now suck."

The saliva that's been used as lube on her hand and now prepping my dick for her mouth, creates an obscene sound that escapes out of my mouth the moment hers takes me in. We may have only been fooling around for half of a year, but in that year we learned *a lot* of things about each other. Like how she has no gag reflex, or how I absolutely die on the spot when her tongue drags across the vein on the underside of my shaft. She clearly remembers, and she does it before hollowing her cheeks out and sucking me as far into her throat as is physically possible.

I hear River utter a "no fucking shit" in the background.

I try to tune him out as I grip Raven's hair tighter in my fist, shoving her down on my dick so far, I know it'll hurt in a few hours. Groaning, I watch her take me in and I spit out expletives as she pulls back to breathe for the second or two that I allow it.

I'm nearly sent to heaven when she repeats the process.

River's grunts of pleasure are closer to me now, and I see he's sitting right next to Raven, one hand on his dick while the other plays with her tits.

She's squirming, but she's still silent. She's *that* determined to avoid my wrath, I suppose. I bite my lip as I watch with heavy lidded eyes while River's hands showcase the difference in skin tones.

She's so deliciously pale, and his tanned skin looks like sand against her. Their contrasting features make my dick pulse in her mouth, and I use my hands to put her hair into a ponytail, tugging on it until I have a firm grip.

I take a moment to inhale before I fuck her face with such force I can see and feel her tits bouncing. I groan and mutter out a "Fuck yes, little bird. Just. Fucking. Like. That."

"Oh hell yeah, Raven, sweet girl, suck him dry," River groans, and I can hear his grunts becoming more labored.

I chance a look in his direction to find his eyes on mine. I bite my lip and a long moan leaves me as I watch him come undone, which forces me to do the same.

My hips stutter and stop as I hit the back of Raven's throat, my cum coating her mouth and filling her so full that it dribbles down through her lips and mixes with our spit that's also coating my dick. My vision goes white, and I slump back in the chair to take a few deep breaths before I raise my fingers and snap, pointing down to my overly wet dick. "Clean up the mess you made, little bird. Then you can go back to your room until you're needed for breakfast in the morning."

I raise a brow in challenge when Phoenix growls, daring him to fuck with me right now. I'm very...*chill,* and I'd like to stay that way.

I watch as River licks his lips while he cleans himself up with his own shirt. It's like he wants to be the one to clean my dick, but I'm not up for that at the moment, so I focus back on the fiery redhead in front of me as she leans forward and begins to suck the juices off of my dick.

I nearly come back for a second round, but it's been a big day for all of us, and I'm not about to go for a marathon here.

The moment she's done cleaning my dick off–swallowing every drop, mind you–I stand up and head toward my shower with a wave.

I don't give the whispers or shuffling a second thought as I go to take the longest cold shower of my life. Whether I'm freezing my feelings out or wishing my blood would cool, the world will never know.

Once I'm finished with my shower and dried off, I enter my room again, only to find it dark and empty. Like the hole in my chest has been for the past year.

Groaning, I lay down flat on top of the blankets, burying my face in my pillows. The sweet smell of strawberry soda calms my racing thoughts and heavily pounding heart before I finally pass out.

The scent of her surrounding me has always been a comfort.

No one needs to know I've kept her this close.

Dear New Boy Living Across The Street,

Momma said you are having a hard time making friends because your momma dragged you here. I don't see why you would have a hard time making friends. It's easy! You just gotta come outside sometimes and play with us...

Jimmy down the street isn't so bad. He's the only other boy I know that doesn't smell like boogers and mud, so maybe you could be friends with him? I don't know. Momma doesn't like him too much but she invites him over for lunch on Saturdays like the rest of the kids.

Oooooh! Come over on Saturday! We'll have the best time. Promise! I think she's ordering pizza this week. Pizza's the best.

Except the kind with pineapples.

Don't eat the kind with pineapples, boy! It's real bad.

TTFN, (that means Ta-Ta for Now),
Raven Hill

raven

Pierce slams the door to the en suite, throwing me off entirely. I'm not able to sit in my thoughts much longer, however, because both Phoenix and River rush toward me in concern. River supplies my bra and hoodie back to me, and they both look away as I dress again.

Strange they don't look away when I remove clothes, but give me privacy when I'm putting them back on.

I sigh once I'm fully dressed again, and when I go to stand, I find Phoenix standing above me, an obvious swell in his jeans as he holds a hand out to me.

Placing my hand in his, I allow him to lift me up, blushing when my leg brushes against his dick. It's innocent, but the size of the monster in there does not go unnoticed. I'm blushing furiously when he lets go of my hand and lifts my chin, his chocolate eyes meeting my blue ones.

"Let's get you back to your room. Tomorrow will be a big day. We start classes, which means we officially kick off advertising for Rush Week." Phoenix's voice is kind, but I can tell he's angered by what went down in this room. His obvious disdain for Pierce's plans perks me up a little bit. I think he's going to be here to protect me through any encounter we have.

As we begin to leave Pierce's room, River follows us out and stops me with a hand to my bicep. It's a soft and kind touch, and when his gaze meets mine, he smiles boyishly, his head dipping in shyness. "Sorry if we took consent away from you, sweet girl. No excuses. I do as the boss says, and sometimes that ain't right. Some of us have too much on the line to worry about right from wrong, ya know? Anyway," he clears his throat, "sorry." Once he's gone, Phoenix brushes a hand lightly across my lower back as we stop by my door.

I'm completely floored that he would apologize, even if he would have probably done it all over again.

Before I can truly think through the situation, Phoenix is pulling me into a sudden hug, brushing his lips along my forehead tenderly, his arms brushing up and down my arms. "You did such a good job in there, Red. You were such a good girl."

I have to stop my thighs from clenching at the 'good girl'. I've recently found myself enjoying the praise. Shaking my head of any lustful thoughts, I pull back and give a soft half smile before backing up toward my door, opening it. I meet Phoenix's gaze once more, and his brows are furrowed as if he can't figure something out. I give him a small wave before closing the door, locking myself in, and taking the deepest breath I can manage.

What I should not do is find myself laying down a minute later, replaying the night with a different lens. One in which the arrangement with the guys was completely consensual. One in which all of us are playing together and we all have a happy ending.

What I should not do is use my hands and fingers to explore my own body, stimulating myself in much the same way River was doing only minutes before.

What I should not do is find my release with Pierce's name on my silent lips.

THE NEXT MORNING, I end up cooking breakfast for what seems like an entire army. It takes a while to clean up, too. I dressed myself up in a sweet sundress, but to kill the sweetness, I picked out a black fabric with little skulls across it. My red hair falls in waves down my back, and my makeup is dark but subtle.

I'm refreshed, and the orgasm last night has something to do with that, I'm sure of it. I can't remember the last time I got off.

My feet are in flats today, which makes it easier to walk around and clean up after annoying frat boys. So when I make it down the hallway for the hundredth time today, I'm more grateful for them. I run right into Pierce. I'd fall on my ass in heels, but I don't wobble on flats, so I remain standing, even though I do stumble backward into the wall. He glares at me with a brow raised, but I could give no fucks what he thinks at this point.

"Little bird, we need to be on campus in ten, so grab whatever the fuck you need and let's get going. The boys are ready, and so am I, so let's go." He barks out commands left and right, continuing his little angry tantrum as we walk toward the front door. I grab the black backpack I left in the coat closet, following him out toward a Jeep Wrangler. River and Phoenix are already sitting inside of it. Phoenix in the driver seat and River in the back.

"Hey sweet girl, have a good night's sleep?" River says, his smile filthy, as if he knows exactly what happened last night after they all left me alone to my own devices.

I blush, which gives me away. He's laughing his ass off as he opens the backdoor for me to climb in. I do so without any help, something I half appreciate and half hate. Chivalry might actually be dead. Well, until I see the glare Phoenix shoots in River's direction, the latter shrugs as he reaches over me to pull the door closed.

"Alright," Pierce says as he enters the front passenger seat, "Get us to the main portion of campus. The little bird can walk to the Arts building. It'll give her something productive to do with all this free time. You," he points toward Phoenix, "are coming with me to the science building. M has some shit for us to see, and I'm not about to put myself in a precarious situation."

I'm curious as to who M is, and why they need a code name, but I simply shrug off the curiosity as I look out of the window and try to ignore the way my stomach flutters when River reaches for my hand, twining our fingers together. I bite my lip to keep my smile at bay when he rubs his thumb along the outside of my hand. Goosebumps rise along my skin, but I pretend they simply don't exist.

He notices though and grins so widely that the white of his teeth shines back at me in the reflection of the window.

Minutes later, we're pulling up to the main courtyard of the Cobalt University campus. I grab my bag and am about to step out of the Jeep when Phoenix rushes out of his door, only to come back to mine and open it for me, holding a hand out.

What should be something so sweet and innocent is nothing but when he pulls me into his body as I slide down the large vehicle. I can feel his dick swell between us, and he winks in such an obscene but endearing way.

"Ignore that, Red," he says softly, placing a kiss on my forehead.

I smile sweetly at him, only to frown when I see the glare Pierce is pointing our way. I back out of Phoenix's embrace and grab my bag that River has held out for me. All three men share a silent conversation before River's sheepish grin widens into something much more jovial.

Wrapping an arm around my shoulders, he walks toward the Arts building. He waves a hand toward the other two, flipping them the bird at the last minute. He smiles softly when he sees my soft grin. "Alright, sweet girl, let's get you to your first class. I don't have a class till like, I dunno, two pm? Again, dunno, but this is my second year here and everyone *loves* me."

He looks ahead to where we are walking making sure we continue on at a brisk pace. We pass countless students who are talking and texting on their phones as they walk. One guy manages to just barely miss walking into a pole. I flinch even though he doesn't run into it. River barks out a laugh that catches attention, but doesn't pay it any mind as we walk on.

Once we make it through the bustling courtyard, we're walking up the stone steps of the cathedral looking building. History says this campus used to be used by some Buddhist monks. When their population had to move for whatever reason, they donated the land for future growth in any fashion. The university was later coined Cobalt University after Sterling Cobalt. It seems like he was an alright guy, which makes me wonder what he'd honestly think of the people that are here now.

"'Kay, so I'll sit in on your first few classes with you, RaeRae, but I'll bounce after lunch to catch my own edumacation." He chucks my chin after I nod. When he catches my gaze he grins. It seems so inviting. His lips pull up into something that looks so comforting that I'd sleep on them if I could.

I bob my head again in affirmation and smile bashfully when he grabs for the hand resting on my shoulder strap, twining our fingers together as we continue our walk down the outside hallway of the building.

Five rooms down, we stop and River opens the door for me, waving me in. I enter the room and am thrown when I see it looks like a simple classroom. A typical college classroom. It's like someone preserved the outside of the building for history's sake, but fixed the insides up to stay with the times. I'm floored, but manage to make my way toward the back of the class.

I soon discover even those in the back of the class have to introduce themselves. The sorority girls absolutely hate me and spend the few minutes of my obvious struggle to shoot me dirty looks.

River eventually speaks up and answers for me. "Her throat is a little sore, teach, if you know what I mean." Looking over to me, he winks dramatically, and the entire class erupts into uncontrollable laughter.

My cheeks heat up, and I bury my face in a romance novel for the rest of class. I'll disappear between the pages of a book where a girl doesn't know who she is or where she came from, only to find out she's connected to five hot guys and gets railed for the majority of the book as a coping mechanism.

She might be onto something...

I PANIC WHEN WE LEAVE, fumbling with all of my things. The teacher gave us his contact information as we were leaving, which I intend to use to send a full email explaining my traumatic mutism and the ways I'm currently able to communicate. I thought Mr. Langston was going to do that for me, but I guess it wasn't important enough for him. It seems like all he wants is for me to help build his stupid Alpha Mu reputation back up.

River grabs my hand as we leave, squeezing in reassurance. "It'll be okay. I dunno why you aren't talking, but honest–"

I interrupt him, pulling him off to the side of the hallway. Lifting my phone, I point to him. He raises a brow, but when I waggle my phone, he gets the point. I snatch his phone and text myself, inserting my name into his contacts. In what seems like lightning fast speed, I text him from my own phone.

> I suffer from traumatic mutism. I can't speak or make noises. I'm not joking, and it isn't funny to me.

River's eyes go wide when he reads the message. He looks at me, back to the phone, and back to me again before he tries to respond.

When he does respond, however, his brows are high when he mutters out a "Well, shit, that's a development. Why not tell Pierce, since he thinks you're simply winning his silent game?"

I shake my head and type again to him, sending the text and waiting out River's notification.

> Let him think what he wants. He deserves to feel vindicated for once.

Sighing, River rolls his eyes and places his arm around my shoulder again and steers me back down the hallway. I have a basic math class next, so we're headed back toward the Gen Ed building. "Alright, RaeRae, as you wish." He tosses a wink my way when my head whips his way in surprise. "Yeah, I've seen The Princess Bride. So what?"

We're headed for a long ass day of classes in which I simply sit silently. River continues to joke that my throat is sore, and I spend my lunch hour furiously typing out emails explaining the reality of my current situation.

THE NEXT DAY, the entire Alpha Mu house is absolutely chaotic. I thought there was an army in here before, but those are the ones opting to stay in the house. I believe the actual frat members currently attending CU count up to 150.

It's absolute insanity.

I'm tempted to use the chaos to get away for a while and read over more of my syllabi from my classes. Before I can take a step in one direction or the other, River slides into the room and places his arm over my shoulders, grinning widely. "Hey RaeRae, wanna come with me to pick out party decorations? We're kind of over the literal 'Greek' theme, and Nixy mentioned you might want to help decide a theme."

I blink up at him. Someone has to be pranking me, honestly. I'm their little bitch right now, so the way he's phrasing 'come shop like a typical female' is strange. But, this is an escape from Pierce's lingering glare, so I shrug and give River a small smile. He's earned one, after all.

"Fuckin' awesome!" He presses a loud kiss to my cheek and drags me from the room where I had barely begun cleaning.

"Hey Pierce, we gotta get going to the store now, so like, you clean up yeah?"

"What the fuck, Riv?" Pierce bellows, rushing from his brooding corner to look at us, "That's her fucking job and you know it. Piss off for a while!" He crosses his arms like a petulant toddler and I look at the ground to hide my smile.

If I'm not mistaken, Phoenix and River are taking small little jabs at Pierce out of preservation for their own sanity as much as fighting in my honor.

"Nah, don't think I will. The store will run out of *every-thing* on this random Tuesday in August at 10 a.m.! Super important we get there like," River checks his watch, "now. Go, Rae, go!" he says, ushering me out of the door with a snicker.

I'm grinning, trying hard not to, but River's antics are the most adorable things ever. He opens the Jeep door for me to get in, and I slide in the passenger side before he closes the door. He gets in the driver's side and, ignoring all safety proto-cols, books it out of the driveway, the wheels spinning in our wake.

Pierce barely makes it to the edge of the driveway before we're off and speeding down the street. River holds his arm across my chest and points to the seat-belt. "Buckle up, butter-cup. We're running from the big bad wolf today!" He turns up some heavy metal song, headbanging and howling like a wolf for the sake of it.

I buckle myself up and chew my lip as I take in River's care-free nature. How he and the other two became friends, I'll never understand. At least Phoenix and Pierce seem to be somewhat the same in their demeanor, but River is an entirely different human. He's too kind for them. Too—well, no I wouldn't say pure.

Ten minutes later, River pulls into a major shopping plaza.

When he kills the engine, my ears are ringing, but my heart is thudding with the adrenaline from the rush of running from Pierce, as well as the excitement of the music pushing through the system. I meet River's gray eyes and see that he looks far too serious, which is concerning.

For a second, I think he's zoned out, but his eyes brighten and widen slightly when he sees me staring. Within seconds, he's leaning forward and planting a kiss on my cheek so loud and wet that I wonder whether or not we're even existing within the same minute.

I smile for him, my lips kicking up on the sides as I look at him. He doesn't give me another moment to look at him, pulling away and getting out of the car before going around and opening my door. Gripping me by the hips, he slides me across the seat, pulling me down so I'm forced to slide along his body when I fall from the passenger side. I lick my lip and bite down a tad, only to startle when River brushes his thumb across it. His eyes burn bright as they focus on the action.

"Don't tempt me, sweet girl, or we'll become far too indecent for a Tuesday morning shopping spree." He pulls my hand into his before slamming the door shortly after.

My heart is pounding in my chest, my breathing harsh as I follow him into the shopping mart. I can't process anything after that moment. I shouldn't be attracted to him. Not in the sense that my heart gets involved. However, as we enter the store and River keeps our fingers twined together like we're a normal couple, I forget my circumstances and simply let myself pretend for a while.

"Alright, so you pick a theme and go for it. Just can't be Greek, got it?" He nods toward the party supplies section, gesturing me into it. I tear my gaze from his beautiful face and look around at all of the possible themes. There's zebra, cheetah, princess, prince, and all sorts of cartoon characters.

Belatedly, I wonder if Pierce would enjoy something in particular, but I push that thought to the side and begin to grab all sorts of crowns and tiaras, gesturing for River to begin grabbing them as well. He pulls one tiara from my grip and places it atop my head, securing it in the red locks and tucking it into my messy bun. He places a crown above his own head, and I let out a few breaths that pass as a laugh for him.

"M'lady Raven, will you please allow me to escort you to the first day of rush week? The theme is your choosing, of course, and I'd hope I could be your chosen date." He looks up and winks at me. My cheeks heat in response, and my smile stretches wide. "Please allow me, a lowly peasant masquerading as a prince, to walk with you on my arm, to dance with you, and to please you in many, many ways." He holds his hand out, reaching for mine, kissing the knuckles as he holds my eyes hostage.

I manage a small dip of my head while swallowing down the lump in my throat. He jumps up in pure elation, picking me up and swinging me around in the middle of the aisle. I let out another breath of laughter, and I think River notices it, because he lets out a soft laugh alongside me.

Setting me down, he kisses the top of my head and begins to snatch up more of the royal ball themed decorations. He manages to throw a gaudy looking purple boa around my neck, using it to bring me in close to him at the end of the aisle. His eyes travel up and down my frame as he pulls me close, our chests now touching as I stare up at him. He licks his lips, my eyes following the movement involuntarily.

He pulls me in closer, his nose touching mine, and whispers so softly, I almost don't hear him, "I wish we'd met under different circumstances. I'd steal a kiss from you and hope I stole your heart in the process, sweet girl."

He pulls away, sliding the boa off of my neck and walking toward the front to check out. I'm left reeling at his confession, wishing he could do as he wished, just this once.

pierce

At four o'clock on the dot, I wonder where the fuck all of my guys are, and where the hell Raven and River got off to.

Hopefully not literally getting off.

I scoff and bring my whiskey to my lips, downing the entirety of it in one go and slamming the glass down onto the counter top.

"Pierce," Phoenix says, coming up to my side and grabbing the whiskey bottle as I go to pour more into my glass. He sets it down and eyes me skeptically before shaking his head. "We have a situation with J."

I growl and push myself away from the counter, heading toward the front door, but Nix grabs me and spins me toward the basement.

"He's claiming some product is fucking stuck somewhere along the line and I don't believe it because he's high as a goddamn kite, PJ."

"Don't fucking call me that," I snap.

My mother used to call me PJ, right up until I turned 14

and Maxwell Langston began dangling her life over my head. From that point on, she was calling me by my first name, and she'd say it in such a monotone voice that I truly don't remember what the hell she sounded like before that.

"I'm about to kill the motherfucker if he doesn't quit inhaling what he needs to be selling," I tell Phoenix.

"Yeah, well," he says, drawing out the last word as he opens the basement door, heading inside first. "Langston'll get him before you can at this point. Don't kill all the chickens in your basket or you won't have any eggs for breakfast."

I huff out a laugh, rolling my eyes at him as we descend the staircase. Once we're at the bottom of the steps, I see Jimmy in all of his skeevy glory being held in place by two of my top guys. They're more on my payroll than Langston's, but I refuse to let anyone else in on that secret. They spy for me. I put food on their tables and clothes on their kids' backs.

"Well, well, well," Jimmy says, spitting out a stream of blood at my feet. His hair is all sorts of mussed up, dirt and dried blood caked within the strands. "Pierce Jackson. Someone stole my shit. Need more."

Half of his words come out slurred, probably from the preemptive beat down my guys have given him. I shake my head as I get closer to him. He tries to lunge for me, but my hired muscles are ex-military and take no fucking prisoners. I pretend like I'm scared for half of a second, only to rear my fist back and cock it forward so fast Jimmy only sees it half a second before it connects with his nose. His howl of pain nearly gets my dick up and going, but I tamp that temptation down and save it for later when Raven is back.

Thoughts of her results in me thrusting my fist back out toward him, a wide grin on my face as I land half a dozen more strikes on his ugly face. I'm laughing at this point, in a manic state of mind as I rearrange all of his features and make them look better than the last time I did this.

Minutes later, Phoenix grabs me by the shoulders, pulling me back. "That's enough. He got the point, Pierce."

Chest heaving, I turn my head to look at Nix, looking back at the passed out and bloodied Jimmy Perkins with a wild grin on my face. I walk over to his limp body and spit on it, kicking his side for good measure before meeting the gaze of the guys above me.

They're both in some sort of strange trance as they watch me, and I don't know if it's because they watched me brutalize this guy for the third time this month or if they don't care and are zoned out.

"Drop him off at his dorm," I tell them, turning on my heel and walking back toward the stairs. "Oh, and boys?" I meet their gazes, "I will fucking cut your dicks off if you allow him near the new secretary. Got it?"

After they nod, I do the same in return. I turn back to walk back up the stairs, since it's stuffy down there all of a sudden.

"Pierce, get cleaned up. Nice suit and tie." Phoenix says, his hand patting me on the shoulder as he passes me once we enter the upstairs hallway.

I close the basement door and look over to him, a brow lifted. "The fuck am I wearing a suit and tie to the first day of rush week for?"

"Red chose the theme. It's now the Royals of Cobalt. Everyone's ecstatic, especially the sororities," Phoenix says as he grins, although doesn't quite reach his eyes. Within such a short amount of time, we have all kept our thoughts of women to only one woman in particular; Raven.

I should be miffed about it, but as long as I know where they are sticking their dicks, or planning to, I can handle it. I guess it'll keep their dicks out of crazy. Nodding to myself, I make my way up the stairs and head toward my room without another word.

Guess we're partying like kings and queens tonight.

TWO HOURS LATER, I'm sipping on yet another glass of whiskey and wondering if I've become an alcoholic like my mom did when I was twelve. I shrug at my own thoughts, and throw a wink at a passing blonde. I sip and sip and sip until the whiskey is gone, the bottle suddenly becoming empty.

Oh, no. I accidentally chugged the whole bottle.

"Slow the fuck down, brother! We still have business to do," Phoenix snaps, snatching away the new bottle of whiskey I'd managed to grab. He looks around and clearly doesn't find what he's looking for before he walks toward the nearest dancing couple and hands them the bottle.

I growl when he returns to me and slaps me on the back a tad too hard. Gritting my teeth, I look around the hall, noting that Raven and River have yet to appear. I got into this damn monkey suit when I could have worn a bedsheet as a toga and been free balling it.

Something tells me that River let Raven pick the theme to fuck with me. He can't listen when I say we aren't going to play nice with the little bird. Slamming my glass down on the bar, I adjust my suit jacket and begin a slow perusal around the room, noting who looks high already and who looks scared shitless. Alpha Mu parties are notorious, nand we recently lost our president and vice president no less than a year ago to drug trafficking charges.

Hence why Maxwell wanted me.

He's an Alpha Mu legacy and doesn't want his precious college days to go to waste. Nah, he's prospered off of too many of the unsuspecting ever since he founded his illegal drug operations.

Not every drug user on campus is a dumb ass, but those of us pushing them for him?

Yeah, we're the dumb asses.

We believe in the false promises he gives to us. We'll be free, we'll prosper greatly, our families will no longer suffer.

He's a flat out liar, because I haven't seen my mom since the quick jaunt into town I made to see Raven graduate high school.

"Holy hell, is that the new secretary?"

"I mean, she's mute, so that must mean she won't drive me up a wall talking, right?"

"Shit she's hot like that."

"Yeah bro, imagine her naked."

I grit my teeth, looking around and cataloging every single person ogling my girl right now. *Not my girl.*

I look around until I find Raven on River's arm as they enter the main party room. I'm frozen when I see the way she is dressed. I'm fucking stunned and I'm so speechless that I have forgotten all words in all of their forms. My mouth goes dry and my brain loses all of its working brain cells. My knees are so weak I'm forced to lean against the nearest wall to keep myself standing up.

She's a goddamn vision.

Her beautiful red locks are curled and cascading down her shoulders and back, a cream A-line gown draping over her frame and sparkling vividly in the party lights. She seems a few inches taller, her chin sitting right at the top of River's shoulder. Black eye shadow and deep red lipstick make her face give off a seductress vibe.

I can't fault my dick for his current attentive nature.

I can, however, fault my heart for thumping so hard against my chest. I might die at this moment from a heart attack.

"Holy shit," Phoenix whispers beside me, his hand rubbing at his solar plexus. I grunt in agreement, finding myself walking toward the red-headed vixen of my dreams—and nightmares.

"Little bird," I say, though my voice is harsh. I remind myself I'm trying to be the bad guy here. "You're late," I snap, swallowing the lump in my throat when her smile drops entirely.

She nods before looking down at her feet, her confidence surely taking a hit now. Phoenix elbows me in the side and fucking bows in front of her like some gentlemen. I swear these two forgot I told them to stop being nice to her. I kick Phoenix in the shin, and he falls to the ground.

Using the fall to his advantage, he moves Raven's dress from in front of her sparkling heels, inspecting them for a moment before he looks up. His face and eyes have hardened, and he tsks in the back of his throat as he looks her up and down.

"The shoes don't quite match the dress, Red. Do you need help getting dressed next time?" He covers her shoe with her dress again. Standing, he dusts off his suit pants, and sends a glare my way, as if to ask if he's performed his job properly.

I nod once, and he spins back around to go do whatever he needs to.

"What's the plan tonight, boss?" River says, and I roll my eyes in response. He knows I hate when he calls me that.

"I've got some cash to collect and some fun to sell, so keep the little bird firmly in your sight. Be a good babysitter, Riv." I tell him, looking Raven up and down once more. "She likes to run."

I don't miss the way Raven flinches at my words, or the way River glares at me as I turn around. I have shit to do tonight and none of it involves those two. At least not until later.

I'm contemplating the logistics of a threesome with my best friend and my ex best friend, a small smirk trying to tempt its way to my lips, when a heavy hand lands on my shoulder. When I turn to see who it is, I balk at Maxwell Langston in all of his former glory.

He's wearing a suit much like my own, and what looks like a legitimate crown on top of his head. It's definitely not one of the plastic ones Raven and River bought for this party.

"The fuck do you want, and why are you here?" I spit out, jerking my shoulder from his touch and heading into the kitchen. I need another whiskey for whatever conversation he wants to have.

"I have a few more bags of E for you to hand out tonight." Maxwell Langston is at least twenty years removed from this damn school, and yet the drug operation he himself created is alive and fucking well. Much to my chagrin, he's roped me in with threats and pretty green paper.

"Max," I say, grinning when he rears back. He hates when I call him anything other than his full name. The pretentious prick. "You already supplied us with ten full bags. We'll struggle to get those out. It's the first night! Too many freshmen here."

"Don't care how you do it, Pierce. Get it the fuck done." He places the bags in my hands, a smile on his face as if he's simply shaking my hand for something else. He leaves with a pointed look toward Raven, and I'm left with a seed of dread in my gut.

Phoenix sidles up next to me, a whiskey in one hand and a beer in the other. He offers the whiskey to me, and sips from the beer as he leans against the wall next to me. "More fun to distribute, I assume?" When I nod, he takes a longer pull of his beer and grunts, "He's getting bolder. This is why Blake and Justin were arrested. Too much product to move at once."

I nod in agreement, keeping my eyes peeled for my runners. They'll do my dirty work and get this shit in the hands of more unsuspecting–or suspecting–people. I hate doing this shit, but I do it for far too many reasons to stop now. Ideally, we can shut Maxwell down for good and steal his money. Like a Robin Hood situation.

Unfortunately, I don't have the manpower, or the current willpower, to do so.

Jimmy Perkins comes sauntering into the room, his face so bruised it looks like a purple grape. I snort, nearly spitting my whiskey out in the process. I point him out to Phoenix, who barks out a quick laugh.

"He looks so pretty now. Does he take house calls, I wonder?" Nix snarks out, sipping his beer.

"I'm sure he's done house calls this whole ass time. Hold on," I tell him.

I make my way across the room, placing my empty glass into one of the Alpha Mu boy's hands once I've finished it. I grin at Jimmy, patting him patronizingly on the cheek, knowing that shit has to hurt. Which is confirmed when he flinches so hard he spills his own beer. "Aw, J-boy. You look so pretty like this. Hopefully you're up for sucking a few later. Just the look of your pretty face has me hard."

A couple of idiots laugh at my dig. Jimmy growls, and I pat

both of his cheeks at the same time, squishing them together. I grin a maniacal grin as I lean in to whisper in his ear, "I have at least fifteen bags of E to get rid of tonight. Be a good boy and exchange them for green, will you?" I back away with one last pat–okay this one is more of a smack.

Raising a brow, I hold out my hand, handing him the bags when he grabs on. I can see his jaw tick in anger. I can't quite give a fuck right now. When I turn my head, I see my fucking girl looking up at River Jacobs like he's a damn god, and I can't have that.

She's mine. Always has been, and I refuse to let her get this damn googly eyed with anyone other than me, dammit!

I'm storming over to them within seconds, pulling her roughly back against me, my hand on the front of her throat, the other clenched against her waist. I place my lips near her ear, unable to stop myself from biting down on the shell of it before growling. I smile a little when the goosebumps rise against her skin, but manage to keep my glare on River as I whisper to her.

"You, little bird, will get yourself in trouble if I find you rubbing up on him again without my permission, do you understand me?" When she nods, I squeeze her throat, not enough to choke her, but to check her pulse rate. What I find is intriguing as shit; her heart doesn't seem to be racing in fear. Her pulse is thundering, sure, but mixed with the way she tries to subtly wiggle her ass against my dick? Yeah, I remember this game. We found it far earlier than when we should have...

"PIERCE, *can we at least try it? We're both adults. We graduate next summer. I'm just...curious...is all.*" *Raven's voice is*

sweet and seductive over the phone, and I find myself getting harder as I listen to her go on about this new thing she found online.

The vixen called me at midnight to tell me this new kink she'd found online.

I didn't even know she searched that type of shit.

We've only been eighteen for a few weeks, and summer is almost over, so her boredom and stress is showing. She's been... exploring...things a bit too much for my liking.

"Rae–"

"Green," she counters, "please?" She whines, but it's not annoying. She's actively pleading with me. "I don't want to go off to college so inexperienced. Just because I'm no longer a virgin doesn't mean I have experience..."

"Why the fuck do you need experience, Blue?" I snap out, standing up and rearranging my quickly fading erection. I change out of my gray sweatpants and into some jeans, knowing I'll do whatever the hell she wants me to do anyway. "Huh? Why?"

"Well," she says. The line goes so quiet that I pull the phone from my ear and check to see if we're still connected. We are. I pull it back up to my ear and look for a shirt while I wait for her answer. "I just...I want to be able to please you better. We have fun but...Green...we're so..." She cuts off.

"We're what, Raven? What the hell are we?" I'm panicking at this point, shuffling into my shoes and nearly tripping over my laces in my haste. I sit on the edge of my bed and begin tying them up so quickly I could win a competition.

What I want to tell her is that we're perfect. But she's been wavering on us lately, and I don't want to scare her off.

Hence my hesitation to get kinky in the physical aspect.

"We're just...the same. We...we have so much to learn and–"

"Shut the hell up with that shit, Raven Hill," I bark out. It sounds like she's trying to break off whatever we've started this summer.

We waited until we were eighteen to try and date each other. What's been going on for only a few weeks has only enhanced the friendship we have. It's only brought to light the way that I need her in every aspect of my mind, body, and soul. She's mine, and I won't let her get away simply by trying to save her already stolen virtue.

"So…" she begins, and I can hear shuffling in the background like she's getting her own shoes on.

"You have three minutes," I tell her, hanging up and placing the phone in my pocket. I look around my room and grin when I find a length of purple paracord.

She's not the only one that does research.

I place the rope in my pocket and look toward my closed door. Fuck it. I shrug and walk directly out of it, leaving the door wide open. Maybe ma will finally care that I go missing tonight. She doesn't any other time. Ignoring the sound of the porn-worthy moans coming from my mother's room, I head downstairs and grab my keys on the way out the front door. With those pocketed, I blink my eyes to quickly get them to adjust to the darkness outside. Streetlights or not, this entire cul de sac is dark as shit.

I place my hands in my pockets as I meander around on the sidewalk, toward Raven's mom's house. Their house backs up to a stretch of forest that leads to an old as-shit abandoned playground. The place is rusted out and in need of a wrecking crew, but we don't mention it ever, and we always find ourselves hanging out there. I whistle a little, letting Rae know where I'm at as I scan for any noise from her.

Maybe she didn't put shoes on after all. Usually, her feet are so damn heavy on the ground I could hear her walking over air, I swear to god.

I bite my lip and hide my groan when I hear a twig break ahead of me.

She has half a minute left now.

Rolling my eyes at the sudden thought in my head, I begin to sing out "One, two, I'm coming for you," which makes my dick harden. Guess I'm into primal play like she is. I'm like a powerful wolf hunting down a scared little sheep right now. And that power is fucking intoxicating as I begin to walk a little slower, a little quieter.

As I get closer to the playground, I hear Raven's footsteps as she walks across the merry-go-round. That thing squeaks so loudly if you breathe on it, so I'm kind of saddened she tries to sneak around on it.

Unless she wants to be found quickly.

I grin, walking as quietly as I can in the thick brush that barricades the playground from view. Biting my lip, I cease all movement and let my eyes do the wandering. Within seconds, I see her bare feet move on the other side of the broken-down climbing wall.

"Tsk tsk, little bird, you haven't hidden very well," I speak just loud enough for her to hear. I hear her intake of breath as I get closer and closer to her, and see her feet as they back up to the wall.

When I round the wall, I don't try to hide my dirty grin when I see her. I can hear her almost panicked breathing, chest heaving, and her entire body is plastered against the wall. She scrambles with her hands to grab onto some of the rocks for support. Her body is coated in a small sheen of sweat.

It's a hundred fucking degrees out here, but the heat between us?

Scorching.

"I've found you." My voice is gravelly and broken. I take in her wide eyes, her pupils blown from lust. I prowl toward her and place one hand on her hip, the other on the side of her head. "Now I can do whatever," I lean in close to her ear, "the fuck," I bite her earlobe, grinning when she shivers from the action, "I want."

"Yes," she breathes out, her hands clenching my wrists as she simply exists between my arms. "Whatever you want, Pierce. Whatever," she says.

I look down at her, meeting those beautiful blues and getting caught in her siren's trap. I smile softly for a moment, placing a gentle kiss on her nose before I step into her more, my body plastered to hers.

"Whatever I want," I say. I hum under my breath while I think, my free hand brushing stray hairs off of her forehead. "Okay, little bird. Down on your knees." I command her, placing my hand atop of her head and gently guiding her down.

We've done this a few times now, both of us quickly learning that Raven is both a quick study and she doesn't have a gag reflex.

Once she adjusts herself on the ground, she reaches to undo my belt, and I'm a fucking goner when her eyes peer up at me through her lashes. I can't fucking concentrate long enough to whip my own dick out. I groan when we finally get it free, and take Raven's bright red locks into my hand. I put them up into a ponytail and fist it. Her hands land on my hips when she leans forward to take me in.

My head falls back on a groan, and the similar whimper that leaves Raven is absolutely sinful. My dick jumps in her mouth, and I grit my teeth to keep myself from coming so damn soon. It'd be embarrassing. Her tongue traces the vein under my shaft, something we've recently found sends me over the edge far too quickly. I look down and meet her gaze, raising a brow, "Shit, you're fucking beautiful at my mercy, baby."

Her hands grip my thighs, her nails digging in as she holds eye contact and continues to flick her tongue around and around my shaft, sucking me deep until her nose is pressed against my stomach. She still maintains eye contact, though her eyes are heavy lidded at this point. She's squirming, and I know she needs to be touched as much as I do at this point.

"Up," I tell her, pulling her off of my aching dick by the hair. "Strip," I tell her, pulling my own shirt off and kicking my pants the rest of the way off of my body.

"Pierce–" she whines, and I step up to her again, helping her with her tank top and shorts, leaning in to kiss the swell of her breast as I unlatch the front clasp of her bra.

"I know, babe," I whisper, pressing kisses along her stomach as I make my way to my knees in front of her. I pull her underwear down her thighs, chancing a glance up at her when I pull them free from her feet. "I know."

I trace my fingers up her ankles, toward her thighs, before I grip her by the ass and lift her, pressing her against the rock wall in the small space where there are no hand or foot holds. Appropriate, since we're both metaphorically free falling right now.

"C-condom," she stutters out, her eyes wide as she wiggles her ass in my hands. Her soaking wet pussy grinds against my skin, coating me in her and only her.

"Fuck," I grit out, squatting down and using one hand to reach into the back pocket of my jeans for my wallet. I come up with the condom and the paracord I had stuffed in my pocket earlier. I hand the condom to her, lifting us both up again and pressing her against the wood with both hands on her hips.

She quickly rips the package open with her teeth. "Shit," I

groan out, burying my head in her shoulder for a moment. "That'll stay in my head forever, Blue."

"That's the plan," she giggles. When I pull back, she fists my cock between us and slides the latex on, maintaining full eye contact. "You're breaking character. You're supposed to fuck me into this wall and make it hurt, Pierce, not be sweet and loving." She rests her head back against the wood, her hand slowly stroking me as her eyes meet mine.

"Fuck, you're perfect," I tell her, leaning in to kiss her softly, sweetly, before I grab her hand, moving it from my dick. I place it beside her head and pin it against the wall. Using my other hand, I position my dick at her entrance and I swear I already see the stars we're headed toward.

Before she realizes what I'm doing, I'm tying her wrists together with the paracord, a large, cocksure grin on my lips when I hear her intake of breath. She squirms underneath me. Once I'm sure the knot I've tied is safe and secure, I place one hand between us, making sure my dick is perfectly aligned with her.

"Fuck me, Pierce," she whimpers, wiggling that little cunt all around the tip of my cock.

"You got it, little bird," I tell her, my eyes looking between us as I thrust inside of her slowly. So achingly slow that I might die before I make it fully inside of her.

"Harder!" She snaps, her glare making me falter.

I bring my hand from between us, and cover her mouth with it, a glare of my own meeting hers. Like a man possessed, I thrust so hard into her I nearly stop. The pained squeak she lets out makes me feel guilty, but the absolute most beautiful moan escapes her afterward. "Ah hell," I say before I pull out and thrust harder into her. It's intoxicating, the way her hips chase mine, her hands clawing at me in any way that they can.

The hand I have pinned to the wood begins to grasp at my

fingers so hard the knuckles turn white. Her pupils are blown so wide, and the way her nipples scrape against my heated skin makes me shudder with my full body as she continues to writhe in my arms.

Her warmth is gripping me like a vice, and I nearly come, but I can't stop yet. I release my hand from her mouth and bring it to her throat, gripping it softly as I stare into those blue eyes. Her lips part and I lean in to take a kiss from her. It's brutal, about as brutal as the pace of my hips as I pick up speed and strength. The wood creaks with our combined weight, and my hips and hers slam against each other.

I couldn't hold back the groans that left me, and they were each met by a moan from Raven. Our combined heavy breathing and panting creates a lot of sound that would scare anyone away from here, if it wasn't already abandoned.

Raven stiffens, and I know she's seconds from exploding around my dick, so I nip at her lower lip and move my hand from her throat, snaking it between us as I meet her gaze again. "You gonna come for me, little bird? Explode and see stars, huh?"

She nods and whimpers, my fingers teasing around her clit as I thrust almost violently into her. I couldn't stop right now unless she asked me to. I'm possessed as I bring my fingers to her clit finally, her eyes shutting closed at the added pleasure I was giving to her body.

"Eyes on me, little bird," I grit out.

She whimpers again, her eyes snapping to mine as she rutted against my ever moving hips and fingers. I use my thumb and forefinger to pinch her clit, and my little bird goes soaring. Her pussy clenches me so tightly that my knees buckle and nearly send us sprawling to the ground. But as she keeps her eyes on me and the world explodes into sensation for her, I continue to massage *the little nub while thrusting inside of her. Once she comes down, a slow whimpering sigh leaves her.*

I grip onto both of her hips, and stare into those pretty blues, losing myself to her body. I'm not thrusting anymore, I'm simply rolling my hips, entering her over and over without rhythm. I roar out my own release, my hips stuttering as I come.

Raven's lips meet mine when I lean my forehead against hers, and the kiss is anything but the hectic primalness of our fuck. And that's what we just did, we fucked.

Our kiss seems to last for an eternity, but I can't find it in myself to release her. My hands snake up into her hair and hold her gently as I explore her mouth with mine.

Pulling back moments later, I smile softly at Raven, placing a quick kiss on her nose. "Ready?" I ask her.

"Mhm."

I pull out of her and gently set her down onto her feet. She wobbles and lets out a soft little laugh that makes my heart clench.

As I begin to put my shoes on, I look over at her. "Why didn't you bring any shoes, you goofball?" I ask her, grinning as she slips back into her clothes and I dispose of the condom. I'll deal with the trash can later. It was getting full anyway.

"I didn't want to be easy to find, and I know my shoes are why I'm always so loud when I walk." She says this sheepishly as she slides her feet into my shoes. They're about five sizes bigger than her tiny feet, so she stumbles a little as she walks toward the merry-go-round. She goes to sit down, placing her ass on the metal and shrieking at the heat. "Holy hell, that's hot!"

I laugh, putting my clothes on before following her. I always follow her.

"Put some damn clothes on, Blue. Ain't that hard." I grin when she swats at my back. Turning, I hover over her until she's

laying in the center of the equipment. I smile, brushing hair away from her skin as it sticks to the sweat. Biting my lip, I watch as her eyes trace my face, her hands rising to rest against my biceps, her fingers stroking the skin there.

"Thank you, Pierce," she says softly, "for trying this."

I scoff and place a slow and languid kiss to her lips, only pulling back because I need to breathe.

"Little bird, I'll always try new things with you. Whatever will help you soar in this life or the next, I'll be right there along-side you."

I TRY to catch my breathing and slow it down as that night flashes in my mind. I blow out a slow breath before pressing my lips against Raven's ear, my hand on her hip tightening. "We'll play later. For now, keep your damn hands to yourself," I grit out, glaring at River and knowing he wants to argue this point.

I pull away from Raven, hiding a grin when she stumbles. I turn away to head toward the bar. I need another goddamn drink before I have to deal with this bullshit.

Like sharing has ever been easy for me to do when it comes to Raven Hill.

Letter from Pierce

Age 8

Dear Blue,

I tried a pizza with pineapple today. I gotta say, Rae, it was really good. I think there's something wrong with you, but I think I can change your mind someday.

We're still going to get married, you and me. Just you wait!

We'll have all the pineapples on all the pizzas, too.

Anyways...I don't want to leave but I have to go to summer camp tomorrow. I don't want you to be sad, so I'm giving you permission to let Jimmy be your best friend.

JUST FOR THIS WEEK ONLY, BLUE!

I'll be back before you know it.

Promise.

Later gator,

Green

raven

The party is dragging, and I've only been here for an hour so far. River won't touch me again, but he also doesn't leave my side. I don't think he has it in him to flip a switch like Phoenix does with his random anger. Logically, I know he's simply pleasing Pierce, but my emotions still get caught up in the way he glares at me and how his voice hardens. It's sad.

I look across the room to where Phoenix and Pierce are talking to a couple, noting that Phoenix hands over a bag with two small white pills in them. Immediately my hackles rise, and my mouth waters. I can't find it in me to stop myself from casing the entire room now, my eyes flitting between couples grinding, singles acting out a little more.

Is everyone in this damn room *high*?

This does not bode well for me.

I clench my fingers together and attempt to look away, but jolt when River comes up behind me, his voice near my ear, though he doesn't touch me. Unfortunately.

"RaeRae, would you like to try some? I see the curiosity in

your eyes," he whispers, placing a little baggie in my hands and bringing it close to my body to hide the evidence. "Free of charge for the beautiful new secretary."

I look toward him with wide eyes, panic rising in the back of my mind. My body is reacting, and I haven't even put it in my mouth yet. When our eyes meet, he grins and dips his head toward my hand. Turning, I open the bag and lift the little white pill to my lips, holding my tongue out to place it there. I let the pill begin to dissolve a little–a trick I learned this past summer–and swallow the remainder.

River hands me a glass of clear liquid, definitely not water, and I'm thankful when I down it and find out its vodka. The mix of this and ecstasy are a fun combination, and they both kept me from the boredom of sitting in an empty house this summer.

With no best friend, no family, and no job, I simply had myself for company.

I found that company within alcohol, drugs, and a pretty little knife that I may or may not enjoy carving myself with.

I clench my thighs together and ignore the way River takes in my body when I do it. His grin turns cocky, and I see him glance over my shoulder before he pulls me in.

"Not your first time, is it, sweet girl?" He rumbles, bringing his nose to my hair, his hands pulling me in by the hips until our bodies are as close and aligned as they were before Pierce came and ruined our moment.

He has us swaying gently for a few moments, but we're full on grinding against each other once a slow and heady beat thrums through the speakers.

Though the theme of the night was kings and queens, we're all dancing like we're wild and free without a care in the world. Letting our minds and body wander as we luxuriate in the feeling of being free, but is anyone actually free?

River's hands slide down and palm my ass, and my eyes grow heavy as I look up at him to find his pupils blown with lust, his eyes red. He must have taken one of the tablets, too. He leans in, nose sliding against mine as we simply breathe each other in.

My hands find purchase on the back of his neck, gripping his hair while I slide my hips against his, my pussy brushing up against his dick in the process, unfortunately through our clothes. My arms wrap around his middle and I let my head rest against his thumping chest.

"The hell's going on, Riv?" I hear someone say, but I pay it no mind.

My body has found its way to a state of bliss that I plan to bask in. If only my little stabby friend were to make an appearance while I felt like this, my life would be absolutely perfect.

I grin when I think about doing the actual chef's kiss emoji but in real life.

I scowl when a little drool falls from my lip.

"Dunno what yer on about, PJ. We're enjoying our time. Flying hiiiiiigh, if you get my drift." River pulls back, having to steady me, though he's unsteady himself. He's as gone as I am, and his hands let go of me to brush at his forehead. "The fuuu-uuck." He looks toward Pierce, or I think it's Pierce. "This is cut with somethin'," he slurs.

The words hardly resonate in my brain before I smile wide enough to make my cheeks hurt. I try to lean forward onto River again, since he was so, so, so, so warm. But, River isn't as close to me anymore, so I stumble. Cursing my luck internally, I reach out to push the ground away from me as it comes up to greet me.

Go away, Mr. Floor.

I let out a breath of laughter, looking around but not seeing anyone anymore. It's dark, and my body is twisted up like a pretzel. When I manage to evade the darkness, I find Phoenix has picked me up and is taking me somewhere. I don't care where since he's as warm as River, and smells like a rainstorm. So I lean into his chest, close my eyes, and take a big sniff.

"Shit you're so gone, Red," he grunts. I think he's bouncing up some stairs, bringing me into a room that isn't mine or Pierce's. I grin wide and flail my arms out, trying to get a feel for his...essence...in here. It's him, alright. All dark, broody, rain-stormy and caring-y. Is that a thing? Probably not.

There's a cloud beneath my body and I snuggle into it, bringing my brooding rainstorm with me and basking in his warmth as I lay my head on his scorching hot shoulder.

"Rest now. I'll be here to watch over you, Raven. You're safe." His lips press to my forehead, and I hear something whispered about Maxwell Langston. My brows furrow right before I find myself caught in a very, very rough nightmare.

I WAKE WITH A START, gasping and gripping my throat. I know whatever I was dreaming about ended with me screaming. I was hoping when I woke I would be screaming. So I'm extremely pissed off to find that I am, in fact, still mute.

I sigh, blinking my eyes to adjust to the light coming from the window on the other side of the room. A room that is not mine. I'm about to bolt entirely out of it when I hear voices coming from down the hall.

"Let me fucking see her, Nix, or I'll cut your nuts off and

feed them to Brittany for lunch!" Pierce yells, my head pounds in response and I rub at my temples.

"She needs to keep resting, so shove off," Phoenix replies. He sounds like he's right outside the doorway. "Go calm River down before he drowns us all in his misery."

"He should be fucking miserable! He was the one who gave the shit to her!" Pierce bellows, and I hear him thump against the door. A few sounds of rustling precedes what sounds like a slap. "What the fuck?!"

"Go away. I'll bring her down for lunch later if she's up for it. You've hit my shit list, PJ. So bug off."

I find myself staring into Phoenix's eyes as he swiftly enters his room, shutting and locking the door before Pierce can enter. Tears are flooding my eyes in moments, and I'm unsure why I let my guard down around him, but I do.

"Shit," he mutters, rushing toward me and bringing me into his arms. "You heard all of that, huh?"

I nod, and he brushes his hand through my hair, pulling me flush against his chest, his fingers brushing through my tangles absentmindedly.

"Sorry, Red. I know you probably feel like shit right now, but I need you to do something for me. No questions right now, okay?" He meets my gaze, imploring me to do as he asks. He looks exhausted, like he's been up all night. Bags under his beautiful chocolate eyes, his black hair mussed up in the knot he had it in.

I nod again with my eyes on his. He helps me stand up and walks me to his en suite. A blush crosses his cheeks but he clears his throat when he opens a drawer and hands me a small cup.

A pee cup.

He wants me to pee in a fucking cup.

I shake my head and go to leave the bathroom, but he quickly lifts me up by the waist and places me further inside of the bathroom.

"Red!" He snaps, then sighs and rubs the bridge of his nose. "You were drugged last night. We think the E River gave to you was cut with something. He already pissed away the evidence, and everyone else that had any has left. So please," he begs, meeting my eyes again, "please pee in this cup so I can take it to get tested."

When our eyes meet again, I'm ensnared by the sincerity of his worry. Not only for River and I, but for the other people who took some of this. I have a feeling these boys are the ones passing this shit around, but they aren't making it, that's for sure. So, in the moments that we stare at each other, I come to the conclusion that I will help them find out whatever this is. I refuse to be part of the reason someone becomes a statistic.

Phoenix hands over the cup before he backs out of the bathroom, and shuts the door, leaving me to myself.

I quickly use the bathroom, filling the cup up as cleanly as I can. I clean the cup and my hands and open the door back up. Holding the cup out with a blush on my cheeks, I walk around Phoenix when he walks toward a cabinet against the wall and places the cup in a small bag. Nodding to himself, he turns toward me and tilts his head before smiling softly.

"I grabbed you a few clothes to change into, so you can take a shower in there before you come out to do whatever for the frat. Most of them have already eaten and cleaned up after the party, so you're off the hook for that."

I smile and do this awkward little bow thing in thanks, shaking my head as my cheeks heat in embarrassment. When I lift back up, Phoenix's brows are furrowed. I tilt my head in question at him and he smiles softly.

"Ah, I think we should work on learning some sign language. There's a class on campus we can all sign up for," Phoenix is smiling brightly, like the idea of doing something so kind for me makes him happy too. "Yeah, I'll get us signed up. Take a shower, Red. Come down when you're ready. I'll order pizza for lunch so you don't have to cook."

He's out of the door so quickly, and I'm blinking back tears. I didn't think anyone would be this kind to me again. Not after all of the bad shit I've done.

I sniff, wiping away the tears as I turn toward the shower and notice the clothes sitting on the dresser near the door. He brought me a pair of black cut-offs and a cream tank top. Simple black socks and some purple lacy underwear are laying atop the clothes, and I shake my head.

He may be kind, but the motherfucker still went through my underwear drawer.

Sighing, I grab the clothes and head into the bathroom. By the time I make it into the water, my body is alive at the thoughts that I had last night. The way I plastered myself to River was sinful. I shut my eyes and let out a long breath as I trail my now wet hands down my body and toward my center.

Before I can get my hands close to my aching cunt, another set of hands joins in. I jerk back, only to be brought close to a hard body. My eyes fly open and I meet the angry green eyes of Pierce Jackson, naked in the same shower as me.

"Not your pretty cunt to play with, little bird," he says, "it's mine." He turns my body and pushes my front against the tiles. The steam from the shower makes my vision hazy. "Hands against the tile, Blue."

I flinch when he calls me by that nickname, but I do as he says and place my hands against the tile, trying to dig my fingers in but finding no purchase. I shiver at the lack of hot water on my skin, but I melt when Pierce's hands begin to roam my skin.

It's as if he's checking me over from last night. Like he's worried and has to verify that I'm fine. His fingers coast across my hands, arms, and shoulders. He trails them down my spine, around to my ribs, barely brushing my breasts before going to my shoulder blades and traveling down my spine again. Every single place his hands touch lights my body up with joy, and I can't say I hate it when I notice his dick hardening against my ass cheeks.

"Fuck, I am so sorry, beautiful. I am so incredibly sorry you got caught up in that shit," he sounds pained. His voice cracking as he leans in and places a kiss to the middle of my shoulder blades.

I'm thrown at the change in him, my world tilted on its axis and rotating out of sync with the rest of the universe. This is the guy who cares, the one who handles me with care and keeps me in check. This is the guy I grew up with and said I'd marry.

Pierce pulls his dick away from me, and trails his hands down to my ass. He squeezes firmly before bringing them down the backs of my thighs, down to my ankles. His breath hits between my cheeks and I clench on instinct, but he brings his hands to my ass and holds me there, placing kisses along the flesh.

"Bend over," he commands. And I do, because he's made me so needy. I'm his little toy lately. "Keep your hands on the wall, and try to keep quiet."

That jab hits right to the very core of my being.

No shit I'll keep quiet, Sherlock.

I'm about to slap him senseless, but he places his mouth over my wet folds and I'm a damn goner. I can fight him later. I haven't gotten off with anything but my own fingers since I've been here, and it's becoming a problem with how many dicks I've seen. It's like a real life porno and I'm simply along for the ride without a release in sight. Until now. Hopefully.

Pierce's tongue lashes out at me, circling my clit before he enters me, thrusting inside over and over again. I buck my hips back, and he pulls away, slapping my ass so sharply I jolt, glaring back at him.

"Stay still, little bird," he tells me, taking a bite of my ass cheek and kissing it better afterwards. He goes back to thrusting his tongue inside of me in such a way that I know I'll combust soon. Landing another slap on my ass, I hear him groan when I clench around his tongue. His finger joins in with his thumb now, thrusting inside of me so obscenely that my body shakes with the movement. I try to stay still, but he makes it hard when his fingers grip my clit and tug on it. My head falls forward, resting on the shower tiles, as I wonder if this is where heaven is after all.

"Fuck, you're delicious," Pierce says, pulling back to breathe. "Come for me, Raven," he growls, leaning in and devouring me all over again. His fingers are playing with my clit in just the right way, and his tongue is practically jack hammering inside of me. His other hand massages my ass before he lands several quick slaps on it, and I'm a damn goner.

I let out a silent scream, knowing I'd wake the whole damn house if I had any sound to give. My eyes are closed so damn tight as I ride this wave. By the time I'm finally down from this, I can't find the need to open them. I jump when Pierce places one last kiss to my ass and stands, gripping my chin and twisting my face to the side so he can kiss me.

"Stay like this," he growls, and his fist touches my ass for a quick moment. By the sounds of his grunts, I surmise he's jerking himself off. "Fuuuck," he groans, long and low. Seconds later, his cum is coating part of my back and the center of my ass.

Coming down from my orgasm, shame immediately ruins the bliss that I had found. My heart clenches painfully and I begin to remove myself from his hold, wrapping my own arms around myself, trying to hide from what we did together.

I blink my eyes open when the air around me goes cold, and I see that Pierce is now toweling off. When our eyes meet one final time, he winks at me.

"Good game," he says, leaving the room.

What the fuck just happened?

ONCE I MAKE it down to the kitchen, Phoenix and River are handing out slices of pizza to the other Alpha Mu boys, and Pierce is already eating a slice at the dining room table, a scowl on his face.

Guess getting off didn't knock the edge off enough for him.

I smile sweetly at River when I make it to where he's standing. He looks like absolute shit right now. As if he was the one to cut the drugs himself and forced me to try them. He drops the slice of pizza he's holding and brings me into his arms for a tight hug, breathing me in.

"Jesus, RaeRae, I am so damn sorry. I feel so damn bad and I promise that I won't give you a single drug ev–"

I silence him with a finger to his lips, shaking my head. I lean in and hug him, shutting my eyes and basking in his warmth. The cold Pierce left behind is quickly replaced, so I'm able to relax. When I pull back, I reach over for a pen and paper that's been on the counter since yesterday afternoon. I write a message down and show it to River.

I'm fine. You had no idea. Don't beat yourself up, k?

When he nods, I smile and am stunned when he presses a quick kiss to my lips before lifting me into a hug. I let out a small laugh–more of a huff of air, but it's a laugh–and River grins ear to ear as he sets me down.

"I'm still paying penance. I'll do all of your chores today, so take a piece of pizza and relax, got it?" When he points toward a stool next to him and a piece of pineapple pizza on the plate, I cringe but sit and begin to meticulously pull the pineapples off of it.

"What the hell are you doing?" Phoenix says, coming up to my plate. He begins putting the pineapples back on my pizza.

I shake my head and snatch my pizza away from him, taking the pineapples back off.

"She's a goddamn crazy person!" River shouts, waving his hands in the air as he looks between me and the pizza.

"Told you not to get pineapple," Pierce says, walking by and grabbing my plate and tossing it in the trash before I can manage a bite. "Maybe let her do what she's supposed to fucking do, dickheads. She's better at making messes than cleaning up, though."

I stare between all three boys before he leaves the room, and I nearly break down there, but I stand strong and promise myself not to shed another single tear over Pierce Jackson.

river

The only thought running through my mind is that I'm seriously pissed right now. I don't quite understand Pierce and why he deemed it appropriate to get rid of Raven's food. We're already being dishonest about what work she's doing for us.

We could use her intelligence to build this frat back up, but nope, Pierce Jackson has it in his head that his high school sweetheart is a cold-hearted bitch. I don't think he knows her at all. I've been watching her since she got here and I think she's truly fucking special. Someone I'd like to cuddle with after sex.

That in itself is a frightening fact which makes me keep to myself and not piss Pierce off.

However...

I smirk, tiptoeing down the hall with a cloth bag in my hand that's filled to the brim with *goodies*.

Reaching up, I knock on Raven's door softly, hoping she's still awake. It's barely past eleven, and Pierce is almost done with the meeting downstairs.

Raven opens the door with a panicked look on her face,

and that in itself is the reason I decided to involve her in this task. I lean forward and press a placating kiss to her forehead, a smile gracing my lips when I see her lips tilt up into a small smile as well.

"Hey, RaeRae," I whisper, holding out my hand and waving her toward Pierce's door. "I feel like getting back at the grumpy boss man, and I think you'll enjoy this as much as I will. Follow me, if you wish to laugh!"

Raven's smile grows a little more as she walks out of her doorway, closing the door behind her. She walks across to Pierce's door and I push forward quickly to unlock it with the key I snagged from his pocket earlier.

He shouldn't have been glaring at Raven so damn hard, and he'd have noticed my hand gripping his ass for nearly half a minute.

Too long?

No.

Not long enough.

I grin when Raven's eyes snap to mine, wide with shock or panic, I'm sure. I gesture her inside, softly closing and locking the door behind us as we walk toward the bed. The cloth bag makes a soft thud on the ground when I drop it, and I crouch down to rifle through the contents. Looking up, I meet Raven's curious blue eyes.

"Alright," I tell her, my voice barely above a whisper, "this prank in itself isn't the absolute worst thing I've ever done, but I think it'll teach Pierce not to shove his ideals down other peoples' throats."

Much like my parents, I think to myself.

I grin, big and fake.

Those thoughts aren't allowed here.

Clearing my throat, I hold up a container filled with sliced pineapples. Pulling out a bottle with my other hand, I show the items to Raven. "Pineapple vodka, pineapple chunks, pineapple juice, pineapple syrup, and actual pineapples. Oh!" I say excitedly, standing up and regretting the way Raven flinches away from me.

Who hurt her is my first question, but then I remember we're pranking the fucker that did.

With an even wilder grin, I head toward Pierce's nightstand and grab a condom out of the top drawer. I take a mental note that the box was unopened, and there aren't open wrappers laying everywhere. Maybe he needs to stick his dick in something other than Rae's mouth. I hold one of the condom wrappers up to my lips and open it with my teeth, winking at Rae when her eyes darken.

I open the bottom drawer of his nightstand and pull out a box of clearly unused sex toys—some are still in their original packaging. With as much exaggeration as possible, I remove a big purple dildo from said box. Inquiring minds will think of this revelation later. I roll the condom onto the dildo, and proceed to lay it flat in the center of Pierce's bed.

I head toward the bag lying at the foot of the bed and pull out a full sized pineapple—the actual biggest I've ever found. I toss it back and forth between my hands before I hand it over to Raven to hold for a moment.

"So, our options are to trash his room or to absolutely destroy it. The consequences will be the same no matter what, and I'm really hoping those consequences involve a dick." I snort at my own joke, grab the vodka bottle, open it up and take a swig before walking toward Rae again. I lift the bottle to her lips and tilt it up ever so slowly. Our eyes lock as she takes a sip, and my own widen when she takes more than two shots worth before I pull it away.

"Good girl," I whisper to her, chewing my lip when I see her thighs clench at the words.

Inhaling a deep breath, I take a drink twice as much as she took, reveling in the taste of her lips on the rim of the bottle. I place it down on the dresser across the room, crossing my arms and turning around as I scrutinize what's left for us to do.

"Place our little pineapple buddy on the bed next to our purple friend. We'll leave a note for him later." Once she does as she's asked, I pull out more pineapple paraphernalia; boxers, towels, a pineapple squish-mellow. It's gonna look like Hawaii came and puked all over this room.

I raise a brow when Raven lifts up Pierce's sheets and grabs for a container of chopped pineapple chunks. She opens it up, and–without hesitation–dumps the entire fucking container on the direct center of the bed. Her eyes are wide and a little bit of mania enters her expression before she meets my gaze in question.

Nodding in approval, I lean into the bag and grab a few more of the food containers, opening them all and spreading the containers across the bed like an offering for her. I spread my arms wide and take a small bow. "As the lady wishes, her revenge is here and it is as cold as Frosty the Snowman's dick."

I wink at her and stand back up with my hands on my hips, watching as she reaches forward for another container of pineapple chunks. It's like she's got a vision in her head. Seconds later, she's leaning in and spreading it all over in various designs, like she's finger painting with the sticky liquid.

I reach forward to grab some pineapple juice in a can, popping the top. Carefully, with a wide smile on my face, I draw a trail in Pierce's carpet. I remember that time he surrounded my bed with hot sauce. When I woke up on the floor the next morning, my face was smeared in the shit. I vowed then and there to get him back.

I hope this shit gets into his eyes.

Probably still won't hurt as bad, though.

When all of the containers are empty, I reach forward and begin to clean them up, tossing them haphazardly into the cloth bag I brought it all in.

Looking around the mess on his bed, I nod and grab the bottle of vodka. Bringing it with me to the side of Pierce's bed, I grab Rae around the waist.

Meeting her gaze, I take another drink of the liquid and place the bottle onto the nightstand. In a moment of pure stupidity, I lean forward and place my lips against Raven's, using my thumb to pry her lips open, opening my own mouth at the same time.

The vodka swirls between our mouths and my tongue meets hers in a passionate and slow dance. Though the drink is a tad sour, I can taste her sweetness and it confirms everything I knew I shouldn't do.

Kissing Raven is like allowing the sun to shine on me after a long day of fog filled views. It dries up all of the sadness that had poured down the night before, and it allows the moment to shine on its own now.

Kissing Raven is the final stampede of fireworks on the fourth of July at a small town carnival.

Kissing Raven? It's the death sentence I know I didn't want to sign yet.

But I do it anyway, and as her hands climb my body and meet behind my neck, scratching the skin there as she plasters herself to me, I find myself in need of a grave partner.

Someone to write my name next to that I'd be proud of.

Fuck, I find myself wanting–no, *needing*–to cuddle.

The vodka–long gone now–leaves a burn in both of our mouths, and so I reluctantly let her go, my hands sliding to her ass and massaging it. My dick takes notice of every curve of her body which is molded to mine. I'm regretting messing up the bed. Now would have been the absolute best time to use it.

So, in lieu of giving myself a happy ending, I settle on the final straws of my revenge plan.

I once again walk to the nightstand and grab out a pad and pen, handing it over to my dear sweet Raven. She grabs it, chewing on her lip. I reach out and stop her with my thumb. "Don't be such a temptress. Leave him a damn good note. We'll pay for this shit hard later, and probably not in a fun way." I pout, and Raven's head shakes back and forth as she tries to write whatever it is she wants to.

Once satisfied, she gestures for me to fix the sheets, so I do. She places the pineapple on the dead center of the bed again with the latex coated dildo, sticking the note in the pineapple leaves like it's a bouquet. I bark out a quick laugh and grab the cloth bag full of evidence, handing it over to Raven. I grab her free hand, cringing at how sticky they are, and pull her from the room quick enough to hide her from the big bad wolf.

Only...the big bad wolf is standing in the hallway when we exit, staring at Raven's door.

Shit.

Clearing my throat, I point down the hall for Raven to head toward my room, and when she does, I fold my arms and hope like hell the smell of pineapple isn't too obvious. "Ya okay, Piercey Jackson?" I ask, shuffling my feet as I await the wrath of all of the gods in one go.

"I'm okay," he says solemnly, turning toward me. He looks as if he's trying to convince himself of something.

When he looks up, and our eyes meet, the tension builds

beneath the surface. It's always been there. At this moment though, I know what he needs, and I won't mention a damn thing about it.

I normally don't, anyway. His request.

So when he walks forward and throws his arms around me, I hold him tight. One of my hands runs up and down his spine, another holds his head on my shoulder as he simply lets himself breathe.

He hasn't needed this in a few weeks, so whatever has him this worked up has me worried like hell.

After a few moments, he pulls back and tries to discreetly wipe a tear from his eye. I catch his jaw in my hand and wipe it away with my thumb, a small smile on my lips. "Tell me what's wrong, Pierce. Can't fix it if I don't know," I whisper, my eyes imploring him.

He stares for a few moments at me, and my heart begins to beat out of rhythm the longer he does. His brows furrow, and I think he's about to admit to something finally, but instead he lets his tongue drift out and lick my thumb that's far too close to his beautiful lips.

"Is that," he says, shaking his head and licking his lips as he pulls away. "Is that pineapple? The fuck did you do, Riv, bathe in it?"

I shrug and try to walk toward my room where Raven should have gone. I tamp down the grin threatening me. I'm halfway to my doorway when I hear him enter his room with a sigh.

Quickly, I reach into my doorway and grab Raven from where she was leaning against the wall beside the door. "Shh," I tell her with a finger to my lips, and when she raises a brow I sigh, "Sorry, sunshine."

I move my grip to Raven's hand, intertwining our still

sticky fingers and tiptoe back down the hallway until we are leaning against the wall near Pierce's door. I pull Raven as close to me as possible and feel her pulse thundering when she rests her chest against mine. I keep myself grounded to her as I wait.

And wait.

And wait...

Just when I'm about to give up...

"What the fuck?!" Pierce roars, and I hear a loud thud. He must have fallen down off of the bed now. I can't help but bark out a laugh. As his thundering footsteps reach his door, we're pouring into my room down the hall. I'm slamming the door, locking it, and shoving a chair against the door handle. "River, I will kick your ass and shove this thing so far up it you won't walk for weeks!! Open this fucking door!"

"No can do, PJ!" I shout back. "I got a scared woman in here and I must defend her!" I laugh loudly, looking at Raven as she shakes her head at me. She's smiling though, which was the plan. She'd been extremely sad ever since he threw her lunch away this afternoon, though I know the food wasn't her only issue.

"River Jacobs," he barks out, pounding against the door, "You can't stay in there forever, fucker." I hear the loud sigh that leaves him before his retreating footsteps pound down the hall. I pull Raven into another hug and place a kiss to the top of her head before tugging her toward my en suite.

"Now, my beautiful little siren, please let me bathe you and treat you as a real queen should be treated while the evil ogre stews in his pineapple scented swamp!" When I see her shake her head, but with a smile on her face, I commend my joke making. I walk toward the shower to turn the water on.

"Strip for me, beautiful," I tell her gently, biting back a

smile when she does. Clearly, I am the superior alpha male in this dynamic.

Once she's naked and in the shower, I strip myself and climb in behind her, shutting the shower door. I trail my hands down her back, getting a good feel of her ass as I lean into her, listening to her breath as it hitches. Grinning, I lean further forward until I can place my lips against the base of her neck. My dick takes its place between us, angry and letting itself be known to us as it brushes against the middle of Raven's back. I couldn't stop myself from grinding against her if I tried.

"Sweet girl," I whisper in her ear, my hand trailing along her skin. "Can I please take a moment and treat you how I would if I had no restraints?" My hand trails through her hair, getting it wet in the steamy water. When Raven nods her head and leans it back onto my shoulder, I groan, twist her face toward me, and slam my lips against hers.

Quickly, this situation has changed from reality to fantasy. I spin her around, and lift her up into my arms, wrapping those pretty little hips around my waist. My dick meets the wetness of her core and I have to keep from entering her. With my lips and hers still entangled, I reach up to the top of the shower door and grab a condom. I keep them here for this purpose. Though they haven't been used since P–

I cut that thought as soon as it enters my brain.

I press Rae up against the cool tile walls, grinning when her skin breaks out into goosebumps. Breaking apart from her to look between us I sheath myself in the latex. Biting my lip, my hand travels between us, and my fingers brush gently across her clit. I'm getting a kick out of teasing the shit out of her. She squirms, grinding on the end of my dick just enough to torture my soul for eternity.

I grit my teeth while I begin to trail my hand up her body,

my hand massaging her breast when it makes contact. My other hand is still holding her up, fingers digging into the meat of her creamy thigh. I lean forward and press my forehead to hers, my eyes locking onto those pretty blues. "Ready, sweetheart?"

When she nods, I enter her in a rushed yet fluid motion. I can feel every goddamn inch of her wrapped around my dick, and the groan that leaves me is so long I wonder if I'll run out of oxygen. Once I'm fully seated inside of her, my eyes land on her half-lidded ones and I smile at her.

"One day," I tell her, pulling back slowly, "I'll fuck you into oblivion while Pierce sits back and watches. For now, however-er," I tell her, both hands now firmly on her hips as I anchor her to the wall, "I'll fuck you into oblivion and keep you to myself."

I thrust inside of her so hard she slides up the wall. I slide one of my hands up to hold onto her shoulder, pushing down enough to keep her steady. My hips piston in and out of her, my dick weeping when I deny him the release that he so desperately wants. I must be biting my lip too hard, because Raven reaches out and puts her hands on my cheeks, pulling my lip from between my teeth with her thumbs before she leans forward and plants a rough kiss to my lips.

She's panting beneath me, and her hands move to grip at my shoulders while I hold her steady and fuck her with the passion of a dying man. My heart is thundering in my chest as I reach between us to rub Raven's nipple with my thumb and forefinger.

She throws her head back at the act, and I can see the moment it finally gets to her. Her eyes roll back when I tug a little harder, and her pussy clamps down on my dick so hard I see stars forming. I lean forward and place a bruising kiss on her now exposed neck, my hand trailing between us until it's pressed over her pubic bone and I can feel myself moving through her body.

"Fuck baby, I can feel myself inside of you," I tell her, biting down on her shoulder as I piston into her faster. I'm going to lose it soon. "I need you to come, sweetheart, or I'll embarrass the hell out of myself. You feel too fucking good," I grit out. Our skin slapping in the shower is hot as shit, and though I can't hear her moans, I can see her body reacting. Her silent pleas for more. Her silent yells.

It's intoxicating.

"Can you come for me, sweet girl?" I ask her, my eyes meeting hers when I begin to rub circles around her little nub. I apply more and more pressure, and the way her cunt grips me nearly sends me to my knees. "Soak my cock, baby girl. Fly with me."

I slam my lips to hers again when I pinch her clit.

I drag the orgasm from her body. As I'm riding her through her high, I find my own. Boy do we fucking fly.

We're so lost in coming down from our orgasms with each other that I hardly recognize it when Pierce rips me from her body. Or when he punches me square in the damn nose, which makes me smile and simply sit down in the shower as he takes Raven out of the room in a towel.

I see the fear in her eyes, but I know I'm better off down here than at the wrath of Pierce Jackson.

I know what it's like to lose, so, in the saddest display of failing to protect the queen I can manage, I merely lay down. I allow the shower to run cold over my aching body.

When I lay in bed that night, still naked but dry and warm, I groan when it's clear that I've let people down again.

Broken more promises I shouldn't have broken.

I may have exploded this entire situation...

Dear Green,

I haven't seen you since I got my cast on. Jimmy's already signed it, and he's hanging out inside with me today watching cartoons. But you weren't even here so you could get to see the color of my cast.

It's purple, obviously.

I tried to talk to your mom but she said you were busy.

Whatcha doing?

Why'd you leave me here without you to help keep the monsters away?

I forgive you. Falling off of your bike was an accident. Momma said it really was my fault for getting onto the front of it anyways.

She took my bike away for the summer.

Please come back...it's lonely without you here... and scary.

TTFN

Blue

raven

I'm terrified. I shouldn't be, but I am. This is my childhood sweetheart. The best friend I've always relied on.

And yet, as he drapes me in a towel and pulls me away from River, I'm shaking from fear and not the sudden cold. I don't know what Pierce Jackson is capable of, and seeing as he deals drugs in plain fucking sight, I don't think I should continue this arrangement. I've already gotten hurt once by the drugs here.

No need to add more heartache or something worse.

Though I'm struggling to see the benefit of not tuning the world out.

Surely going about life while unaware of the casual bull-shittery that's going on should make for a happy...well a happier life than seeing all of the shit and not understanding how to change it.

Right as we make it to the tiny ass maid's room that was given to me my first day here, Pierce places me on the ground and pushes me up against the wall. He wraps his hand around my throat and squeezes hard enough my pulse begins to race.

Leaning in, his voice is low as he speaks. "I told you over and over to keep your damn hands off of my friends, Raven! You are not my friend anymore!" He shouts, and I flinch backward, my head slamming against the wall. His nostrils flare as he opens up the door, shoving me inside.

I have to scramble to keep my feet underneath me, my hands clawing at his wrist to get him to let me go.

"You have *no* free will, Raven!" He grits out. "You are a goddamn slave here. You do as *I* say or I will tell Langston how much of a useless little shit you actually are. You'll lose your place here and be forced to go back home to be all alone and be a miserable fucking bitch for the rest of your life!" He lets go of me, and I clutch at my throat, staring up at him with tears threatening.

Holding the towel to myself, I furiously blink back the tears when Pierce stands straighter and crosses his arms, his eyes hardening more as he clenches his jaw.

"So here's what's gonna happen," he grits out. "You're here. You don't fucking speak."

Does he seriously think I'm giving him the cold shoulder?

"You don't look at my damn friends. Eyes and hands to yourself unless I command them to be any fucking different. Aside from that," Pierce grips my door handle and begins to close it, "you don't fuckin' exist, Raven. You wanted it to be like this, so have it your fucking way."

The door is slammed roughly in my face, and I jump, dropping the towel. When I reach out for the handle, I find it locked.

He fucking locked me into this glorified closet!

I want to yell and scream and commit murder at this point.

Instead, I let the flood of tears fall and try not to choke on them while I pound on the door with my fists, my feet, and all that I have. I know it's not going to work, but by the time I hear Pierce updating both Phoenix and River on his plans, I recognize the loudest sound in the room is the sound of my soul shattering.

Pierce Jackson had my heart once...

I just didn't let him know that...

And now he's gripped it in his dirty fucking hands and crushed the thing into a million pieces.

What I would do to exact some fucking revenge at this point...

THE DAY after being locked in the room, I went up to the administrator and tried desperately to plead my way out of the scholarship stipulation forcing me to live with the frat. It was mostly through written notepads on my part, and rolled eyes on hers. She answered slowly as if I were an idiot and it made me want to pop all of her damn tires.

Eventually, I was told the conditions of my scholarship are strict. I can't break a single portion of the conditions. If I give the scholarship up now...I also won't have a spot at this school.

Two weeks later, we're entering into a steady normal.

I keep my head down, the boys keep their hands to them-selves, and Pierce continues to spear me with every single scathing look he sends my way.

I'd say I couldn't care less, but I probably could. My mind is so much of a spiraling mass of emotions that I find myself giving into them every single night at this point. Surprised I have tears left, honestly.

It's after lunch, and I am now meticulously cleaning the counter tops until they shine. Pierce told me he and the boys will be gone until late tonight, so once I'm satisfied with the state of the kitchen, I make myself scarce in my room. The only other places I have had access to these last two weeks have been the kitchen, bathroom and whatever room I'm cleaning.

When I finally hear the boys enter the house around 3 am, I've managed to read an entire book featuring a female serial killer and the FBI agent she manages to fall madly in love with.

Morally gray characters are fantastic in fiction but not even close to amazing in person.

See: Pierce Jackson.

OCTOBER.

I'm pissed at myself that I've allowed this situation to continue for a month and a half. I should have fought harder to get out of it, but without anyone to go home to, and no real friends, I've given up and given in. Pierce can own me, body and soul, like he always has. I'm too far into the dark to see a good way out, anyway.

A damsel in distress I am not.

No. I am a damsel in depression.

It's been a hell of a few days getting ready for this upcoming Halloween party that the boys are hosting for the entire school. They have been more stressed lately, and although River took me to get an outfit for the party, I've hardly seen the guys or even know what's going on. I was told to simply clean the house spotless before getting myself dressed and ready to go.

I demanded a mirror in here a few days after Pierce locked

me in, and he also revealed an en suite attached to the maid's room. He had it hidden behind a large bookcase.

I take a deep breath, and let it out. Today is my favorite holiday, and I won't let any circumstance ruin it for me.

I love Halloween.

It's when the monsters come out to play in full force; most of them are actually wearing their real faces tonight. Some of these monsters I've grown up with, others I've loved. Though I have come to hate one monster in particular.

But he's not worth a tick of the clock tonight.

No. Tonight is my night to change the course of fate and turn my forced silence into something more powerful. Something that I can finally own rather than shy away from.

I'm looking at myself in the mirror, studying the way my hair cascades in waves halfway down my back, nearly at my tailbone now. I'm wearing neon purple contacts, and my makeup looks sexy as hell—but that's going to be covered by my knock-off purge mask, so my perfect cat eyeliner is pretty much pointless, as are my black stained lips.

The mask itself is off-white, the mouth and eyes stitched out and bloodied. I situate the white tutu which barely covers my ass and hangs over the white corset bodysuit I decided on. The stockings I'm wearing have little devils and angels stitched into the design that runs up the front and back of my legs. To top it all off, I'm wearing probably the highest heels I've ever worn. I think they're about five inches, which brings my five foot seven up to a whopping six feet.

I look like a grade-A slut, and I can't say I hate it.

Pierce will, though.

I roll my eyes before situating the mask over my face, securing the back with a double knot, and stuffing my phone and ID into my cleavage. Should have thought about storage when I came up with this costume idea, to be honest. But I was more concerned with how to hide from Pierce, since he has no fucking idea what my costume is. He was too busy to come shopping with River and me, so I get to be a little bit stealthy tonight.

Hence the mask.

I stumble my way out of my room, closing the door behind me. The boys, so kindly, left it unlocked earlier so I could come down on my own time–that's how busy they are in preparation for this event today. I heard them talking about something to do with Maxwell. They also talked about the drugs that were tossed around during rush week. I'm concerned about taking any tonight, so I'll make sure to guard my own drinks.

These boys may act like they care about me, but the fact of the matter is they don't care enough to get me out of Pierce's clutches. They still do as they're told when it comes to him and that does not settle well with me.

Even if River's dick is magic and Phoenix tends to be the most caring of the three.

"Fucking watch it!" some douche nozzle yells, pushing past me and nearly making me collide with the wall. I don't bother to react, it's not worth it anymore. These idiots don't care about me. No one's ever cared.

Okay, that's wrong, Pierce cared. But that was a long time ago, back when I believed in Once Upon a Times and Happily Ever Afters. I won't allow myself to believe in those things anymore.

"Is that...," some girl whispers as she points to me, turning to her friend while her gaze stays in my direction. The rest of their conversation is blotted out by the fucks I don't give and the fucks I don't have.

I've spent my time at CU in utter solitude so far, aside from the Alpha Mu boys. It makes my classes hard, since group participation tends to be a portion of my grade. I typically have to email my professors and do extra credit to get away with it.

People finally understand that I have an actual condition, and while it's been hard as hell to communicate, I'm learning it has its perks. Like not getting to know the dick-wads who attend this school.

I don't need to converse with anyone. I want to get a creative writing degree, maybe become a social media influencer or blogger. I'll take off across the country while living the van life. I don't want to be here anymore.

There's a thick, pulsing, heavy beat coming through the stairway as I descend it. The stench of sweat and booze is overwhelming, but that's a typical college smell, so we all pretend it's acceptable and move on. The decorations are top notch, with glow-in-the-dark spider webs cascading across the railings, walls, and hanging from the ceiling. String lights bracketed by black lights sit across the top of every wall, some adorning the stairs off to the side.

I have to hold back a full on cackle at the centerpiece of the room. A set of four skeletons, one female and three males, are in a compromising position. The female skeleton–distinguishable by the tight, sparkly black dress covering its frame–is sprawled sideways across an armchair, face down ass up. One of the male forms is thrusting in from behind. Boning her, get it? Another is in front of the female's face, presumably getting a blowjob. The third male is knelt at the front of the armchair, hands curled under the female's form.

Looks like fun.

Turning my attention away, I reach in and hold out my ID to the guy at the bottom of the stairs. He takes in my figure slowly, and I raise my mask to prove my identity before snatching it out of his hand. He sneers at me for a split second for ruining his fun, but shakes his head and hands me a glowing bright pink wristband. I place my mask back over my face, and walk away with as much sway to my hips as possible.

Fucking sleazes get teases. Blue balls will serve them well.

I slip through the crowd towards the bar at the right side of the room. I have to shove people out of my way in order to get there. The guy tending the bar bows his head at me and I bow slightly in return as I grab a glowing blue drink inside a martini glass. Tipping the glass towards the guy, I lift my mask and take a sip, nearly spitting the concoction out of my mouth.

Bar guy chuckles. "The pledges got heavy on the drink and not enough on the mix tonight, sorry. Best to down it." He winks and I roll my eyes before downing the whole thing. I grab another and walk away before he tries to get chatty.

I can't chat.

I sip on this drink, though I'd rather burn my throat intentionally. I had a few shots of Jack before I left my room, and by a few, I mean I drank a fourth of the bottle before I got dressed. My body sways and bops to the beat right alongside my classmates, but my mind isn't here. Never is. I do at least have a good buzz going, and I'm definitely headed towards tipsy territory after I downed the horrid blue drinks.

I'm surprised when hands land on my shoulders, but I grin wide behind my mask when I see River. His hair is a tad messier than usual and is spotted with red. He's wearing a white and black plaid shirt opened over top a bloodied white tank top. The blood looks incredibly real, and I commend him for it. He leans in to hug me, but steals my drink on the way. I try to snatch it back, but he shakes his head and laughs when he pulls back.

"Now, sweet girl, we shouldn't get completely sloshed

tonight. Lots of business to do and I can't keep track of you if you're not acting properly." He sips from the drink I had, tempting me to lift the mask from my face so I can glare at him, but it's not worth Pierce spotting me this early on in the party.

I fold my arms for a moment in contemplation, but I simply shrug, moving onto the dance floor where there is a bit of free space. I begin to gyrate my body to the slow and sexy beat that has begun and River quickly abandons the drink, coming up to me and placing his hands on my hips. He digs his fingers into my hips as he follows the slow movement of my body. I shut my eyes and simply feel, my heart pounding hard in my chest when he presses his entire frame against mine. We become one moving muscle at this point, sliding this way and that, grinding against each other.

River spins me around and slides a leg between my thighs, and I quickly find myself seeking the sweet friction I've been deprived of for weeks now. I know I'm wet by the time the song ends, and River's cocksure smile tells me he knows it just as much as I do. He leans in and presses his lips to my exposed collarbone, goosebumps appearing in his wake.

"Fuck I miss you, my sweet Raven," he whispers hoarsely. "I'm sorry it's been hard for you recently. Pierce won't give in. I've tried so hard to get him to give in." He places another kiss along my collarbone and up my neck. He lingers there, his tongue lashing out and tracing patterns in my ever heating skin. One of his hands trails down to my ass and squeezes as we begin another dance to the overly sensual music.

My hands slide up and rest at the nape of his neck, my head falling back to allow him access to my throat. He groans and places kisses there as well, my eyes rolling into the back of my head in response.

"I'd find you soaking for me now, wouldn't I?" He questions in a low voice.

He quickly brings me up with a hand on the back of my head after I nod. His free hand abandons my ass and removes my mask, pressing his lips to mine in a feverish kiss.

We both know Pierce is watching. We could sense him the moment he entered the room. But we knew he'd be too busy to stop us.

My costume gave me a tad more time.

But River pulling my mask up has opened me up to whatever punishment Pierce needs to dish out.

My tongue plays with River's, his hand gripping my hair and anchoring me to him, as he tilts my head to his own liking. His groans are barely audible above the music, but I can sense them, and he can feel my needy body pressing against him. My fingers are digging so far into his skin I'm sure I'm drawing blood.

This only goes on for a few minutes, however, long enough for one single song to play, before Pierce is gripping me by the shoulders and frog marching me to the edge of the room. River's complaints are loud as he trails behind us.

"Now tell me you aren't actually rubbing your body all over my best friend, again, after being strictly told not to? And not only that, you're here, in a clear line of sight, looking like the biggest slut in the room." The dark, low tone to Pierce's voice is so terrifying, I don't attempt to open my eyes.

My nostrils flare on a deep inhale, and I let my breath out slowly. I don't move. I don't try to think past this point. If I stand still, maybe he'll go away. He's good at that, anyway.

No such luck, though.

He moves closer. The familiar scent of mahogany attempts

to overwhelm my senses. So goddamn addicting. Or it used to be.

Fingers on my chin. A thumb sweeping across my cheek.

A fucking tear falls from the corner of my lashes.

I inhale sharply and attempt to rip my head away, but his hold tightens and he growls at me. And on that pleasant note, I open my eyes and they lock immediately with his forest green orbs so easily. Those familiar, piercing eyes glare down at me.

"Rae, Rae, Rae," his tone is so sharp and calming at the same time. He's the biggest contradiction known to man. "I thought I told you to stop acting like a fucking whore." He nearly shouts the last word. He steps closer, pushing me further back into the wall with his body. His warm, broad, hard...

STOP.

I try to shove him off of me, but this only makes him more mad. His other hand comes to grip the hair at the back of my head, tugging so I'm forced to look up at him, which forces him to look down on me. He wants a reaction from me, but he won't get one.

I won't react.

I can't react.

I don't react.

"You know I love the silent treatment, little bird. Keep it up, see what happens." His thumb strokes my cheek again, before he shoves me until my head smacks lightly against the wall. I nearly tip over, but right myself with a hand on a nearby table. It's demeaning, but I look down to keep my eyes away from his. "Get some fucking proper clothes on, Raven. There will be consequences."

pierce

I watch as Raven walks out of the room. I'm half-hard watching her ass as she leaves. Fucking ridiculous and tempting woman.

Bringing my phone from my back pocket, I tap a few buttons and bring it up to my ear as I begin walking toward the kitchen. I grab a handful of chips on the way toward the staircase. This call is long overdue and I'm hoping to find some fucking relief from Satan himself by announcing my new ownership of the bird.

"Pierce, what the fuck are you bothering me this late for? Got a death wish, boy?" The gruff voice on the other end of the line sounds a bit...winded. Let's hope he's running.

I huff out a short laugh and attempt to clear my head of the visual of him definitely not running.

"I'm about to lock her up and throw away the key if you don't let me fucking go, Maxwell." He doesn't need to know I've already locked her up for the last month and a half. I probably do have a death wish.

The not running, definitely huffing, Maxwell Langston

nearly bellows through the line next. "You will do as I say and keep an eye on and your hands OFF her, Pierce Jackson!" The sound of a screech and a fist hitting wood sounds over the phone before a door slamming and the tell-tale signs of a belt being done up invade my ear drums. "I don't care how the hell you have to get the recipe from her. She has to have it. She has to know what that bitch stole from me all those years ago. She has to. Figure it out, Pierce or there will be consequences."

Click.

I slam my fist into the hallway mirror before storming into my room. Funny how I keep taking things that don't belong to me. Raven never did, anyway. Not that she knew that. I loved and cherished her, right up until she fucked me over and caused the current events that are taking over my fucking life.

I want to leave.

But I can't.

"Hey there, Piercey Jackson!" River's annoyingly happy sing-song voice filters through my anger and I swivel my head to find him star-fished across my black sheets. They've been cleaned a dozen times in the past two weeks, and I hope he doesn't think the pineapple incident is forgotten. I still smell the shit daily and now I think I might hate the fruit.

"The hell you doin' on my bed like that, River? Also, stop fucking calling me that!" I grab the closest object to my left, a stapler, and toss it towards his head.

He dodges it, falls off the bed with a loud thump and laughs loudly before climbing up on all fours, situating himself until he's standing. His gray eyes are alight with humor and his face is a bit flushed. Running his hands through his hair, he grins at me, flexing his muscles. This fucker thinks I'm into him. Nobody needs to know he's right, so I shoulder past him as he comes near me and I sit down on the edge of my bed.

"Bro, please let me have some spicy fun times with RaeRae again!" He folds his arms and tilts his head in such a goddamn endearing way that I want to rip his throat out. After wrapping his lips around my dick, of course.

I clear my throat and shake my head. "No."

"No?" He fumbles backward like I just hit him.

"Yep, I said no. Now get the fuck out."

"C'mon!" He groans, arms outstretched as he looks at me pleadingly. My heart thumps in my chest hard as I stare him down. I need him to leave. He's as tempting as she is. "Sharing is caring, PJ!"

My eyes meet his and my jaw tics. He knows I won't fucking budge right now, if ever. Doesn't matter if the idea is thrilling and makes my blood heat.

"Fine...fucking...fine." He storms out of my room like an overgrown toddler. The door rattles the wall as it slams, knocking down a picture frame from the nearby dresser.

I groan and lean back until I'm lying flat on the bed and bring my hands up, running them across my face. I wish it was this easy to wash the pain and useless feelings away. Of course it isn't, so I bite off a curse and look around my room.

I thought about keeping Raven inside of my walk-in closet instead, but Phoenix almost murdered me before the words left my lips.

Looking towards my walk-in closet, I tilt my head as the thoughts of playing in a similar closet with Rae cross my mind. I stand and walk towards the door and open it. Flicking on the light, I lean against the door frame as I reminisce.

"GREEN! C'MON!" Her voice is a whisper but I hear it. I always hear her.

"Shh, Blue! We can't be found or the monster will grab us and keep us in his secret lab! They really like 10 year olds!"

She giggles, and sometimes I wonder if I'm allowed to make her giggle for our whole lives. It's the best sound in the world to me.

"There are no such things as monsters," she tells me seriously, her blue eyes catching in the small sliver of light coming through the slats of the closet door.

"Rae...there's always monsters. We don't always get to see them in their true forms until it's too late."

She snickers and shakes her head, shoving me until I fall on my butt on the closet floor. Joke's on her. I hug her tight and bring her down with me until we lie side by side.

"Hey Pierce...?"

"Yeah Rae?" I tangle my fingers in her hair. It's so smooth to the touch, like a soft blanket.

"If there are monsters...you won't let them get me, will you?"

I shake my head and turn to look at her. Our noses brush each other's as I stare at her. "No, Rae, I won't let them get you."

PROMISES ARE MEANT to be broken, after all.

So, is keeping your childhood sweetheart locked away fucked up?

Probably.

Am I going to keep doing it?

Abso-fucking-lutely.

Bitch had it coming.

I cross the room and pick up the picture frame that fell,

studying it with a deep and incessant thrumming to my heart. The frame is old wood and gray, nearly broken down but the picture on the inside is well taken care of. It showcases a boy and a girl dressed in swim gear, skin covered in mud, and big, bright smiles as they huddle close for the person taking the picture.

If only things could be as simple again as a girl and a boy growing up playing together...

WHEN I HEAD BACK DOWNSTAIRS ten minutes later, I notice I can't find River, Raven, or Phoenix.

I've been impatient all night, I know. I don't want to watch her enjoy herself. I haven't let her out of her room nearly as much as I should, and I'm fucking tired of locking her up like I'm the Beast, and she's Belle, here to do my bidding and not bitch about it.

She hasn't spoken or yelled or even given a hint that she's going to open up and speak to me, so I think that's what keeps me from letting her out. Her silent treatment is kind of on point. Can't say I blame her, but she is the one who asked for this last year.

Shit...has it really almost been a year since...

Shaking my head to rid myself of those thoughts, I pull myself out of the stupor I've found myself in and when I finally see the *three of them*, I'm barreling toward them as I watch their bodies greedily.

Raven is in the middle of River and Phoenix. She has a smile on her face that looks far too drunk for my liking. That little purge outfit got my dick hard the moment I knew it was her, and when the mask was removed, I nearly came in my pants. She's a fucking vision all of the time, but the way she pulls off the dark and demented vixen sometimes blows me away far too quickly.

I must be in slow motion as I make my way toward them, pushing people out of the way. My eyes eat up the way that River is grinding his dick against Raven, one of his legs between her thighs. Phoenix is pressed up against her back, a hand between her and River, holding her throat as her head leans back on his shoulder. Her eyes are shut in what looks to be absolute euphoria, and I panic for a moment before realizing the drug we're set to make and distribute here soon hasn't even been made yet—mainly since we need that fucking recipe.

River's eyes find mine and shine with delight. He's fucking drunk.

"Rae has made this party," *hiccup*, "absolutely epic!" He hip thrusts into Raven, and all I see from that moment is red.

I don't think about what I do. I simply step between them all, push my boys to the side, and grip Raven by the hair. I lean in close to her ear and growl, "Get the fuck up those stairs, Raven, before I embarrass you in front of the whole school."

I push her forward.

She whirls on me, her fist ready to fly fast and hard, but I grip her wrist and lean in so she can hear me over the music that's still pulsing. "Ah, ah, ah, little birdie. It's rude to hit your captors. Quite dumb, too, yeah?" I smirk, gripping her jaw with my free hand, and forcing her glazed eyes to meet mine. Her lips are pursed from my grip, and my dick takes notice of how pretty her pump little lips are.

"She, uh, she," *hiccup*, "She's trying to fight the monsters, PJ!" River says, cackling like a lunatic. I roll my eyes, hoping I find the answers to all of my problems somewhere in the back of my head.

"River?" I say.

"Yeah boss?" He slurs.

"Get a goddamn clue and walk away," I bark. I side eye him, waiting for his response.

"Aye, aye, captain!" He salutes me, winks at Raven, and proceeds to walk away...sideways.

I jerk Raven's head, forcing her wandering eyes back to mine. I narrow my eyes at her, hoping she'll open up and confess all of her sins to me, though I've seen most of them as of late. I notice she shrinks in on herself, and I hate myself for it. But...I continue on. I'm a glutton for punishment.

"Alright, birdie," I tell her, "It's time to bring you up to your cage and get you nice and comfortable for me. We have a little errand to run tomorrow morning, and I refuse to bring some hungover whore out to play on a Monday. So," I say, my eyes flitting between her panicked but drunk eyes, "no more booze–or fun–for you."

I pat her cheek, and drag her toward the main staircase. People stop and stare, of course, but with a sharp glare from me their eyes and heads swivel and search for other things to find interest in.

I usher Raven in front of me, then follow her. I'm on her heels as she stumbles in what looks like a panic up the stairs. Her breathing is hard, and I know both River and Phoenix are behind me. I turn toward them and fold my arms.

"Shut the fuck up," I tell them, "and go back downstairs. I'll be back down there. We have more business to attend to."

I glare at River, "I told you to keep your fucking hands off of her, so this is the consequence for not doing so." I shoo them away, impatiently waiting for them to leave. They do reluctantly, so Raven and I continue on.

Once we're at Raven's door, I push it open and pull the key

out of my pocket. Shoving her inside, I have to try hard to keep from helping pick her up when she falls onto her hands and knees. I keep my arms crossed, dangling the key from my fingers, my eyes meet hers once she turns her head to look at me. She's so fucking angry, and it makes her absolutely beautiful. Beautiful in the way a fire is before it destroys everything in its wake.

"A pretty cage for a pretty bird," I muse, my voice low and dangerous. "Funny we spent so many years hiding from monsters together, Rae. You didn't know I was one of them all along." I frown, but fake another grin while I take a step back toward the hall.

She rushes forward, of course, but I manage to slam the door before she crosses the threshold. I hear the thud of her body hitting it and cringe as I lock the door, chuckling when she pounds on the door with her fists and feet. She'd have to She-Hulk her way out of that door to get out, and no one will hear her with the party going.

She's trapped, just like I want her to be.

"See you later, Blue."

Letter from Pierce
Age 11

Dear Blue,

She left me alone again today. Slammed some peanut butter and bread down in front of me and told me to stay inside.

It's been 8 hours so far, and now I'm just sitting in my room, staring at you from across the street as you play with Jimmy.

I feel abandoned.

I don't want to break the rules, Blue.

But she abandoned me just like Matilda's parents did in the movie.

Please don't ever leave me, Raven Hill.

You're supposed to marry me and we're gonna eat pineapple pizzas, remember?

Later gator,

Green

PS: Jimmy sucks at basketball. I could beat him blindfolded.

warning!

The chapter you are about to read contains a full, described in detail, non-consensual scene mixed with a bit of dubious consent. I, as the author, struggled with writing this and fully understand if it is not your jam, or you can't read it. As a survivor myself, I chose to put this page in as a final reminder that you DO NOT have to read Chapter 9 in order to read the rest of Pierce Me. Chapter 10 references it enough, and by Chapter 11 things start to turn around for our dear sweet Raven. Please don't continue if you do not think you can handle this—I fully understand and support that decision. Take care of yourself, please.

raven

What seems like a decade of time after Pierce locks me back up into my room, but is actually only a few hours, I hear the sounds of male voices yelling, slurring their speech, laughing. A scuffle follows after all of that, and if I'm correct in my quick investigation, Pierce and River are arguing. River is definitely more drunk now, which seems like an Olympic sized task from how drunk he was earlier.

"Pierce...man...I think...," Phoenix grits out, and my head pops up from my pillow as I look toward the door. Their voices sound extremely close. Suddenly, there's a thud followed by River's drunk chuckle and a growl from Pierce.

"If you so much as...as...If you want to stay in the crew, you will follow my flucking orders, Nix!" Another thud follows Pierce's voice before I hear the slap of skin on skin. "River...be a good boy and bring our girl to my room. I got some frustrations to take out on our birdie."

"Aye," hiccup "aye," snort "capitaaan!" River sing-songs

snickering as he comes closer and I back up as far as I can, my pulse skyrocketing.

A loud thud sounds out, and I hear cackling at the door before River opens it. Did he...did he just face-plant the door?

"Pierce...you guys are far too drunk...sleep it off, man." Nix is nearly silent, being drowned out by my thundering pulse.

"Nix, kindly, go fluck yourself!" Pierce barks out, right as River finally gets the door open, stumbling inside. "Grab her, Riv, and bring her here."

River's bright grin doesn't shift even a little as he stumbles inside of my room and grips my wrist, tugging me into his body. He may be plastered, but that only benefits him. His body is so warm right now. He chuckles a bit, and I bristle, trying to feign indifference to him.

I thought we were on good terms...I should know better. I try to tug out of his hold, but he only grips me around the waist and practically carries me across the hall to Pierce's room.

After being tossed unceremoniously onto the bed, I scramble up into a ball, meeting the green eyes of my past. I swallow hard and his eyes track the movement while he starts to take his shirt off. He tosses it onto the floor, points to River, then to me. "Restrain her. She's good at esc-" hiccup "escaping monsters."

River's gray eyes meet my glare and he tilts his head in what looks like an apology, but he can shove that up his ass. I don't want it. I try to dart off of the bed, but River's entire body plants on top of mine, his hard length grinding into my upper belly as we wrestle for control.

I want to growl. I want to yell. I want to scream for help. But...I can't.

"C'mon Rae, let's make the Big Bad Wolf happy, yeah? He

wants a little fun time with you. Don't worry, we'll put you safely back in your box, baby." River grins down at me and plants a quick kiss to my nose.

Before I get what's happening, my hands are unceremoniously hand-cuffed to the headboard and Pierce is holding my ankles, putting them into cuffs of their own. Tears spring to my eyes, and I meet Phoenix's pissed off gaze across the room, watching as his jaw tics, but he does nothing.

"Strip her." Pierce barks at River. My head snaps toward him, the tears finally falling down my face when I shake my head.

I don't know his intentions right now, but it can't be good. My heart is thundering in my chest and my blood is roaring in my ears. This is not the boy I grew to love. No...this is the monster that our world created.

Quickly, and with far too much ease now that I am cuffed, River has my shirt resting above my shoulders, my bra undone, and my pants and underwear pulled to my ankles. I'm bared to them all. Without a single chance to fight them back. I close my eyes and swallow hard, attempting to take a deep breath to hold off the panic.

Unfortunately, I don't get a full breath out before a hand is at my throat, squeezing hard until my eyes pop open from pure fear. I'm met with those greens, my own eyes pouring tears down my cheeks now as I inhale a lungful of his scent. He still smells of the trees we climbed, the water we splashed in...our childhood.

I nearly lose all of my consciousness before a rough voice speaks up.

"Stop. You'll kill her." Phoenix says. Why is he trying to save me, now? Doesn't he know that death would be preferable to the torment I'm sure I'm about to be put under?

Releasing my neck, Pierce narrows his eyes at me before whipping his head towards Nix who is standing against the door to the room. He shakes his head before stepping back from the bed and snapping his fingers at River, who so easily comes over.

"Play with her, Riv. I want you to bring her to the brink, but don't let her come. She doesn't fucking deserve it." Pierce sits down in a chair off to the side of the room and undoes his jeans as he watches me. My chest is heaving, my skin begins to break out in goosebumps.

I'm hyper-aware of River stumbling towards me before he is laying on the bed beside me, his hands cupping my jaw as he looks down at me. His pupils are blown and his face is red with how drunk he is. I can feel his cock harden through his jeans, resting against my hip. I sniffle a little and he catches a tear with his finger before putting it onto his own tongue, swallowing it down while his eyes take in the rest of my body.

"Don't worry, baby bird, I'll make it good for you, 'kay?" His words seem jumbled together, but his eyes are intense as he begins to trail a finger down my neck, between the swells of my breasts. I inhale sharply, more goosebumps forming across my flesh. My nipples harden of their own accord and I slam my eyes shut, fisting my hands in the headboard as best as I can.

"Eyes, Raven." Pierce barks, and my eyes snap open to find him in the dark. He grins a big drunken grin and leans his head back against the chair, his hand on his dick that's still in his boxers.

I watch with panic and arousal mixing in my veins. River's touch has always caused me pleasure before tonight, so my brain and hormones are confused. Pierce holds his dick in his hand, stroking it as he watches me. For a minute, I wonder if he is going to take it all back and stop this train wreck, but he simply shifts his gaze toward River and nods once.

River's hands are reverent toward me, proving how much he missed my body. I try to focus on hands that have showered me in praise and pleasure before, biting down on my lip as I keep my eyes on Pierce and his greedy eyes. He's hardly abused the sexual favor card, and I'm disappointed he'd use it like this.

I can't fight them off, as I'm strapped to the bed at this point. Can't yell. Can't fight back. A tear falls from my eye again, and I shut my eyes, shutting out the bad in this situation, simply giving up and giving in to the physical. I'll try and process this later.

My back arches and my nipples pebble when River brings his hands and lips up my torso, his fingers tracing my tight buds before his lips descend down onto them. I toss my head back and let out a long breath, gripping at the headboard again as River trails his free hand down toward my wet folds. I can do nothing but give in to the pleasure, my hips bucking and seeking more of his fingers, but he only pushes one inside of me, his thumb placing the slightest pressure against my clit as he groans out how sweet I am, how perfect I am.

I tune them all out. Pierce's muffled grunts as he strokes himself, Phoenix's shuffling against the door as he tries to hide the obvious bulge he has going, and River's sweet words. I escape to a world all on my own in this moment, hoping and praying to a god I don't believe in that I'll forget this.

I dissociate for so long I nearly escape my own skin when I hear Pierce grit out a low "Enough," to River, and he stops his hands and mouth from playing with me.

I open my eyes and glare at Pierce. I was on my way to an orgasm. He smirks as he walks closer to me with his dick out. I realize River has his out as well, and I sniff back tears.

I understand they're drunk, but usually it's the drunk ones who are the most honest, after all.

Both of them stand over me now, jerking their cocks like it's an Olympic sport, and in seconds they are coming all over my stomach and breasts. I feel extremely sticky and debased at the same time and it gets worse when Pierce leans over me, pushing his finger through it. With the way his finger glides through the cum and across my skin, I'm convinced that he wrote his name on me. Once he's done, he smears it into my skin like it's a lotion.

Running his finger all the way up to my lips, he shoves it into my mouth and in a voice that both terrifies me and arouses me, he says "Suck."

I do, and I'm confused by my own body's reaction to this situation. I glare at him while I do it, of course, and I keep my breathing steady as I lick the cum from his finger. Once his finger is clean, I bite down hard on it, shooting him a shit eating grin when he curses and brings his finger away from me.

"Bitch," he snarls out. He turns, pulling his cock back into his pants and waving River away from me. The latter looks at me with longing and regret in his eyes at the same time. I close my eyes, not wanting to try and forgive at the moment, if I ever can. My body is alight with confusion for the longest of moments, but I manage to open my eyes right as Pierce points to Phoenix. He points toward me right afterward with a raised brow.

Once Phoenix nods, uncrossing his arms and heading toward me, Pierce and River leave the room. I shut my eyes to finally let the torrent of tears fall.

I should be more angry at what they took from me...

Instead, I'm angry with myself.

I shouldn't have liked what happened to me, and my body shouldn't have gotten close to feeling pleasure.

Instead, I found myself lost in it, ignoring the clear abuse happening to me.

Fuck you, Pierce Jackson.

CHAPTER TEN

T have the worst motherfuckers for best friends, honestly. I sat and watched these dick-holes debase Raven as if she's nothing more than a typical Tuesday night cum-slut. I quite frankly want to murder them both.

After Pierce leaves the room, I sit and wait for River to do himself back up. He's too drunk to notice how absolutely devastated Raven looks. She's lost in her own world at this point, dissociating and trying to black herself out.

River looks at me, glassy-eyed and teetering as he stumbles toward the door. With a slap to my shoulder, and the dumbest grin, he walks out after Pierce and disappears down the hall. I should probably follow to make sure he makes it somewhere safe. But...that would make it far too easy to rack up murder charges.

So I shut and lock the door, and take a deep breath before turning back to the broken shell of a woman on the bed.

She's covered in cum and sweat, her tears are pooling on the pillow, and as I begin to walk toward her, she's looking at me with panic all over her face. I sigh and hold my hands up, tilting my head to the side as I peer down at her form, taking in the state of her.

I'd be lying if I said my cock wasn't hard as stone in my pants, but she isn't truly consenting to us. She's here on the terms of a scholarship that I know she knows is bogus at this point.

I lean down to begin untying her and softly croon out to her, "Shh, Red, it'll be okay. I won't touch you without your consent, okay?"

I keep eye contact with her, waiting for some semblance of acknowledgment. She gives a short nod, and more tears fall over the sides of her face. Shaking my head, I lean over and brush my thumb over one, catching it before it has the chance to join the others on the bed. I reach over and untie each of her limbs, gently rubbing at the marks as I go. There's an intake of breath when I massage her right wrist, so I make sure to remember to grab a bandage to keep it clean.

In the moments following, I have to ignore the scent of sex on her. She nearly had an orgasm against her own will, and she hates herself for it.

Fucking idiot friends, I tell you.

I shake my head as we enter the en suite. Only Pierce Jackson would have one this elaborate, and I know for a fact it's newly installed. I was the chump stuck watching the install.

I set Raven down on the counter, and brush the hair from her face, so I can study her. I know she's mute, so I've studied up on human behavior a bit in order to learn how to read her. The silence scares some people, but I find it oddly comforting.

My old band-mates would die a slow death at those words.

I press a feather light kiss to her sweat covered forehead, before I turn toward the bath. It's one of those jacuzzi styles with too many jets.

Only the best for Pierce.

The water comes out cold as hell at first, but I quickly get it to a warmer temperature before putting the stop on the drain. Reaching up, I grab a bottle of bubble bath and quirk a grin. Strawberry soda smells fucking divine on her, and it seems Pierce knows this woman's scent perfectly.

As the scent of her envelopes the room, I turn back towards Raven, lifting my hands in a placating gesture as I speak, "Your choice, but I'd like to clean the heathens off of you, Red. May I?"

She looks me up and down, her bottom lip trapped between her teeth as she studies me. I'm hoping she stops soon so that I don't give her a show. I exhale a deep breath when she nods her head and looks toward the nearly full bath.

"So here's how this will go," I speak calmly as I slowly approach her, "you have all the power here. You have to hold your hand out to stop me. That's all, okay?"

As I reach her, she's got those beautiful blues locked on me, and I'm reminded of the many times we've shared this... tension. Our eyes have locked a lot, but this is the first time I'm allowed to do anything about how I feel for her. But I won't. She's delicate, broken, and shattered at the moment. So instead of threading my fingers through her thick red locks, I exhale a breath and lift her from the counter, bridal style.

Of course I can't help but bury my face in the top of her hair and inhale deeply before crossing the room.

She inhales sharply as I lay her in the bath, quickly righting herself and trapping that plump lip between her teeth again.

"You need to stop that," I murmur, taking her lower lip between my thumb and forefinger. "I may be your only friend tonight, love. Don't test my limits, 'kay?"

She nods as her tongue lashes out to wet her lips, and I

nearly come all over myself from the act. Shaking my head, I reach over and turn the water off before I accidentally drown the woman. I turn toward her and reach out slowly, maintaining eye contact after her nod of consent. It's all she can give me. All she's ever given me has been those silent nods.

When my hands reach her cheek, I stroke it softly before sliding my hand to the back of her head and situating her hair behind her. "Sink into the water, Red. Let me wash your hair."

Once she does as I ask her, her eyes spark with fear before she nods once more, seemingly to herself this time. She surprises the shit out of me, however, by closing those beautiful blues. It's insanity, the trust she gives me despite her fear. But it's earned.

Or it was until tonight.

I slide both of my hands through her hair, soaking the beautiful red strands all the way through before tugging at her a bit to get her to sit up. I keep eye contact with her as she rises, and I notice the column of her throat as she swallows. She's fucking nervous. Smart to be, of course, with a predator so in control of his prey.

As I'm reaching for the shampoo, Raven's eyes widen as she takes in the familiar product. Her eyelashes flutter and kiss her cheeks as an errant tear escapes, but as she reaches out to swipe it away, I quickly reach out to take it from her. It's my job to care for her right now, she shouldn't be dealing with her sadness alone.

"He cares about you, y'know. Whether he'll ever admit it or not...he...," I sigh and shake my head, placing a generous amount of shampoo onto my palm before rubbing both hands together and sliding along the rim of the tub to get closer to her.

Her eyes are closed again once my hands reach her scalp,

and I bring my bottom lip between my teeth as I go to work washing her hair.

It's a methodical process, washing someone, but I'm not only washing her. Instead, I'm worshiping the body that the other two so cruelly violated.

As I work to finish her hair and go to work washing her body, I shift in my position. It's hard to ignore the stiffness in my pants, but I do.

Once she's washed and dried, I walk her back into Pierce's room and root around for one of his shirts to place on her. Strangely, I find one of my old band's shirts folded up in a drawer and it draws an arrogant grin to my lips. I twist around and place the black material over Red's head, careful of the towel I wrapped her hair in. The shirt lends itself as an over-sized dress, but damn if she doesn't radiate the same beauty she always does.

"Sit," I say, pointing towards the end of the bed as I walk into the bathroom. I grab a comb off of the counter and head back into the room, only to find her perched on her haunches, her hands in her lap.

And now I'm thinking how beautiful she looks in such a submissive stance...

"I'm going to fix your hair for you. Afterward, you'll go to bed. Understand?" I can't help the dominance that comes from me. She's a natural sub and it's fucking delightful. Too many women have tried to be my submissive, but all they want is to be brats so they can get spanked.

Too much work.

Just ask to be spanked; much simpler.

As I watch Raven dip her head, she plucks at the ends of the shirt and I sigh. The boys broke something in her tonight. It's frustrating to see something so beautiful crack.

I'm crawling on the bed behind her when I hear her sniffle, and it makes me growl low in my throat before I reach around to her front, grab her chin between my thumb and forefinger, and yank her head so I can see her in profile. "Do. Not. Break. You're fucking strong as hell, Red. Stay that way." She bobs her head as best she can in my hold and I gently massage the marks my fingers left before I release her and turn her head forward.

For the next half hour, I run my fingers and the comb through those beautiful red locks of hers. I ensure the hair is only damp, and free of tangles before I begin to style her hair into one long braid that reaches down half her spine.

It's intoxicating–caring for her–and it seems I'm the only one of us three willing to do it.

Pierce is a fucking idiot.

Once I'm done, I wrap my hand around the base of the braid near her scalp and give it a small tug to get her to look at me.

Our eyes meet.

My heart skips a beat.

She's looking at me in a way that makes heat spread through my entire body. I shake my head and wet my lips before I meet her gaze full on. "Bed, okay, Red? I have to lock you in there but know this; I don't fucking want to. Don't break. You didn't before and you won't now, do you hear me?"

My tone makes her flinch at the end, but she nods, so I let her go. She scurries off towards her bedroom, her head hung low as she does. Turning, she takes the final step backwards into her current jail cell and I cringe inwardly.

I want to deck the fuck out of my best friend right now, but I understand his need to do this.

All of it.

So I place a firm but caring kiss in the center of Raven's

forehead, brush a strand of hair behind her ear, and reluctantly back away.

Closing the door is hard.

Locking it is harder.

But worst of all?

The tear in my soul as I leave for work that night, knowing there are two fucking idiots out there, idiots I call friends, actively breaking the one thing we shouldn't be playing with.

Death is coming for us all.

Letter from Raven
Age 12

Dear Green,

I know I just saw you, but I really need to tell you this. I'm kind of glad that you came to Thanksgiving with us. Momma and I have been alone for a long, long time. I know you were sad that your mom wasn't here again...but the addition of you in our day made it so much better.

We laughed more. It's been a while since we've laughed, Green.

A long while. =(← Trying emojis in my letters, don't make fun of me.

Anyways, when will you see your mom again? I feel like it's been weeks, Pierce. Weeks.

At least ask her if you can stay with us while she's gone. I don't like the idea of you being alone.

No one should have to be alone, ever, but especially during holidays...

She's not a very good mom, Pierce...and I'm so sorry that you have to be alone for the holidays again.

TTFN,

Blue

PS: Thanks for being so nice to Jimmy today. He's becoming a really great friend to me, and I'm glad you guys can be friends now, too!

CHAPTER ELEVEN

raven

I'm silently crying for hours. The tears won't stop, and my mind is constantly flipping between the acute pain of my heart shattering to bits over the way Pierce is treating me, but I'm wondering why Phoenix is treating me the way he is.

He acts like he knows me better than just two people passing by in the hallways and silently brooding through group therapy together. The only real feeling I have around him is an immeasurable amount of trust. It's like our souls are connected and I know, even when he's being silent and broody, that he's a protector. He cares for me far more than I deserve.

It's unfortunate that I didn't get to know him better.

It's more unfortunate that I have to endure this house of terrors with more questions running through my brain.

I know I won't sleep at all tonight. My body is too sore, even after the tenderness in which Phoenix treated me. I wished like hell I could have vocalized the absolute pleasure running through me when he was washing my hair...brushing it...braiding it.

The last person to braid my hair, excluding myself, was my mother, two days before her death.

I didn't wash my hair for a week after that, until the braid was so tangled I had to cut out the hair tie holding it in place. It took me two hours to simply brush my hair before I could even think about washing it.

That feels like such a lifetime ago...

I nearly jump out of my own skin, letting out a silent scream when the door opens and the pounding of loud music echoes from the hallway of the frat house. I hear a few grunts, a quiet 'motherfucker'. The door closes and the sound of the lock engaging sends my heart rate spiking in alarm.

I'm wiping away my tears and shuffling as far back against my headboard as possible when I see him.

Pierce.

Green eyes glare at me for a moment, before he sits down on his ass, leaning against the door like he's a sentry awaiting my escape. Pulling his knees up to his chest, Pierce rests his arms on them, his chin resting on top before he exhales loudly and just...keeps...staring.

I finish wiping the tears from my face, inhale deeply, and stare right back at him. Our eyes collide in a powerful moment of memories and what could have beens.

I want to yell at him so bad, but I can't. So I settle for glaring as hard as I can at him, wishing it could do physical damage.

"I don't want to do this, Raven," he grumbles, exhaling again before shaking his head. Those green eyes are still staring into my soul, pleading for answers. "I've never wanted to do this." His voice is darker, raspier, deeper. I'm sure I could feel it rumbling in my own chest if I were closer.

I snatch the blanket off of the bed as quickly as I can and

wrap it around my body tightly, making sure I keep my eyes on his. I don't trust him. Not sober. Not drunk. Just...not at all.

I shake my head as I watch him, my brows drawing in as I try to process his words. If he doesn't want to do this to me, why the fuck is he? He's simply using me at this point, right? So why the pity party with himself. I didn't ask to get invited to it.

"I don't know why you're choosing to keep silent. I've heard you speak so many times, Raven. You're being so...such a...," he inhales, growls, and shoots up to his feet before sneering at me. "You're being a stubborn fucking bitch, Raven Hill!" He yells, his voice nearly booming through the room. "SPEAK. TO. ME!"

When our eyes clash harder this time, I don't move. I don't breathe. I do nothing but stare.

A second passes.

Ten.

Thirty seconds of pure hatred emanates from him before he slams the door and locks me inside once more. His fist loudly collides with the door itself.

"You've ruined my fucking life. I'm going to enjoy the fuck out of ruining yours, little bird."

The sound of his body hitting his mattress is the last sound I truly hear, my ears ringing, my heart pounding, and my vision blurring as I find myself passing out from pure exhaustion.

He's truly going to ruin me, and he doesn't care how.

THE NEXT MORNING, I'm escorted by the lovely, bouncing, far too much energy for his own good, River. I'm exhausted as all hell, and I look it, too.

Even though I spent an hour getting ready this morning, time didn't rejuvenate me like I thought it would. I spent most of it rehashing the events of the night before and how absolutely broken Pierce looked. He knew what he did was bad, but he kept doing it anyway, so I've been dealing with my own emotions, pushing them to the side while pulling on my big girl pants.

While doing my makeup, I had fingermarks to cover up on my throat, and a hickey between my breasts. Both of these I didn't notice were there when Phoenix was washing me last night. I had to spend extra time to make myself look like a boss bitch by putting more makeup on my face than normal. A typical day in my life.

I scoff and shake my head, holding my chin high as I walk beside the man-puppy attached to me. He's holding my hand in a show of ownership, but he's doing it in such a way that I don't truly mind it. It's comforting, in a 'this guy just ate me out and almost made me come against my own will' sort of way.

"Okay, Rae, I'm gonna need you to be a reeeaaallly good girl today. Absolutely perfect. River has a headache and quite honestly, I'd rather perform a self-lobotomy than attend classes." He pats me on the head, shuffles me forward to my first class of the day, and slaps me on the ass in such a patronizing way. I'm forced to keep his murder only inside of my head. He follows behind me as I go to sit in my normal seat.

Pierce is here, of course. Even though the scumbag doesn't take this class.

I roll my eyes as I sit in the seat directly in front of him, my shoulders high. His gaze burns the back of my head, but I don't let him see the effect he has on me. He doesn't have to know that I sense him everywhere.

He also doesn't need to know that I can still feel the ghost of his fingers around my throat, his eyes staring into my soul, and his cum smeared across my body like the silkiest of lotions.

He doesn't need to know that I secretly enjoyed the deprivation.

So I sit confidently, bring out what I need for class, and spend the next 90 minutes acutely aware of Pierce's gaze, River's snores, and my pulse thundering in my ears. It's a difficult feat to fully pay attention, but I manage to finish my assignment and turn it in before class ends. I book it out of class ahead of the guys in order to have time to myself.

I almost make it to the bathroom alone before all three men make themselves known.

River checks all the stalls, Phoenix locks the door and leans on it like the guard dog he is, and Pierce crowds me against one of the sinks, his glare hot on my skin as if it holds actual heat. I swallow hard as I methodically meet all of their gazes.

Phoenix looks devastating in a black Henley, his leather jacket, black jeans, and combat boots. His brown eyes remind me of chocolate cake at the moment—sue me, I'm starving.

River looks like he'd rather be in bed, but he's still dressed in a clean pair of blue jeans, a dark blue t-shirt, his hair covering his stormy gray eyes.

Pierce...well...he looks like a god among men. It's almost significant, the way he dresses.

He's wearing a leather jacket, almost exactly the same as Phoenix's, except Pierce's has all sorts of pins, buttons, and patches on them. Too much to take stock in at the moment. Underneath that is an unzipped, plain, black hoodie, which is covering a plain black t-shirt.

What strikes me, however, is his goddamn pants.

LEATHER.

HE'S WEARING LEATHER PANTS!

I may be internally drooling, my face, however, must give me away. Pierce can't hide the cocky little smirk that graces his pouty lips while he leans in on me, crowding into me more. My eyes are wide, and I'm trembling.

PS: Not from fear.

My breathing picks up as those green eyes sear into my soul. I'm trying to take a more calming, deep breath, but Pierce runs his right hand from the tips of my fingers all the way up to the shell of my ear. His touch is electrifying and, after last night, I shouldn't want it.

Goosebumps rise along my skin anyway. The hair along my arms lift, and take my soaring heart with it as my childhood best friend leans closer...closer...and as his nose brushes mine, my eyes flutter shut.

"Little bird, you smell so fucking delicious...," he rumbles, and his breath races down my throat as I attempt to pull back. It's a fruitless task. He shakes his head and tsks twice before tightening his grip on me.

One hand on my hip, the other still at my head. It's excruciating. I want him to let go.

I want him to pull me closer.

"River?" Pierce barks, and I nearly fly out of my skin.

"Yeah, PJ?" He's grinning and bright eyed as he leans into our space, his nose between ours. His eyes are bouncing back and forth between us.

"First," Pierce huffs, shoving him out of our space with a hand to the face, "back the fuck up. Second, could you maybe get our birdie wet for me? I think I need an afternoon snack."

"Sure thing, brother!" River is nearly bouncing with excitement at this prospect, and I'm left cold and confused as Pierce pushes away from me.

I stumble against the sink, my breath coming out in pants as I survey the room, my eyes darting between the men. I don't know whether to panic or to submit, but I guess I don't get much of a choice when River takes the place of Pierce, placing his hands on my hips and lifting me until I sit on the sink.

I meet Pierce's gaze over his shoulder, watching as he leans against one of the stalls. He crosses his ankles, puts his hands in his pockets, and settles in for the show he ordered. It's degrading, and I'm beginning to wonder if I've discovered a new kink. It's like unlocking achievements in a video game. Pinging off one at a time until the entire list is uncovered.

New kink unlocked - 300 points!

Pierce probably knows the whole list at this point.

My thoughts take a sharp turn as River's hands are shoving my dress up over my hips. My gaze swings to his sharply, and the way he groans from finding me already wet...it forces me to shift my thighs together.

Which he also notices, and his hands become firm against my thighs. I tempt fate by trying to struggle, but the almost imperceptible shake of River's head is enough for me to give in to what my body wants.

Fuck my heart. I don't need it anyway.

With the tiniest growl escaping, River becomes almost ravenous as he descends upon my clothed pussy. It's enough to make me gasp loudly, one hand flying to the side of the sink and the other finding purchase in his hair. I'm gripping him like he's my lifeline, and I'm not ashamed of that fact.

With fingers digging into my thigh hard enough to bruise for a solid week, River's tongue rubs against the red lace covering my folds. It's as if he has a homing beacon directly to my clit. He hits his mark immediately, and the wetness soaks through the lace, the material becoming useless aside from the friction it provides. Between the lace and River's overeager tongue, I'm overwhelmed, bucking so hard into his face, I'm sure I could suffocate him like this.

What a way to kill a man.

I allow my lips to tilt up into a tiny little smirk, which is ruined when his tongue plunges deep inside of me. I gasp, and he forces the lace of my underwear to rub inside and outside of me. It's overwhelming, and if he could just...keep...going–

"Enough!" Pierce barks, tugging River away from me by the scruff of his shirt. He practically flings the guy into a stall door. River recovers quickly, wiping his hand on his cheek. He stares directly at me while he slowly licks his lips clean.

He ruins the sexy thing by winking though, and I'm tempted to roll my eyes. Fucking playboy.

A hand grips my jaw, thumb on my lower lip, the rest covering nearly half of my head with its size. My eyes are forced to meet Pierce's, and I wish they hadn't. He reaches down, unseeing, with his left hand and runs it up my thigh before meeting the soaked lace. I'm so worked up that if he'd touch my clit once, I'd soar to new heights.

He knows this, though, and the little smirk on his face is more infuriating when he avoids my clit altogether, runs his finger under the lace, and plunges it into the wetness which proves how much I'm enjoying this predicament I've found myself in.

My hips buck against his hand of their own accord, and I shut my eyes against the onslaught of emotions it brings on. I can't keep them closed for long, however. Pierce's grip on my jaw tightens to the point of pain and I'm forced to open my eyes to glare a hole directly into his soul and hope it drops him dead.

"Eyes. On. Me." He growls. His eyes are on mine and

finally manage to keep me hostage as he brings his hand from my soaked cunt only to lift his finger to my mouth.

He pops my lips open by squeezing his fingers against my cheeks. Before I can attempt to move away, he shoves his finger into my mouth. Immediately I'm overwhelmed by the taste of my own arousal.

Then he kisses me.

He fucking kisses me!

Both of his hands are on the sides of my face, his erection pressing into me as he pulls me closer to him, and his tongue plunges into the depths of my soul rather than my mouth. He groans, I slam my eyes shut and wish I could murder the bastard in broad daylight and get away with it.

He's not supposed to do this shit.

He's not supposed to send my heart soaring with the depth of this kiss and the reminders of what was.

I don't want to remember.

It's too fucking difficult for me...

"I EXPECT *you to be back here by sunset, Raven!"*

"Yes, mom!" I yell. She probably doesn't hear me though since I'm halfway out of the front door and slamming it before her name escapes my lips.

I'm grinning ear to ear as I race across the cul de sac towards Green's house. His mom isn't home. I saw her leave with a strange man in a nice car about half an hour ago, so I asked mine if I could go check on him and maybe go to the park.

It's our spot now.

Even if it is abandoned.

It's 6:30 right now, but I've been done with dinner for ages and sunset isn't for another hour and a half. So we have time before my mom's yelling the block down trying to find me.

As I reach his front door, Pierce bursts out of it, nearly barreling into me.

"Ah hell," he says, steadying me with hands on my shoulders, "you okay, Rae?"

I nod stiffly, taking a breath to steady my heart before I take a small step backwards. I hook a thumb over my shoulder, pointing back the way I came, "Park?" I ask.

Looking nervous, Pierce looks behind him, shutting the door quickly before we make our way off of the porch.

We're quiet as we walk across the street. Even more silent as we head around my house and towards the open field behind it. The silence nearly kills me by the time we finally make it to the old playground.

It's been around for years, decades. It's all rusted over, but Pierce and I don't mind it. It's all ours.

"What'd ya want to talk about, Blue?" he says as we make our way to the merry-go-round. I go to lay down on it like usual, but before I can, Pierce has taken his hoodie off and laid it down, looking almost confused after he's done it. "Uh...there was...dirt. Don't want your...," he clears his throat, "don't want your mom to be mad about dirty clothes. Yeah." Shaking his head, he lays down on the opposite end of the merry-go-round, his head laying just a tad bit from where mine falls when I finally settle atop his hoodie.

"I wanted to check with you," I say in a small voice. His gesture is cute, but it sparks something in me.

We turned fourteen the other day and, honestly, I see him differently now. We start high school in a little over a month.

Things are going to be so different.

"I'm good, Raven," he says. His tone is clipped, and I know he's lying.

A minute goes by as he uses his long legs for good by spinning us.

It's silent.

"Sorry," is whispered across the small space, and I can hear sadness in his tone.

I sigh and sit up, getting my bearings before turning around and sitting on my butt, legs crossed in front of me. I pick at the ends of my jean shorts and wait. I know he's going to mirror my position. This has almost become our nightly routine this past summer.

His mother goes out with a strange man. Sometimes the same one, sometimes not. He's left alone but seems to always be so angry...so I go find him and bring him to our spot.

We talk. We laugh. And, when the sun begins to set, we walk arm in arm back to my house. He has to walk alone back to his house. His mom returns home shortly after, and all is a little better in the world.

But I'm at this point now where I feel things for him. I want to hug him, hold his hand...kiss him. But never once does he try to kiss me when he drops me off.

I've avoided Jimmy from down the street for weeks now. He's always trying to kiss me.

I don't want my first kiss to be with Jimmy.

"Rae?"

I don't want to think about giving someone other than my best friend the honor.

"Hey, Raven?"

Why won't he even hold my hand?!

"Raven!" Pierce is shouting now, and his hand meets my jaw, lifting it so our eyes meet.

My heart lurches, and the world seems to fall away as we stare at each other. This could possibly be the perfect first kiss moment...and yet...

"What's goin' on in that head of yours, Blue?" He says it, a grin on his lips. He shakes his head and lets his hand fall to his own lap.

I swallow, lick my lips, and lean in close to him with my nose nearly touching his.

"Uh...personal space, Raven?" His voice is shaking, even as he tries to tease me.

We stare, still as statues, and I watch as, FINALLY, his eyes fall to my lips before they flick back to my eyes in an almost panic.

One beat.

Two...

What the hell is he doing?!

I sigh and place my hands on his shoulders, grounding us both.

"Are you just gonna sit there and stare, or are you gonna kiss me, ya doofus?"

In the blink of an eye, my scared best friend becomes confident in himself for what seems like the first time, and our lips meet right as thunder rolls in. Rain droplets begin falling all around and the heavens fully part for us.

By the time we finally make it back to my house, we're soaked through to the bone, shivering, and grinning from ear to ear.

raven

It's almost comical how wide River's eyes are after Pierce releases me from the kiss. You can tell the guy just doesn't get it.

Unfortunately for Pierce and I, however, Phoenix does.

His brooding is next level right now, and he's glaring at Pierce as if he's broken all sorts of rules. I kind of want to laugh, and since Pierce is currently turned around, I let a small little huff of laughter escape me. It comes out in breaths, of course, but his back is to me, and he's probably thinking of the next challenge to take on, so he doesn't hear or see me.

River and Phoenix see it, but River is well...River...and he stares with an open mouth, comically wide eyes, and presses a hand to his heart, as if I'm affecting him in any way that is meaningful.

Phoenix lets his eyes slither that much closer to closed as he glares at Pierce. He shakes his head and straightens up, tilting his head to one side, then the other, the telltale sound of his bones cracking echoing through the now almost silent room.

As Pierce goes to turn around, the loud ringing of a phone

startles all four of us, reminding us of the world outside of this bathroom.

This public bathroom.

My face flushes and I fix my dress and chew on my lower lip as I await whatever the guys are going to do next.

This is their show. Not mine.

"Ah fuck. Nix, take Raven to Junk, I'll meet you there as soon as I can." Pierce is barking orders again. Surprise, fucking surprise. "Riv, grow the fuck up, put your tongue back in your mouth, and follow me."

Before the rest of us can react, Pierce has pushed through the door, his voice coming out extremely tense when he answers with a "Yeah?"

It's silent for a beat before River passes by me, grips my hand in his and places the most gentle of kisses to my knuckles. "Till next time, Rae." Of course he winks again, too.

He's out the door in a flash and I'm left alone with Phoenix. Again.

Guess he's been relegated to the babysitter role.

I scoff and slide down the sink, turning to wash my hands and fix my face and hair. I don't need to look as though I've been ravaged. Even if it is the truth.

"Here, Red," Phoenix speaks low, presenting me with a comb. It nearly makes me tear up with how affectionate he is.

My eyes meet his in the mirror and I have to swallow to keep my emotions at bay.

Before I can reach out and grab for the comb, he pauses and swallows, his Adam's apple bobbing against his tattooed throat. "May I?" He asks so gently, it's almost like this tall, muscular, tattooed man is simply a facade.

I nod before I can think better of it. My eyes fall down to watch as my hands white knuckle the edges of the sink.

The absolute comfort Phoenix brings to me when his hands run through my hair, and as he begins to brush through it with the comb...it's unfathomable. I should not feel safe in the situation I've agreed to be in. I'm allowing these assholes to use and abuse my body...and yet...

Safe *is* what I feel at this moment.

A tear falls before my head is being jerked to the side so I can see Phoenix's hard gaze out of the corner of my eye.

"Don't break, Red. Promise me you won't?" His voice is so damn sincere it nearly breaks me apart.

My chest heaves as I struggle to take in enough oxygen, but I manage a small nod before he leans in and kisses my cheek affectionately. It stuns me, and I don't move even after he releases my jaw and continues to brush my hair.

It's almost as if taking care of me is his way of trying to atone for the bullshit he and his friends are doing.

TWENTY MINUTES LATER, Phoenix and I are walking towards the edge of the student parking lot. I don't know where the fuck we're going seeing as it's hardly ten in the morning, but I figure I might as well settle into my new normal.

I exhale loudly, and Phoenix looks at me with an arched brow.

I arch mine back.

His lips tilt up in a small smile before he shakes his head, focusing his attention in front of him again.

I'm almost about to ask where the fuck we're going when a singular street bike comes into view. I halt my steps, nearly skidding to a stop ten feet away from the beast.

My head is shaking back and forth, and before I know what I'm doing, I'm turning on my heel and attempting to power walk my ass back toward the library.

No. Fucking. Way. Nuh-uh. Not happening.

About twenty feet from where I took off, I'm suddenly soaring in the air, hands and legs flailing while Phoenix grabs me. He tosses me over his shoulder and carries me right back to that bike.

He huffs as he sets me down on the ground in front of it, growls as I fight him to put on the helmet. I'm nearly tossed on my ass before he manages to place me on the back of the bike itself, his hand brushing my upper thigh as he throws his leg over the bike seat.

"Get the fuck over it, Red. We're headed to Junk, so sit that pretty little ass on my bike and settle the fuck in. Fight me, and I'll make sure you get a little more torture tonight from Pierce."

With that little tidbit from tall, dark and silent, I shut my mouth and nearly choke him to death when he pats my thigh patronizingly. He makes a satisfied noise in the back of his throat, and twists the key to turn the bike on.

The rumble of the engine nearly sends me flying, but I stay put and place my feet up on the pegs, hug my thighs to the outside of Phoenix's legs, and place my helmeted head against the center of his back.

My hands snake their way forward and I clutch to the edges of his leather jacket with all that I have.

Don't kill me, please, I wish I could say.

Instead I'm silent as he begins our journey towards wherever the fuck they want to take me.

The campus begins to fade away from us, the small town

surrounding it flying by within minutes until all that's left to see are trees. So. Many. Trees.

The forest which swallows our whole state is enchanting, to say the least. It's a beautiful thing, when you aren't being kidnapped, abused, and used for others' pleasure. So, as a big fuck you to Pierce fucking Jackson and his merry gang of fuck wits, I shut my eyes and pretend my heart doesn't beat out of my chest with the thrill of riding on a street bike.

It seems like hours later, instead of minutes, when the bike slows and my curiosity is peaked enough for me to open my eyes and peer through the helmet visor.

What I see...well it shocks the ever-loving shit out of me.

We're parked outside of a large gate with JUNKYARD spelled out above it with various old sign pieces. It's vintage AF and I honestly admire the fuck out of it. It looks like it was put together by hand. The gate and the surrounding fence look the same. Walls upon walls of cars, metal scraps, and tires are pieced together so you can hardly see inside of it. The wall itself must be about ten feet high, with the gate raising above it another five or so feet.

It's fucking glorious.

As Phoenix pushes the bike with his feet closer to the gate, he hits a button on his key-chain, and the gate begins to open inwards.

It reveals such a lush, serene greenery and I feel like I'm transported to fucking Narnia all of a sudden. I'm spellbound. Frozen. I feel utterly speechless.

When the gates are fully opened, Phoenix kicks his feet back up and moves us forward. We're going slow enough that I'm able to drink in every detail of the hidden world presented to me.

I see the makings of a dirt trail–we're currently driving

over it—as well as what looks like an actual freaking garden. Like...one of those container gardens. This looks taken care of and it has plenty of what looks like peppers and tomatoes inside of it.

Unsure what the rest of the green shit is, but I'm impressed, nonetheless.

I mean...

I'm not impressed.

Ahem.

I am appalled.

I shake my head to rid it of the thoughts of comfort, letting out a long breath once we reach a building.

It's old brick, climbing with healthy, green vines, and as the garage door on one side opens, I'm met with the interior of what used to be a junkyard garage...but much, much more modern.

As Phoenix pulls inside and parks the bike, he taps my thigh in a clear command to get off of it. I do as he asks, removing the helmet once my feet are secure on solid ground again.

When I point to the green space and tilt my head in question, Phoenix grins and walks over toward where I'm standing at the front of the open garage.

"The guys and I refurbished this place entirely over the last few months, mostly over the summer. We wanted an escape, y'know?"

But why? They have the frat house to live, eat, fuck, and shit in. It's insulting they'd need an 'escape' from Cobalt University frat life. They're living the fucking dream, right?

Spoiled assholes.

My body is still thrumming from the motorcycle ride, heat running throughout the entirety of my spine from the drive here, but I shove away the need that's demanding attention, and turn to look around the garage.

There are other bikes here, at least half a dozen in various states of disrepair. Two vehicles sit beside where Phoenix parked—a black Jeep Wrangler and what looks like a cherry red Shelby Mustang GT. The latter has me nearly coming on the spot. I ignore it, with much gathered strength, and begin my journey towards the only other door in the room. Before I can reach out, however, Phoenix is there with a key and unlocks it, pushing it open wide with an arm held out in invitation.

My eyes meet his chocolate ones, and I push past him in clear dismissal. He scoffs, slams the door behind us, and I nearly round on him when the snick of the lock sounds.

I'm still here. I'm not fighting. So why do they insist on locking me up?!

I roll my eyes and begin my Tour de Fuckwits' hangout, taking in every single detail the modern home provides.

That's what this is: it's a home.

It may be the absolute epitome of a bachelor pad, but it's glorious in its own right.

What used to be the shop side of this business has been transformed into a modernized loft area. Wall to wall windows on one side—facing the inside of the junkyard—and the back wall holds the stairs and what I assume is an actual loft bedroom. I can see the edges of the bed from here.

Everything is dark mahogany wood, with a rich black leather sectional facing the windows. The walls and accents are all black, putting us into an almost pitch dark room if it wasn't for the windows open to all of the greenery we are surrounded by. Up the metal stairs there is a bedroom—with the bed I saw, a king—and a bathroom and walk-in closet near the edge of the space.

It's magnificent, and from the looks of the pool and Foosball tables, as well as the bar and kitchen lining the downstairs space, the boys have made a safe haven for themselves. Beats me why they need it, but I can tell by the scattered personal items that they don't bring many people here.

This is where they let go of their masks.

But will they let them down for me, too?

I shake my head. Quite honestly, I don't care. I want to stay strong. Afterward, I want to get the hell out of here and travel far, far away.

But I don't know how to sustain that lifestyle yet.

The sound of the gate creaking open halts my movements along the loft railing upstairs, and I lean against the black metal, my forearms taking most of my weight while I watch two other street bikes enter the sanctuary.

Pierce and River are here.

I must look panicked. When Phoenix looks up and meets my eyes, he tilts his head a bit before smiling at me reassuringly.

"S'okay. You're freer here in this cage than you are in the other, Red." He disappears below the loft floor and into the kitchen, where I hear the fridge open.

The rest of the sounds are drowned out by the garage door opening and closing, my eyes taking in the junkyard itself.

Cars are stacked upon others, yes, but it's almost done in an artistic way. My mind is torn between who these boys are and who Pierce used to be. This screams of his artistic talent as we grew up. He wanted to be an architect when we were younger, and you can almost see that dream has come to fruition in some small, minuscule part of the world.

Unfortunately, as he and River make it inside of the loft, his glare is firmly on the side of my head. Anger rises within me and I turn to meet him as he rises among the metal stairs, boots clanging against them hard. As he makes it to the top, my gaze meets his, and I find myself pushing my shoulders back and standing as straight as possible while I raise my chin in defiance.

I do not want to back down. I do not want to be weak, meek, or any other version of a small female at the hands of men.

"Pierce!" Phoenix barks. Is he trying to protect me?

I inhale sharply when Pierce reaches me, his hand circling my throat as he begins to shuffle me back towards the bed.

"Little bird, meet your new fucking cage. Leave it without one of us and I'll slit your throat myself. Otherwise, stay, enjoy the fruits of my hard fucking labor, and do as you're asked."

The backs of my knees hit the bed, my pulse speeds up, and I'm panicking. My hands find purchase in his wrist, my nails burrowing into his skin and instantly drawing blood.

He roars.

Shoves me back against the bedding so hard my breath is caught in my lungs.

He's on me in nanoseconds.

"I do not," he speaks, his hands gripping the material of my dress and sliding it up my body, "appreciate," he punctuates this with ripping the material above my pelvic bone, "your fucking attitude." My dress is now over my head, trapping my arms above me, my legs spread open, with him between them.

My body is a live wire of hate and terror, and yet, when he skims his fingers up my thighs, his eyes flashing with pain and longing for the briefest of seconds, I find myself wanting him in the most carnal of ways. I don't show this to him, though. Well, until his hands meet the juncture of my thighs, his fingers finding my lace panties absolutely soaked once again for him. I inhale sharply as he shoves two fingers inside of me, forcing the lace to rub against the most sensitive of places. All it does is make me wetter.

I should absolutely be ashamed of myself right now, but when he leans down and runs his tongue up the center of me, I do what I do best when it comes to Pierce Jackson; I give in. I give up the fight.

My back arches, and Pierce stiffens for a beat, his eyes meeting mine as I clamp down on my lower lip.

Everything in me is pulsating right now.

There's only a split second for me to change this direction into something either terrible or pleasurable.

I choose the latter.

He sees it.

He's tearing my underwear away, tossing it aside, and plunging his tongue into my cunt in a rapid manner. My legs clamp around his head tightly, trying to gain back some of the power that I've lost here.

"Fuck, little bird, you taste so much better than I remember," he growls, and those vibrations force my whole body to sing for him. His fingers are gripping my thighs, holding me to him and bruising me.

At least I want these bruises.

My lower stomach clenches with each new swipe of his tongue inside of me, and when he brings two fingers up, shoves them inside of me violently, I'm forced to inhale deeply to keep from coming too quickly. I own him right now, and I'm damn sure going to steal this moment while I can. It's almost unbearable to keep myself held back. Almost. Yet, as Pierce continues to eat me like a starving man, I soak the sheets minutes later until he brings my clit between his lips and sucks, hard.

All of my muscles clench, my back shoots off of the bed with how high it arches, and I can't breathe. I'd panic if I didn't feel the gush of my cum covering Pierce's face. His eyes lock on mine, his fingers, lips and tongue help me ride out the orgasm.

As I come down, my body satiated in a way it hasn't been, consensually at least, Pierce climbs up my body and seals his lips to mine.

I'm so incredibly turned on by the taste of myself on his tongue, my hips rock upwards into the hard erection Pierce is frantically trying to free from his pants. It's almost like he knows I'm emotionally here with him, too. We both accept that it's truly just us at this moment.

"Please tell me you're here with me. Tell me you feel this," he punctuates his words by pressing his hard dick onto my core, my hands grip at his hair, tugging it tightly, keeping his face near mine. "Speak to me, Rae...don't stay silent anymore."

Our eyes lock, and a tear falls. I wish I could. In this exact moment, I truly wish I could speak to him.

He growls and loses all of the sweetness that overtook him, pushing off of me and doing up his pants again. His eyes are cold as fucking ice right now, and I shiver in their depths. My entire body is left cold from where he was, and my heart is left to break ten times over again.

"Raven! SPEAK. TO. ME! Stop fucking hiding behind this silent, cold shoulder shit. I listened to you talk and yammer on for our entire fucking lives."

He stares.

I stare back.

River and Phoenix appear at the top of the stairs, frantic, as if they were worried about this exact thing happening.

As I stay silent—not out of choice—Pierce rushes the bed, rears his hand back, and punches the headboard right beside my head.

All hell breaks loose after that.

Phoenix rushes forward, River grabs Pierce, and I flinch so hard the top of my head smacks the headboard. I wince and grip at my pounding skull.

My tears go forgotten as I watch River drag Pierce down the stairs as he roars obscenities at me. He won't believe me if I told him what happened, so there's no point in telling him.

As Phoenix unpins my arms and checks my head, I'm left questioning how to gain Pierce's trust back.

Afterward, while I'm wrapped up in Phoenix's arms and brought to another jacuzzi style tub to bathe, I'm heartbroken for the boy who wanted to give it all up for me.

Later that night, when I'm curled up on the bed, silently sobbing, my soul crumbles.

I know, without a single ounce of doubt, I may never earn the trust, love, or loyalty back from the boy who made my entire world shine.

So much for our wedding plans, huh, Green?

Dear Blue,

I can't really believe that we're starting middle school soon. Can we finally just pretend we don't know Jimmy? Guy gives me the creeps, Rae.

I don't know how many classes we will have together, but at least we can ride our bikes together on the way there and back.

Maybe our new tradition can be to get ice cream and french fries after?

Think your mom will go for that if I pay her with my money?

Anyways, Rae,

This is a big moment for us.

We can't let it change us okay?

You are my BFF always,

Later gator,

Green

pierce

I'm so pissed the fuck off right now, I hardly feel the way River manhandles me, tosses me on my ass outside of the garage, and how my ass lands on a sharp as hell rock embedded in the dirt.

I bring my knees up and put my head between them, attempting to ease the panic bubbling up in me.

I didn't want to give up on the moment Rae and I had. It was just us up there in the loft. It was as if time had finally ceased to exist and we were us again.

Green and his Blue.

But of course, I had to go and fucking ruin it with my need for her to end her damn cold shoulder towards me. I was so incredibly frustrated that she didn't moan, grunt, say my name, whisper. She didn't do anything.

And it attacked my goddamn ego. Unless my eyes were staring into the depths of her pretty blues, I wouldn't have truly known how much she was into it, aside from the wetness of her sweet cunt.

I'm aching. Blue balls, anger issues, and trust issues are

roaring their protests in my mind, so when River crouches down in front of me with none of the humor that is his typical personality, I rear back and punch him square in the nose so hard that blood splatters against my face and shirt.

Halfway towards the garden, River's yelling a muffled, "WHAT THE FUCK?!" and I'm flipping him off with my bloodied-from-the-headboard knuckles on full show.

I hear the sound of the garage door closing, but I don't give a shit. Let them lock me out. It's best for Raven anyways.

Regardless of my behavior, I give way too many shits about that girl, and I never fucking stopped. So, in the midst of my anger, I go to take it out on weeds, bugs, and snag myself a fresh jalapeño to snack on while I work with my hands in the dirt. It grounds me to work in this garden, and we decided a while ago, us three, to try and sustain ourselves here in the event of a major fuck up by Maxwell Langston.

Junk has been our safe haven for over six months now, and Phoenix joined in over the summer. We corralled him in for his connections to the local music scene, hoping it would get us more profits for Langston. It worked, and now he's one of us. We protect him, he protects us, yada yada.

We're a team, and I'm damn determined to keep us together.

And that *us* has always included Raven Hill.

AN HOUR LATER, I'm covered in dirt from head to toe. I've eaten a half dozen jalapeños like the psychopath I truly am, and my shirt was taken off long ago to be used as a sweat rag.

My anger has dissipated and quite honestly, I'm feeling like a human again. Calm. Collected enough to go back inside, eat with my team, shower, then fuck off to the corner of the couch and conk out.

Of course that's when Langston attempts to call me. It's fucking dinnertime, and all this fucker thinks about is himself. And I better be ready to ask 'how high' when he tells me to fucking jump. I roll my eyes while I swipe to accept his call, walking towards the garage and wiping my face clean of sweat with my shirt.

"Langston. What a fucking pleasure!" I'm impressed with my ability to make that statement sound genuine. It nearly makes me laugh.

"Jackson. Where the fuck did you take her? Where the fuck are you? I specifically told you to keep her on campus so I could keep my eyes on her while she's here." He grunts, and I hear a smack before a feminine squeal and the fakest of all moans fill the dead air between his statement and my answer.

"Having a good ole time, Maxwell? Couldn't have waited another five seconds to blow your load before calling me?" I sneer, my back resting against the cool brick of the garage as I stand in the shaded area below an apple tree. I reach up to grab one, admiring the red of it as I would Raven's hair. I take a large bite out of it and try to ignore the groan that fills the call.

"Thanks, Daddy," echoes through the call, followed by the sounds of a dismissal from Langston and the slam of a door.

"Alright, Jackson, I asked you a question," he grumbles through the line, and I finish the bite of my apple before I attempt to answer him.

"I've got her somewhere away from the product. I don't trust anyone but my boys, and you know that."

A snick of a lighter precedes a long inhale—a cigar, I'd wager—and a longer exhale. "Alright. I can admire you getting her away from it, but I'd like to have eyes on her, son."

"First off," I snap, "I'm not, nor have I ever been, your son. Second," I take a deep breath, "I thought you trusted me? Why give me this job if you're not going to trust me to get it done, huh?"

"Pierce…" he sighs and I hear him take another drag before he speaks a moment later, "I do. I trust you. Don't make me regret it."

"How long until D-Day, Langston?"

"New Year's. Enough drunks out that the new product will fall in without a hitch." I hear a knock on his door through the line, followed by some shuffling as he stands to go answer it, no doubt. "I'll test it over Christmas with the kids that stay here."

"So I've got less than eight weeks to get it to you, for you to create and pre-test it, and for it to be bagged and handed out?" I groan inwardly, shaking my head, "Maxwell, it can't–"

"It can, and will be done, Pierce. You've done harder things than that, yeah?" Another knock, louder this time. "I gotta go. Get it done, or I'll make another visit to dear old Chloe soon." He laughs before hanging up the phone.

I roar a challenge, though he can't hear me, and smash my knuckles into the tree in front of me. The act destroys my already beat up knuckles, of course, but I don't quite give a fuck at the moment. Shoving my hands in my pockets, I go to turn the corner and face plant directly into Phoenix.

"Ah fuck!" I yell.

"I've taken care of her, and she's in bed. The fuck was all that about with Langston?" he questions, gripping my shoulder and glaring at me in a way that makes my skin boil.

"The fuck off me, Nix. I don't answer to you, you answer to me." I shake him off and walk toward the main garage door. I've got bikes to fix, and a woman to avoid.

"I don't give a shit who you answer to, PJ–"

"Don't fucking call me that!"

Our eyes meet, and Nix grins before raising a brow as we finally enter the garage, making our way towards the broken down bikes in the back. I want extra bikes, in case some of ours run into trouble.

Rae could use one too, so long as she doesn't run.

Yeah, like she'd use it at all...

"Anyway, PJ," Nix says, and I growl at him but continue toward my tools. "If we're all in this together, we should all know everything."

"Riv doesn't give a shit," I tell him, quirking a brow, though he can't see it.

"Yeah but River would follow you across an ocean of rusty nails without question, so your point is lost on me, dumb ass." Nix hands me over the red flashlight I was looking for, and I snatch it from his hands.

"Fine," I grumble, squatting before a busted up Kawasaki Ninja ZX-10R. It's beginning to rust, but I can sand and repaint if I need to.

All of our bikes are the same make and model. I don't trust anything else and I make sure they all end up matte black by the time I'm done with them. Each of us has a special under glow that we use, but only when we aren't running from something or trying real fucking hard to stay hidden on a job.

"Waiting," Nix snaps, planting his ass against the toolbox and crossing his arms.

"Maxwell wants the recipe soon. So soon, in fact," I plop my ass down and lay back, turning the flashlight on, "that he wants to deliver the final product on New Year's Eve, so all the drunk little boys and girls can get addicted that night."

"No fucking way is that possible! We don't have the fucking recipe, Pierce!" Nix turns and kicks the toolbox. Tools clatter across the floor as he kneels down next to me and glares, like this is somehow my fucking fault.

"The fuck's goin' on out here Piercey Jackson?" River says as he enters the garage, closing the door to the loft as softly as his dumb ass can, "You're gonna wake RaeRae up, and I ain't as good as Daddy Nix at takin' care of her. So...like...shut the fuck up, maybe?"

"Tell him, PJ," Nix shakes his head as he gets up and walks towards his own bike, checking it over to make sure it's at peak performance.

Perfectionist prick.

I lean up and brush a bit of rust off of the engine with my fingers, grumbling. Not enough of it is coming off. I'll need to take the whole fucking thing apart at this point.

"Alright, listen," I say as I slide out from under the busted bike. I lean back against the bigger part of the body and sigh, turning off the flashlight and shoving it in my pocket. "Max-well wants the product by New Year's Eve."

"Easy," River says excitedly and with a raised brow like we've lost our minds with the tension in the room.

"He wants Rapture by New Year's Eve," Nix punctuates the word Rapture almost with a growl. He hates this line of work, but we keep him housed and fed, so fuck him, and his holier-than-thou bullshit.

Whatever keeps my mom safe, I'll do it.

Even if she is a fucking whore.

"That's not fucking possible, PJ!" River shouts, his hands flailing in the air like they're both dead fish.

"I don't care what's possible, we're gonna MAKE it possible!"

"How?" River looks at me, raising a brow and crossing his arms.

"We'll go back to our hometown over Thanksgiving break, take the bird with us, making sure to distract the ever loving shit out of her while we overturn the whole damn house."

"That still only leaves a fucking month, assuming we find the damn thing in the house. I still think Maxwell's blowing smoke up our asses, but whatever, PJ–"

"STOP. FUCKING. CALLING ME THAT!" I roar, tossing the nearest thing to me–a wrench of all things–and I try not to laugh as it hits Phoenix square in the chest and he grunts in pain.

River doesn't win his battle against the laughter, however, and snorts before busting out into the loudest of laughs I've heard from him. He's doubled over, hardly breathing, when Nix chucks the wrench on the ground and launches himself at River with a roar of rage.

Within seconds, the tension is broken and I'm laughing my ass off, too.

We're brothers, and this is how it's supposed to be.

We fight hard, and we love harder.

I join in on the fight for a bit, throwing half-assed punches and kicks. River mounts me, grinning down at me like the devil he is, with my arm held in between both of his as he squeezes the life out of me. My veins are bulging on the side of my head as I hold myself back from tapping out.

"Tap, PJ, tap!" River says, and he's half bouncing on top of my crotch, forcing a grunt out of me in a mix of pain and frustration.

"Stop," I grunt, "fucking," I shift my hips to try and get him off of me, "calling me," I succeed in twisting so that I'm on top of him, and free my arm, my hand going around his throat, "PJ!"

Nix is laughing harder now, cheering us on in stride, but River soon notices the hardness of my dick, and I notice his.

This is an unspoken thing between us, so within seconds he taps and shifts away, trying to hide himself since he's in sweats and doesn't want to showcase how deep our bromance could go if we let it.

I clear my throat and try to straighten my clothes, staring at my brothers in earnest, a plea in my gaze as I meet each of their eyes.

"We need to do this, guys. For my mom's sake, okay?" I hold my hands up in a prayer motion, pleading.

River nods and chews on his lip as we both look towards Phoenix, who looks lost in his thoughts, a deep "V" in his brows.

"Nix–"

"Alright," he clears his throat, "But we need to convince Red that we're taking her home for the right reasons. When's the last time you saw your mom, Pierce?"

And therein lies another fucking problem...

CHAPTER FOURTEEN

raven

I'm woken by the sound of Pierce's voice, though I can't make out his words. My body is slick with sweat, and I'm sticking to something that feels a hell of a lot like skin.

Jolting upright, I cringe at the way my skin separates from the person wrapped around me, nearly falling off the bed as I scramble away. Fixing my clothes, my eyes rake over the form covered in the blankets. I'm absolutely certain I was alone in this bed last night.

Dirty blonde hair covers his head, and half of the muscular back is showcasing all sorts of magnificent tattoos. The biggest, and most prominent tattoo grabs my attention instantly. A large raven takes flight across his back, its wings going from one broad shoulder to the other. The shading is glorious, and I can almost sense its feathers gliding across my fingertips.

I'm practically hunched over when one of those strong arms bands across my waist and brings me back onto the bed. I pound against the arm, but I'm still half distracted by the tattoo and its meaning to fight River as he brings me back in to snuggle.

"Don't leave the bed, yet, Rae. I like my morning snuggles with coffee, and Phoenix went to go get some while grumpy Jackson downstairs bitches at people." He opens one eye, and the playfulness I see in his gaze has me partly relenting in his grip. My head rests on the pillow as I stare into the endless sea of gray that stares back at me.

He brings a hand up from my waist, trailing his fingers across the bare skin of my midriff. It's excruciating, mentally, to want him right now. The goosebumps showing up along my skin are cursed in my mind. The way my nipples pebble when his fingers barely brush my breast on their way up to my jaw... well...I'll hate myself later for that, too.

"You're so beautiful, Rae. Like a rainbow in the middle of a bunch of storms," River whispers, both eyes now open and flashing across my body.

His words sink into me, and stupidly, I let them.

It's moments like these that make me see I may not be truly seen as property to these men. Maybe there's something else within their words I should be looking into. Pierce's, specifically.

This entire situation is fucked up, truthfully, but I feel like I'm missing something...something big.

As I'm frozen, staring into the storm filled eyes of River Jacobs, my entire body alight at his touch, I hear the screech of the junkyard gate opening, and the roaring of a motorcycle.

Phoenix.

He's a mystery to me, as much as he was when I met him, and the way he takes care of me is such a strong offset to the way Pierce treats me that I'm constantly warring with myself. Should I trust him? Trusting him implies that he's someone who will do me no harm, and so far, he hasn't taken part in any of the sick shit that the other two have done.

But he hasn't stopped it either…

In all reality, River only does as he's told by Pierce, who is the ringleader of this entire fucked up situation. He's the one who wanted to claim me, and it's clear to see he's got the trust of the other boys. They do whatever the hell he says. But why?

I'm pulled from my thoughts when the smell of warm donuts and coffee permeates the air. The donuts; I'm all for them. The coffee makes me scrunch my nose in disgust and attempt to cover it with the blanket, pulling it from underneath mine and River's bodies as the smell of it gets closer, the sound of Phoenix's steps also getting louder and louder.

"Alright," Phoenix says as he rounds the railing and comes towards the bed. "Went to that coffee shop off the corner of Cobalt Drive and grabbed the first batch. I dunno how you take your morning coffee, Red, so I kept it black and brought all the extras with me."

As he says the words, River is taking in my look of disgust, his brow raising as he looks from me to the coffee. I nearly gag when he hands me the cup, and I'm shaking my head vehemently when he tries to pry the blanket from my nose.

"Holy hell," he whispers, "Nix…she doesn't like coffee!"

"Coulda told you dumb asses that, had you sought to fuckin' confer with me this morning." Pierce's footsteps were silent, so his voice scares the ever loving hell out of me. I jump and fall off of the bed.

Only, I don't make contact with the floor. I look up in shock at Phoenix, who still has the drink holder in one hand and now has me in the other arm. His brow is also raised.

They think I'm a damn alien now.

"Here's your reminder that she hates pineapple on her pizza," Pierce jabs, reaching out to snag me from the floor before placing a possessive kiss to my brow.

My brows jump to my hairline in surprise at the tender action, and I'm certain I'll fall where I'm standing the moment he lets go. This is the old Pierce. This is Green. My best fr–

His voice is a mere whisper when his lips make contact with my ear, "What other secrets should I share this morning, or will you finally speak to me?"

I want to punch the fucker in the face, but I settle for shutting my eyes and shaking my head, my heart in tatters on the floor at our feet.

Green has been gone for a while now, Rae.

He growls before spinning me around, my back to his chest, his hand sliding around until it covers my throat. The action shouldn't make me wet, but here we are and denial is a girl's best friend.

"I was also her first kiss, and she fuckin' sucked at it, though she was begging for it." His grip on my throat tightens, almost as if he knows I want to whirl around and deck him.

My eyes open, only for a tear to slide past the defense of my lashes and slip down my cheek.

"Pierce," Phoenix barks, glaring at him over my shoulder, "let her eat." His eyes track to meet mine, and he offers a small smile, trying to placate my panic. "What can I get you to drink, Red?"

It takes him a moment to understand I can't answer. I wouldn't be able to with Pierce's hand around my throat anyway, but my mutism provides its first real challenge within this arrangement. River slides across the bed and produces a pen and a notepad from the nightstand. Standing he brings it to me, placing both in my hands.

I nod in thanks before writing down my answer.

Hot chocolate, please? Or a soda...

Pushing the note outwards, unable to move due to Pierce's hold on me, I implore Phoenix with my eyes to come take it.

He does, smiling softly before shaking his head. "Hot chocolate it is. I'll head to the store later and grab some sodas for the fridge." He places the notepad on the bed, then points at the box of donuts. "Eat. I'll bring a warm drink up here."

Phoenix leaves the room, River heading downstairs shortly after him, which leaves Pierce and I all alone.

Silence.

We never used to have uncomfortable silences, and yet, when the loft is empty of the other two...all that seems to happen is this uncomfortable silence. It's almost as if Pierce is conflicted on how to treat me anymore. As if his actions up until this moment were planned and now he's free falling.

We've been free falling since our first kiss, it seems.

His fingers tighten almost imperceptibly over my pulse point before he grunts and lets me go.

I stumble forward, but manage to catch myself and stand upright, whirling around to glare at him, hands on my hips. His brows are furrowed, but once he sees my glare, he shakes his head and waves me off before heading towards the bathroom.

Minutes later, the water in the shower turns on, but the door is cracked.

Boy's lost his mind if he thinks I'm taking that invitation.

I grab one of the chocolate glazed donuts and make my way down the cold metal stairs, looking out of the windows towards the junkyard and the greenery the boys have managed to salvage out of seemingly nowhere. It's a gorgeous set up, and in any other circumstance, it'd be a paradise of sorts.

This feels like home.

I chomp down the rest of the donut, swallowing it and my thoughts down. We don't get heartwarming, happy thoughts here. That's not what life has given me.

I'm halfway down the stairs when Phoenix emerges from around the corner, a coffee mug full of hot chocolate–with marshmallows–steaming in his hand. We nearly bump into each other, as his attention is on the phone in his other hand, but I manage to grab the mug and keep it from spilling. I give a small smile to him in thanks. Skirting around him, I begin my appraisal of the converted shop.

The dark leathers of the furniture call to me. I want to grab my steamiest romance novel and curl up under a blanket for ages. It'd be nice to let go every once in a while.

"Raven," Phoenix says, following after me and shoving the phone into his dark jeans, "it's still early, but let me give you a ride to campus today. I have the Jeep Wrangler. We can take it if you aren't comfortable on the bike?"

His gaze is penetrating and as warm as the hot chocolate that slides down my throat. I assess him, admiring the warmth of his eyes as they peruse my body in a not nice way. I cross my arms to cover my pebbled nipples, and sip once more from the mug. My footsteps are quick as I head back toward the stairs I recently descended from.

"Uhm...shit...," he says, following after me again, "the notepad is upstairs. Just, uh, write down either bike or Jeep, yeah?" He coughs to clear his throat, and I let a tiny smile surface as I ascend the metal step. I hide it once I clear the top step so he doesn't see.

After all, if you let them see your happiness, they'll know how to use it against you.

Once I'm at the bed again, I grab the notepad and write the

word bike down. I show it to Phoenix, his brows rising in surprise. He may have had to forcefully put me onto the thing, but I enjoyed it enough to get back on with him.

Only him.

"Okay then. I brought you some clothes from your room," he points to a box sitting near the closet. "Wear some pants and closed-toed shoes, and I'll loan you some leather if you don't have one."

I nod and chew on my lip as he backs up a few steps, before turning and heading downstairs again, his hand ruffling through his hair in a show of frustration and stress.

Turning and walking towards the closet, I rifle through the box that was brought. Most of my clothes are in here, it seems. I pick out a pair of tight black jeans with frayed holes up and down the front of the legs, in rebellion to Phoenix's penchant for my safety, of course. I also grab a purple crop top with a skull face across the front of it, some socks, and my shit kicker boots that I bought right before I came here.

I need something to make me a bad-ass, alright?

It's humorous to think I use them as armor, rather than a weapon as intended.

When the shower doesn't turn off after a few minutes of me glaring at the cracked doorway, I exhale the breath I'm holding and begin to strip my clothes off. Nothing they haven't seen, anyways, and if I smell it's their fault.

Minutes later, I'm fumbling with a braid in my hair on the way down the steps, only to come in contact with Phoenix again as he holds out a black leather jacket far too big for me.

"Sorry, Red," he sighs, turning me and putting my arms through the holes like I'm a child, "this is all I've got here. I want to get a better jacket for you, soon, 'kay?"

When I nod, he pats the shoulders of the jacket down.

Taking the half-assed braid out of my hands, he begins to undo it, running his fingers through my red locks. I'd groan if I could, but I settle for letting a long breath out and closing my eyes, falling into the soft–yet most likely false–security that is this man taking care of me. I truly, truly should not let him in like this, but he seems to enjoy it and it sure is nice to let someone take the reins on my care for a moment.

I'm broken, surely.

After he has the braid done, one of his hands sneaks around and wraps around my throat in a possessive manner, and the other wraps around the base of the braid. Using both, he tugs my head back so I'm forced to look at him nearly upside down. My pulse skyrockets at the caring and heat I find in his brown eyes, and we're locked in this space while he looks like he wants to say something.

"Yo dudes and dudette," River shouts, bringing us out of the moment, "We gotta go or else we're gonna be fuckin' late, and I can't be late to this class again or I'll fail it!"

Phoenix brushes his hand along my collarbone, my shoulder, and before he lets me go, he releases my braid and head, backing up and brushing his hands along his own leather jacket. I take a deep breath and regret it. The sweet smell of rain encompasses me, and it's a scent I've come to learn is solely Phoenix.

He smirks cockily as if he knows how he's affected me.

I glare and spin around, only to crash into Pierce as he buttons his own jacket up. He doesn't catch me. Nope.

The ass-hat lets me bounce off his broad frame, and I find myself falling sideways into River, who bunches me up in a hug and sniffs me like a dog.

"Ah, hell," he whines, "now my dick's hard and I gotta take this damn class. I hate numbers, guys, I truly fucking do!"

"We know," both Pierce and Phoenix bark at the same time. Phoenix follows up by smacking his hand on top of River's shoulder. "Let her go, Tweedledum, she's riding with me."

"Wait," Pierce whirls on us, halfway to the garage door already, "She's *willingly* riding your bike?" His eyes lock onto mine, and he's angry as fuck about it.

Phoenix merely grips my hand, ripping me from River's hold, and proceeds to shoulder check Pierce on his way out to the vehicles. "See what happens when you're nice to someone, PJ?"

I see the smirk.

River sees the smirk.

Pierce definitely sees the smirk.

Once Phoenix has me on the back of his bike, a loud laugh escapes him after Pierce growls out something I don't quite hear thanks to the loud roaring of the bike.

Boys.

Green,

I swear to all the heavens ever thought of,
JIMMY IS THE WORST KISSER IN THE WORLD.

I didn't enjoy it, I didn't want to enjoy it, and when Patricia Gardner came up to me and slapped me for kissing him, I wanted to tell her she could have him, but my traitorous body just broke down in tears.

I went home today and didn't tell you, and now I feel bad.

So have this letter, my apologies for ever kissing Jimmy (I was curious, okay?)

I know you said we shouldn't be boyfriend and girlfriend until we're seniors, but, Pierce, I seriously do not want to try to spend time with other boys. They are all so fricken' annoying.

Please, for all that is good in the world,
Be my boyfriend?
Keep the other gross boys out of the way.
Blue
PS: Jimmy said he's gonna kick your butt for telling on him for peeking under my skirt.

pierce

I'm pissed. More than pissed.

Not only is River wearing a shit eating grin, but Phoenix has taken my girl on the back of his bike, *with her fucking consent* I might add.

On top of it all?

I see the tiniest of smiles as Nix places his spare helmet on her head. It's almost impossible to see, but I've been looking at her since the day we fucking met so I fucking see it.

Bitch, I want to say. Instead, I grumble, lock the door and get on my own bike. River and Nix have taken up outside of the junkyard gates, so I hit the button for the automatic garage door, hitting it again for the gates once we cross the barrier.

Time to face the fucking music.

We're halfway to the school when I veer off the side of the road and wave the others onward. I know better than to make a bigger show of it than that. Nix drives on by, and Riv makes the dumb phone sign with his hand, making me roll my eyes.

Pulling the bike onto the dirt track hidden in the trees, I

slow down to a safe speed, keeping my eyes open for passersby while I make my way towards the empty dirt lot behind the school.

I'm glad no one knows this is here. Maxwell is a complete idiot for having HQ be this close, but here we are, the under-bosses for his stupid fucking business, running the shots and hurting people who don't follow the rules.

Comical, seeing as how it's a fucking criminal organization.

I sigh as I round the last curve, slowing the bike and hopping off of it. Flexing my fingers in and out of a fist as I stare at the dumb fuck who sits waiting for me in the empty dirt lot. I try to ignore the watchful eyes on me from behind the moving cameras that are plastered around as I walk toward my childhood nemesis.

"Ah, if it isn't ol' PJ," he says, his tone jovial and his smile far too fucking bright for my liking.

"Don't call me that. You bring the fuckin' cash, J?" I bark at him, grinding my molars as he runs a hand through his dusty brown hair. His bright blues are far too fucking close to Raven's, and I'm forced to swallow down the need to punch him in the dick.

"Yeah, yeah, all's you want is the green, huh?" He taunts, reaching around to his motorcycle and lifting the bag of cash from his saddlebag. "Gonna suck me off for bein' such a good boy?"

"Jimmy!" I growl, fisting my hands in my pockets as I watch him fiddle with the bag like he might put it back on his bike.

"Aye, old friends need to be kind to each other. It's what dear old ma would tell me, anyways." He grins, big and fucking wide, and I'm left seething in his presence, like normal.

"I've given you about a dozen black eyes over the years, Jim Boy," I snark. He visibly flinches and walks toward me with the bag. "Want another?" I ask.

He clears his throat, flexing his fingers on the bag as he holds it out toward me, his eyes now on his fucking feet like the coward he is. "Nah...just take it, yeah?" He's almost silent.

I get a sick sense of pleasure from taking cash from this fucker every week. I didn't want to see him after I left my hometown, but he showed up the same week as I did at CU and I wanted to murder him more than I wanted to take my first breath.

He took what I wanted.

At that thought, and once I've got the bag in hand, I ball my right hand and punch him square in the nose. It's comical how fast the man falls to his ass, dirtying up his jeans. He never was good at scrapping with me, anyways. I let out a loud laugh, tossing the bag of cash onto the ground near my bike. No one else is here to take it.

Within a few seconds, I'm on top of Jimmy, pounding my fists into his face, my knee into his nuts, and I'm grinning so wide it hurts.

But boy does my soul fucking sing.

He hardly gets half a hit in before I remind him exactly why the fuck he left Raven Hill alone back when we were kids.

Ah hell...

"SERIOUSLY? *You look like an old bitty right now, Rae!*" I shout, *bunching my fists on the inside of my suit pants.*

We're all dressed up for prom, and she chose to go with

fucking Jimmy. It's disgraceful, hurtful, and out of pure spite, I'm bringing Patricia Gardner.

At least I'll get something to take the edge off tonight.

"I don't look like an old bitty, you ass!" Rae shouts. Her red hair is cascading across her shoulders and back like a waterfall of blood and it's got me hard in places I shouldn't be when it comes to my best friend. She's a goddamn vision in that black dress. The fringes on the bottom make me want to run my fingers through them to see which way they'll tangle.

"Whatever, ya old bitty, let's fuckin' go, 'kay? The limo has been outside for twenty minutes." I glare at the heels she's putting on, and at the same moment, put my suit jacket on, buttoning what I can before she grabs her clutch and wraps her hand around my bicep.

Too bad I chickened the fuck out of asking her to our junior prom.

Maybe senior prom will be different for us.

"'Kay, so just cause I'm goin' with Jimmy doesn't mean I don't want to dance with you at least once, Pierce, got me?" She side-eyes me. The smokiness of her eye makeup and the dark, blood-red lipstick on her lips only enhances the darkness in her gaze.

I wet my lips and nod, clearing my throat as we cross the front room and come into contact with Everlyn, Raven's mother.

"Aw hell, you two look a vision, don't you?" She croons, smushing my cheeks and kissing my forehead in the way she always does. It's patronizing sometimes.

She repeats the action with Raven and I cough to cover my laugh when she tries to wipe the dark lipstick off of her daughter's lips, only to wince when said daughter stomps her heel down on my foot.

"Shit, Rae," I mutter, wiggling the toes that I'm sure were gone seconds ago.

"Mm, not sorry," she grins, swatting her mother away.

Twenty minutes later, we're halfway to the school after taking far too many fucking pictures for my liking.

She's too exposed, I think, but I smile, crack a few jokes with Patricia and Jimmy, and try to ignore the way Raven is leaning into him like he's her best fucking friend.

Once we reach the school, I realize how fucking dumb this whole night is. In this podunk town–population 2,000–it's clear as day that they are particular with their money. I shouldn't be surprised when all the PTO moms and their high society daughters take up the role of greeting people like this is some big fancy red carpet event in New York or LA.

I nearly forget my date while I glare at the way Jimmy places his hand possessively on Rae's lower back. Patricia reminds me she's there, though, by digging her gold talons into my arm and smiling brightly at the student-run cameras, her jewelry glinting at the flash and making me want to be anywhere but here.

The only jewelry Raven owns? A locket I got her for Christmas when we were 13. Each side holds a picture of us, with our hands outstretched making a half heart. Together the sides make a full heart with our hands.

She cried.

I preened.

It was an eventful Christmas, to say the least.

Once inside, I offer to grab everyone's drinks, attempting to get away from my date–and Raven's. I can't stand another fucking minute in their presence, the jealousy radiating off of me is probably palpable at this point.

With the punch in hand–probably spiked–I make my way back across the room towards the girl I swore I'd marry one day.

Only, she's sat up on Jimmy's lap like it's her own personal fucking throne and I'm tempted to toss my drink in his face.

"Thanks, honey," Patricia says, gathering a drink in her manicured hands and grinning as she sips from the fruity concoction.

I try not to snort as the drink goes a little up her nose. She squishes her face up, and I especially don't laugh when the liquid dribbles down her chin. Nope, I cover my indiscretion with a cough, grab a napkin, and offer it to her–albeit a tad roughly. I'm handing Raven and Jimmy's drinks over when Patty shrieks her anger about it being spiked, laughing far too hard when she stomps her way across toward the ladies' room.

"Here, darlin'," Jimmy says, his eyes all for my girl as he places his hand along the outside of her upper thigh. "Take it slow, it's spiked with vodka."

Raven grins the tiniest of bits, sipping from the drink without a sign of weakness, her eyes meeting mine across the rim.

This is not our first rodeo with alcohol.

Jimmy's eyes are wide and his pupils are large after watching her brazenly drink the liquid, and he's nearly jumping out of his seat when she chugs the whole thing.

"C'mere, handsome," she says, sliding off his lap and pulling him with her towards the dance floor.

I'm crushed and dateless as I watch them dance for seemingly hours after that. My date bails with some girlfriends, tears threatening her perfect makeup. So now my night is extra lonely, and my girl is on the arm of some jackass who's wearing an even more expensive monkey suit than the one my mom was able to get for me at the last minute.

The end of the night couldn't come soon enough.

I sigh, bringing what seems like my tenth glass of spiked

punch to my lips and chugging it down as Raven drags Jimmy towards the doors with a wave towards me.

Oh hell no.

I'm up out of my seat before I can register the movement, but the drinks I've had are far too much for my system, so I'm stumbling as I make my way towards the doors. In minutes—though it seems like hours—I'm in the parking lot looking for them both. Everyone knows what happens on prom night.

What I should have been offering up to Rae on prom night.

I can't fucking find them though, so I'm stuck leaning against the outside wall and trying to stomp down my worry, my fear, and my absolute anguish at how brazen she is tonight. It's a sad occasion for me as I wait for nearly ten minutes before I see a light flash as a car door opens, and by fucking god, my girl looks like she'd rather be anywhere else but near that fucking dick.

So I move.

I haven't moved this quickly ever in my life, and yet my fist is making contact with Jimmy's face faster than my eyes can close to blink. Blood is everywhere, my knee is to his groin—his pants are fucking undone!—and I'm left in a whirlwind of activity for what seems like a damn century before hands grab me, and arms are holding me back. I quickly find myself staring into the beautiful deep blue ocean of Raven's eyes.

Eyes filled with tears.

Did he put them there?

"You...are...," she sniffles, bringing a hand up underneath her nose to clear it, "you're an asshole, Pierce Jackson!" She rears her hand back and—

SMACK!

Never in my life has Raven Hill hit me. Not on purpose, and not that fucking hard.

My skin is burning as hot as the fucking sun, my girl has tears in her eyes that I now register as tears I put there.

And as I make eye contact with Jimmy, he's grinning wildly, though his face is bloodied. His grin grows and grows as my girl spins toward him, helping him leave so he can get home.

While I spend the goddamn night at the precinct.

CHAPTER SIXTEEN

raven

Curious as I am to why Pierce ditched us all halfway to school, I don't try to bring it up. Communication aside, I don't want to give in to my curiosities about him. I want to stay in my lane and continue to hate him. It's easier that way. Can't get my heart broken again.

The moment Phoenix lowers the kickstand of his bike, I'm off, thrusting the helmet into his lap, and halfway across the parking lot before either he or River catches up.

It's easy to run from them and their expectations of this situation. Easier, even, to ignore the possibilities of what could be if I gave in to the kindnesses they've decided to show me–Pierce aside.

Class is slow. I'm hardly paying attention, so when the door opens and slams against the interior wall, I'm shocked out of my skin.

Pierce stands there, bloodied, with dirt all over his leather jacket and black jeans. It's a fucking miracle he's not at the hospital right now with how much blood is covering his body. He's gunning it for me, pushing students and their desks away as he beelines it for my spot in the room, and I'm shuffling to get out of the way.

Whatever this is, I do not want to be a victim to hurricane Pierce.

What stops me in my tracks, however, is that this man is smiling. It's a shock to my system. This is a real smile from him. Not a smirk, not a cocky grin. This is an honest-to-shit smile.

I'm frozen, and he's still grinning like a Cheshire cat when he slides along my desk, sits on the top of the surface, grips both my cheeks in his hands, and plants the loudest kiss on my lips, leaving me and half the classroom stunned.

My eyes are wide when he pulls away, and I nearly swallow my heart whole when he brushes his thumb across my lower lip, his eyes cascading across my stunned face like a warm blanket.

I should not be comforted when he tugs me from my classroom, my bag slung over his arm as he wraps his arm around my shoulders. I shouldn't be reminded of home while he guides me through the hallways.

He breaks through that thought bubble, however. In a move that doesn't even surprise me, he shoves me into a study room, flips on the light, and turns the lock.

"Knees, little bird, I need your fucking mouth on me," he barks the orders at me, his hand slowly caressing my scalp as it travels to the top of my head. Once there, the pressure from his palm indicates I should lower myself for him.

I glare and shake my head, though my wet panties are an indication of how turned on I am at seeing him so jovial. I preen when I hear the command in his tone. His guidance is like a warm hug sometimes, allowing me to shut my brain off and listen for a while.

He's glaring at me, but with mischief in his gaze. Tossing

my bag on the floor, he points at it–another command. I'm almost certain I might kill this motherfucker one day.

Till death do us part, eh?

Hi, I'm death.

I grin, but look down at the ground to hide it, my braid falling across my right shoulder as I lower myself to do as he asks. It's not a hardship to suck a dick–only his. Without any more preamble, I reach out to lower his zipper, my hand sneaking into his jeans to find him already half hard. I bite my lip and take as deep a breath as I can manage before lowering his jeans and boxers enough to free his shaft.

Licking my lips, I go to put him in my mouth only to be stopped short when Pierce leans down into my face, the hand that's not on my scalp reaching out to tip my jaw up so I can look in his eyes. "Eyes on me, little bird. I need to see you as you suck my dick."

I blink up at him with outrage simmering in my veins, only for him to pop my mouth open with his thumb, "Open up, baby, and drool for me."

Before I can attempt to fight against him, my mouth is filled with his flaming hot cock and I'm halfway to coming from the way he's treating me.

Who knew we'd develop kinks of the darkest varieties?

We've come a long, long way from home, Green.

I'd gag with the size of him, if I had a gag reflex. He pushes to the back of my throat, but I manage to swallow as much as possible. Drool immediately coats my mouth, and as he pulls out of me, the long line between his dick and my lips should be absolutely disgusting. And yet I find myself squirming on top of my bag, my hands finding purchase in Pierce's thighs as he pushes his way past my lips again.

He taps my cheek with his hand, a light slap, and growls out, "Eyes."

My blues meet his greens and the lust I see there is enough to drown in. I'm salivating all over his dick and running my tongue around the veins there, tracing him, relearning him.

"Fuck yes," he moans, the hand in my hair tightening to the point of pain.

With our eyes connected, I can't hide the lust in mine, the way my pupils are blown and my body is reacting. There are goosebumps all over me as he thrusts his dick into me. He groans and a fire lights along my entire being. I'm lost in him, and in another time where something like this wasn't feasible. I was always too scared to do this, but I'm doing it now. My cheeks hollow out as I suck him in, swallowing him down past my gag reflex until I'm forced to breathe through my nose or suffocate.

What a way to go though, yeah?

With a few final thrusts, Pierce holds my head so far toward his crotch, all I see are his abs as he constricts inside of me, pulsing until a spurt of hot liquid travels down my throat. He doesn't give me time to swallow when he pulls out, opening my mouth until my tongue pops out, his cum on it to show him what he's done.

He grins, eyes flaring as he spits on my tongue, falls to his knees, and kisses me with such passion, I become dizzy.

Our tongues tangle, and he forces me to comply with his pace and movement. Pierce groans at his own taste on my tongue, and I'm hardly functioning enough to take in the contrast of his spit versus mine.

It's intoxicating in the worst ways. Between the depravity, I see glimpses of the boy who practiced kissing with me for hours, and in those glimpses, my heart is still shattered.

"Up," he barks, killing the kiss of a thousand kisses. I swallow our combined juices and chew my lip as I watch him put himself away. He, of course, does not deem to help me get up or get off, so I let out a huff as I climb to my feet, wiping the remainder of the evidence off of my lips with my tongue.

He watches the motion, eyes flared with lust again. He grabs my bag and places it over my shoulders for me. Before I can slap, kick, punch or maim him for his bullshit, he's flipping the light off in the study room and exiting it, the door forcing me to choose whether to stay put or follow.

I follow, of course.

Don't mind me, just a glutton for fucking punishment coming through.

I sigh, placing my hands on the straps of my bag as I make my way down the hall behind him. I don't bother trying to go back to class, there's hardly any point to Intro to Business anyways. I'm here to earn a degree to appease the scholarship gods and those who will hire me based on four years of half-assed attention being paid over someone with tons of life experience and no shiny piece of paper worth thousands of dollars.

Pathetic, how society puts those expectations on us.

As we exit the building, I take in the dark clouds surrounding us and sigh, knowing I'll get soaked to the bone when we ride back to the junkyard. I tug the jacket closed and force myself to breathe while I follow Pierce down to the parking lot.

Only, when we make it to the opposite side and pass the guys' bikes, my curiosity peaks.

"Gotta make a few stops, and you're my little pet right now."

And that's how I find myself smack dab in the middle of

the nurse's office with a pretty little blonde staring at Pierce like he hangs the moon, the sun, and all the stars.

Yet she glares at me like I'm destroying the whole entire universe by simply existing.

Bitch, you can have him.

It's insulting when women always glare at women who are hanging out with guys. Girls and guys can be friends. That's not an actual issue. Plus, my issue with these guys might be solved if they all fucked around and got distracted by Betty Blondes and their fake tits.

I sigh, shaking my head and plopping my ass in the waiting room. Pierce has already been gone for twenty minutes and I'm finding it hard as shit to stem my curiosity while we're here. I don't need to deal with his business, and maybe while he's back there, he can confirm whether or not he's given me any diseases that I should be aware of.

Too bad you can't really cure heartbreak.

I'M STARTLED AWAKE, my body being jostled against something warm. It smells like the ocean all of a sudden, and I find myself relaxing into the scent, hoping I can drift off and wake up again on an actual beach somewhere far the fuck away from here.

That's not the case, however. Minutes later someone is pressing a soft kiss to my forehead and attempting to wake me.

"Rae," River whispers, "Hey, pretty girl, can you wake up for me? Can't take you on my bike while you're asleep." His voice rumbles through his chest and I'm caught in a silent war with myself.

Do I lean against him and never leave his warmth, or do I

wake long enough to curl up in the soft as hell bed at the guys' place?

The bed wins out after a moment, and my eyes flutter open to find River grinning down at me, his pretty gray eyes mimicking the storm clouds above us.

"Y'awake now? Gotta have your senses about you when we ride, RaeRae. Don't wanna turn into a pancake." He snorts, placing me slowly down onto my feet.

"She'd be a pretty pancake, though," Phoenix says from beside us, and Pierce rolls his eyes in my peripherals.

"Get your helmet on, baby doll," River grins and winks at me. Plopping the spare helmet onto my head, he helps me climb on the back of his bike, pulling me as close as possible. When that's not enough for him, he places his left hand on my upper thigh and digs his fingers in possessively, grounding us to each other.

I rest the front of the helmet against the center of his back, and wrap my arms around him, holding onto my own hands as I put my safety in his. It's a dumb notion to feel safe in his arms, but I do. I run with it and allow myself to relax on the way back to the junkyard.

And with the luck I have, we end up fucking drenched by the time we cross into the gates.

Blue,

This cold shoulder thing you've got going is bullshit.

I beat the living fuck out of Jimmy for talking dirty things about you, and you get mad at me?!?!?! Tell me, please, how the fuck that makes any damn sense!!!

Whatever, I'll shove this under your door or something later...

I only do this shit to keep you safe anyway....

As I always do....

LG,

Green

PS: I'm fine, by the way.

CHAPTER SEVENTEEN

river

She's goddamn warm against me on the way home, even as she trembles in the thunderstorm that shouldn't have taken us by surprise.

I laugh as I pull into the garage and wrench my kickstand down with a screech. I'm damn near doubled over when I see her crop top is stuck to her like a second skin, and it's dripping into her pants since she didn't zip up the leather jacket Phoenix gave to her.

It's too big to keep her safe from the rain, anyway, but at least she wouldn't be plastered with the storm had she zipped the damn thing up.

Silly girl.

I grin as I undo the helmet, lifting it from her half wet hair and tossing it toward one of the guys. I hear the grunt as they catch it, but I don't care. I lift Raven up into my arms bridal style and carry her inside, up the stairs of the loft and across to the shower, uncaring about the trail of rainwater and mud I leave behind.

If Pierce wants me to be his little bitch in this scheme of

his, he can do a little bit of cleanup while we do damage control on the girl.

S'all he's good for, anyway.

Without a care for what the other guys want, I shut myself in the bathroom with Raven, toeing off my boots after setting her on the long counter. She's nearly keeling over as she looks out of the skylight and wall height window behind the jacuzzi tub. It's like she didn't truly get a chance to take it in when Phoenix bathed her yesterday.

Nix has taken to caring for her like she's a child, and I don't know whether to be concerned about that or not.

Whatever.

With a grin larger than my face should allow, I pull off Raven's shit kickers, tossing them in a pile with mine. My hands roam up her wet jeans, my nails making the tiniest of contacts with her skin in each of the frayed holes.

Wonder if her pussy is as soaked as her clothes?

"Hey, Rae, did the grump let you get off at least once today?" My eyes are taking her in, watching as her breath hitches when my fingers reach the tops of her thighs and how her nostrils flare when I dig in that much more.

She shakes her head at my question, taking her lower lip between her teeth. I let out a small growl, both at my asshole boss and at the look of her lip becoming swollen under her ministrations.

"Pity," I grunt, stopping my kneading of her only to unbutton her jeans and tug them down as best I can, "Lift."

She does, and I grin at her compliance. I'd give her a good girl for it, but I'm not as much of an asshole as my friends are, and I haven't truly earned the consent to give her terms of endearments or honorifics.

She does, however, reach down and pull her panties down

alongside her jeans, pushing my hands away to finish the job by herself. And as I'm standing there stunned like an idiot, she's letting the leather fall to the side and lifting her top above her head.

Squirming under my blatant ogling, Rae flinches when I reach forward. I was about to undo the front clasp of her bra, but I back away and lift my hands to show that I can and will listen and watch her body language.

I'm not a guy who likes to take, take, take. What I did the other night while I was drunk pisses me off entirely. I know I did it with the express intention of keeping Pierce's fucking sadistic hands off of Raven's pretty pale skin. Still not proud of it, and I'll get her off a thousand times, apologize a million, and still not be comfortable in her presence.

With shaking hands, Raven unclasps her bra and stares at me for far too long before she lets her breasts free and drops the item on the pile of the rest of her clothes. And as she stands there searching my gaze for something, I don't know, she reaches forward and grabs my hands, pulling them to her chest in a move I think surprises both of us.

I'm unable to hold back the groan, my hands flex across the globes and my thumbs find their rightful fucking forever home on her nipples. She's so fucking pale almost everywhere, but the little tinges of pink that call to me? They're the best shade of pink I've ever seen in my life.

My eyes are imploring as I look at her, bending at the waist and waiting for the almost imperceptible nod she gives before my tongue lashes out and wraps around the little bud.

Goosebumps erupt all along her chest, and as I knead both breasts, thumb one nipple, and leisurely lap at the other? Dear god, the woman nearly vibrates with need. Her not getting off during all of this sexual play is forcing her to fall apart fairly quickly under me, and I'm sure it'd take one good brush of her clit before she erupts all over me.

With the strength of a thousand gods, I lift my head and trace my hands away from her breasts, my fingers making the softest of contact with her skin until both my hands are bracketing her jaw. I search her eyes, a silent question in mine as I tilt her head the way I want it.

Her pupils are blown with desire and give me the consent I seek, but Pierce has taken too much from Raven, and given Phoenix and I far more than he should have.

So I wait, and wait, and fucking wait for her to find whatever it is she needs to find.

Finally, she nods, a silent yes playing out on her lips, and I dive forward to accept the gift she's giving me.

Kissing her shouldn't be like the world has been set alight, leaving her and I on our own island, swallowed by water and sand and safety.

Kissing her definitely shouldn't be like fireworks being set off in the middle of a country road, lighting the whole ass sky up with the wondrous colors of burning shrapnel.

As our lips barely part for us to take a breath, our tongues tangle in the sexiest of dances, and my knees begin to shake. My heart is cracking wide the fuck open for this girl, and my body goes dizzy from the lack of oxygen. I don't need oxygen anymore, I only need her.

I grip her hair and tug her head back, exposing the column of her throat to me. I dive in like a starving man looking through the window of a buffet and groan as her strawberry taste explodes on my tongue, the taste of rainwater mixing in.

I nuzzle into her neck and take a soft nip, and she takes a sharp breath. Backing away, I keep my eyes on her as I unbutton my pants and let them and my boxers fall to the floor. I reach behind me and take my shirt off by bunching it in my hands at the back and pulling it over my head. It's a complete show for Rae. I know the girls like it when we pull magic tricks while we pull clothing off.

I'm only here for the women and the booze.

And I'm all out of booze.

Raven's eyes are wide, her lower lip between her teeth as she takes me in, and I belatedly remember to snag a condom from the back of my wet jeans before I turn towards the tub. I turn the shower on, since I have the insane need to rail her against the wet tile rather than let her ride me where the water can give us away.

I want this moment with her. For some fucking reason.

As the double shower head turns on, I turn toward her and grip her chin in my hand. With all the seriousness left in my body right now, I keep my eyes on her and ask, "Can I fuck you, sweet girl?"

My heart pounds in my chest and my blood roars in my ears as I stare into the depths of her deep blues. My breathing comes to a halt when she nods. I crush my mouth to hers, lifting her into my arms, and blindly climbing into the shower with her. I slam the privacy screen shut and push her up against the now wet tiles. Bracing one forearm at the side of her head, the other grips her hip as I grind myself into her molten heat.

Just the tip, just a second, just to see how it feels.

Groaning, I nip at her shoulder, biting down harder when she tightens her legs around my hips and grinds herself on me. It's intoxicating, and I allow her to chase her own pleasure for a few moments. She nearly takes me out when she bites down on my shoulder in return, those little canines almost drawing blood when they find purchase.

Leaning back, I bite my lip as I take in her flushed skin,

pinkened by my touch and kisses. Her lips are swollen from mine, her pupils wide with lust. "Naughty girl."

Lips parted, she shakes slightly but holds herself on me with her hands on my shoulders, her heels biting into my ass and urging me forward.

"Just," I grunt, shifting my aching cock away from her, "hold on a sec, doll." Opening the condom wrapper with my teeth, I spit the trash on the ground and roll the latex over myself, giving a few short strokes before placing myself at her entrance. I pause and make eye contact with her again, "Two taps," I say, "right to the back of my neck, and I'll stop, got it?"

Consent is fucking key right now, and since she can't utter a damn word or make a single sound, we have to find a way to get around it. I grin like a snake when she smiles, a 'yes' playing on her lips as her hands slide to rest at the nape of my neck and patting me twice. I ground myself to the sensation and nod in satisfaction, eyes still on those intoxicating blues.

"Alright, love, hold on. It's gonna be a fun ride down the River," I wink at her and when she glares at me, no doubt hating the joke, I push inside in one full thrust, unable to keep from tossing my head back on a groan.

She's goddamn glorious. Tight, warm, and sopping wet as I drive into her relentlessly. The sounds our bodies make are enough to spur me on, my hands finding purchase on her hips as I thrust into her, possessed. She gives me these tiny little sharp intakes of breath, and I keep on going. My lips find her neck again, and I let my tongue lave at her, luxuriating in the way she constricts around me when my teeth make contact with her pulse point. I bite down a little bit harder, pull her skin between my lips, and suck. Hard.

Her whole fucking body lights up and tightens. I groan and nearly come on the spot, but I hold back. She needs to come. It's been days of torture for her and I refuse to walk out of here without at least reciprocating. Let's not talk about the fact that I haven't come either. I'm sexually frustrated, sure, and I'd have taken care of it by now if it weren't for this siren currently in my arms.

My hand makes its way between our bodies and my fingers find her clit. I rub circles around it slowly at first, my thrusts matching the pace of my fingers. When she clenches around me, I pull her clit between two of my fingers and pinch.

Her breathing stutters, then stops, her eyes roll to the back of her head, and the way her pussy clamps over my cock nearly kills me on the spot. My orgasm hits me harder than I could have imagined.

My vision clouds as I thrust into her without rhythm, and it's almost a complete and utter shock that I manage to ride her through her own orgasm, milking both of us for all we're worth. Seated inside of her, I still and bring my lips to hers for another heated kiss.

Except it's not heated, it's sweet, and not something I'd normally give a girl.

To stave off any feelings we both might catch, I nip at her nose and unceremoniously place her on her shaking legs. "Let's clean up and get warm. Nix is making pizza."

I slap her on the ass to get her moving, leaving her shocked as I turn around and look for my soap. Once I find it, I quickly wash and get out to dry myself off, leaving a shocked Raven at my back, and strongly fucking regretting sticking my dick in something that will definitely call to me for the rest of my miserable existence.

Pierce scares the hell out of me when I exit the bathroom, still naked. I watch as his eyes round, but his pupils flare at my dick. I grin but hide it behind my hair as I flip it over my shoulder to dry it out. "Sup, Piercey Jackson?"

"Shut the fuck up, RJ," he barks.

I growl.

We sound like a bunch of fucking animals in here.

"I got a job in a week, but there's a party at the frat scheduled. Take care of it for me, will you?" He glares at me while giving the command, his hand on the bathroom door.

I sigh, brushing my hair with my fingers as I traipse toward the closet to change.

Aye, fucking, aye, captain I'm in love with my childhood best friend.

raven

I'm feeling extremely off-kilter.

The boys have done nothing but dote on me this last week, hand and fucking foot. I've gotten a few orgasms out of the deal from River, denied pleasure by Pierce, and Phoenix has taken care of me after every single encounter.

Today, however, has all three of them tense and serious in a way I haven't seen before–even Pierce.

I don't know what's going on tonight, only I'm to dress up for a party and be ready to let loose. River's words.

It's hard to do that, however, when all the boys look like they're about to go to fucking war. They think I don't see the guns on their backs or the knives in their boots? It's comical they think I'm that dense.

I shake my head and finish curling my hair, letting the red locks fall down along my shoulders and back. Setting the curling iron down, I stare into the mirror at my smoky eyes, my black lips, and the skin-tight black leather dress I chose for the night. It's strapless and pushes my tits up far past their usual spot.

I shrug, letting a small smile befall my lips as I begin to turn toward the bathroom door, but I'm shocked when Pierce bursts through the door, forcing it to slam against the wall. It's almost embarrassing how far I jump, my hip slamming against the counter corner and I hiss in pain, gripping for it.

Pierce grips my throat, leaning me backward so my back is bowed over the sink as he stares into my eyes. "You have rules tonight, little bird. Are you listening?'

I swallow and nod, my eyelids fluttering as I try to keep the tears at bay. He's never scared me until this year. He's never shown anger towards me, so I'm always thrown off by his tantrums. His forceful hands.

He inhales, eyes and nostrils flaring as he stares me down. "River is the person you listen to the most today, got me? You follow him like a lonesome little puppy and you don't let him out of your sight. Phoenix will be at your six at all times, so don't think now is the time for you to run. You don't look at or touch another man besides my boys, got it?" He jostles me until I dip my head, then leans in to press a firm kiss on my lips. This is something he's been doing since we kissed only a week ago. He's claiming me and continuing to possess me in ways I don't wish to divulge.

I hate myself at this moment, but, in true Raven Hill fashion, I square my shoulders, look him dead in the eyes, and let him pull me to a stand in front of him.

"You look like a slut, little bird," he growls, his eyes raking over my form. "Just don't fucking act like one in public."

He leaves the bathroom, leaving me to the tears that want to fall. I won't cry for him. I haven't in a week now, and I don't want to restart the process of grieving my best friend.

If the worst thing I've ever done for the guy was to send his college application in, what would happen if I really pulled some shit on him?

I shake my head and bolster myself before walking out of the bathroom, noting Pierce is already half out of the gates by the time I get my heels on. Phoenix is driving the jeep tonight, so I don't have to wear sensible shoes for the bikes.

With a soft smile, River approaches me from the stairs, a bag in his hand. He looks sheepish. Dare I say...embarrassed?

I tilt my head at him in question, something he's finally caught onto as this situation continues for us all. The boys haven't been too frustrated at my silence–except for Pierce who is still convinced I'm choosing to be stubborn–so we've all learned each other's body language over the last week.

Words are spoken less around here, but intentions are far louder now.

Closed mouths tend to open hearts, I've learned.

When Phoenix comes up the stairs behind River with a large grin on his face, I'm caught in the boys' looks. It takes me a moment to notice River has now opened the garment bag he's holding, presenting me with something that I've secretly been excited about since the moment it was mentioned.

My leather. My own jacket to wear while we ride.

I want to fall to my knees and sob right now, but I don't. I stand strong and turn around, Phoenix quickly taking up a spot behind me to lift my hair–he has a fascination for it. River takes the cue to put my arms through the jacket. When Phoenix releases my hair, River turns me toward both of them and flattens the collar.

Immediately I notice how warm it is, how comfortable and safe it makes me feel. I'm running my fingers across the arms in an almost embrace when Phoenix slides up behind me, pushing my hair across one shoulder as he leans in to place warm lips against my neck. I sigh in contentment, a small smile lifting my lips as my eyes flutter closed.

It's enough to make a girl feel special.

I can't put another thought through my brain when River plasters himself to my front, his lips taking mine in a slow and sweet kiss. My heart stutters and I'm left in a moment of pure bliss as he places a hand on my hip, and another in my hair. With both of their bodies against mine, I want to float.

I don't want to think about the outside world, or Pierce, or hate, or sadness.

I just want to fucking let go for once.

When I think they might accept my silent plea–my always silent plea–they fix my stance, Phoenix fluffs my hair, and River shows me a cocky wink the moment my eyes flutter open.

"Time to ride, pretty girl. I want to take you for a whirl on the dance floor tonight." He grins wide, and I shake my head while rolling my eyes. It's an easy dismissal of his nature, but he takes it in stride as I walk down the stairs and spend the next few minutes trying to hide my smile.

I'm tempted to ignore them both and take a bike of my own, but Phoenix guides me with a hand on my back, leading me towards the front seat of the jeep. "Front seat for the queen," he grins when my gaze snaps across to him.

"Oy! What about the king?!" River barks, bounding over towards us and trying to throw himself inside, but Phoenix pushes me through and slams the door shut.

Not before I hear him mutter, "King of the man whores, maybe."

My shoulders are bouncing at the crack. Before I know it, the boys are in the jeep, staring at me in confusion. The little huffs of air posing as my silent laughter are shocking to them.

I haven't laughed this hard in months.

It feels too fucking good to be true, but tears are falling from my eyes and the boys are looking at me like they're deer in headlights. The looks they cast to each other and back to me make me laugh harder, and I double over and clench my sides as I let it free.

Soon enough, both of them are laughing, too. They can't help themselves. It's contagious as hell and I find myself bopping along to the music as we head towards campus for the second time today.

Fixing my mascara the moment the jeep slows, I see the guys cast a glance at each other, before River grins, nodding while Phoenix looks at me with what looks like guilt in his eyes. It's enough to make me take stock, but I outwardly ignore their silent conversation in lieu of getting out of the jeep myself.

I'm my only backup plan. My only cheerleader. My only safety net. So I need to take their silent conversation and remind myself they're still keeping me captive in some way. Still keeping me as a possession.

Dubious consent does not enthusiastic consent make.

I sigh when River slams his door, closing mine shortly after. He grabs my hand and places it on his bicep, reminding me of prom and all the things that happened after. My face heats with a blush right alongside the deep seated anger.

Pierce ruined that fucking night for me.

It should have been him to take my virginity, but he was too damn chicken to do it.

So there's Jimmy, and, well, it sucked.

But at least I wasn't the only girl at her prom to leave a virgin. Well, to leave prom night. I was hoping Jimmy would fucking take me back to his house or some shit. Everyone knows his mom went MIA on his ass more often than not. So when he proceeded to take my virginity in the back of that trashy ass truck of his, well, I was the absolute opposite of flattered.

Took me a week after that to teach myself to come for the first time.

A few months after was when Pierce and I decided to fool around with each other.

What a fucking summer that was.

I sigh, my eyes tracking my footsteps on the ground as we walk towards the guys' frat house.

It's an absolute wreck, and I can smell the stench of beer and vomit instantly. No fucking wonder they stay at the junkyard.

As we're ushered inside, however, I notice there are hardly any lights on inside, and the windows are blacked out. This is close to the Halloween party...only darker. There's an erotic and horror-themed feel to the party decor. It's giving me shivers as we walk through the halls and towards the open living room that houses the dance floor.

The beat pulses through my body, sending shots of desire to my core as I watch the other party-goers grind against each other, almost porn worthy. River grins when he turns his head, gripping my hand and bringing me toward the dance floor. He instantly plasters me to his front.

My hands slide to his neck, and I move with him as our bodies guide each other to the beat and thrum of the music surrounding us.

Phoenix leans in between us and places a soft kiss on my cheek. "I'll be at the bar," he states. He leaves and gets himself lost to the darkness surrounding us all.

"Fuck yeah, grind with me, baby. I wanna show you the fuck off." River shouts over the music, twisting me until my ass is pressed against the hard ridge of him and my back is against his chest. His hands glide down my shoulders and arms, until our fingers lock. Bringing them up along my thighs, he locks our arms around each other across my ribs.

Our bodies continue to twist to the beat as River hums and sings along. The heat of our encounter, the eyes of those around us, and the sheer amount of people in this room with their eyes on us is causing my body to become slick with sweat and desire.

I close my eyes and simply exist here. I want to stop and feel this moment; the smell of River, who is the ocean personified; the bass thrumming through my body; his hands and body gliding against mine. It's fucking intoxicating and I can't find a single fuck to give as I let go.

Dumb? Yes.

After a few songs I'm abruptly yanked into another hard body and I instantly know it does not belong to one of my three guys.

My eyes fly open and the first thought that comes to mind is...Jimmy?!

Letter from Raven
Age 16

Pierce,

You're a goddamn asshole, y'know that? Jimmy was in no way going to replace you in my life, but he sure as hell filled the holes you wouldn't.

(Yes that was an innuendo. I can use those just like you can, you motherfucker!)

I hope you know that I will never, ever forgive you for interrupting us. If you can get your rocks off, so can I, asshole!

TTFE (That's ta-ta forever, dick!)

Raven

"Nix, baby, I haven't seen you in weeeeeeks," Lucy whines. I'm half-listening to her while the rest of the room continues on around me.

To be fair, she's not lying.

I haven't done anything except care for and protect Raven for the last two weeks. She's been all I can focus on. Not only to protect her from the other shit, but to keep her at least feeling safe around Pierce.

We're running out of time, and I feel like a noose is being tightened around my goddamn neck as each day passes. Maxwell won't let us get off easy anymore. We have to find that recipe and it's clear as fucking day Raven has nothing and no one to care for.

School's a way station for her, same as me and the guys. So there's nothing keeping her here, and nothing calling her home.

We're out of ideas, but, at the last minute, I told Pierce to back the fuck off so River and I could get close to Red. So here we are treating her to a night of dancing and debauchery. It's going as fucking brilliantly as I could have hoped. The girl in question is smiling, biting her lip, and grinding against River in the way I wish she could grind against me.

I grin to myself and take a sip of the whiskey in my glass.

"Phoeeeniiixxx," Lucy slurs, her nails trailing up my leather-covered arm.

"Fuck off, Barbie, I don't have time for your shit again." I brush her off and continue my watch party of Raven and River. They're a fucking sight to behold, to be honest. She'd be happy if it was only him trying to own her, I'm sure of it.

I'm fucking chopped liver most days. Except for when I'm pampering the fuck out of her.

Someone needs to take care of her. Not a single other soul does.

"Niiix," Lucy says again, pushing her tits out and getting in front of me. She blanches at my glare and attempts to square her shoulders up to me like Raven so successfully does daily. "I want to be your girl again, baby. We had fun, yeah?"

I grunt and finish my whiskey, before I shuffle her to the side with a pointed glare, "You cheated on me with your own fucking uncle. Why in the absolute hell would I want you after that? Excuse me." I growl out, turning to grab another whiskey, only I'm pulled up short. From the corner of my eye I see Jimmy reach out and snatch Raven from River's arms.

I see fucking red. So, much, red.

And it's about to be Jimmy's blood all over the damn dance floor.

I beeline it across the room, balling my fists up and getting ready for a fight. Or a murder.

Only fate truly knows the direction this will go.

"Get your hands off of her before I shove yours so far up

your own ass you'll be the new name for a yoga pose!" River barks. I choke on my laughter as I reach them.

His hands are balled up like mine are, and I know that if Raven wasn't in between both guys, he'd have had Jimmy on the floor or outside in a hole in seconds.

Raven's eyes meet mine over her shoulder, and I'm stunned when I see tears spill over her cheeks. This girl doesn't cry much, since the world has taken enough from her.

The unfortunate side effect of losing everything you've ever loved? It takes infinitely more pain for you to truly feel it.

I narrow my eyes to slits and meet Jimmy's smug—and fucking high—eyes over my girl's head. "Let. Her. Go." I grind out, but Raven lifts her leg and stomps her tiny little heel down onto his toes, and he shrieks like a little bitch as she crosses to me.

Me, not River.

I'll dissect that later.

My arms are wrapped around her and I'm holding her close to me, her arms reaching around behind my back and her face burying into my chest. Her entire body is shaking when I meet River's gaze. His eyes flash between mine before turning toward Jimmy. I nod, silently telling him to deal with it. I'm halfway down the hallway and toward a bathroom with Raven before the first anguished cry is sounded.

I smirk a little but tamp it down when I close Raven and myself into the bathroom. I flip the light and caress her frame, beginning with her face. My thumbs find her tears, wiping them away before I bring my hands down across her shivering frame. Cold or fear, she'll never let me know. She reaches out and surprises the shit out of me by hugging me. Not out of holding herself together, but out of thanks.

We stand there for minutes, one hand in her hair massaging

her scalp, the other lightly caressing her back as I shush her. It seems like our own little world in here right now, and I'm fucked if I think I want to rejoin the rest of the world outside of this room.

It's silent for a long time, so long in fact that my ears are ringing by the time a solid knock lands on the door, and River's voice bursts the quiet solitude we've found, "He's cryin' like a little bitch. Let's fucking go."

THIRTY MINUTES LATER, we find ourselves outside of a rather ugly-looking green mansion, with a literal white picket fence, a playground and trampoline visible in the backyard, and a few trees to line the property.

Jared and his bitch of a wife Melissa reside here. We don't like Jared. He's a two-timing scam of a man who treats women like slaves and throws his responsibilities off until the last minute before blaming said women for things going awry. To top it all off, he blames everyone but himself when his own plans go belly up.

He's also the reason a few of our drug dealers have gone off half-cocked and fucked over some girls on campus. His propensity to hurt women is low-key, but it's still there.

And so, today, on the day of post-Halloween pranks, we are lined up outside of his driveway, having given Raven a carton of eggs, while River and I hold onto some rolls of toilet paper. By some, I mean we have two 24-packs, and we're locked and fucking loaded.

Raven's eyes are wide as she looks between us, the eggs, and the house. I grin slightly and tilt my head, "He deserves it, promise."

River hoots and hollers as he taunts Jared from the street, his grin as wide as ever as he plays the loudest music possible to annoy the fucker.

"The moment he comes outside, start pelting him, 'kay Raven?" I grin at her, nodding toward the egg carton before raising a brow.

She shakes her head, inhales, and opens the carton before turning towards the front door and squaring her shoulders.

"Atta girl," I mutter, and I have to bite back my groan at the way she shivers and goosebumps flow over her pale skin. God, I wish this circumstance was different. I'd show her so many ways she could get tied up with me.

Figuratively and literally.

"Yoo-hoo, Jared!" River shouts, bouncing on his toes as he keeps his own blood pumping. "Melissa! I want to see egg-zactly what you're up to tonight!" He looks at us and grins wide, waggling his brows like he thinks his joke is funny.

His face falls when he's met with mine and Raven's blank stares.

"Fuckin' buzz killers," he grumbles, but his face lights up again when Jared comes out, red-faced and absolutely fucking livid. "GET 'EM BABY GIRL, GO!"

Raven inhales, and grabs an egg. With a force of strength I shouldn't be surprised by, she pelts Jared directly in the face with an egg.

I've never seen a smile as radiant as the one that she wears on her face after that.

That one egg cracking on the dude's face results in Red's armor splitting wide open. I can't complain when she turns and chucks one at River and me, and I truly can't be bothered to bitch at her when she's running us out of all the eggs we brought—about five dozen, mind you. She nails those eggs in the worst places all over the Leatherwood's yard. Places they might not ever get the raw egg out of, and I'm fucking here for it.

River and I are off at a sprint, tossing toilet paper all over their yard and making sure that shit sticks to the eggy mess left all over by our girl. I'm grinning far wider than necessary, but this is something I can feel free doing. I'm a young adult, feeling free for the first time in ages, and I'm by my best friend and our girl's side while I do it.

By the time the cops are pulling up, we're already down the road and laughing wildly. Even if Raven's laugh is silent, I still see her. I see her happiness, and it's glorious.

The sticky mess we're in is an unfortunate side effect of today's fun, so when we pass the junkyard gates, I look at both of them and raise a brow, barking out a command. "Strip."

And my dick immediately flies high when Raven removes her jacket and tosses it to the center console. I nearly run the jeep right into the garage door while I take in the way her chest heaves and her tits rise and fall with her heavy breathing.

Parking right outside of the garage–because eggs–I take off my shirt and toss it with River's once he's placed it over Raven's jacket. We're all silent but for our collective heaving breaths, and it's so erotic that I'm going to replay the sound for the rest of my fucking life. My eyes meet those deep blues and I lick my lips, and she bites hers in response. With a tentative hand, I reach out and slide my fingertips across her heated skin, reaching for the zipper at the back of her dress.

Our eyes meet, she nods, and I let out a loud exhale before lowering it until there's nowhere else to go. The black material splits open at her back and I can see down to her panty line, only there's—

"You fucking dirty girl," River says, leaning forward to

plant a thankful kiss on Raven's cheek. It's loud and wet, and when he pulls back, he eyes me as if he's waiting for my next command.

"Out of the car," I bark, "both of you."

They both comply, and I sit and watch as River helps Raven down, only to crowd her against the car and lean in to kiss her lips like a dying man who's found water. I'm closing the car door and rounding the front of the vehicle. "Come." They do. "Against the wall," I point, they obey.

Red's eyes meet mine and I'm lost for a moment before I shake my head and reach out to turn the outdoor water on, gripping the end of the hose and letting it slowly flow out of the end. I don't wait for it to set any normal temperature. I walk toward them, lean my body against Raven's, and allow the stream of water to fall over all three of us, and against that brick wall as I watch her body's reactions to ours.

My dick is aching to be freed, aching to have any sort of relief that's not my own damn hand.

Once we're all soaked to the bone and Raven is shivering from the cold and her own desire, I drop the hose and quickly turn the water off. It's excruciating to watch River snag her up around him, but I don't mind when I get a show of her bare ass when he lifts her dress up to wind her legs around his hips. He winks at me over her shoulder, and I can't find the sense to care that I'm watching him with her.

Guess I'm a voyeur now. Whatever.

I'm the one left to unlock and open the doors to the garage and loft, and also the one left to close them back up, but by the time I'm upstairs and River's got her splayed out on top of a towel on the bed, I'm ready to fucking explode from the heat traveling up my spine.

I'm raring to fucking go as I look over River's shoulder

while he's laid across her, his face on her chest and his hands traveling up her entire body. This is a bit like that first night, but I see the consent written all over Raven as she grips at River's hair, shoulders, and neck. I groan when she wraps her legs around him, and I can't help but palm my stiff dick when she scrunches her face up in pleasure.

"Fuck, baby girl, let's share with Nixy-boy, 'kay?" River grunts out, removing her hand from the back of his head and shuffling backward until he's standing at the end of the bed and waving me over.

I'm naked by the time I make it to her, realizing that her dress has finally made it off of her body and onto the floor where it should be. I grin as I lean down and place my face only inches from hers, my fingers on her jaw as I take in the flushed state of her skin, and how heated it is. She smiles at me, and it takes me off guard for a moment before I lean in and press my nose to the bridge of hers, letting it glide along the length as I take in her aroused scent.

"You gonna let us both have you tonight, Red?" River speaks, his hand brushing through Raven's hair as he sits at the top of the bed, his free hand on his naked dick. "You gonna let us play with you in all the fun ways we've had planned?"

Yeah, we don't have plans, but the intake of breath has me thinking Raven doesn't mind as much as she wants to. So instead of calling River out, I let my nose trail a line to her ear and suck on her earlobe a bit. After I tug on it with my teeth, I groan in her ear, and her entire body trembles. "Be our little fucktoy tonight, Red? I promise you'll enjoy it. I've wanted to play with you for far," I bite her earlobe, "far," lick down her neck, "too long." I find purchase with my canines in her pulse point and god how I wish I could hear her moan for me, but the way her nails are scraping down the bare skin of my back is enough for me to know precisely how much I'm affecting her.

"On your knees, Red," I bark, leaning back on my haunches and slapping her softly on the hip twice to get her moving.

The quickness in which she obeys me tells me far more about her than I think even she knows, and I grin when I meet River's stunned eyes. I shrug and go back to watching our little vixen as she presents her ass to me and her arms bracket River's thighs immediately.

Ah hell, she's seen some shit.

"Good fucking girl, Red," I growl, sliding my hands from the bottom of her feet, over her ankles and calves, up toward her thighs. I knead the delectable globe of her ass before rearing my hand back and smacking it hard enough to create a solid print with my hand. Raven jolts, but the second she pushes her ass back into my hand, I'm a goddamn goner for her, if I wasn't already. I massage the place where I spanked her, and look towards River, meeting his gray eyes over the sea of red hair covering Raven's head.

"Fuck yes, she loved that, do it again!" River says, gripping Raven's jaw in his thumb and forefinger and watching her as I light her ass up again on the other cheek. Gooseflesh travels across her entire body once the smack radiates around the room, and I knead her flesh with both hands, leaning forward to drop a soft kiss to the spot right above her ass. I groan when she rocks back against me, and trail a finger down to her mound, tracing around the spot where she wants me a few times before I thrust two fingers into her, thrusting at such a quick speed that her body is practically bouncing between my hand and River's.

It's a miracle I don't fucking come all over myself when I hear her fucking pant.

This teasing bullshit is for the birds when you've gone as long as I have with only solo play, so I incline my head to the nightstand, rolling my eyes at River's quiet laughter. He grabs a condom and tosses it towards me before settling against the headboard, his thighs now on either side of Raven's head. A head that is, thankfully, now hiding his dick.

I'm all for pleasing a woman with my friends, but I'd rather not cross swords while I'm doing it.

I plant a few more kisses on Raven's ass as I continue to ruthlessly finger fuck her. After a few moments, I rear back and fumble to open the condom before I finally cover my shaft. I give it a few quick tugs, checking to make sure I don't blow the second I seat myself inside of her.

Leaning over Raven's back, I bring my hand to the back of her head and grip her hair, tight enough to control her but not tight enough to hurt her. Plastering my lips against her ear, I speak. "I want you to put his dick so far down your throat that you don't know where either one of us begins or ends once I'm finally inside of you. Two taps to his thighs for stop, one for slow, got it?"

Once she nods, I lower her head over River's thick dick and groan at the way her drool falls all over his lap already. "Good, Red, good fucking girl. Drool all over him and suck him as fantastically as I know you can."

River groans, fisting Raven's hair and knocking my hand off of her head. I look up and glare at him, flipping him off as he grins at me with half-lidded eyes.

Annoying prick.

As I lean back on my haunches again, I watch as Raven shakes her ass at me, and I know she's taunting me. I land a few good smacks on her ass for the audacity. She does something that makes River's hips stutter while he face fucks her, and once he starts up his relentless pace again, I plan my entrance of her with one of his thrusts.

I enter her wet cunt the same moment he pushes his dick so far down her throat, I can sense her struggle for breath. It's an out-of-body experience I have in that moment, and I'm barely able to hold onto my load. I have to hold onto her hips and slow her wiggling as I shut my eyes and take deep breaths. "Oh...fuck," I murmur.

Once I've got myself situated and under control, I tap her hip and begin a slow roll of my hips into hers. I wait and find that sweet, sweet spot inside of her, and when her whole body shudders, I keep the pace and make sure to drag the crown of my dick along her g-spot in the same way over and over until she's squirming and panting. I see sweat building up along the arch of her spine, so I move her hair from her neck and blow a line of cool air across her.

She shivers. River lets out a string of expletives.

I do it again, and River looks up at me with a glare. He doesn't want to come too soon.

I grip Raven's hair in my hand once more, twisting it over my knuckles a few times until I find purchase, pulling her off of his dick and watching as drool and pre-cum slither from her lips in the most intoxicating line of fluids I've seen in a while. I bite the shell of her ear and meet River's eyes when I speak the next words. "He almost blew his load too early, Red. Naughty girl. Get back down there and fucking make him come this time."

I toss her forward and push her head down over his dick again, and she eagerly takes him in. I let out a moan at the sight of her cheeks hollowing out. She's become a pro at sucking dick lately—Pierce's doing probably, with how much he stuffs his down her throat. River's taken full advantage of her soft spot towards him, and I'm finally glad to be able to get my own dick involved in this little group.

I grin and land a few more smacks on Rae's ass, luxuriating in the way that her pussy clamps down over me when I do. I score my nails down her spine, taking note of the goosebumps dotting her skin. She clamps down on me hard and I curse as my thrusts falter.

She likes pain—noted.

I grip her hip in one hand and snake my free hand down and around until my fingers find her clit. I can't fucking hold on anymore, so as I circle that little bud slowly but roughly, I say, "We own all your pleasure, Red. This little bundle of nerves right here?" I tap it, and she jolts. "Yeah. It's ours. So when I tell you to fucking come—no, not yet," I growl. She squeezes my dick tightly, and I slow my thrusts so I can speak to her. "When I touch this pretty clit and tell you to fucking come—you will fucking come. Ready?" I bite out.

She nods.

"Fucking come," I bark, pinching her clit harder than I think she's ever experienced. The resulting climax taking over all three of us is enough to cause the universe to explode.

At least that's what it's like for me.

The moment Raven lets go, her cunt squeezes me so tight I think she's taken full ownership of my dick and won't let go. I grip her hips so hard I know there's bruises, and River is holding her head down over his cock like he's trying to see how long she can hold her breath. The explosion erupting from me is brutal. Black spots dot my vision, and the resulting aftereffects of Raven's orgasm makes my dick attempt to stir back to life.

Only it can't.

We're all fucking dead at this point.

We have to be, because the next thing I know Pierce is glaring at us from the end of the bed, his arms crossed over his leather jacket and his jaw grinding back and forth so hard that I know we're fucking in for it.

I'd rather be dead than face the wrath of Pierce Jackson.

raven

I'm hardly aware of my surroundings when I wake, but what I am aware of is the absolute lethality of the voices I hear coming from downstairs. The guys sound like they're at a whole ass UFC fight and they might burn the world down with their voices alone.

My whole body aches, and I'm grateful for the oxygen that I'm able to take in now that I don't have River's dick in my mouth. I swear I'd cock warm for him if I had the chance. He tastes like a warm summer day and I can't quite give a shit that it shouldn't be a real taste.

"I don't give a flying fucking monkey's ass what we have to do to get her to come back to our hometown, Phoenix! We're fucking going and you can't say shit about it. She doesn't need pretense–she's a big fucking girl!" Pierce's voice echoes along the walls and the noise gets louder as he bounds up the stairs toward me.

His boots cause the metal to reverberate, and I'm trembling as I wrap the blanket around me, my eyes finding his instantly as he rounds the top step. "Good, you're fucking awake.

Remind the boys what a big girl you are, Raven. Remind them," he grits out, tossing clothes at me, "how you–YOU–chose to fucking sentence me to this goddamn life with your sneaky ass hands and your lying ass mouth–THAT CAN SPEAK, BY THE WAY, stubborn bit–"

"ENOUGH!" Phoenix's loud roar makes me jolt so hard I fall off the bed, wincing as my hip lands awkwardly on the floor.

I grab the clothes that were thrown at me and fumble up to my feet, holding them to my chest as I back up towards the bathroom, my eyes flipping between all three guys now that Phoenix and River have come upstairs. My shaking hands are noticed by both of them, and the lethal glares they shoot toward Pierce almost feel physical.

"Shower, Rae, it'll all be okay," River croons, pointing towards the bathroom and putting himself between me and Pierce.

I meet Phoenix's gaze while I back up onto the tiles. The last thing I see before I shut the bathroom door is the toughest blow to a throat I've ever seen, and Pierce falling roughly to his knees within a millisecond of it happening.

Locking the door, I drop the clothes onto the counter top, wincing when I see the bruises along my skin. If I didn't know what happened last night, I'd think I was bruised and battered in a fight, but I see the fingerprint indents and the little love bites all up and down my throat. My skin is a story to be told, for sure, and I think I'm going to hold this one close to my heart.

I let go last night entirely. From the moment I stepped out and saw the way the guys' eyes tracked my every movement, to the way my whole soul sang when River had me in his arms. The boy can dance, that's for sure. Even Jimmy couldn't fully tamper down the rest of the night. Egging a misogynist's house was definitely on the list of top ten most fun things to do, and afterward?

Well.

I bite my lip and trail my fingers across my skin. I look flushed and happy, with a radiant glow to my skin that wasn't there before. It's intoxicating and beautiful to see myself like this.

Grabbing the hairbrush, I run it through my tangled locks before placing it back down and getting myself a much-needed solo shower. River has invited himself into all of my showers lately. I want to be pissed, but he's treated me like a damn queen–as Phoenix called me last night–and I can't find myself regretting any moment of the tenderness I show those two.

If only Pierce were to allow you back in, my brain snarks.

Fuck you, evil thoughtress, I snark back.

I'm out of the shower twenty minutes later, makeup done, and in a pair of black skinny jeans, a plain white long sleeve shirt, and my hair is up in a high as hell ponytail.

A fucking power move, if I do say so myself.

As I exit the bathroom, Phoenix is sitting on the bed, his elbows on his knees as he leans forward on them. His hands are clasped so tightly together I think he might hurt himself, so I walk towards him and plant myself between his legs, my hands falling onto his shoulders.

I begin to knead his taut muscles, finding countless knots and forcing them to loosen. A small smile plays on my lips when he groans and loosens his body, his hands snaking around my waist until they find purchase on the back of my thighs.

I look down at him, but he buries his face in my stomach, a long sigh leaving him.

"We don't deserve the goodness you show us, Red," he murmurs, and I run a hand up the back of his neck, scoring my nails across his scalp.

He shudders, and I tug on his hair to get him to look up at me. When our eyes meet, the chemistry swirls between us as I slowly, so slowly, lean down to press my lips to his for the first time.

The butterflies in my stomach are throwing a thousand parties all on their own, celebrating a victory I didn't know they wanted. My heart leaps from my chest and plants itself firmly in his hold as our lips press so sweetly together.

I sigh, allowing my lips to open in invitation, and when our tongues begin to tangle, Phoenix holds firm to my thighs. I guess I'm trembling.

We're like this for minutes, hours it seems. When there's nothing left to give of my soul, Phoenix pulls back and runs a thumb along my lower lip. His eyes take in my kiss-bitten flesh like he's never seen such a beautiful thing before.

"That was exactly what I'd always imagined kissing to be like," he whispers.

I blink and tilt my head, my brows furrowing in question.

"Thank you," he says, clearing his throat and abruptly standing up, his hands scoring across my body until he's got me in a tight hug. "Finish getting dressed, we gotta go."

He lets me go, before walking down the stairs.

I stay there for a while, wondering if he really did just confess to me being his first ever kiss.

AFTER TAKING a moment to compose myself, I find long socks to fit under my boots. I head downstairs and look around at the guys. I refuse to look at Phoenix. I still can't believe what he's confessed to me. River looks like he'd rather be eating pig shit than sitting down on the couch sans any movement.

My gaze rakes over their stock still form, the way they're all tensed up. In milliseconds, my eyes snap to Pierce's, and though he's holding an ice pack to what I'm sure is a filthy bruise on his throat, he looks formidable.

"Alright," he says, his voice raspy from the damage to his windpipe, "we're going home for Thanksgiving in a few hours. It's a good six-hour drive, so we have to take the jeep. You'll pack a damn bag and come with us. I'm not letting you loose on campus so you can get loose on campus."

"Pierce!" Phoenix barks, glaring at the man in question.

Rolling his eyes, Pierce glares at me harder–if that's possible. "Let's go, little bird. I'm already fucking tired from this vacation."

I hold a hand up and reach for the pocket of my leather jacket to pull out a notepad–a gift from Phoenix. I write a few words in it.

School? Back when?

Ripping the page, I ball it up and toss it at Pierce's grumpy ass face. River chokes out a strangled laugh. I fail to hide my tiny smile, so I chew my lip instead as the men stand off against each other.

"Fuck school, not important," Pierce grits out. Eventually, he sighs, tossing the paper on the coffee table. "We'll be back the Sunday after Thanksgiving break. Gives us a solid week and a half there." Meeting Phoenix's gaze, both men silently communicate with each other before Pierce looks back at me,

"I miss my ma, Rae. Don't think she's doin' too well right now."

I'm furiously blinking back tears, worrying about someone else's mom being taken from them–by death or other means. Pierce shoves up, tosses the ice pack to Phoenix, shoulder checking me so hard that I fall backward and nearly land on my ass. Phoenix sighs, gripping my arms as he checks me over. He dips his head in silent acceptance of my outfit.

"I already packed a bag for you, Red," he says softly, running a hand along my jaw before kissing my forehead. "Get your boots on and let's go. The ride is too damn long to make boss man any grumpier than he usually is."

With a patronizing–yet endearing–pat on the ass, he sends me towards the garage. He's not lying though. He and River are on my heels and Phoenix grabs a purple duffle bag on our way out of the loft.

As I approach the jeep, I avoid the front seat like it's on fire. Pierce is sitting in the driver's seat, looking out at the green forest that's grown into the junkyard itself. The trees and vines are finding purchase between man-made parts and it's as if nature itself is reclaiming the planet.

Fitting, since Pierce is reclaiming me in more ways than he should right now.

River smacks me on the ass playfully as I climb into the back seat, and I turn my head to grin at him, meeting his gaze right before he winks. I know I blush, and his grin grows wider than I thought possible before he puts both hands on my ass, and begins to shove me into the car as if I'm stuck or something.

My silent laughter must catch Pierce's attention. He honks the horn and yells, "LET'S FUCKING GO ALREADY!"

I sigh and sit properly in the middle of the seat, knowing

full well it'll irritate the shit out of him. And I'm right. No less than a minute later, after both Phoenix and River have settled in, Pierce guns the gas so hard River's forced to hold me tighter when I'm jolted with the motion.

"Chill the fuck out, Piercey Jackson," River grits out, trying to stay in his usual playful mood.

I know something's off with them, though. River never has to fight to stay in a good mood.

Ever.

"I'll chill the fuck out once you take your filthy fucking paws off my girl," Pierce snaps.

My eyes meet his in the mirror and his eyes shutter before they go cold.

"The girl. The bitch. Whatever," he snarks, turning up the music and drowning out the rest of us as we drift down the road.

PIERCE'S VOICE comes out a low rumble, and I'm sure I miss some words, but I do hear it when he says, "Grab the bitch and take her inside. I don't care where the fuck she sleeps. Give me time over there, yeah?"

My heart is shattered by his blatant hatred of me. I get it, I do. What I did to him wasn't okay, but he had to leave, dammit!

I try to discreetly wipe my tear on Phoenix's shirt, only for him to help me wipe it off. My eyes flutter open and meet the deep, chocolate brown eyes I've grown so fond of. He shakes his head and leans down to press a soft kiss on my forehead, and my breathing hitches before he helps me sit up and right my clothes.

"Let's get you inside, sweetheart," he says solemnly as Pierce slams the jeep door closed so hard the entire frame rattles in its wake.

"He's fucking unhinged, Nix," River grits out, looking toward me and offering a soft smile and a hand to help me out of the vehicle.

I don't need the help, but they're offering more than simple, sweet gestures. They're trying to soften all of Pierce's blows with their kindnesses. I wish I could tell them that placing band-aids over bullet wounds won't do shit, but I allow them to placate themselves, gripping River's hand tightly and leaning against him as he ushers me inside the house that scared the hell out of me for far too long.

Our hometown consisted of far too many children and not enough parents. Mostly, single moms, our cul de sac was the perfect place to fuck around and find out. The mothers were gone to work, fathers were gone to 'get milk', and the kids grew up with a ton of curiosity and nobody to watch over them.

We had fun, but it wasn't innocent.

Each house in this cul de sac–all four of them—are colonial houses and they're all the same fucking color with the same shutters and the same doors and even the same damn garden in the front.

Pierce's mom's house, however, has overgrown weeds all over the yard, trash littering the sidewalks and half the drive-way, and it looks so decrepit you wouldn't trust someone was living in it right now. I'm absolutely shocked to hell when I see Pierce open the door willy nilly. I didn't see a key, so, was it unlocked?

I shrug out of my thoughts, wiggling my body around and trying to get feeling back to all of my extremities. River runs his hand across my shoulders as we walk inside, where I proceed to sneeze so hard I'm surprised I didn't scare every dust bunny within miles.

Pierce glares at me over his shoulder, meets River's gaze, and points down the hallway. Great, I get to use the fucking guest room that's probably not been touched in five years.

The moment my mom learned I had kissed Pierce–the same night it happened–we were no longer allowed to come over here. She knew Pierce's mom would let us do whatever, so she didn't trust us to be alone in a house without proper supervision.

Too bad she didn't know what we'd been doing while we were at the park.

I bite back my smile at the memories and try as hard as I can to keep the bitterness and sadness away. I haven't seen his mom since my mom's funeral. Such a sad realization.

As we creep into the guest room, I have to cover my nose to keep myself from smelling the stench of near fucking death that is this room.

"Oh...oh nope. Nuh uh, not happening, PJ!" River yells, grabbing my hand and tugging me back the way we came. "Raven, sweetheart, can we stay at your house?"

His eyes are imploring and pleading, almost as if it pains him to ask me, but it'd be more painful for us to stay in this hell hole. How it isn't condemned, I don't know. I let in a breath of fresh air the moment we cross back outside, and nearly gag when my body revolts against the sensations.

I point across the road towards my house–much more kept up since I hired someone to do it–and Phoenix exhales loudly. Leading us across the street, he grabs my duffle bag from the back of the jeep as we go.

Once we hit the front steps, I have to swallow hard to keep the emotion at bay. I haven't been back since I moved into the dorms. The emotions barrel into me and I'm almost doubled over when Pierce takes the key from my hand roughly and jams it into the lock.

"Fuck's sakes, stop being a pussy," he growls, shoving the door open hard like he always does.

A picture frame falls and breaks, and my heart shatters with it as I fall to my knees and let the tears fall with me.

The boys take the bags to the different rooms. It seems like I'm going to be relegated to my mother's room, which is somewhere that I haven't stepped foot since the moment she was put in hospice.

My heart is utterly shattered as I meander around, my feet scuffing on the ground and my hands wringing tightly as I take in my familiar surroundings. It's like I've walked into a waking nightmare and quite frankly, I'd rather be lost in my nightmares while I slept.

At least in my nightmares, my body is on autopilot.

This current pilot isn't working so well with the waking part.

I sigh as I round the corner to the kitchen downstairs, avoiding Pierce's gaze as he leans back in the recliner which used to be my mother's comfort spot. I'm tempted to toss a shoe at him to get him to move, but I don't.

He's not worth the effort at the moment.

Even though I'm here under slight duress, it's probably healing for me to be back in my home. I was gone for so long... I'd forgotten what my mother smells like. The full scent of jasmine and vanilla encompasses the entire house, and I'm truly a goner when I see Phoenix wearing her purple apron as he cooks at the stove. The tears come hard and fast, taking me by surprise, and I'm doubling over until my forehead is leaning on the stone island counter.

River comes up behind me and forces my head off of the cold stone, pulling me up into his arms and wrapping me in a tight embrace. One hand snakes up my spine and into my hair, tugging on the strands. My head moves with his palm, and when our eyes meet, I sniff to try and keep the tears at bay.

"Let the tears fall, baby girl," he whispers, his eyes flickering between mine. "I'll be right here when you're ready to stand on your own again."

He begins to sway us, trying hard to get me to fall into the motion with him, humming a tune I truly don't know. I fall into a weird numbness that could call itself calm, I suppose. I'm drowning in his comfort, and my eyes remain unseeing as we begin to float around the kitchen in a slow dance.

He's distracting me.

Music turns on to drown out River's hum, and we begin dancing to The Gambler by Fun until I'm twirling under his arm, my feet and heart are light across the space, and a smile stretches so far across my face my cheeks hurt. River brings me into his chest, running a hand along my cheek and wiping away any remaining tears. He spins me again and I let out a breath of laughter, wishing it was full of sound instead of air. The sentiment rings through, however, and River's bright eyes and large grin returns

"Food's ready," Phoenix says, breaking me from the reverie River and I have fallen into, but when I manage to look up at his face and meet his warm chocolate eyes, he's grinning in a way I haven't seen before.

His emotions have been all over the place and hard to read, but when he's taking care of me, or the other guys, I find he's truly in his element.

Unfortunately for those of us who like to smile for a living, Pierce enters the room and dampens the whole mood when he shuts off the music that's playing through the kitchen's sound system. It was a gift from me to my mom after I got my first ever paycheck.

I chew my lip, making my way towards the stools lining around the counter, keeping my eyes downcast to avoid all three guys' stares. I'm flayed open right now and don't need anyone else to add to my emotional distress.

I end up squished between River and Phoenix once spaghetti is served to me, and my body gets all sorts of heated each time their arms brush mine, and I about jump out of my skin when Phoenix's hand lands on my knee, his thumb and fingers digging in on either side of my flesh.

"Eat, Red," he commands in that low tone of his, causing me to almost immediately obey.

I should be offended that we've fallen into a shit version of a Dominant/submissive relationship without a conversation about it, but are we even in a real relationship to begin with?

I grit my teeth and give a small smile, lifting my fork and eating a healthy bite of the sauce covered noodles. It's a bit hot in my mouth, so I'm instantly regretting the big mouthful I try to take, spitting it back out onto the plate and huffing, waving my hand frantically in front of me.

River laughs and smacks his hand on the counter as he tries to stem his sudden choking fit, his eyes welling up as he meets my gaze. I see Phoenix in the corner of my eye shaking his head and pushing a water glass toward me, tilting his head toward it in a silent direction.

I'm grateful for the cool liquid, so I meet Phoenix's gaze and give him a small smile. A reward for his kindness, I suppose.

His lips quirk up and he shakes his head in exasperation, turning back to his own plate as we all continue our silent rebellion of ignoring Pierce and the lonely little storm cloud above his head.

The clean-up crew ends up being River and me, and I can't say I'm mad about it. I don't think I've done something this domestic with a guy ever–wait that's wrong, I did a lot of these things with Pierce.

I sigh, and River takes his bubble covered hand and lifts my chin with it, leaving behind a soap bubble beard in its wake.

"Chin up, RaeRae, it'll all be fine, you'll see." He boops my nose with his finger–leaving more bubbles behind–and actually makes the 'boop' noise!

I'm laughing, hard, the breaths that come out fanning over the bubbles in the sink as the happy tears fall from my eyes. I can't help what happens next. Swear.

Lifting both of my hands from the water–I think River overdid it on the soap on purpose–I bring up a large handful of bubbles and blow them as hard as I can, grinning wildly when they splash all over his face.

River's face contorts with mock rage, and my smile grows as I begin backing up from whatever mischief is now shining in his eyes.

"Oh, so that's how it is, huh?" He snaps, his lower lip twitching. He attempts to be angry with me, but he's failing miserably. His lips are turned down so far, he looks like a grumpy clown. In a blink, he's reaching out for me, lifting me over his shoulder. "Pierce, come stick your dick down our girl's throat. She needs to be taught a lesson."

My face blanches. The last thing I want to do is to spend time with Pierce in this place again. I don't need the memories to overcome me any more than they already have. I'm beating like hell all over River's back, but it's a fruitless task to escape.

He has me in my room and plastered to my bed before I can think up a feasible escape plan.

I at least had the title going; **Codename: Caveman Escape.**

It's a work in progress.

All three guys are surrounding me in minutes and my body heats as I watch them watch me. My chest is heaving with the heavy intakes of breaths that are needed to keep the blood firmly in my brain, but it doesn't work. The second River has my body spun with my head hanging off of the end of the bed, I know his intentions, clear as day.

I like to read and watch my porn, 'kay?

I lick my lips, and someone in the room groans–Phoenix, I think.

This is a little too close to what happened the night of the Halloween party, but I shove that thought far into the trenches of Things We Never Deal With. I chew my lip while the guys gain positions of comfortability in the room. Phoenix, in a chair in the corner, eyes blazing with heat. Pierce, undoing his jeans as he walks towards me. River, my lovely River, crawling onto the bed after stripping to complete nudity.

I ignore the sight of Pierce's dick in favor of watching the hair atop River's head cascade over his face as he leans down to press a soft kiss to the small sliver of skin between my jeans and shirt. He traces his hands up my thighs, lifting my shirt slowly once he grips the material so tortuously slow that I'd yell at him if I could.

I sigh loudly, and glare down at him with so much venom I'm sure I've poisoned him with it. The cocky shit only grins and licks a path up the center of my abdomen until I need to help him by removing my arms and head from the shirt. He places a soft kiss against the swell of both of my breasts, unhooking the front clasp of my lacy black bra.

Tired of my attention not being on him, Pierce grips my chin from above me and tilts my head until it's hanging off of the edge of the mattress. Our eyes meet, and his are flickering between pure lust and absolute hatred.

I'm going to ignore the love simmering there.

Neither one of us truly deserves love anymore.

Gritting his jaw, Pierce leans down, popping his thumb into my mouth, "Open," he snaps, and when I do, he exhales sharply before leaning as close to me as he dares. He opens his mouth and lets a line of drool trail from his tongue to land on mine. When he's satisfied he's sullied me–he hasn't–he lands a patronizing smack against my cheek and leans back up to a standing position.

"Stay," he barks. I do, but mostly due to River having managed to take my pants and underwear down my legs. I couldn't close my mouth if I wanted to when River's mouth makes full contact with my wet cunt.

My body jerks, but I manage to keep my head still, mouth open wide enough. I'm prepared for it when Pierce takes no prisoners, shoving his dick down my throat seconds later. I think he has come to terms with the fact that I'm truly suffering from mutism. The amount of times he's fucked my throat is getting insane, and the noises most people make have not once left my vocal cords.

The realization finally hits him. It's clear as day. Although he still thrusts into me, his eyes soften drastically, anguish clear in his features, and I'm pretty sure I see a tear fall down his cheek. My heart breaks for him all over again, but it quickly forgets its turmoil as River continues his relentless pace with his tongue against my pussy, adding a finger to the mix to help spread me open, his shoulders brandishing my thighs like armor as he leans in further, tongue fucking me in a way that has my body writhing.

Pierce thrusts into my mouth and forces me to shift down the bed and onto River's waiting tongue. When River's nose brushes my clit, I'm flying up the bed and taking Pierce further down my throat again, twisting my tongue around the head of his cock and hollowing out my cheeks as best I can to squeeze him inside of me.

Minutes into this little adventure and my hands are gripping so hard to the bedsheets I'm sure I'll break through the fabric. My eyes are shut tight while I let them both use and please me at the same time. A heady sensation of power overtakes me at the realization that I'm causing all of these reactions. River is practically fucking the mattress, Pierce is gritting his teeth to hold back his release, as he reverently strokes my throat, feeling himself inside of me.

I still when another body moves onto the bed, Phoenix. My hand reaches out and grips at River's dirty blond hair as I squirm under his ministrations. Pierce grunts when my other hand reaches out and lands on his thigh, nails digging in, but he doesn't stop fucking my face.

Phoenix leans down and whispers into my ear, "Ready to come for them, Red? Ready to soak River's face so much that he resembles his namesake?"

I nod as best as I can, my eyes trying to meet his gaze around Pierce's thigh as I suck him in. The man gives me a break to breathe, but seconds later, he's tracing his finger around my lips and pushing slowly, so fucking slowly, back down my throat. Phoenix trails a kiss down my throat, over where I'm sure he can feel Pierce's dick moving.

"Come for us, Red," he growls, biting my nipple at the same time that River bites my clit.

The intake of my breath, the arch of my spine, and the sweat seeping from my pores is euphoric. A cacophony of groans escapes from all three men, and it's heady.

I swallow down Pierce's release, and I'm barely aware of Phoenix lifting up and heading towards the bathroom, while River leans up and jacks himself off over me until his cum is covering my stomach and chest.

When Pierce pulls his dick from my mouth, he leans down, cupping my jaw with too much tenderness. My heart rate tries to pick up, but the bliss that the orgasm has left me in is enough for me to lean into his hand instead of away, a tear falling as I meet his softened gaze.

"I'm sorry," he whispers.

His lips meet mine for a barely there peck on the lips reminiscent of our first kiss, before he leaves the room, footsteps echoing down the hallway. We hear him descend the stairs, followed by the front door opening and closing with a snick.

I lay there for a while, staring at the ceiling, with my soul splayed open and Pierce's words acting as the salt to all of my open wounds.

Well, fuck.

Blue,

I could just come talk to you, but I feel like this deserves to go into a letter to immortalize (did I spell that right??) the moment that I questioned our choices, and how you subsequently turned my ideas down, and we end up doing shit your way no matter the risks involved.

I'm off work now, and I know you don't like when I just disappear, so I brought you some sappy cute shit from my trip. Used my own money, too. You'd be proud.

Anyway, my request is that we go tour colleges in the next few months. We don't have to go to Cobalt University, y'know? I think we could get into Harvard or Yale, if you're looking for prestige. You could get in.

I'll follow you anywhere, B, you know that.

Love,

Green (your future husband, remember?)

pierce

I want to run far the fuck away from the scene at Raven's house...

But I don't go as far as I intend to in my mind.

I had to leave before more soft words were spoken by the other guys. I can't handle the way her eyes warm to them. She smiles and laughs for them.

For some goddamn reason, over the last few months, I had myself convinced Raven had perfected the cold shoulder ice queen persona to the point that she was actually this quiet by choice.

Watching River take care of her with his mouth, though? While I fucked her throat? She should have been making some sound, any sound. Why it took a sexscapade to get me to see that she wasn't bullshitting anyone, I don't know. I suppose I chose to think she wasn't harmed. It's better to think that than to think I may never hear her pretty voice ever again.

All those nights where we spent time at the playground...in our tree house...or even on my bed in the dead of night. I'd listen to her sing at the top of her lungs, then I'd fall asleep to the sweet lilt of her voice as she spoke to me about her day while we talked on the phone until they died or the sun came up.

I inhale deeply, kicking a stray box out of the way on my trek up to my mom's house. I don't remember the last time I stepped foot in here when it was clean. Honestly, I think my penchant for having such a clean area is due to the state of our house, always. I was the one left to clean. To cook. To put myself to bed after bathing and doing homework. Half of the time, I'd lock myself in the room to hide from the random dude's mom would deem 'babysitters' for that particular day.

Already wiping my hands off on my pants, I make my way inside the house, toeing the door closed with my boot. I can see our footprints from when we were inside earlier, and it's a goddamn shame.

Not that mom would care what her house looks like. I haven't seen her since right before Raven's mom went into hospice.

It's the last time I saw Raven before she came to CU.

Is that really the last time I heard Rae's voice?

Shaking my head, I glare around at my surroundings and wonder if this place is worth the effort. Probably never was, and neither am I, but here I am so I begin the slow process of wiping down dust and sweeping the floor. We have to be able to stay here, or at least hang out here. The guys and I need time to look for the damn recipe at Rae's house.

If we find it in the next few days, I can give it to Maxwell; possibly with a rectal insertion. I can't fathom why the fuck I'm helping this guy. It can't be due to his half-assed hostage situation of my mother.

Chloe Jackson has been a working girl her whole life—and I

mean that she sells her body to the highest bidder every single night. I don't know a night in which she's taken off, ever.

More power to those who are in the sex work industry, but the least she could have done is see her son and take care of him every once in a while.

Or, I dunno, let me stay with the Hills when she was gone.

Nope, Chloe locked me inside of the house more often than not, leaving a young boy alone with a stranger every single night. The stranger would typically be some douche bag who got to fuck her cunt after she returned. He'd leave sweaty and with a wave in my direction like I was some dude bro he was hangin' with.

I cannot, in any universe, condone child neglect. There's not a single good circumstance for leaving your children high and dry. I learned how to steal simply because I needed a jar of peanut butter to survive one week. Learned how to hide because she invited one too many curious guys into the house.

Chloe Jackson does not deserve my love and loyalty, but she has it anyway. She's all I have left in this world.

That's not true, I think, Raven is right there, and you have her under your thumb.

I scoff at my own thoughts, rolling my eyes as I bring the bottom of my shirt up to wipe my now sweaty brow. In the process of my internal war on life, I've managed to sweep the living room, kitchen and hallways. Still without a single clue as to what the stench is, but as I make my way closer toward the end of the hallway and the guest bedroom, I set the broom against the corner wall and lift my shirt to cover my nose.

My eyes water as I enter the room, making it harder to look around through a blurry gaze. Walking inside, I flick the light switch upwards, only to stop in my tracks so quickly I stumble and nearly fall on my ass.

Right there, in the center of the bed, is a black cat. It's dead, clear as fucking day, with guts strewn about the mattress and floor. There's not a note, not a single trace of who sent this, but I know.

Maxwell's not playing, and he wants me to know I'm out of chances.

LATER, I have the house up to my standards, spotless and smelling more like Pinesol than a Pinesol factory, and the dead cat has been tossed in Jimmy's trash can. I know he's not here, but the sentiment remains the same. I feel better knowing I tarnished something of his.

The house looks more deserted now that the dust bunnies are gone. It's like the souls of our ancestors have been sitting on the surfaces, and I kicked them all out in favor of the strong scent of lemons.

I'm putting the last dry dish away when I hear the door open and close quietly. Shutting the cabinet, I look over my shoulder and turn with a raised brow at River's choice to walk around in nothing but gray sweats and his blonde locks mussed up from earlier. I really, truly try not to stare. My face is burning when River pulls up a stool and sits at the island counter.

"The fuck you doing, Pierce? It's two in the morning and I know you typically pass out for a solid eight after fucking somethin'." River's slight country drawl is something most of the girls are drawn to, and sometimes, I get lost in the way his voice warms over my body like butter and biscuits on a cold Sunday morning.

"We gotta, uhm," I clear my throat, and shake my head,

trying to ignore the lust burning for him. "We gotta have a place to hang outside of Raven's house. Can't search it if she's there, y'know?"

"Bullshit." He curses. His lips pull up into a shit eating grin. "She's easily distracted, dude. Ever noticed that?"

Rolling my eyes, I turn and busy myself by picking up a trash bag, and heading towards the front door so I can get rid of the last of the stench that lingers.

I barely make it past River, though, before he's grabbing my bicep and spinning me to him. Our chests crash together and I grit my teeth when the trash bag falls to the ground at our side. "Fuck off, Riv," I grunt.

"Nah, don't think I will." He says, leaning in until our noses touch, and my breathing hitches.

Reaching out, I put my palms on his pecs, ignoring the hardness of his nipples and the way both of our dicks grow against each other. "Go. I'm almost done here. I'm going to go search Rae's basement while she's passed out." I shove him away from me and grab the trash bag again.

I'm halfway across the street after depositing the bag when I hear him grunt out, "Pussy," before slamming the door to my mom's house so loud it causes the dogs along the street to bark.

I refuse to let River entice me right now. I'm not good enough for him. Not good enough for anyone, if I'm being honest. Look at the state of Raven, for example.

Shoving my hands into my pockets, I walk back across the street towards Raven's house and toe my shoes off the moment I'm inside. I pad along the hallway and toward the basement door in my socks, keeping my steps light so I don't wake anyone else. River must have had a sixth sense to have known I was still out.

He tends to find me no matter where I am at any given point in time.

I should probably treat him better for his loyalty.

But instead, I'll keep pushing him away. It's my talent at this point.

As I make my way downstairs, I use the light from my cell phone until I reach the bottom step. I flick the light, flooding the room with bright fluorescents and effectively blinding myself until I feel the burn in my soul.

Rubbing the burn away from my eyes, I walk around and survey the empty space. Raven's mom never did anything with this space, so it became our little hangout as we got older. It went from a play space, to a hangout for tweens, to a full on gaming area for teens. We played way too much Mario Party down here with the rest of the kids. I crack a genuine grin when I see the scoreboard still standing. We started it when we were juniors.

Fuck, that summer was the best...

"I EXPECT *you two to behave down here. I have to go to work, Raven, and I know Pierce's mom isn't home, so right now,"* the woman tries to hide her smile as she points between us, *"behave, children."*

"Yes, mom!" Raven drawls.

"Yes ma'am," I say, grateful she even let me stay. She knows Chloe's a treacherous wench, so she tends to help me out every now and again out of pure spite at this point.

Everlyn grins and waves us both down the stairs before she grabs her car keys and leaves.

Instantly, I sense trouble, and her name is Raven Hill.

"Nope," I say, brushing past her, heading towards the mini fridge to snag us both drinks. Cherry coke for Raven, Cherry Pepsi for myself.

It's highly competitive around here.

"Pierce, I said nothing!" Raven whines, throwing her hands up before snatching the Coke from my hands.

"Don't give a shit, Blue," I grumble, popping the tab on the can and taking a sip, coughing on the bubbles attempting to choke me. "You know how I fucking feel about Jimmy. We ain't friends. You ain't friends with him anymore, and just," I plop my happy ass on my permanent spot for the next six hours, "no." Raising a brow, my gaze bores into the pretty blues of hers, and I can't resist grinning when she harrumphs and plops herself down next to me. Her shoulder and elbow knock into my side and I spill a bit of my soda over my hand. "Brat," I snark.

She grins at me, facing me full on. "I know you are, but what am I?" She completes the sassy statement by sticking her tongue out.

She squeaks when I set my soda down, and she's halfway up the stairs when I grab her around the waist and bring her over my shoulder, making my way back down into the trenches of a fucking war she decided to start.

"Pierce! I'm sorry!" She laughs, slapping at my back with her tiny little fists, as if she's getting a single ounce of my forgiveness without earning it. "Please! Let me down!"

Tossing her onto the couch, I lean over her, my nose touching hers as I attempt to maintain my glare. It's nearly impossible not to grin when she snorts out laughter as I tickle her sides, but I maintain my game, ruthlessly pushing into her flesh with my fingertips.

"Say it!" I bark out, tickling her more and trying to keep her from making both of us fall off the couch.

"No!" She screeches, bringing her knee up precariously close to my balls.

"Alright," I drag out the word as I pull her shirt up to show off her belly button. I intended to blow raspberries and make her laugh harder, but I'm pulled up short when I see the diamond stud in her navel. "The fuck?!" I bark, my glare turning real this time.

"Shit," she breathes, her eyes and nostrils flaring wide. She attempts to push me off, shoving her shirt down, but failing when I pull it back up.

"Tell me this is fake," I whisper, inspecting the redness around the jewel. It's fucking real, all right, and I was not prepared to see this kind of shit. "Who the fuck–"

"Doesn't matter, does it?" She successfully pushes me off of her, forcing me to catch myself on my knees or hit my head on the coffee table. "It's done. I like it. Leave me alone or I'll show you the tramp stamp I got, too."

I blink, shooting up and trying to see her lower back, keeping my hands to myself in favor of leaving my balls intact–I was the one who taught her how to kick a dude in the balls, after all.

"Joking, you freak," she says, taunting me. She grins, but the guilt on her face is obvious.

"Rae, we said we wouldn't do shit like this alone! It's sketchy as hell near that shop. The fuck were you thinking, huh?" I snatch the controller she'd snagged and hold it up above her head. She huffs out and stomps her foot like a toddler, crossing her arms and avoiding my gaze. "Rae! Answer me, dammit! You could have been fucking killed or drugged or worse, y–"

"Nuh uh, stop. I went with Patty and I'm fine. She got one, too. You'd know that if you went to the damn party. Instead, you're trying to be a goddamn protector or white knight or something. Can we fucking play the game?"

The tears in her eyes bring me up short, and I slowly lower the controller back down so she can grab it and sit back down on the couch.

I huff and sit down beside her, pulling her into my side minutes later as we play Mario Party and ignore the very real possibility that she did not heed my warnings about that damn tattoo shop.

This would have been a perfect time to let her know exactly how dangerous that side of town is, but I'd like to keep her in the dark on how twisted and sadistic her real father is. Especially since she doesn't know the guy exists.

CHAPTER TWENTY-TWO

raven

I don't know what wakes me up, but I nearly jump out of bed in fright when I feel the weight of eyes on me. My whole entire being is covered in a sheen of sweat, but not a single soul is around me, so I'm equally confused as I am terrified.

The effects last night had on me...well...my body was exhausted.

Looking over, I see the alarm clock on the nightstand reads 4 a.m. I sigh, bringing my head back to look up at the ceiling. This is the time I would have woken up with my mom to give her pain meds, so it makes sense I would wake up now while staying here. A tear falls before I angrily wipe it away and wrap my arms around myself.

I get up and head toward the kitchen, grabbing a glass and filling it with ice and cold water from the machine in the fridge door—the best invention, honestly. Music sounds from somewhere, so I pad my way toward the noise, only to stop short when I see the basement door is cracked open and a faint light is coming from downstairs. My brows knit together in confusion, not understanding who would be down there, or for what reason.

The stairs are cold under my bare feet, but I'm grateful that at least my body is covered by one of the guys' hoodies–River's by the faint smell of the ocean on it. The chill as I descend into one of my old sanctuaries reminds me of how long it's been since I've been down here.

My feet hardly make contact with the carpet when I'm stopped short at the sight of Pierce curled up on the couch on his side, a letter in the hand clutched to his chest. Instantly on guard, I slam my water glass down onto the coffee table in front of the couch and snatch the paper from his grip, tossing it inside the box laying on the floor and closing the lid as loudly as possible.

The glare I shoot toward Pierce should burn the fucker alive, and yet, as he wipes the sleep from his overly tired eyes, he meets my gaze unflinchingly.

"Oh goodie," he grumbles, annoyed at getting caught out more than anything. "Just let me finish reading those. You can burn them to fucking ashes or some shit. Use 'em to make your morning hot chocolate or something." He reaches out to take the box, and I stand in front of him, crossing my arms and glaring.

His hand moves to the right, and I move in front. His hand moves to the left, and I move with him. He doesn't deserve these fucking letters and he knows it.

Grunting, he reaches to the right again, and as I go to intercept his movements, he pulls back at the last second and snatches the box up, standing and walking toward the stairs. I should have honestly seen that coming, but I haven't always been smart around him.

"I've got a lot of reading to do right now, Blue, could you possibly just–"

He's interrupted by me tackling him to the ground like a pro, straddling his back as I kick the box off to the side, spilling the contents of both of our hearts all across the floor.

Belatedly, I realize how dumb that was. Now I have a decade of letters to pick up, but it's fitting they're so splayed open; matches my soul, honestly.

"The fuck off me, Raven," Pierce growls, trying to twist around, but we've played this game before. He's the one who taught me how to fight off boys and scrap with girls. The reason I can punch so hard and knee a guy in the exact right spot to make it hurt worse than an untrained knee ever could.

But as he twists around and my knee grip loosens, I also remember he's the reason my heart knows love. The sweet kind. The messy kind. The kind that shatters expectations by being the one to set them in the first place.

He's the reason my breathing stops and my heart rate picks up.

The reason I can't seem to stay angry when I rightfully should.

Pierce Jackson is the reason my soul sings and my heart beats.

So when he reaches out to grip my hips, it's not in anger, or to truly hold me down. No, his grip is to anchor me to him in the physical sense. We're already bound together by our souls.

A tear falls as I realize he isn't being angry with me for the first time in almost a year. He's being tender, and it's for longer than a minute. Our breaths are a collective rise and fall of both of our chests, and his fingers are massaging the exposed skin of my thigh. Our eyes lock and it's extremely intoxicating. I'm almost dizzy as we continue to simply exist together right now.

In a moment so fleeting it might blow away on an exhale, I lean my head down toward Pierce, my eyes never leaving his. When I get close enough, I tilt my head to the side, our lips close enough for our breaths to mingle. I can taste the Pepsi on his tongue, and I could cry at the memories. I don't. Instead, I feather my lips over Pierce's in the most real kiss we've had since being back in each other's presence.

The sharp intake of his breath is surprising to me, and I know that his groan mirrors the one I could make for him. His fingers dig into my hips as he presses his lips more firmly to mine. We're simply luxuriating in this moment together, and yet, I know there's not a single moment that follows this where we will ever share the same intimacy.

"Well, fucking, well," we hear, before River's face appears right next to ours, a shit eating grin on his face. "Makeup yet, folks?"

I freeze, my eyes meeting his right as he winks for me.

Pierce practically throws me off of his body, and I land on the ground with a hard thud. I wince, gripping my already hurting and bruised hip, but he doesn't care, simply standing and grabbing another box I hadn't seen sitting near the couch. It has the college's logo on it, so I'm confused as to why it's in here since I can't fathom who would have brought CU para-phernalia back here.

Pierce storms up the stairs and the sound of his footsteps fades as he heads to the room he's staying in.

"Fuckin' idiot," River mutters before he's lifting the hoodie away from my hip and checking the ever growing bruise. "Damn. Sorry, RaeRae. Let's get you some meds for that, 'cause it's gonna fuckin' hurt."

He lifts me into his arms and I can't quite seem to mind

being carried up the stairs bridal style. It gives me a solid moment to live in the emotional pain Pierce has left me in yet again.

Reminding me why being soft with him is a bad idea.

That boy didn't deserve a second of my time back in October, and now he's consuming every millisecond.

Something has to give.

And that something is *not* me.

LATER IN THE MORNING, Phoenix finds River and I cuddling up on the couch watching The Princess Bride. A classic, if I do say so myself. River heartily disagrees, even as he hits play, winks, and quotes, "As you wish."

He's seen this, and he's fucking lying about it. The sap.

"We need to get food for Thanksgiving," Phoenix says, walking in front of the television right as the characters were about to kiss.

I toss the remote at his chest, and River throws an empty popsicle stick at him, both of us in outrage.

"Best damn part and you put your ass right in front of it?" River yells, chuckling when Phoenix darts toward him and proceeds to put a pillow over his still yelling mouth.

Looking at me, he grins and holds a hand out, "Come with me, Red?"

I eagerly nod, needing to get farther away from Pierce. Maybe a trip to the store will let me breathe for a change.

"Upstairs," he grunts, backing up as he releases the pillow from River's red face, "I'll deal with the mess you've made of your hair, yeah?"

I chew my lip and grin, trying hard to keep it at bay as I walk around the boys before they start an unsanctioned UFC fight in my living room.

When I make it upstairs, I peek down the left hallway and note that Pierce is still locked up in the guest bedroom. I curse myself, turning towards the master–which I guess is now mine, not mom's–and slamming the door shut out of spite. Hope to fuck I broke whatever concentration he was holding.

After getting myself dressed in a black halter dress adorned with little skulls all over it, I'm sitting at my vanity putting my face on when Phoenix walks into the room, brandishing a soft smile as he saunters toward me.

The man is sexy, and he knows it. His abs are constricting against his tight black shirt, and the belt holding his black jeans on his frame calls to me in a way it shouldn't. I'm chewing my lip when he finally makes his way behind me, our eyes meeting in the mirror.

His hand snakes through my hair, pulling until my head tilts back and I'm looking at him upside down. I swallow, and he notices the movement, grinning cockily.

"I think you want to be a good girl for me, Red," he says, leaning down to place a feather-light kiss on my forehead. My heart lurches in response. "Are you looking to be my good girl, Raven?" When I nod, he reaches out to grab my hair brush, pushing my head back up until our gazes meet in the vanity again.

I take a deep breath as he begins to brush through my strands, my entire body simply leaning into his care. It's like the moment he's around me and taking care of the simplest of tasks for me...well...my brain shuts off. I'm simply allowed to exist, and it's a much needed side effect of Phoenix West.

"We'll discuss our terms and conditions later," he says in a soothing voice. My eyes open slowly–they fluttered closed while he was running the brush through the mass of tangles atop my head. "Since I haven't been here before, I'll let you take charge of our shopping spree. I've got a list to fulfill, but you will get whatever you think you need or want while we're here. We have about 6 more days here. Only 3 until Thanksgiving, so we need to take all of that into account."

I attempt to nod, but he grips my hair, tugging until my eyes meet his. He places the hairbrush atop my lap for a moment and brandishes his free hand, showing the American Sign Language motion for yes, to which I immediately show him back.

I've worked with basic sign language since the onset of my mutism, so it's not a chore to do these. Phoenix has been begging me to learn more, and it has made school a tad easier since I can communicate with almost everyone around me in a quick fashion.

The notepad will hopefully become obsolete as I learn more signs, but for now, simple one-word answers are the only ones we all know.

He smiles approvingly when I show the sign, and I smile in return when he picks up the brush again. "Good girl. I promise I'll have the others learning ASL as soon as I can. It's important to me that our communication be effective, especially since–"

I meet his gaze, but his has become guarded now, and he brushes my hair a tad rougher for a few seconds before exhaling. Guess he's done with that train of thought.

Clearing his throat, Phoenix places the brush down and begins braiding my hair, pointing toward hair ties to ensure I hold them for him like usual. "Anyway. Today we'll get food.

Afterwards, I think maybe you could show us around? You could show us your favorite places?"

He laughs a bit, shaking his head when I narrow my eyes to slits and shake my head, warding off the panic.

"Alright, we'll find something else to do, I suppose."

A few minutes later, my hair is braided down my back, and Phoenix is presenting me with the red leather jacket. I'm wondering when I'll get the same beautiful raven on the back of it like the one on the back of the guys' jackets, but no one has mentioned it to me.

I may be a bit biased toward those black birds at this point since my name is Raven. My eyes flit to the side of Phoenix's throat, where I see a black feather there. Again, they think I don't notice these things, but I do.

Pierce has made something of himself and the guys under his wings. He's created something we have discussed many times.

The loft. The garden. The green space hidden from the rest of the world. The motorcycles.

I notice it all, and I appreciate it in quiet contemplation each day while I watch them go about their fraternity duties. They never leave me alone, but they haven't taken me back to the Alpha Mu house since the night after the Halloween party, outside of random check ins and other parties. They refuse to let me step foot in there alone. I wish I knew why, but I'm also eternally grateful that they don't take me around their frat bros anymore.

My anger rises again at what he coerced me to do, and it only grows as I stomp down the stairs to find him pouring himself a cup of fucking coffee in my mother's kitchen.

We didn't drink coffee in here, ever. The smell was making my mom sick, so she stopped drinking it. I never took up the habit of coffee, as the taste was too strong no matter how much you cut it with sugar and cream.

Pierce is chugging from a mug while he stares me down now, and I know my glare is burning a hole in him. I see the second he pauses in his movements, and I'm hoping he backs down and stops taunting me with bullshit.

He doesn't give a shit, however, his brow quirking up as he chugs the rest of the coffee, only to turn toward the pot and fill his mug again. He makes an obnoxious "Aahh!" sound at the end of another long chug, and I flip him the finger, turn toward the door, and put my flats on before I exit the house.

Pierce Jackson can fuck all the way off right now, and it still wouldn't be enough.

River yells out, "See you later honey butter!" and I breathe out a bit of a laugh, shaking my head and attempting to stamp out any anger as I round the jeep and hop into the passenger seat, closing my door at the same second Phoenix does.

"Alright, Red," he says, turning a wild grin on me as he turns on the vehicle, "let's go act like a normal couple for two point five seconds."

As we take off down the road toward town, my eyes taking in every second of our journey to the only grocery store available, I'm transported to a time when a task like this was much different and much sadder. An ache begins in my chest, and it nearly takes me out.

"I'LL BE BACK, *mom, 'kay? Pierce is taking me to the store, but Chloe is downstairs if you need anything.*"

Slowly, my mom manages a nod, a soft but trembling smile on her lips.

"Kay...I'll be back," I repeat in a whisper, turning on a dime and rushing swiftly out of her room and down the hallway. I swipe away a few errant tears as I come into my bedroom, the purple walls adorned with pictures from my youth. I feel so far from that time. Though I've barely turned 18, my life is intrinsically more difficult than it probably should be.

"She's not getting better, Green," I sniff, choking out a quiet sob as I climb onto my best friend's waiting lap.

Wrapping his arms around me, Pierce presses a kiss to the top of my head and rocks me gently, his hand rubbing up and down my arm soothingly. "She will, I promise."

I choke on my next cry and shake my head, not even close to embarrassed about the snot trailing from my nose, mixing with my tears. "Don't make promises you can't keep, PJ. Ain't nice."

He sighs at the nickname, one he hates to the bottom of his soul thanks to the way his mother lets her lovers call him that at all times. He doesn't say a word about it, though. He simply holds me tight, humming softly while I silently mourn my mother.

"Let's go get some food. Thanksgiving is in a few days and I think both our moms will like that we made somethin', y'know?" He presses a kiss to my cheek after I nod. He helps me stand on my own two feet again–literally and figuratively.

"It's," I hiccup and wipe my nose with the tissue he offers, "It's such a domestic task. Guess we're close to bein' married after all, huh?" I turn toward him and grin wide, though we both know the action is forced and fake.

"Yeah, guess so," he mutters, rolling his eyes and wrapping one arm around my shoulders.

I grab my clutch from my desk, walking alongside him until we have to separate at the stairs or risk falling down them–not a fun activity to do alone or with a friend.

"We're headed to the grocery store, ma," Pierce says as we pass

her, half waving at her and half waving her off while we exit my mom's house.

Once we make it to the beat-up truck Pierce managed to get a few weeks ago, we're off down the street and headed toward our local grocery. The only grocery. It's a small mom and pop shop that hardly gets what we want, but we don't have any other choice in an emergency situation. Like a dying woman's last Thanksgiving.

Minutes into our shopping trip, I realize how out of touch with this town I am. Patty Gardner is working the register while Jimmy holds a bottle blonde under his arm and flaunts her and his big ass box of micro-condoms around.

I snort and point it out to Pierce, which results in him and Jimmy holding a full blown stare off that might result in the world exploding.

I leave them to it as I begin my trip around the store, grabbing the things we'd need for Thanksgiving.

We've shared this holiday with the Jacksons for as long as I can remember, and sometimes Jimmy, too. Jimmy's not been to one since we were 14, though. His mom found a new beau and effectively changed her whole lifestyle for the guy. Wish she'd have moved, though. Jimmy's been a twat ever since I caught him with Patty at the end of the school year and told him to fucking beat it.

Didn't mean his dick, but at least he's leaving me alone.

"That guy's got some serious fucking balls, I tell you," Pierce says next to me and I jump. I hadn't even noticed him coming down the aisle.

"Fucking hell, dickhead, warn a lady before you come all up in her space!" I yell at him, smacking him across his broad chest. He's filled out so much in the last year and I don't particularly

hate it. Though, the thought of him being a man now is kind of laughable.

He proves that as he tries to tamp down the laughter that wants to bubble out of him, only to lose the battle and laugh so loud it echoes through the store.

"Stop it, it wasn't that funny," I snark, biting down on my tongue to keep from joining in. We're causing a damn scene in the Shop N Mart.

Seriously, that's the name. Wish I was jokin'.

"That's-" he begins.

I glare and point a finger in his face so close that my fingertip touches his nose. "Nuh-uh."

"That's what she said!" He barks out another laugh and swats my hand out of his face, reaching forward to pull me under his arm, guiding me down toward the turkeys. "And look, what beautiful breasts they have on display, Rae!"

"Oh my god you are the most insufferable and embarrassing best friend on the planet and I want a refund!" He laughs and holds me to him tighter, and my heart warms as I grin, looking at the prices for the turkeys on sale.

"Can your mom eat solids?" Pierce says in a whisper.

"No," I say sharply, looking up at him apologetically before I reach out and grab a smaller turkey. It'll only be Pierce, Chloe, and I eating. No need for anything bigger than this. "They'll give her some pureed bullshit that tastes worse than baby food, but you know she'll tell us to do it up right."

"Maybe she'll perk up and get better so she can kill us off?" He grins, trying to lighten the mood up again like he usually does.

I shrug, and his grin falls as we continue our shopping trip. I can't find it in me to smile at all for the rest of our trip. I can't smile when Pierce buys me a king-size peanut butter cup, knowing I hardly have the cash to buy it myself. As we make the trek back to the car, load up, and head back home, I think maybe he shouldn't be staying behind with me for this. Maybe, just maybe, he'd be better off as a solo act.

The Pierce and Raven show has gone on for as long as it can. Time to change channels.

Dear Green,

This letter seems absolutely silly, cause we're sitting next to each other. I just wanted to write down our silliness, because we just spent the last hour arguing over who wins in Mario Kart and how I kicked your ass every. single. time.

(I just giggled writing that and had to fight you off so that I could finish this letter).

Anyway, I love you. So much, and I hope that when we compile our letters through the years that our kids can read them, and we can showcase our relationship to them.

I hope we get a nice big house with a big back-yard and a park down the street—not abandoned, btw.

Love,
Your Future Wife,
Blue

pierce

They're gone for so goddamn long, and I don't quite believe Phoenix only took her to the grocery store.

I've had the time to go over every damn document inside of ten fucking boxes, and not a single thing looks like a recipe for anything, much less a synthetic drug to make people lose their fucking minds for twelve hours.

I slam another box down on the ground in the guest bedroom, kicking it to the side and cursing the action since it makes me stub my bare fucking toe on the corner. "FUCK!" I yell, leaning forward to rub the aching appendage. River comes rushing in like the house is on fire instead of the nerve endings of my big toe.

"The hell, Piercey Jackson? You tryna give me a heart attack?" He looks around at the copious amounts of boxes lining the room, raising both brows in surprise. "Well, hell, brother, I didn't know you'd become a damn detective overnight."

"Shut the fuck up, Riv, and get out. You ain't helpin' much

anyway," I grumble, knowing I'm the one who kicked his ass out after the first hour of him 'helping'.

His version of helping involved tossing the papers everywhere until he thought he saw the right one. It was like pulling teeth to get him to walk the hell out of here, and so he's been watching Supernatural for the past two hours.

"Alright, alright," he holds his hands up in mock surrender, "I'll keep watching Sam and Dean deny the sexy thruple, which could happen if they'd finally let Cass in." The fucker winks and I rear back.

"Sam and Dean are brothers, ya fuck!"

"Yeah but ask me if I care, Pierce," River snarks. "C'mon, ask me!"

"No," I bark.

"Okay fine, I'll tell you anyway." He walks toward me, leans down, puts his lips to my ear, and I shiver involuntarily. I can tell he notices by the way his lips curve up against my skin. "I don't care."

He pulls back and evades my swinging fists, walking backward out of the room, laughing wildly. His loud ass footsteps echo in the back of my skull like an incessant drumbeat.

I swear he was dropped on his head as a child. It's extremely fucking evident.

Groaning, I lean back in the chair and cross my arms, looking around the room and trying to think of any hiding spots Everlyn would have. I know Maxwell said she and David took Raven and the drug recipe, but I'm beginning to think I'm on a wild goose chase and I'll ultimately fail so Maxwell can finally off my mother. After her, he'll find a way to off me, too. He's hated me since I stopped allowing him to cut the product that I personally put on the streets.

I may help sell drugs, but I'm not about to sell shitty ones which could result in more deaths than their more legitimate parent product.

The door downstairs opens and I hear the rustle of bags for a solid ten minutes before I decide to make my way down the steps. The scene I come across makes my heart clench. It reminds me of a better time, but also of a time when Raven and I entered the house like this. Bags in tow, food ready to make, only to come back, finding an ambulance and nearly every first responder on the property.

Rae's mom took a dive that night.

And my dumb ass decided to tank the friendship I had cultivated and reveled in for my entire life.

Watching Rae move around my friends so comfortably, smiling cheekily when River smacks her ass as he passes by, well, it has me boiling with rage. I had her, for a split fucking second this morning I had her. I'm reminded that she only glares at me, so surely the pure fucking want and willingness of her to be sweet with me was a goddamn daydream.

So, like the idiot I am—though I'm feeling more like a genius—I pushed her away. The anger has been surfacing in her gaze every single time she looks at me today, and I can't quite figure out how to get back to where we were that day.

She may have pushed me here, but I know it was out of the pure goodness of her heart.

She didn't want me to suffer alongside her.

I sigh and make my way toward the fridge, grabbing a beer and popping the lid before chugging the whole thing in one go. I vaguely hear River and Phoenix crooning and laughing and flirting with my girl, but I drown it, and my sorrows, alongside that beer. Once I'm done, I toss it into the trash can and look around at the scene in front of me.

"I'm taking Raven for a walk," I say.

The room falls silent and the woman in question stares at me like I've lost my ever loving mind.

Right back atcha, sweetheart.

I grin and wave the others off, walking toward the screen door at the back of the kitchen. The hesitation Raven makes loud and fucking clear is enough to make me rethink all of my life choices up until this moment. Is she scared of me? The guys sure as fuck don't seem to care what happens, so long as they reap my fucking rewards.

I refuse to touch her more than enough to get her mouth on me.

I refuse to be the reason she comes.

She doesn't truly deserve relief at my hands, and yet, as she walks out of the door, heading down our man-made path from so many years walking it, I'm wondering why in the hell I truly care that she sent in my college application behind my back?

I may have been shot forward a few months by graduating high school early and joining college shortly after, and I may be stuck under her biological dad's thumb, but I know she was only taking care of me. In the heat of the moment, I belatedly–a year and a half too late–understand my anger is all for Maxwell, and I have an ass load of apologizing and groveling to do in order to gain the trust and love of my best friend back.

As we walk through the back gates, I'm looking more toward the sky than to my surroundings. Not a problem for walking around. I know this area like the back of my hand. So many nights were spent in the playground, wandering around and hiding from other people.

Raven and I were just...us. We never meant to get so caught up in each other, but it happened.

The Raven and Pierce Show. Couldn't find one of us without the other.

I sigh as we enter the playground, watching Raven walk slowly through the decrepit swings, slides, and other equipment. Her hand brushes along the merry-go-round that used to house all of our secrets, and she grips onto the bar, her knuckles going white.

Our eyes meet, and I swallow when I see a tear track down her cheek.

I'm gutted at this point.

This was the last place I remember hearing her voice. The last place we were ever the old us, and I can't begin to fathom why I let her so easily push me away. My heart begins to race as I take a step forward toward her, my hands itching to make purchase with her skin...

"RAVEN HILL, *what the actual fuck have you done?" I bellow, heading toward her before walking back toward the swings.*

I've been pacing for nearly an hour now, my heart in shambles at my feet, the mere panic in my tone enough to force half the kids away from the playground. They know to leave when we show up, anyway, so that's nothing new.

"I–" she begins, but I hold up a hand to cut her off.

"No. You weren't thinking, were you?" I spin around and glare at her, my arms open wide, my hands splayed open. "All you wanted to do was get rid of me, yeah? You didn't want to let me in on the hard stuff, so you pushed me out the only way you knew how!"

"I didn't–"

"Stop fucking speaking. I don't want to listen to you right now. You've done your talking loud and fucking clear by sending

that application in," I snarl, my eyes raking across her now trembling form. She's crying, and while it hurts me, I can't quite find a true fuck to give since I found the acceptance letter in my mother's mailbox.

"Pierce," Raven pleads, her eyes full of tears as she tries to stand up to me, squaring her shoulders and lifting her chin. "You need to go. I have to stay here, but you don't."

"I DO have to stay here, Raven!" I yell, my voice making her flinch. Sighing, I place my hands on her shoulders, caressing them and trying to comfort her. "I do have to stay here," I whisper.

She hiccups and places her forehead against my chest, soaking my shirt with her tears instantly. I bring one arm around her back, holding her tight, and place the other on her head, securing her to me.

"Why?" She says, almost too quietly.

Lifting her head back away from me, I hold both of her cheeks, my eyes flicking between those pretty blues. "Raven Hill, I need to stay here for you. We promised each other forever so many years ago, and it hasn't been forever yet, babe."

She pushes me away from her, and the look in her eyes changes before hardening seconds later. I'm shocked, honestly. She brings her hand up to swipe away the tears, glaring at me as she continues to put distance between us.

"Rae, wha–"

"I," she whispers. Walking back to me, she lifts her chin in defiance again, "do not," she puts her hands on my pecs, her hands digging in for a second, "WANT YOU HERE!"

The scream she releases, followed by the push, forces me onto my ass in the wood chips.

"You don't mean that, Blue."

"Don't call me that," she snaps.

"Raven, I want to stay here and help you!" I yell at her again, my voice pleading, my heart aching, my soul shattering far and fast. I scramble to my feet and walk after her now retreating form.

"I don't want you to be here. It's not how this is going to happen."

I reach for her, barely gripping her shirt before she's too far from me again. "Rae."

She spins back in my direction, glaring at me and holding her fists up like she's gonna scrap with me. I hold my hands up in surrender, my eyes pleading with her as my soul cracks down the middle.

"I need to be here for you." My voice is low now, and I'm breathing heavily, starting to panic. "I need to be able to hold you at night and make sure you are okay during this. I love you, Raven, and I don't want you to be alone through any of this."

I know she's about to cut me with her next words.

"Well, I don't love you!" She screeches, her voice breaking as she spins back around and takes off at a sprint.

Not that I'd follow her, anyway. I'm stuck standing here, staring blankly at the spot where my best friend tossed us aside like nothing.

Thought she was gonna cut me, but I didn't expect a bloody execution.

"RAE," I whisper, my eyes now on her heaving chest. It's like she can remember the words we shared that night. How she tore us down in a single-handed blow to the very core of my being.

I try to keep the tears at bay, I really do. I'm a man now, and big men don't cry, right?

It's not an easy task, and it proves fruitless when I notice Raven is shaking, her chest heaving so hard I can't imagine she has space left in her tiny body for the air. Tears fall freely down my cheeks and I choke them back enough to reach out and take her hands in mine, running my fingers along the backs of her hands.

"You ruined us here, Rae," I say. My voice is so soft it's a wonder it's truly mine. "I wish I knew why. You don't have to tell me. You had your reasons. Life was hard for you. Hell, it still is."

She pulls back from me and turns, wiping her tears with her shirt as she goes to sit down. She stares down at her hands, wringing them tightly between her knees.

I'm suddenly angry. Despite the fact I'm being soft with her, that I'm crying and remembering with her, she's blocking me out.

I walk backward a few steps, turn around in a circle, and my hands come up to my hair, pulling until my scalp burns. I growl and kick a rock, watching as it sails only a few feet away. I yell so loud and birds fly from trees and I know the cops may get called.

Who the hell cares about what happens out here anyway?

Turning toward Raven again, I glare at her, our eyes searing into each other with heat and venom and hate and love and longing. It'd be intoxicating, except I'm not here to feel these feelings. I'm not here to be broken like this. Growling, I kick the side of the merry-go-round Raven is sitting on, her silence now more deafening than it has been.

I see her reach for her phone, and she raises a finger, so I wait, albeit impatiently, as she types out a message. Less than a minute later my phone pings.

RAVEN:

It was a necessary step to save you. I'm not sorry.

I blink, scoff, and stuff my phone back into my pocket as Raven stands and begins walking back toward the house.

She's dismissing me so easily.

So quickly.

Again.

Except this time I won't let her. I grab her bicep and twist her around to face me. The hatred in her gaze pisses me off.

"Sit the fuck down and listen to me," I snap, leading her to the rusted metal again. I wait until she is still, and tamp down the panic. "You lied to me in this exact fucking spot almost exactly a year ago."

She shakes her head vehemently, and I grit my teeth.

"Don't fucking deny it. A year ago," I begin to say, kicking my foot against the metal again, calming at the introduction of physical pain. "A year ago you lied to my face and told me you didn't love me. Why?"

Raven shakes her head. Shrugs. Chews her lip as she avoids my gaze.

"Goddamnit Raven!" I bellow. "You spend so much fucking time rubbing up on my friends. My new best friends by the way. But you won't let me the fuck in! You look at me with such a fiery fucking hatred in your eyes but you've gone and frozen me out, pushed me so far away that I'm in the fucking antarctic!"

I place my hands on either side of her, gripping the rusted

metal as I look at her. The next words out of my mouth crack as they're delivered. "Just let me in, Rae. I've needed you for every damn second you've been gone and I'll need you for every damn second I'm drawing breath."

I swallow after my admission. The hurts I'm causing her are still truly unknown to her, so the absolute hatred she has of me is almost unfounded. She blinks as she stares up at me, tears falling from her lashes. I bring a hand up to caress her cheek, brushing away errant tears. I feather a soft kiss on her forehead and sigh as I take in the strawberry soda scent she wears.

"Just let me in baby so I can try to fix us," I whisper.

It's silent as we stay like that. Only the hoots of owls and the sound of rustling leaves. I don't know how else to plead with her, so I simply breathe her in. My eyes are drinking her in, taking in all of her micro-expressions. I see the panic as it rises, the defiance as it takes its place. Eventually, her gaze fills with what I can only determine is acceptance.

Her lips part, and I'm almost elated in the belief that she might finally speak. She must sense this, shaking her head once before mouthing 'Okay.'

I don't try to dissect anymore of her after that. I simply reach out for her face, my thumbs brushing her cheeks as my eyes flick between hers. "Okay?" I ask. I'm a desperate, dying man finding water for the first time in months.

She mouths the word again, and I crush my lips to hers roughly. I bruise her. Mark her. Make her mine all over again—she never wasn't mine. She presses herself to me, her dainty and familiar hands drifting up to grab at my wrists, clutching them in her grasp.

My heart thunders inside of my chest, beating so erratically I wonder if I might die here.

What a way to go.

I grin, my lips curving against Raven's for a second before I open my mouth and drift my tongue out to meet her lips. Lips I consumed for years. Her tongue is soft and I taste chocolate on her, a groan escaping me. As I tentatively explore her mouth, one of my hands drifts to her hip to pull her closer to me, and the other goes to the back of her head, holding her hair and tugging to angle her in a way I need her, ensuring my lips have better access to hers, my tongue tangling with her soft one.

I explore a whole new part of Blue; a woman who has endured far too much in our short time on this planet.

I relearn the fierceness she grew into. The strength of her heart and passions and emotions.

Relearn this woman who is the one I had planned to grow old with–the whole wedding was planned when we were 12 and she found a bridal magazine.

I relearn what it's like to let my walls down and feel something.

And what I feel after nearly a full year without the love of my life?

Serenity.

I'm leaning into her now, her back pressed against the unforgiving metal on the merry-go-round, and her hands snake to the back of my head. It's a glorious thing to have her grip tighten in my hair. I move my hand from her hip and slowly reach out as we continue to kiss, pushing up underneath her shirt and resting against her skin. It's so smooth, familiar and yet different from when we were last like this.

An ache begins to build within me, my dick growing hard as she's panting beneath me, her fingers scratching down my skin and trying to find purchase within my shirt, my hair, my shoulders. She practically teleports with how quickly she climbs my frame, her legs wrapping around my hips.

I pull my head back when my hands are forced to hold her thighs or drop her, and I'm grinning wide–something I'm not used to doing. I lick my lips, the taste of her sweet strawberry scent mixing with the chocolate she had. My eyes fall to her chest, moving rapidly. When I look back up and see the lust in her eyes, I nearly come undone. I'm about to lean back in to kiss her when the rain begins to fall.

And by begins to fall, I mean a full on downpour. A tsunami from the sky. A typhoon. A hurricane. It goes from nothing to just...dropping onto us.

I laugh as I catch the frustration in Raven's gaze, a little bit of her fire coming back to her. I've missed this...since before her mother died.

Rae's body begins to shiver under the onslaught of the rain, and I catch a peak of her nipples through her shirt. They're hard and I know it's from lust rather than the cold. Okay, maybe a bit from the cold. My dick tries to shrivel up and die a slow death as I continue staring at her while we get soaked. I'm staring at her like a bumbling idiot with a girl in his arms for the first time.

Probably true, honestly.

Raven pats my shoulder and attempts to get down from my hips and I put her down on her feet, only to spin around and tap the middle of my back. "Up, little bird, let me help you fly."

I'm eternally grateful when she gets up onto my back, trusting me to carry her back to the house. And though we're soaked to the bone, the heat remains between us when I walk through the back door, glaring at the guys in a clear 'Leave us the fuck alone' look.

Said look and my rushing movements makes Rae laugh–

something I know by the way her body bounces in the silence. I miss her laugh so damn much I wonder if I'll remember it correctly.

Shaking those thoughts away, I plaster a wide grin on my face when I enter the master bedroom–the one the guys and I set up for her to stay in. She doesn't need to use her old room–that's kind of our headquarters right now anyway. Unsure why I set up there but whatever.

I place Raven down on the floor in the en suite, turning her toward the mirror in the bathroom. Our eyes meet, and though some of my anger is remaining, right now I am far too joyful she's let me in, not allowing us to waste a single moment of this time together. As we continue to gaze at each other, I bring my hand up to the sides of her shirt, tilting my head in silent question. After she nods, I bring the shirt up above her, revealing her black lace bra and groaning when her pale skin is in my full view.

Her nipples are poking through the lace. I reach up with one hand and tweak one, biting down on my lip when her body shivers. I toss the shirt to the floor, reaching with both hands to the clasp of her bra and undoing it. Sliding it over her arms, my eyes follow the straps as they fall away and reveal the sweetness of Raven Hill.

I bite my lip when I notice her doing the same, my eyes struggling to decide whether to lock on her deep blues or to trace every delectable inch of her skin. My eyes probably look wild in their indecision, but that's okay.

I'm like a free bird at the moment.

I'm able to do whatever my mind sets itself to. I'm able to lean forward and press my hard dick against her shorts, my hands gripping her hips as I dig in, grinding against her to relieve some of the ache. It's torturous, but I see the way the denial of a quick fuck is getting her all hot and bothered, so I continue the slow actions.

I continue to torture her with sweet pleasure as I bring my lips to the back of her neck, licking up her sweet taste and the rainwater. I kiss and lick and place barely there hickeys along her spine as best I can, bending at the waist when I reach the spot right above her ass. The dimples there have been tantalizing to me ever since I saw them the first time, and right now I have the freedom to do what I've always wanted to–bite them. So I do, and the hitch in Rae's breathing is intoxicating.

Ever since I learned she hasn't been a stone-cold bitch by giving everyone the cold shoulder, it has been easier to read her movements. Though, of course, it's only been a day.

I roll my eyes at myself, realizing Maxwell has his claws in me too far–but he's not worth the thoughts at the moment.

Ignoring all thoughts of Maxwell Langston, I continue with my kisses on the sweet skin in front of me, my hands landing barely below Raven's knees and my fingers trailing light as feathers up her thighs until I reach the top of her shorts. I take in every single goosebump coming to life on her creamy skin, grinning when her body shudders as I place a soft kiss to the center of her dimples.

I pull her shorts down slowly watching the way Raven glares, the way she shifts her hips, and rubs her thighs together. Yeah, when I take her tonight it will be with the patience of a saint–and a saint I am not.

Raven reaches back and pulls at my hair, and my head tilts up. I look at her, and a smile tilts my lips up when I see how absolutely frustrated she is. She's panting, her chest heaving, her pupils blown in lust. It's absolutely addicting to see her this way.

When I tap her ankle, Raven steps out of her shorts, and

before she can move anywhere else, my lips land at her panty-line. I nip, suck, lick, bite, and do anything I can on top of her underwear. I'm sure she'd growl if she could and the fact she can't is turning me on at this moment, which I understand is absolutely not okay.

I grip her thighs and push her forward so she's leaning against the counter, bent over with her stomach resting on the cold surface. I bring my lips above her ass and grip the lace material in my teeth and begin to pull it down her skin, my teeth scraping along her flesh and leaving barely there score marks.

My dick is weeping at this point, about to combust of its own accord and without my permission. I reach down and unbutton my jeans, freeing it and running a hand along it, squeezing barely enough to take the pressure off as I remove Raven's underwear.

The moment she steps out of them, I'm rising to my feet, dick still in hand, while the other traces along her legs and up to her ass to squeeze firmly. I catch a small gasp and grin to myself, keeping my head tilted downward as I look up through my lashes at her in the mirror.

Her entire complexion is flushed, her wet hair stuck to her skin like the most delectable art. I reach forward and pull her hair behind her head, the water droplets falling between her breasts force my eyes to follow their path. I chew my lip and lean in, placing a kiss on her shoulder as I meet her gaze again.

"Raven, I know that you expect me to make love to you, but that's not how I do things." I trail my hand around to her throat, gripping it and tilting her head up with my thumb, ensuring her eyes are looking down at me–what she should rightfully do always.

"I do want you to know something first, though."

Kissing the side of her neck softly as I reach out with my free hand and grab a condom from the drawer of the sink. I rip it open with my teeth and sheath myself, trying not to be too cocky about the way she stares at me, squirming her little ass against my cock like it'll magically find its rightful place.

"You have the power here," I meet her gaze and raise a brow, "do you understand?"

She nods, biting her lip as her breathing nearly stills while I squeeze her throat a little–just enough–using my other hand to place my dick at her entrance, my feet knocking at hers to get her legs to spread wider for me.

"Alright," I say as I push Raven down against the counter, her tits resting comfortably on the counter top. My hand moves around her throat until it's on the back of her neck, and our eyes meet in the mirror again.

Holding her in this position, I squeeze a little tighter as I bring my dick to her entrance. "Something to learn about me, little bird, is that I do not make love," I pause for a moment for those words to register in her head, and then continue, gritting out "I fuck," and punctuating the last word by entering her so forcefully I have to hold her back from smashing her nose into the mirror.

It'd be funny if I didn't nearly cross over into fifteen different heavens with the way her slick cunt takes my dick, like it'd been begging for it. I'm seated at the throne inside my version of heaven. My eyes roll to the back of my head when I still inside of her, allowing us time to adjust to each other once more.

The last time we'd done this was the week before last Thanksgiving–before our world went to shit.

Our bodies get reacquainted, but as with everything, it's

like placing a missing piece back into its puzzle. Our souls can connect once again.

When she wiggles her ass, I grin and meet her gaze. The fingers on my hand flex over her pulse point and the other hand grips her hip, digging into the delectable skin with my fingers. I want to leave her bruised. I need to leave my mark on her. I have a feeling this thing with my friends won't stop just because she and I are having a moment.

I should care more about that, but the idea of sharing her isn't as off-putting as I'd have thought before I'd first seen her with River. The idea itself gets me harder than I'll ever admit.

I grunt as I anchor myself to her and meet her gaze once more, my jaw ticking in anger. "You're fucking mine," I punctuate the statement with a thrust, pulling out slowly so I can take in every single pulse point in her sweet cunt.

It's amazing what someone's body telegraphs, like how when I pull Rae's hair a tad harder, her cunt grips around me like a vice. The heat from her traveling through my dick and up my spine. "Fuck yes, little bird, grip me like you'll never let go."

Her eyes flash with the lust that's overtaken us both right as I thrust into her. Her hips pressing into the counter over and over again as I begin to pound relentlessly into her. I aim to make her mine with the way I fuck her. My sole purpose is to show her just how fucking good we are together. My dick is absolutely throbbing, and the sound of slapping skin is echoing in the bathroom, only broken by the sounds of my grunts and Raven's panting. I notice her eyes begin to roll back when I hit a particular spot inside of her. Bringing my hand from her hip, I trail my fingers around her clit with enough pressure to make her entire body freeze up.

The whites of her eyes show as they roll to the back of her head. It's intoxicating, knowing I've taken her body over and possessed it in this way. I'm forced to still my breathing. I take my other hand and wrap it around the front of her neck, squeezing enough to make her breathing cease, her face turning shades of red.

At this point, I know she'll be seeing spots, so right as I bring her clit between two of my fingers and pinch, squeezing it, rubbing it in circles in a relentless pattern, I let her throat go and let myself come at the same time her body shatters beneath me.

Her knees shake as I ride her orgasm out with my fingers massaging her clit, my own knees wobbling precariously. Once I'm able to take a deep enough breath, I pull out of her but don't let her get far as I rid myself of the condom.

I walk over to turn on the tap for the bath, plugging the drain and putting in her strawberry scented shit. Turning, I pull her into a tender embrace. My head rests on hers when she presses the side of her face into my chest, her arms wrapping around my middle and holding on for dear life.

We both are careful with each other as we bathe together, cleaning our bodies. I'm extra tender with the bruises I've left her with, placing kisses among them and thanking her for each one.

And as we get out of the bathroom, I find Phoenix has supplied us both with a change of clothes and some midnight snacks–strawberries and chocolate, ironically enough. We change and enjoy the snacks, and when we're pressed as close as two humans possibly could be, I find myself drifting off with my head in her lap as we simply exist together in a state of peace I haven't truly known in what feels like forever.

We'll sort the rest of the bullshit out later.

For now, we press *Resume* on the Pierce and Raven Show.

raven

Waking up the next morning is a strange experience. The familiarity of Pierce's arms should concern me first, but I cuddle into his body and simply exist with him. Pretending the last year hasn't happened at all.

We're able to be us again.

The dream is ruined a little when River comes pouncing through the room. He lands on the bed behind me, squishing me into Pierce, grinding his dick against my ass. I have to fight back the silent laughter trying to bubble up.

I've laughed more lately than I think is natural. I wonder if I should be laughing in this situation. But, instead of fighting off the need to cuddle into both of the guys' frames, I grab River's hand and place it across my stomach, intertwining our fingers as I press my forehead into the center of Pierce's shoulder blades. I breathe him in as I settle myself, purposefully grinding my ass against River's dick and he shoots off a curse and a groan at the same time.

"Tempting little vixen this morning...," he lets out, placing a soft and playful kiss to my exposed skin. He bites down on my shoulder and I jump a little, my ass grinding against him again. "Shit, stop or we'll have to wake Pierce up for some happy fun times and he isn't ready for the group spicy times yet. Not in the way I want, anyway," he murmurs.

Something tells me River wants more than a simple bromance with Pierce, but I'll keep that thought to myself entirely as I watch it unfold.

Should be something fun to keep myself occupied with as time goes on.

Maybe they'll let me be the ham in that sandwich. Though I guess I wouldn't mind being the bread, either.

I grin and try to hide it by burrowing my face further into Pierce's back. He turns, however, and tries to pull me into his arms tightly, but I'm stopped by River's hand and arm tightening to keep me in his hold as well. Pierce stiffens and opens one eye, staring me down.

"The fuck?" he grumbles. He lifts his head to see over my shoulder. "Riv, get the hell out."

"Nah, I want cuddles too, PJ!" River exclaims, bouncing a bit on the bed. All three of us end up squished tighter together, much to his amusement, if his growing dick is anything to go by.

I sigh and settle between them, closing my eyes again as I let them deal with their own shit. I've found myself in quite the dream world. Three guys doting on me, though Phoenix is nowhere to be found in this room. He's probably making breakfast.

"Alright, get your hands off my girl and go find something useful to do. Didn't we *lose something* that we have to find before we leave on Sunday, Riv?" Pierce's voice sounds so serious, and River's body stiffens in a not fun way.

"Shit...yeah, okay. But," River starts to say, landing a loud and wet kiss on my cheek, "She's our girl, not just yours. Don't even try to argue with me on this one."

He gets up, landing a smack on my ass followed by a risky one on Pierce's ass as well. I bite my lip so I don't laugh, but fail when Pierce's glare lands on me. I don't want to pay for River's shit, so I try to shuffle quickly off of the mattress.

Of course, Pierce has always been the fastest of us all, so he easily catches up with me before I can make it to the en suite. He does nearly lose a finger when I try to slam the door, however.

Grabbing me around the waist, he lifts me up and places me on the counter of the sink. He moves between my thighs, bracketing my hips with his hands. His nose barely touching mine. The grin on his face is something magical and so rare that I pause to take it in and make a mental picture, trying to keep from looking anywhere else.

He's always been attractive to me, but ever since I got to Cobalt University, I've found it near impossible to ignore the way he looks. His chest is broad and defined, as are his abs. He has this easy dark tan about him that makes me want to visit the beach constantly so I might be able to catch up with him.

There's also his curly black locks which only barely crest his ears and cover his eyes. I reach up and freely run my fingers through it, knowing brushing it won't fix the craziness atop his head. It's adorable, and I find myself relaxing more as I brush my fingers through his hair and along his scalp. My eyes meet his and I find the tenderness in his gaze comforting.

My body is alight like a match right now, and I could explode at any second with sensation. So when Pierce leans forward and kisses me, the world tilts on its axis before righting itself all over again.

The universe was not prepared for us last year, and I don't care if it is now.

We're ready for us.

Even if the universe gave me two extra men who are beginning to steal my heart.

His hands find my hips and I reach up with my free hand to place it at the base of his neck, gripping what hair I can there. He grinds his growing erection against me until I'm squirming, searching and pleading for the friction that will get me there. Pierce groans when he finds the right spot for himself, and I let out a silent giggle, grinning up at him sheepishly when he pauses to take me in.

A small smile graces his lips, his eyes glossed over with sleep and sex and I can't find it in me to stop it when I lean up to press my lips to his in such a languid kiss. Our souls reach out and pull each other close once again. A small tear falls from one of my eyes, and Pierce pauses our kiss, backing up to wipe it away with his thumb.

Pressing the drop of liquid to his lips, he licks it up, quirks a cocky smile and says, "I love the taste of the tears that you drop for me, little bird, but I especially love the taste of your happy ones."

I quirk a brow at him and let out a huff, trying to escape him. I begin laughing when he starts to tangle himself around me. He tickles me and forces the silent laughter to bubble up. He tracks every movement of my chest and stomach, watching the actions of my laughter even if he can't hear it. It makes me wonder if our memories are strong enough for him to have the sound still echoing in his head.

"Fuck," he sighs, as he rests his head on my bare stomach, wrapping his hands around my waist. He pulls me as close to him as possible and rests his body between my legs. He simply holds me there for what seems like an eternity. Placing a few sweet kisses to my stomach, he rests his chin there, looking up at me with a deep regret shining in those forest green eyes.

I shake my head and place a finger to his lips, not wanting him to speak on this topic right now. I'm not ready for it, and he's not either.

We're still too fresh right now. We've been flayed open, salt poured onto our wounds before we were able to clean them.

We're still healing, and that's okay.

I toss a cocky grin his way, before wrapping my legs around his shoulders so suddenly his eyes flash with panic and surprise. I grin down at him, his eyes half lidded while I bite my lip and squirm under his gaze.

"You cocky little shit," he says, though it's not in anger, it's in amusement. "I taught you half of the things you know, so I don't know why you think you got one up on me."

I raise a brow at him in challenge, and bite my lip when his tongue reaches out to wet his lips. His eyes take in my heaving chest and flushed skin, still slick with the sweat we created by sleeping directly against each other last night—the only downside to cuddling, honestly.

"You're so beautiful and I am so sorry if I've ever made you feel unworthy of any of the attention and love you deserve, Raven." Pierce's voice is so sincere and loving that I nearly choke on the affection. "I'll fix us Blue, promise," he chokes out.

And since I can't handle the mushy shit anymore this morning, I lean down and press my lips furiously to his. His lips part and our tongues begin dueling as my body tries to align itself with his. I'm wet, and we both know it. Our lips are fused together so tightly at this point that our breaths are shared, and I can't find it in me to care.

We could be the end of the other right here, right now.

His hands slide down my body, making it to my ass and holding me onto his hard dick while he pushes up and rubs against me to find his own small relief. It's intoxicating and the small pressure to my clit has my whole body lit like a live wire. I break from our kiss to breathe better and bite at Pierce's lower lip. I do it once more, and he grunts before releasing a low growl in warning.

I grin as I look down at him, and bite my lip to try to stifle it. He narrows his eyes and points to the little bowl on the counter top where I see a box of condoms the guys must have brought. I turn and reach over the counter to grab one out of the box. Once I have one in hand, I go to turn around. I am shocked to all hell when Pierce lands the loudest and most painful smack to my ass imaginable. The warmth comes first, followed by the sting. His hand is there to massage it and I let my head fall forward in relief. My hair brackets me, clothing me in a small bit of darkness as I try to steady my breathing.

"Up. Come ride me to the ends of Hell, Blue," he commands me, grabbing my hips and spinning me until I'm straddling him again, my ass firmly planted on the cool counter top sighing when it soothes my aching ass cheeks. He quickly grabs the condom and rips it open with his teeth—all three of the boys have done that at this point and I'm pretty sure it's a talent they've practiced together. I stare at him, taking in his naked frame, and as I sink down onto his waiting cock, I let out a small breath that becomes staccato as he fills me up in ways unimaginable before last night.

My hands fall to his chest and I find a good enough grip as my hips meet his. We both exhale loudly and I grin, peeking an eye open to see his eyes are also on me. Pierce brings his hands up my thighs to my hips and anchors me where he wants me.

He quickly tugs my hips forward, forcing the entirety of the friction onto my swollen clit. I'm alight with the sensation, and when he rocks me over him again, my eyes fly to his in an almost panic. I should NOT come this quickly. It's unfathomable.

"I don't have much stamina this morning, Blue, so you'll have to excuse me for," he thrusts up with the next grind of my clit on his pelvic bone and I throw my head back, my nails digging into his skin, "playing your body like a fiddle." He grunts the last word out, his fingers digging in further.

I grind against him in the way he showed me, and as I get closer and closer to my climax, my eyes dive into Pierce's forest green ones. I let out a silent scream of pleasure when I reach my crescendo, my breath leaving me when he thrusts into me at an inhuman pace. His dick hits the right spot inside of me to send me barreling into a second orgasm at the same moment he reaches his own peak.

We ride this one out together while he mutters curses and my broken breaths meet in between us before he takes me into a heated kiss. One of his hands is still on my hip while the other grips my scalp in a bruising hold. We roll our hips together and ride the wave until we can't anymore, our lips continuing to show our love for one another as our bodies attempt to fail us. We eventually collapse together, my back resting against the mirror and Pierce resting on me while his hands continue to explore my slick skin.

We rest there for I don't know how long, before two sets of hands clapping scare Pierce so much he jumps backward, his back hitting the wall and his head hitting the towel rack. I scramble to check he's okay while I laugh.

I'm not embarrassed by the other guys finding us. I'm

incredibly amused, while also being kind of disappointed they didn't think to join in.

There's always next time, Rae...

"Okay, boys and girl," Phoenix says, his chocolate eyes alight in amusement as Pierce shoots him a filthy glare from his perch on the ground. "We have to get a move on today, yeah? Separate showers—you too, River. We have a busy ass few days ahead of us." He points toward the shower and looks directly at me, his eyes traveling my skin and lighting it up all over again.

I saunter toward Phoenix and his perch at the bathroom door. His brow raises and his lips try hard to maintain their current scowl. I grin sweetly and lean up onto my tiptoes, pressing a soft kiss to his lips. He doesn't return it, simply grabbing me by the biceps to move me and physically putting distance between us.

"Shower, Red, or your ass will be brighter than your namesake." He walks out of the room leaving me standing there, pouting. River plants a wet kiss to my cheek as he walks out, finger-gunning in my direction and winking like a dork. Pierce walks past me a few seconds later and kisses the crown of my head.

I stand there stunned at the affection all three of the guys just showed me. I tilt my head, frowning. I expected a tad more from Pierce this morning.

A few words, maybe, as he left me standing naked and alone in the room?

I sigh and twist around, going to my bag and grabbing some jeans and a sweater, along with a matching set of red underwear. I'll make sure to let them show a little today to fuck with all three of them. I make my way into the bathroom and take a shower, lingering as I look at the bite marks and fingerprints on my body, remembering each of them were kissed reverently by Pierce last night as he both apologized and thanked me for them.

I blush as I finish up in the shower, a small smile cresting my lips when I get out to dry off. Meeting my own gaze in the mirror, I'm shocked to find actual happiness there. Something I didn't think I would see for so long that it's almost jarring.

It takes me a while, but I manage to put my hair in some sort of order–a messy top knot–and I clean my face of all makeup. I put on the black sweater and the blue jeans, putting red fuzzy socks on my feet to keep them warm. I tend to run cold–my inpatient therapy was hard on me, more so since it was always so cold in the hospital–so I'm always, always, always in something to keep me extra warm.

Making my way down the stairs, I hear the guys mumbling feverishly about something, but I don't catch the words before they see me and their entire conversation stops.

You could hear a pin drop with how silent the room goes, and the hackles on the back of my neck begin to rise to an intense degree.

Resuming my descent of the stairs, I make it toward the guys finally and grab a plate of fresh eggs and hash browns that were made for me. I dip my head in thanks to Phoenix. He's the only one who tries to cook decently around here. I plop my butt down at the kitchen island, taking one big bite as I watch the guys while they attempt to continue their conversation without speaking.

They forget I've been mute for so long that I've learned to pick up on body language a lot better since I've been working on perfecting my own. So when I take a large bite of eggs, I sit straight and watch their expressions.

Phoenix raises a brow and points his head in my direction.

River bobs his head, too enthusiastically for it to be subtle.

Pierce rolls his eyes and glares so hard at River that I fear for his life.

I huff out a laugh, spitting food out onto the counter in front of me.

Luckily–or unluckily, depending on who you are–this releases the tension in the room and Pierce heaves a huge sigh, coming to my side and throwing an arm around me, his hand landing on my shoulder as he tugs me into his side.

"Fine," he grits out, glaring at Phoenix now as he pulls me from the stool I'm sitting on.

"Story time, story time!" River yells out, bounding into the living room and tugging Pierce by the hand so we're forced to follow him. I stumble a few steps before I manage to catch myself. I sit down on Pierce's lap when he pulls me down to do so, banding his arm around me and tugging me so close to him. I'm already terrified of what River looks far too excited about.

Once Phoenix makes it inside the living room finally, he places his hand on my shoulder and gives it a squeeze before placing a soft kiss to the top of my head. He walks away and sits down in the recliner that's angled toward the sectional Pierce and River are sitting on with me. I curl my arms around Pierce's, and clutch my hands onto his forearms, waiting for the bomb they're about to drop on me.

"Okay," Pierce says before he takes a deep breath, tightening his hold on me. "So, here's our dilemma..." he stalls for a moment, looking around at both of the other guys and getting his reassurance before he begins his story.

"Alpha Mu is currently a frat house running the drug trade through Cobalt University. It has since the 1980s when Maxwell Langston was the president. The entire drug trade began with him and a group of friends," he takes a deep breath and begins again. "Since they began, this entire school has become a part of the operation in one form or the other. Maxwell funds the whole thing, the science wing creates them, the medical facility pushes the test runs out, and Alpha Mu distributes to other people through parties and other means. We are the head honchos and everyone brings the cash back to us, which we bring to Maxwell whenever we accumulate too much cash. He pays us, we live here for free so long as we *don't* fuck up."

The boys make eye contact with each other for a moment, and I wait until Pierce's eyes find mine again before I nod, a silent plea for him to continue.

"Since I've been here–six months earlier than planned," he glares at me but quirks a grin before he rolls his eyes and places a placating kiss on my nose. "Maxwell needed someone to train up and become the next Alpha Mu president, so...here I am." He meets the guys' eyes again and I see Phoenix roll his eyes before shaking his head and looking down at his ankle when he crosses it over his thigh. "And now that I'm the president, well, Maxwell takes advantage of that and my newfound business sense to make me the top dog around here."

River sits up straighter and looks at me before he speaks, "We've essentially become Pierce's bitches. Nixy boy and I are here to help him, but all in all... when Maxwell tells us to jump we all ask how high."

I raise a brow. For some reason, these guys don't seem like the type to just...do what they're told by someone random. I reach out for the notepad that was left on the coffee table and smile softly when Phoenix hands me a pen. When I'm done writing, I lift the pad to show Pierce what I've written.

What's Maxwell have over your heads?

"Smart girl," Phoenix says after he has a chance to read the pad, passing it to River. "He's got a lot of shit over our heads, and it's not that important at the moment."

I roll my eyes and shake my head, folding my arms as I glare around at all three of them as they remain tight lipped on this. Throwing my hands up, I go to stand up so I can get some space to think about all of this, but Pierce grabs me and holds me to him again.

"It's heavy shit we don't talk about a lot. We'll tell you in time. But for now," he says, massaging small circles in my upper thighs to try and calm some of my anger.

Of course it fucking works. His hands are calming and warm to me. Familiar.

"For now, we have to find something he has been looking for. He swears up and down it's here in your mother's house." When my head snaps to meet Pierce's gaze, he dips his head once. "Yeah, that's what I was looking for downstairs when I found our letters. River and I have looked through a lot of shit upstairs but we can't seem to find anything that even looks like a recipe, much less one for an illegal synthetic drug."

I grab the notepad and write on it again while the guys remain silent. It would be an awkward silence, but we've all grown accustomed to my communication styles lately. Though our sign language classes have been truly helpful with the little things, we're a long way away from communicating full sentences.

Phoenix grabs the notepad and reads it aloud for everyone, skipping the need to pass it around. "She says there are dozens of boxes in the house but she went through them all before heading to therapy in January."

He looks up and meets my gaze and I smile softly before looking away. Clearing his throat, he continues to read my note. "The only place she hasn't looked through yet has been a safety deposit box at the bank in town. She has the key," he pauses when Pierce shoves me off of him in his haste to get up. He shoves his shoes and jacket on quickly. "She has the key in the top drawer of the dresser upstairs," Phoenix finishes reading.

"Got it," Pierce says, booking it up the stairs so quickly I start to wonder if he didn't teleport up there.

I look at the other two with my arms folded once more and tap my foot, hoping one of them will spill the rest of their secrets. Unfortunately, I see it won't work. Now they're working on getting dressed. It's not like the bank is a hard place to go on a solo tour to, so this recipe must be extremely important.

I sigh and go to put my boots on, sliding my feet in, working on the zippers and the buckles at the top. I stand up to my full height at the same moment Pierce makes it back down with the key to my mother's safety deposit box. When he holds it up in front of me, silently asking if that's the right one, I nod. He grins so wide it makes my heart hurt.

I go to comfort both of us with a tight hug around his middle, my hands clasping together at his back as I rest my cheek against his chest, and he rests his chin atop my head. His hands rest above my butt, his fingers splaying out underneath my sweater and forcing a shiver out of me.

"Fuck Rae," he whispers. After my heart has skipped enough beats, he places a kiss to the top of my head before releasing me.

I stand there stunned for a moment, huff out a breath, and grab my coat, angrily shoving my arms into the holes.

Phoenix comes up to me during my struggle and helps me out of the tangled mess, helping me get into it properly. Placing a soft kiss to my forehead, he lifts my head with his forefinger and thumb, meeting my watery gaze.

"Time heals all wounds," he says.

When I go to move my head away, he jerks my head back to him, looking at me sternly. I lick my lip, accidentally licking his thumb as well. His nostrils flare wide and his eyes darken before he tightens his grip on me.

"We'll play later, Red. I have plans for you," he says before he leans down, placing a chaste but promising kiss to my lips.

My heart skips a beat and I gasp for air when he walks backward out of my reach, a little cocksure smile on his face. I bring my own hand up to my mouth and brush my fingers over my lips as I watch him go to get his own cold weather gear. A few seconds later, Pierce is heading back toward the front door and River is hounding after him, dragging me by the hand after the two of them.

His grin is infectious, and I smile wildly with him when he pulls me into the back seat of the jeep, cuddling close to me as he secures my seat-belt. Pressing a kiss to my lips, he murmurs against them, "I'm so fuckin' proud of you, little vixen." He kisses me more firmly before pulling back with a promise of more in his eyes.

"Alright, calm it the fuck down," Pierce barks, his glare meeting my eyes followed by River's in the rear-view mirror.

Phoenix enters the jeep on the front passenger side, and quickly checks over us all to make sure our seat-belts are secure. River leans in between the front seats to look at him with a large grin, waggling his brows.

"Proud Daddy?! We put our seat-belts on by ourselves this time!" River cackles and swerves out of the way to make sure Phoenix can't punch him like he tries to. He glares at River before Pierce shoves the jeep into gear and reverses out of the driveway.

We're heading toward town again and I'm biting back more of a smile as I take in the familiar surroundings. Everything is so damn similar to last year, and I suddenly find it hard to properly catch my breath...

"ALRIGHT," *Pierce says, a wide grin on his face stretching his cheeks and making them pinken from the strain. "Are we playing rock paper scissors to determine who cooks the turkey or...?"*

I roll my eyes and chuck a gummy bear at his head, groaning when he catches it in his mouth instead of on the side of his face like I had planned. "No. We'll work together. Don't try to get out of it, lazy ass."

Chewing the gummy bear, he contemplates his next move as we continue to make our way down the road. He took the long way around town, past the bank, and down the longer 'scenic' view. He wants to give me a reprieve, but I want to get back to my mom. Anything could happen at this point.

"Oh!" He shouts, sitting up straighter. He turns his head toward me. I panic and point toward the road, flicking him in the forehead for his recklessness and he flinches in response. "Ouch! Shit, Blue, cut your claws!" He barks, rubbing his forehead with one hand while he steers with the other.

"Drive fucking responsibly, Pierce Jackson or I will murder you in your sleep!" I yell at him, clutching the oh shit handle—not for the first time in this vehicle.

"Alright alright, damn," he mutters, putting both hands on the wheel and rolling his eyes as he watches the road again.

"We'll work together, and it'll be done sooner so you can spend more time..." he pauses, his brows furrowing.

The red and blue lights infiltrate our vision before we can take in the sight of the police cars, firetrucks and ambulances.

"Your mother," he finishes, pulling us up onto his driveway and putting the vehicle in park.

I'm out of the truck before he can get that far though, ignoring his panicked shout as I rush across the road toward my mom's house and nearly tripping over myself as I push through first responders.

My heart is thundering so hard in my chest I feel like I might have a heart attack.

Guess it's good all these people are here.

I'm halfway up my own driveway when an EMT stops me with an arm around my waist. I kick and scream and cry and battle the fuck out of him, but he doesn't let me go until Pierce is pulling me into his arms firmly, pressing my head into his chest.

He doesn't hide my gaze fast enough, though. I still see how lifeless my mother looks on the stretcher. I still see how they've had to intubate her. How the sheet covering her is only a foot from being what I'll see in a morgue.

No.

Pierce doesn't hide me from the doctors telling me she's at the end stages and I should go ahead and arrange her funeral.

He can't hide me from anything when I send in his college application three days later.

He can't hide me from my mother's death once he's graduated from high school early and left for CU before me—and alone.

Not a single soul saves me or protects me when I lose the ability to speak or make a single sound.

I'm physically left standing in his arms, but in all other forms, I'm left on a plane of existence that is my own.

"RAVEN," a voice comes through the fog. "Raven, hey!" The voice yells at me, a soft tap on my cheek has my head turning away, but another hand presses against the same cheek and pushes my head back.

My eyes flutter open, sure, but all I see are the red and blue lights and I don't want to see them anymore. I reach out and bat the hands away from me, only to be restrained by them and forced to remain in my motionless state. I keep my eyes tightly shut, avoiding the bright light that seems to be blinking above me.

"Raven, sweet girl," another voice says, calming but in a panic, "open those pretty blue eyes."

A body seems to invade my space before I'm being suffocated, or what feels like suffocation, until lips press to mine. I'm struggling to breathe again, much like I was before I remembered that night. The night they put my mother into hospice care and told me she was as good as dead. I sit up in a panic. I can't fucking go back there! I want to yell.

Shit, am I yelling?

My eyes fly open, and my mouth is open in a silent scream as my hands scramble at my throat, trying to pull the noise out. I want to make a noise.

Green eyes meet my blues and my breathing grows more erratic, the panic becoming far too tangible for my liking. Gripping me around my hips and pulling me in, Pierce presses his lips to my ear, his cheek lining up with mine. He ensures my legs are around his waist and he lowers us to the ground.

I don't remember leaving the car.

The panic rises at the thought and I find the world going dark until the stubble on Pierce's cheek scratches me, and my back is being rubbed gently up and down by another hand–Phoenix. My breathing begins to match Pierce's as he presses our chests so close together that I can sense his every heartbeat.

Hands grip mine and manipulate them until they're wrapped around Pierce's neck.

All three boys are putting me in a position where no one would tell where Pierce begins and I end. It's so fucking endearing and yet my panicked breathing comes back until I'm clutching so hard at Pierce that I rip a hole into the shirt poking up from the collar of his coat.

"Shit," he breathes before he pulls back. Seconds later, he presses his lips back to mine firmly, forcing my lips to part with his tongue as he steals what little breath I have left. He pulls me further into his body, just as Phoenix brings his hand to my hair, massaging my scalp while also moving my head as much as he can to keep this kiss as deep as possible. They're all trying to ensure Pierce's kiss is a kiss of life.

Moments into the kiss, my breathing slows and my heartbeat is a regular rhythm again. I'm still panting, but that's due to the fact that all three men are touching me and Pierce has spent the last sixty seconds–at least–grinding his growing erection into my center. Confirmed by the rigid bulge in his jeans when I go to grind down on him, distracting myself from the inevitable conversation we'll all be having due to whatever just happened.

Pierce raises a brow at me, placing a soft kiss to my nose before pulling back and firming his hands on my hips to still me. "Enough of that. We need to get this taken care of. Then, we need to talk about what happened."

See? There it is.

I go to shake my head but Phoenix's hand in my hair holds my head still as he leans down to whisper in my ear, "Don't fuckin' lie, Red. That was a PTSD attack and it's important we know what sets that shit off, got it?" He makes me bob my head before placing a kiss on my forehead. Releasing me, he places a hand on River's shoulder. They both walk through the front doors of the bank, no doubt waiting inside for Pierce and I to join them.

"Rae," Pierce whispers, his voice near my ear again as he tries to slow his own breathing. His arms wrap around me and hold me in a comforting hug. "I don't care what's happened, you should have mentioned you could have attacks that bad. You took off while the car was still moving, baby." His voice is pained, and when I rear back in surprise to look up at him with wide eyes, he nods and chews on his lip.

Pierce brushes the hair from my face and we stare in each other's eyes for a while before he places a kiss on my forehead. We stand up together, and he steadies me, helping me brush my clothes clean of dirt and gravel. My body hurts as if I've been through a fight, so I assume I must have hit the ground hard.

"Let's go get this document, and we can get you back home so you can let us know about these attacks, okay?" I look up at Pierce before I nod. He wraps my hand around his arm and escorts me inside of the bank. When we make it to the counter, I find my mother's attorney, Henry, smiling brightly at me while also side-eyeing my companions.

"Miss Raven!" Henry says, shuffling quickly around the counter so he can come and grab my hand gently, shaking it as he takes me in. "I am so happy to see you! How was therapy? Did it work well for you? How's school? How's–"

"Yo, dude," River says, his voice harder than normal, "It didn't work. So stop with the questions."

Henry's face blanches and he bows in apology, which I find a bit too amusing, so I hide my face in Pierce's shoulder.

"We have a key," Phoenix says, all business and demanding at the same time. "It goes to the late Miss Hill's security deposit box here and Raven would like to obtain the contents now."

Henry bobs his head enthusiastically as he finally makes his way behind the counter again. He shuffles some paperwork around before sliding one sheet across the counter with a pen attached. Meeting my eyes, he says "Just sign this and you can come in and grab whatever is left."

I sign the paperwork, passing it back to Henry. He shakily grabs the paper, looking between me and the boys several times while putting it back where it needs to go. I think the boys are scaring the hell out of him. Pierce abruptly grabs my hand and walks us toward the hall Henry ushers us down.

"I doubt there's anything in there but the box number is 5225, so go ahead and enter here," he says, opening up a door halfway down the hallway and gesturing us inside. "You're good to go. I'll be at the counter if you need anything. Short staffed and all that," he tries to joke, but when no one laughs and all of the guys continue their glaring contest, he leaves.

"Somethin' feel off to you, Nix?" Pierce questions in a harsh whisper.

With a shrug, Phoenix wanders the rows of boxes until he reaches the one which belongs to my mother. "Possibly, or he's scared shitless. Who knows."

I head toward the row showcasing the boxes beginning with 5, and soon after find box 5225. I lift the key from my pocket and am about to turn it when I sense the growing presence of all three guys behind me. Pierce on my right, River my left, and Phoenix walks up close and presses himself against my back. His hands land on my hips as he leans in to whisper a gentle encouragement.

"You can do it," he says before placing a kiss against my cheek. He waits with as much bated breath as the rest of us.

I take a deep breath before fully turning the key and sliding the box open.

Inside is...

Nothing.

"The fuck?" Pierce barks out, shoving in front of me, sliding his hands into the box and trying to find what isn't there.

I stumble a little until I slam into River and nearly fall over, but he catches me at the same time Phoenix smacks Pierce in the back of the head for shoving me. I lean against River's front while watching Pierce frantically search for the recipe.

After a few minutes of him looking through the empty box and still not finding anything–surprise, surprise–Phoenix pulls him back and shakes him.

"Breathe, brother," he says to him soothingly, glaring into his eyes to get him to stop and think for a moment. "We'll find it."

"Who the fuck did you let in here, Raven?" Pierce bellows, rushing me and placing a hand on my throat as he steps in and glares at me. My face blanches in panic, but he doesn't stop. He manages to get me out from River's hold and press me against the wall of boxes, one of them digging into the skin above my pants and under my sweater. I frown and try to escape his hold, nearly choking myself in the process.

I see Phoenix and River having a silent conversation over Pierce's shoulders, but they don't move. They don't try to save me at all.

I narrow my eyes on them, only to find Pierce in my line of sight again as he stares down at me. His hand tightens on my throat a little more and my vision goes spotty. Clawing at his wrist, I know I draw blood. I'm gasping for air at this point, my legs going weak as he holds me there.

"Where," he grits out, "the fuck," his voice grows louder, "is it?" He yells, his spittle hitting my face, and I flinch.

I shake my head, keeping my eyes shut tightly, opening myself up to the possibility of passing out.

Quite frankly, the oblivion of death would be preferable to this. He won't trust me for a long time. I get that. But this is pure violence and hatred. I don't exactly know when that happy little boy became this brutal man in front of me, but I have a feeling it happened before our blow up last Thanksgiving.

The way the other two are simply standing there, allowing Pierce to do this to me and spit his anger out so viciously? Yeah, it's a problem now. My heart is in shambles right now as I wonder if I die here, would it be easier than facing the wrath of three ruthless men and their unjustified anger at an empty box. As if I was the one who came here and emptied it out! As if I was the one who sent them on a wild as hell goose chase to another town!

My body begins to go limp finally and I'm about to grace the blackness when I'm freed, River's arms banding around me and hoisting me up bridal style in his arms. His frame is vibrating in anger, but he manages to keep composure long enough to get me out of the bank. I hear the other two yelling, but I allow myself to fall asleep in River's warm embrace.

Ignoring my problems is sometimes self-care, too.

Letter from Pierce
Age 19

Raven,

You won't see this, ever. I'll probably burn this fucking thing the moment that I finish with it anyway. So I don't even know why I'm writing it other than I'm really fucking pissed off.

I watched you cross that stage, and I didn't cheer for you. Hardly anyone did, and at the moment I thought that's what you fucking get, but then I felt like shit. Felt even worse when I walked down that hallway, looking at all of our usual hiding spots, and heard Jimmy bragging about some bullshit that I *wish* I never heard. I beat the living fuck out of him for you, babe, but you won't even know it because I won't send this letter.

The guys are hounding me, so I'm gonna just not write anymore now...

I fucking hate...love you, Blue...

Later gator,

Green

pierce

I run after River and Raven, my entire body heated from the realization I may have failed this one last chance to keep myself in Maxwell's good graces.

Right as I hit the doorway, though, Phoenix reaches out and slams his hand on the center of my back, forcing me to fall forward.

Before my head hits the ground, he grabs me by the scruff of my neck and pulls me back into the room, slamming the door before he slams me face first into a row of the security deposit boxes. My face collides with some of the metal used for the handles and locks and I instantly feel the blood trickling along my skin. My nose is also busted, but that's not enough to shock me right now. I turn my head and shoot a glare at Phoenix, his own angry stare meeting mine right back without hesitation.

"You are so fucking far out of line right now, Nixy boy," I growl out, but he slams a hand to the side of my face to keep it firmly against the boxes.

Stepping into me, his body presses mine flat. His voice is so low of a whisper I have to strain to hear him. "If I ever catch you touching or yelling at her like that again, I will end you without a second of hesitation. Fuck your deadbeat mother. Fuck River's parents. Fuck it all. I've got nothing left to lose, and you were so far out of line. I'd enjoy the goddamn prison sentence."

The sound of our heavy breathing echoes through the room before I nod, grunting when he releases me. My knees buckle and I nearly fall on my ass. He pats me on the head like a fucking dog and I'm about to go three rounds in an octagon with him for it, but think better of it when I turn around to see how truly fucking angry he is with me right now. I don't quite understand the vitriol of his anger at the moment, so I simply shoulder past him and out into the hallway.

Once around the corner, I swipe the blood from my face before I glare at Henry through the glass that separates customers and employees of the bank. "We need to talk."

"Uh, well I, uhm," he fidgets with his hands, his eyes shifting across the entire lobby as if someone will come in and save his ass.

Spoiler alert: they won't.

"Now, Henry, we're friends," I tell him, splaying my hands out to show him I'm not a harm to him–a lie, of course. "I need to know the exact fucking reason box 5225 was completely empty."

"I-I-I r-really can't...t-tell you that, s-s-sir," Henry tells me.

I smirk. I love when men below me know they're outmatched–the stuttering is my favorite. Typically they piss their pants next, but I don't like that part, so I move forward quickly and press my hands to the glass, glaring through it at the man as he trembles behind his safety net.

"You need to figure it the fuck out. Whether you can tell

me or whether you lose your job, Henry. I can be very, very convincing, after all. So," I say, leaning back and placing my hands casually inside of my pockets, a small smile playing on my lips as he scrambles around in his paperwork and file cabinets.

Phoenix comes up next to me, his shoulder pressing against mine as we both stand there watching the man flit around. "This bank needs to be brought up to the next fucking century if nothing else," he grumbles.

"Whole town does, but it won't," I tell him, and he grunts in reply.

What seems like an hour later, Henry comes forward with a sign-in sheet that looks so dated I'm surprised it's on paper and not stone somewhere near a burning bush. I snatch it from his hand, hiding the chuckle trying to leave me when he gets a paper cut. As I look over the names signed in back in August, roughly a week after Raven got to CU, Henry reaches through the window in the glass and points toward one name in particular, one which isn't a name after all but a set of initials.

"J.C.?" I say aloud, looking up at Henry with my brow furrowed.

"No idea. She looked unwell, but she said Miss Raven was in a hurry to get whatever was in there. She said," Henry swallows audibly as he pulls his arm back through the little window. "She said Miss Raven could become very wealthy with whatever was in there. I'm not sure if I was meant to hear that part, though, but I did. That's all the information I have!" He says quickly, holding his hands up in surrender as he stares at Phoenix and I.

I bob my head a few times before meeting Phoenix's gaze. He dips his head in return and we simply...walk away.

Henry will wonder when we'll come for him, and that kind of torture is free to dole out and isn't a crime.

"We should probably get her real name and a full description of her, honestly," I muse aloud.

Phoenix looks over to me, pushing the bank doors open, "We'll figure it out. It would have all been lies, anyway. I don't want a fake name or a fake description rolling around in my head while I'm trying to piece information together. Too many false clues will confuse us all."

"I guess that makes sense."

As we reach the jeep where River has Raven, I peer in through the back window, sighing when I see her head laid in his lap peacefully, and his face looking contemplative as he strokes her hair.

He senses me though, like he always does, and his head snaps up. The glare he shoots my way has me skipping around the vehicle and getting in the driver's seat far faster than I normally would.

We all need a little distance.

AFTER RAVEN HAS WOKEN and River and Phoenix have made sure she's not seriously ill from passing out, we're all in the basement, brooding and brainstorming all in one.

Our little team is broken, and I can't help but to feel like I'm the only real broken piece.

Unfortunately for us all, I'm the pivotal piece in it all, so as I call the shots, they all give me attitudes, but they still listen. I grin when Raven slams a stack of papers down in front of me and spins on her heel. She walks over toward the large sofa in front of the television and game system we played on for so many hours when we were younger.

"Oh hell yeah, game break!" River barks out, tossing papers down in front of him as he goes to follow her, gripping her in his arms and pulling her down onto his lap. He bands his arm across her midsection and accepts a controller when she hands him one.

"The fuck?" I bark out, glaring at them both, but I'm ignored.

Phoenix shrugs, placing down the pile he was looking through, and places his happy ass next to River, grabbing a third controller and leaning back to get himself comfortable. His eyes meet mine in question, and I growl before standing up and squishing myself in on the other side of River, grabbing the last controller to the Nintendo 64.

Raven and I never could enjoy any other console as much as this one.

I shake my head when she turns Mario Kart on, and selects Princess Peach as her character, followed by Rainbow Road for the track. Meeting her eyes, I blindly select Bowser as my character, arching a brow at her.

He is the one who stole the princess away for himself, after all.

Her cheeks pinken as she quickly looks back at the 64-inch TV.

"Phoenix, be a bro and play Luigi so I can play Mario and we can team up to save the princess?" River says.

"No thanks," Nix says simply, attempting to select Toad.

"Bro!" River yells, nearly jumping up but remembering Raven is on his lap, so he holds her closer to him, placing his chin on her shoulder as he shoots puppy dog eyes toward

Phoenix. "Come on...we can team up against Pierce, and he'll lose every time."

"So will we, numb-nuts," Phoenix says, raising a dangerous brow when River pokes his lips out in the weirdest looking pout ever. "Plus, it's Mario Kart. We don't have teams."

Shaking his head, River leans in on Raven's other side–the one closest to me–and whispers loudly, "It's fine, I'll keep saving you from the beast whenever you need me to, princess." He places a wet kiss on her cheek and I shove him with my thigh, growling in warning.

The game begins, and sure enough, River takes his promise to heart. He's constantly fighting against me and ignoring the fact we should all be racing against each other. Phoenix, however, has no qualms in whooping Rae's ass so hard I'm surprised I can't hear it. Her face is lit up in anger and challenge. She could always beat anyone on this track, so to find someone that can beat her is a tad bit of a surprise to us both.

When Phoenix beats her in the next round by a hair, I'm jumping up and dancing like a lunatic. I point at Nix, the widest grin on my face, "Over. A. Decade," I begin, "she has not been beat on this track in over a DECADE, Nix!"

Raven glares up at me, crossing her arms over her chest. Which only serves as an extra push up for her tits. I bite my lip as I take her in, but am thrown off balance when Phoenix shoves me from the side. "The fuck, Nix?!" I rub my side a little as I sit down, still looking at him questioningly.

"Shut the fuck up and don't brag," he barks out before taking a calming breath and sitting back down, all poised and shit. "We don't flaunt it when we dethrone people, Pierce."

When the next round begins, it turns out Phoenix can keep up with his ass beating of Raven in a video game she used to be undefeated on. He looks over and grins at her, raising a brow as he points to his cheek, getting the kiss he expected from Raven in return. He meets my gaze again and winks like a douche bag, and says, "We don't flaunt it *much* when we dethrone people."

I scoff and throw my hands up, elbowing River when he barks out a loud laugh. I grin and shake my head as we continue to play well into the middle of the night, forgetting the rising panic in my chest at what could happen if I don't find this fucking recipe. My mother's entire livelihood is on the line, as is my own. I couldn't afford college without Maxwell and his fucking empire.

"She's asleep," River whispers, leaning into me as he gets comfortable. He's been trying to get physically close to me lately and I don't truly know how to feel about it, but while we're all tired like this, I don't have the energy to fight off my emotions. So in a moment that shocks all of us, I think, I bring my arm around River and rest my head on the back of the couch, placing my controller down so I can run my fingers through Raven's hair.

I could seriously get used to this shit. I'm unseasonably warm with them both next to me like this. The broken organ in my chest tries to come back to life, but I tamp it down and blow out a long breath, staring up at the ceiling as I contemplate what to do if we don't find the drug recipe.

"You owe her a fucking apology, Pierce," Phoenix says in a harsh whisper as he stands and comes toward the three of us. He swats at River's hands. River lets go of Raven, and Phoenix lifts her into his arms, cradling her against him with a soft as hell look on his face.

For a moment, we're all staring at her in awe. This gorgeous little bird who's taken us all under her spell. I crinkle my brow and meet a furious glare from Phoenix.

"The fuck for?"

"Think with the head on your shoulders, dumb fuck," River grits out, smacking me upside the head.

"We do no work tomorrow. I bought enough food to treat her to a proper Thanksgiving, so that's what we're doing," Phoenix says as he begins to walk toward the bottom of the stairs. Turning to look at us before ascending, he meets my gaze once more, "You will apologize for the way you treated her today. I won't have it." He heads up the stairs with my girl in his arms and I flop back on the couch, groaning and rubbing a hand across my face.

River is far too silent, but he takes a few deep breaths before he leans on me again, his head resting on my shoulder. I don't ask him to move, and I'm battling whether I want him to or not.

We don't say a damn thing as we stay there in silence for what seems like forever.

"It's okay, Pierce," River whispers.

And though I know he's right, and that he's fought for this his entire life...I gently remove myself from the comfort of him and head toward the guest bedroom to sleep.

I'm not ready to face much more than what I already have this week, but I do know I have to apologize for manhandling Raven if I want her to stay with me and not leave.

Everyone always leaves.

I don't want her to be included in that everyone.

I WAKE WITH A GROAN, rolling over on the uncomfortable mattress as I attempt to bat away the incessant sound of an alarm. It sounds like a damn foghorn with how loud it is, only it's on repeat and practically *in* my ear.

My hand makes contact with skin and I hear a muffled "ouch" before my eyes snap open. I'm met with River's gray eyes, smiling lips, and his phone halfway toward my face. I roll over onto my back and regret it immediately. Riv straddles my stomach and keeps the phone blaring at me.

When I glare at him, he laughs, hopping off of me. He narrowly avoids hurting my dick and getting hit by my swinging fist in the process. I shut my eyes and think of a million things to get my erection to cease its existence.

Baseball. Hockey. Teletubbies. Sperm Whales. My mom in a speedo.

"Phoenix is helping you with your apology, PJ, so you might as well get going. I brought it up for you so you don't have to go downstairs. You're welcome," he winks at me before disappearing down the stairs. His feet sound like jackhammers with how loud they are.

I can hear the pots and pans being used downstairs, and I know Phoenix will be making this meal on his own if we don't get down there and help him. He'll guilt trip us all for not helping and we'll owe him random shit we don't want to owe him.

With that thought in my head, I stand up and fix my sweatpants, looking down and deciding against a shirt.

She'll appreciate the gray sweatpant look, I've seen her social media accounts. Thirsty bitch.

I grin and walk toward the door, grabbing the tray River placed on top of the dresser as I walk out. The fucking hardwood floor is cold as shit, so I make a note to help Rae into some of her favorite fuzzy socks before she exits the room in which I—yep, can confirm—know is a sauna.

Immediately I break out into a sweat with how hot she has this fucking room. I'm tempted to crack a window, but I know

I'm here to begin my groveling, so I simply walk toward the bed. She's curled up into a ball under what seems like a dozen blankets.

"I'll never understand you, Blue," I whisper as I place the tray down onto her nightstand. I sit down on the bed beside her and begin to uncover her sleeping form, one blanket at a time.

Once I finally have her uncovered, I begin to trail my fingers along her exposed and heated skin, from her wrists, up her arms, and toward her face. It takes a few moments, but once I have half of her face exposed, her eyes flutter open sleepily.

I get the most glorious smile from her as she begins to wake. One of relief and adoration.

Doesn't fuckin' take long before it's transformed into a scowl though.

Should have expected that.

She scrambles up to sit cross legged, crossing her arms over her chest and glaring at me. I hold my hands up in surrender as I try to keep my eyes on innocent places. The anger in her eyes makes my dick grow, because I'm sick like that. She's at her most beautiful when she's explosive.

"Brought you breakfast...," I begin to say, fumbling with my words and what to do with my hands. I settle on placing them on the bed near her, gripping the blankets in my fists to keep from leaning forward and taking her in them. "I know I'm a long way from your forgiveness for yesterday, but I do want you to know how incredibly," I swallow back the bile rising in my throat, "terribly sorry I am."

I look up, meeting her gaze and gritting my teeth when I see that her eyes are watery. This is so unacceptable to me, and I know I need to learn to control my emotions better if I'm going to get to keep her. "I'll work better on me, and I'm on Phoenix's last strike list, so in an effort to keep my life, I'll make sure to not be as angry with you in the future. I won't grab you again in anger," I look up and meet her gaze again, swallowing hard once more, my Adam's apple bobbing in my throat. Her eyes follow the motion, and she licks her lips in response. My dick comes right back the fuck to life at full force. I hide the groan behind a hand on my face before meeting her gaze. "I promise to keep my shit together as best as I can, okay, little bird?"

Our eyes meet, and we simply stare for a while, as her hands slowly move to pick at the hem of her sleep shirt–one of the guys' shirts by the looks of it. After what seems like a century of silence, she nods, biting her lip when she looks toward the tray I brought in.

Reaching toward it, I grab the whole thing and place it between us. I only want to break the space between us so I can bring her into my arms and hold her there for eternity.

I lift the lid from the covered plate and watch Raven's expression when she takes in the cinnamon oatmeal with diced apple pieces on top of it. It smells fucking divine, and I can't help it when I grab the spoon and take a bite for myself before getting another spoonful and lifting it up toward Raven's pouty lips. Her whole face is extra puffy in the morning, and since she sleeps like the devil in the heat, her skin is flushed and slick with sweat, which is the sexiest vision in the morning.

I raise a brow when she hesitates to take the bite of oatmeal. I lean forward over the tray and bring the spoon closer to her mouth, my eyes staying on her pretty blues the entire time. Her eyes darken with lust the closer I get, and I hide my growing grin by biting my lip. I could die the moment her lips part for me to feed her, and I nearly do when her eyes roll in the back of her head in pleasure from the taste of the food.

Phoenix is a damned good cook, and if it makes my girl this happy? Fuck yes, I'll keep this dynamic the way it has been.

I lean forward after I watch her swallow and press my lips to hers in a frantic kiss, groaning at the explosive taste of her and the oatmeal mixing together on my tongue.

I'm in fucking heaven and I don't want to leave.

When she clutches at my biceps, I nearly kick the whole tray off of the bed so we can devour each other instead of food, but her stomach growls loudly and I can't help the chuckle that bubbles out of me. Placing a few quick pecks against her lips, I lean back and push the tray closer to her. "Eat up, Blue, Phoenix will want all of our help in the kitchen today."

I wink and press a kiss to her nose as I stand and walk out of the room, hoping I can swing a quick shower to relieve myself of the pressure in my aching cock before we have to deal with Phoenix and his dictatorship.

THE ENTIRE DAY is full of making food in one form or another. Phoenix takes care of the turkey. He does not trust a single soul to handle that bird. His words.

Raven is set at the stove to stir things and make sure nothing boils over or burns.

This leaves River and I to cut up random shit and make rolls. They have to be homemade, Phoenix says.

It takes me until probably three in the afternoon to note this is the first Thanksgiving where Phoenix and Raven don't have their families. That realization has me pausing and staring between both of them, noticing how subdued they are.

Phoenix only barks orders, and Raven hardly looks up from her position at the stove.

It's been River and I communicating all day. I've been belligerent like always, and River has mostly held the conversations and made the jokes–extra dumb to try and draw the tiniest of smiles from our girl.

Our girl? The fuck have I gotten myself into.

I groan and toss the knife I was using to butter some of the bread into the sink, wiping my hands off on a towel as I make my way toward the fridge. I grab a beer and offer one up to Riv, popping the top and taking a long drink from it as I look around at the absolute destruction of this kitchen.

It's a reminder of last year and how Rae and I didn't have this holiday for the first time in a decade. We were spending more of that time in the hospital, and she was beginning to pull away from me even then.

Chugging the rest of my beer, I slam the bottle down and make my way toward Raven, turning on the sound system to an upbeat song on the way. I grab her around the waist, tossing her wooden spoon onto the counter top before spinning her and beginning to dance. It's a quick swing dance, reminiscent of all of the school dances our mothers made us attend.

I pull her into my body, and spin her outward as soon as we make it to more of an open space in the dining room. I see the smile she finally lets free, and laugh when I see how hard she hides it when she spins back into my body.

Phoenix is glaring from the dining room table, but his eyes soften once he sees the smile on Rae's gorgeous face.

River's eyes are alight as he watches, beginning to move his body to the beat as well.

I bark out a quick laugh when he joins us, his hands grabbing onto Rae when she twirls out of my hold once more. He holds her waist and dips her, placing a gentle kiss on her lips and whispering something only she can hear into her ear before pulling her back up.

She's flushed, but the smile on her face is so blinding that I nearly stumble in my made-up dance moves before I grab her again, pulling her into me as the song changes to a slow and romantic beat.

I should change it, but Lookalike by Conan Gray effectively stops my heartbeat.

We listen to the lyrics together, her arms wrapped around my neck, mine around her waist. All I see in this room is her right now, and yet, as River presses himself into her back, he takes up space, but it's not as if he takes it away from her.

No. River makes new space, growing this situation into what could be for us, one of his hands trailing to my hip as the other goes to Raven's head, brushing her hair to one side so he can lean in and press a soft kiss to her neck.

My dick and heart finally work together in this moment, and I'm stunned by what I feel. This is like last night with them both in my arms.

I'm comfortable.

I'm...happy.

I'm home.

I swallow hard and pull back, twisting to go check on the stove since we've left it alone. Phoenix meets my eyes when I go to grab another dish to put shit into, and the sadness there—for me—is annoying as shit, so I flip him off and he shakes his head as he goes back to watching River woo Raven with his not smooth moves.

But even though he stumbles, sometimes on purpose, she's still smiling, though there's a hint of sadness in her eyes when our gazes meet at the end of the next song.

I ignore it in favor of bringing things to the table.

Phoenix has it so we're all at one end of the large oak dining table, with Raven at one end, River and I on her left side, leaving the spot on her right side for him. He made sure we all dressed the part for a fancy dinner party of four.

It's pointless, but no one wants to piss him off today.

As I go to sit down, I watch as Phoenix pulls the chair out for Rae, glaring at River and I when we sit down without waiting for her.

Chivalry has died a quick and fiery death since Raven cut me down last year.

Shit, I'm supposed to be groveling...

Without thinking too much about it, I begin to fill Raven's empty wine glass with a healthy portion from a bottle of red we brought up to cool earlier. When she's sat down, I help get her plate filled, passing her items as she gestures for them and not filling my plate at all until everyone else has had their fill.

See, I can be courteous too, dickhead, I think as I look at Phoenix with a bit of an accomplished smile on my lips.

He rolls his eyes and we wait for Raven to begin eating.

No one says grace.

We're all out of patience for deities here.

They leave us alone, so we leave them alone.

Seems fitting.

Once Raven finally takes a bite of the turkey, a small grin on her face as she looks toward Phoenix, we all begin to dig in appreciatively. It's almost like all of the hard work we put in for this meal has made it tastier simply because it's the reward at the end of our day.

"Mmm," River holds up a finger, asking us to wait for a moment, and when Phoenix and I pause to stare at him, he finishes the bite in his mouth. I try not to notice the little bit of shine on his lower lip after he licks it clean.

He notices me staring and winks before looking around the table. "Did anyone think of anything for dessert? Because we didn't get dessert and that's a fuckin' travesty, guys." He nearly whines, and I roll my eyes.

"Well," Phoenix says, clearing his throat and staring at Raven, his eyes darkening, "I've thought of dessert plenty. So eat up boys, but save some room in your appetite." He winks at Rae once she catches onto what he's thinking, her cheeks growing pink at the innuendo.

"Fuck yes," River says, digging into his food in a complete caveman fashion. Rae is gaping at him when his mouth becomes so full he can hardly chew, much less breathe.

I finish the bite in my mouth and grab his fork and plate, moving it away from him with a pointed glare. "You'll choke and die, dumb ass. Chill. We aren't going anywhere until Sunday at the latest. We have time," I tell him.

He tries to swallow and nearly chokes, confirming my suspicions of his impending doom. I breathe a sigh of relief when he finally empties his mouth, passing his plate back to him with a pointed glare. He nods at my silent plea, and we all go back to eating, Phoenix and Raven eating without much more fanfare.

Their subdued nature brings the mood down as we all think about who we *aren't* having this meal with right now.

My mom would be here, as would Rae's mom, but we are living in a different time entirely. I don't know where the hell my mom is right now, only she's probably doing something Maxwell is requesting of her. She makes the most on holidays, after all.

Once we finish eating, Phoenix orders River and I to clear

the table, and so we do. River has a bounce in his step, and I can clearly see his excitement level through the bulge in his black slacks. I roll my eyes and pat him hard on the back as I pass him, heading back toward the dining room.

"Calm down, brother, or you'll poke someone's eye out with that thing before it's polite to do so."

He barks out a laugh and follows after me, placing his arm around my shoulders as we enter the dining room.

I stop short of where Raven is, stunned at the scene that I find.

raven

TEN MINUTES BEFORE…

Watching Pierce and River leave the room with the rest of the dishes, I'm caught off guard when Phoenix grabs my chair and it screeches across the hardwood. He brings me in close to him and uses his fingers to lift my chin to meet his gaze. His eyes are dark with lust, and I chance a look down to–yep, he's hard. I bite my lip, and Phoenix uses his thumb to pull it from between my teeth.

"Raven, will you be my good girl tonight and trust me to provide you with the pleasure you deserve?" His voice is deep and sultry, and my pulse skyrockets.

I shiver when his hand trails from my jaw to the side of my face, and finally, to the back of my head. His thumb is at the shell of my ear and he strokes it as he brings my head in toward him, a small grin on his face as he notices my entire body going flush from my reaction to him.

I finally nod in response, delayed due to his ministrations of me without doing much. My eyes are heavy lidded now and I know my pupils are blown with lust. They looked so delectable in their suits tonight, and I felt like a princess in my black dress. It helped when Pierce and River danced with me, letting me flit around in the kitchen as if it were an actual dance floor.

I felt cherished for the first time in a while.

Just like I feel every single time Phoenix looks at me the way he's looking at me now, with eyes so heated they could burn right through me if it were possible to do so.

My nipples are pebbled in my dress, a delicious friction happening between my skin and the silk.

Phoenix notices, a grin curling up his lips as he pulls me closer to him, our noses touching and our breaths mingling. My breathing picks up as he brings his free hand behind me to begin unzipping my dress.

"If you're going to be my good girl, I expect you to dress like my good girl, do you understand?" He asks, and I nod, trying not to bite my lip again, since he's asked me to stop countless times now.

I'd rather do as he asks, as that gets me pleasure far sooner than being a brat does.

As he slides the zipper down my back, his lips come to mine in a kiss so promising I clench my thighs together, seeking sweet friction where I need it most. Phoenix notices and pulls back, moving the hand from my hair and placing it on my thigh, pressing my leg down onto the chair to anchor me there.

His chocolate eyes bore into me in command as he manages to bring the zipper to the end. His hand slides up the skin of my back, finding the emptiness there since I skipped the bra tonight.

That information spurs Him on as he pushes the straps of my dress down my shoulders, his eyes burning a line into my skin as it falls down to my waist.

"Up," he grits out, and I stand, his hand at my waist

helping to keep me steady. "Good girl," he murmurs, almost absentmindedly.

I squirm under his gaze, and throw my head back on a silent plea for *something* as he moves his hands onto my dress and pulls it from my body achingly slow. I sense the moment he notices my lack of underwear, and he lets out a curse, his hands stuttering in their movements for a split second. He practically sends me flying with how quickly he lifts me into his arms, my dress falling to the floor at his feet.

Bringing my hand to the back of his neck, I meet his fiery gaze with my own, licking my lips in a clear invitation.

He doesn't see it though. He simply lays me down on the table and I watch as he leans back, his hands tracing along both of my sides in reverence until he's standing up at the head of the table looking down on me. His head snaps up and meets the gaze of the other two who either recently walked in or have been standing there for a while.

"Here's how this goes," Phoenix begins, beginning to take his suit jacket off, laying it across the back of the chair he's standing in front of. "We are a team. We work together. We fight together. We cry together. We *fuck* together." His eyes meet mine when he says the last words, and I shiver.

"Fuck yes!" River shouts out, already half naked with his suit jacket thrown haphazardly on a chair, his shirt nearly all the way unbuttoned when his hands begin to undo the button on his pants.

"Jesus...*what*?" Pierce grits out, his eyes taking me in but also half watching River strip down at lightning speed.

"Not the first time we've done this, Pierce," Phoenix says seriously, looking at him pointedly. He gestures with his hand around the room. "This is the first time anyone has acknowledged the dynamic. We'll discuss more details later on, but for tonight, we're all here to catch a release and treat our princess in the process. She deserves it, and, if we're going to keep doing this, I figure we need to call it as it is."

Slowly, Pierce begins to strip his own jacket and shirt off, and my eyes follow his movements.

My head is laid down on the oak table and my body is becoming slick with anticipation. I'm squirming, and Phoenix places a hand on my hip bone to keep me anchored so I can't move too much. My eyes snap to his and I take a deep breath when I see the fire in his gaze.

The command to do as I'm told.

When I nod, he grins and pats my hip in silent praise before he looks back toward River and Pierce. I follow his gaze and the intake of breath I have is sharp and loud enough for all three of them to snap their eyes to me.

I bite my lip and try not to squirm too much since Phoenix is staring at me right now, my hands reaching out and trying to find purchase on the table. I'm a meal laid out for the taking and I don't absolutely hate it.

Instead, I feel like the most cherished jewel on the planet. A woman with her own group of men to worship her.

The universe hasn't given me much to appreciate, but this...this I can be thankful for.

Having a silent conversation, Phoenix nods at River, followed by Pierce. They shoot into action. Pierce walks to the head of the table and tugs on my ankles, and my eyes go wide in surprise when I slide down until my ass is hanging precariously over the edge.

I'm more surprised when he sits his naked ass on the chair and pulls it up to the table, his hands snaking up my ankles, my calves, my thighs, until they find purchase around my upper thighs and anchor us together.

Finding my eyes, he promises me the world with his before he leans in and presses the faintest of kisses to my clit. My entire body lights up and my hips *attempt* to buck against his hold. He doesn't allow me to move, however. Forcing my legs over his shoulders, he leans in and licks up my center in such a drawn out motion I nearly combust in anticipation.

I'm distracted when Phoenix comes to one side of the table, grabbing my right hand and running it over his now naked and thickened erection. My eyes fly to his as I bite down on my lip. I love all of my guys' dicks, but Phoenix's happens to be the one I admire the most.

My thumb caresses the sensitive area around his tip, and I have to bite my lip when he throws his head back on a groan. I arch my back, and I can hear it when Pierce presses a finger into me, I'm that soaking wet. His tongue flicks my clit, and my eyes roll back from the sensations.

River finally joins us, coming up on my left and leaning over the table to take one of my nipples into his mouth. I throw my head back so fast I smack it on the wood. Phoenix looks down at me and raises a brow.

"Careful, Red," he says, "we're the only ones doing the banging tonight."

Pierce pulls his mouth away from my center, raising a brow at Phoenix, "Horrible joke. Leave those to River."

River pops off of my breast, letting go of the other one he was massaging. I glare around at the guys as they begin to bicker, and in a so-not-me move, I take my hands and begin to move them across my own body.

By the time I have one hand on my breast and the other nearly at my pussy, all the boys are silent and watching me in a mix of anger, shock, and lust. I bite back my grin as I finally drag a finger into my wet folds, closing my eyes as the sensation of them watching me, mixed with my own ministrations, becomes a bit too much.

"Red," Phoenix grits out, reaching out to grab both of my hands, "You aren't being a very good girl right now."

My eyes pop wide and I'm suddenly worried he won't allow me the pleasure he promised. He grins. Realizing the panic in my eyes, he leans down and whispers into my ear. "If you start acting like a slut, I might have to call you one."

My entire body flushes and heats at his words. The dirty chuckle he lets out makes my hips buck, seeking any sort of relief I can find.

"Seems Red here likes being called a little slut, and I think that fits her right now. What do you boys think?" He says, bringing my hands together and binding my wrists with the tie from his suit. My breathing is heavy now, the background noise to the boys shuffling around as they descend on me like a pack of ravenous wolves.

I'm incredibly hot right now, and the wetness between my thighs is becoming far more obvious to me. I lick my lips as I look between my boys, hoping one of them will crack and help me anytime soon.

"Pierce," Phoenix barks out, snapping his fingers and pointing somewhere I can't see. With Phoenix holding my wrists by the tie, it's hard for me to see much unless I want to strain my neck uncomfortably.

I hear the chair at the head of the table creek right before Pierce's hands land on my hips as he strokes my skin. "You're lucky I like you, Nix. I'm about to bust six ways from Sunday and she looks like the best meal I'll ever have."

"There's a condom in my suit jacket," Phoenix says, his voice taking on an edge of anger, "Suit up and fuck our girl until she's on the edge, but don't let her come. Her punishment for trying to take pleasure when it's ours to take tonight." The grin Phoenix shoots down at me has me squirming again. He shakes his head, leaning down to nip at my ear lobe.

"What do you want me to do, Nixy boy?" River asks. His voice is light, but I hear the thinly veiled restraint in his tone, goosebumps rising on my skin.

River may be playful, but he can be as much of an alpha male as the other two when he wants to, and that's generally in the bedroom.

"Straddle her chest and stick your dick down her throat," Phoenix barks out, pulling back from me and shooting a pointed look at my wrists before meeting my eyes again. "Come down that pretty throat and show her who owns her. Got it?"

My eyes are wide, and breathing becomes hard when River remarks in the affirmative, climbing onto the table and straddling my chest. Pierce has finally sheathed himself in the condom with his hands on my thighs, positioning himself at my entrance.

When River presses his dick to my lips, my eyes fly up to meet his storm gray eyes, and I'm lost in them as he looks down at me with so much affection that I'm caught off guard.

Sure this is sexy as hell, but to be doted on at the same time? My heart is getting involved now and I don't know if I love or hate it here anymore.

I look over toward Phoenix as he grabs a chair and sits off to the side of the dining room, taking us in as he reaches for his own dick. I see the glistening drop of pre-cum on the top. My tongue darts out at the sight and I *accidentally* lick the tip of River's dick.

He hisses out a breath, and Pierce groans when he runs a finger through my wet folds, finding me dripping for all three of them.

I'm aching for someone to fill me somewhere at this point. I don't care where they fill me, only that they do it soon.

"You good, sweet girl?" River questions, running a finger along my lips as he strokes his dick a few times, watching my eyes for consent as I nod to him. "Alright, baby girl, open wide and show me how much you love being owned."

I open my mouth and let my tongue trail out over my bottom lip, saliva coating it in order to help him enter me easier. I see him look back at Pierce for a second. River shoves his dick into my mouth at the same time Pierce shoves his into my cunt.

Bliss.

That's the only feeling I'll remember from this moment on.

My body becomes theirs as River pushes as far down my throat as possible and Pierce pushes so far into me our pelvic bones meet. I twist my hips, seeking more, but suddenly Phoenix's hands are gripping the restraint on my wrists and he's holding me hostage, his eyes boring into mine as Pierce and River pull out and push back in again.

My eyes roll to the back of my head at the sensation, but I make sure to twirl my tongue around the crown of River's dick while it's pulling out again. He bucks his hips and slows at the same time, while curses leave his lips.

I squeeze around Pierce, my wetness coating him. He enters me easier with each thrust, curses leaving his mouth as often as River's. I attempt to see both of them, hoping they're working through their own shit, but Phoenix leans down and presses a kiss to my forehead before pressing his lips near my ear and talking, seeming unbothered by River's dick being so close to his face as well.

"You take their cocks so fucking good, don't you baby girl?

You gonna let them use and abuse your sweet little body while you lay out on this table like a fucking meal for them?" He grins when I nod, gripping my wrists a little tighter in his hold. My nails scratch at his skin when I grip at him, my hips twisting and meeting Pierce with each thrust, and I force myself to go slack jawed for River to enjoy the back of my throat as he enters me the next time.

"Holy fuuuuuck," River groans out, and my pussy clenches at the sound.

"Shit," Pierce grits out, his hands holding firmer onto my hips as he begins to slam into me now, uncaring for how it moves River deeper into my throat, or how my body slides across the now sweat-slick table.

Phoenix lets out a little growl, and I squirm, clenching around him again. "You're our little plaything right now. Our pretty little slutty princess with not a care in the world but to milk our cocks dry, aren't you?" When I don't respond, he bites at my ear lobe, and my breathing hitches. "Answer me, Raven."

When I dip my head in answer, he chuckles all low and dirty again. He leans up, probably looking at the other two boys. "Our little slut wants to milk you both dry, so I guess you better use her little body as best as you can right now."

"*Holyshitballs*," River moans when my tongue traces the vein at the underside of his shaft, and when my eyes meet his shocked ones, his hips stutter. "Pierce, I c-can't..."

"Yeah, yeah, with you Riv," Pierce grits out, moaning when my walls clench around him. My hips circling and trying to find friction for myself. I know they won't let me come, though, so I'm left seeking nothing as Pierce thrusts into me faster, gripping my hips harder.

"Ah, shiiiiiit–" River groans, his dick hitting the back of my throat before his cum spills down it. His hands are on the top of my head, holding me down, and the act alone makes my pussy walls clench again.

Pierce moans out a string of expletives as he finishes inside of me, filling the condom as he rocks into me. My clit finally gets the stimulation it needs, and I chase it, only for Phoenix to grip my hands tight again and glare down at me, shaking his head when our eyes meet.

"Off," he says, looking at both River and Pierce. Once they both leave my body, each of them placing sweet kisses to my lips as they go to sit on their unoccupied chairs to catch their breathing, Phoenix sits in the chair at the head of the table and slides me down the table, his hands firmly on my hips once I make it to the edge. "Now, you're going to ride me until you come so hard you can't see straight. Got it, Red?"

When I nod eagerly, because holy fuck I need to come soon, he brings me closer to him. I panic for a second but finally notice he's wearing a condom. He must have put it on when I was otherwise occupied. Phoenix holds himself steady before sliding slowly into me. Once he's in a bit, he brings both of his hands under my arms and up my back, and his hands sit firmly on my shoulders.

Our eyes meet, and he pulls me down roughly. My head is thrown back in pure fucking bliss, and I let my eyes close as I get lost in the sensation. I rock my hips each time I come down on his shaft, and I'm frantically trying to sink back onto his cock each time he pulls out.

It's a beautiful and cruel sense of pleasure Phoenix gives to me tonight. He's anchoring me to him, placing sweet kisses and love bites along my skin.

"Fucking ride me, Red," he grits out, groaning when I rock down on him again. My undulating hips cause my clit to hit the right spot to light me up from the inside out. Phoenix moves his hands down to my hips and holds me there, rocking up into me and spurring me on to undulate my hips again.

"Fuck, you fuck like a porn star, my little slut," he groans out, his head pressed back against the chair now as he looks down between us. He snakes one hand between us, pressing against my lower stomach in order to feel himself as he thrusts up into me. He lets out the loudest moan I've ever heard from his lips.

"Holy hell," is whispered, but I don't know if it's from River or Pierce.

Phoenix notices how close I am and puts a hand around my throat, flexing his fingers until he can sense how hard my pulse is thundering. He thrusts up into me faster, but makes sure our bodies grind against my clit in the best of ways as he does so. "Your pleasure is ours, Red. So fucking come for me like a good little slut." My eyes shutter closed at his words and he grits out, "Fucking come for me."

That last command has me exploding all over his cock, my movements stuttering and falling so far out of rhythm that I simply let Phoenix control me from that point as my body moves with the waves which take me over. I hear muttered curses closer to me, but all I experience is complete warmth as I ride out the intense climax. Phoenix grits out a curse as he finds his own release, and the warmth of him filling the condom inside of me. My pussy walls clench again, which drags another curse out of him.

It takes a while to catch my breath, and I lean my body onto Phoenix's chest, unable to move at this point. It's intoxicating to be this comfortable with him. I let his heartbeat control my own as we all catch our breathing, and when I finally come down, I open my eyes to find River sitting in a chair next to me, Pierce sitting next to him. They both look like they could use a damn shot of whiskey and a good night's sleep.

I let my lips stretch up into a sleepy grin, and River lets out a loud laugh, his head thrown back against the chair.

"Hey sweet girl," I look up to meet Phoenix's gaze, his lips pressing against mine sweetly before pulling me away from him. Strangely, I'm a tad stickier than I thought I would be after this encounter. "These idiots didn't give a warning before...coming over here."

"No," Pierce groans out, wiping a hand over his face. "Seriously, Nix, leave the bad jokes to Riv."

"Shut up, my jokes are *not* bad!" River yells, slapping a hand upside Pierce's head.

I blink, trying to understand what the hell they're going on about. I look between Phoenix and I, seeing I'm not only covered in sweat, but the unmistakable sticky white substance. I throw my head back on a silent groan, wishing I could yell at them. Since I can't do that, I hold up both of my hands and meet the gaze of all three boys before I flip them off with both hands.

All that does is make them laugh heartily while Phoenix stands with me in his arms. We begin our near-nightly ritual of him bathing me, as well as brushing and braiding my hair.

It may not be perfect between all of us, but for right now I can allow myself to bask in the pleasure and contentment of the moment.

Something tells me we need tonight to keep us going for the future...

Pierce,

You're all gone now. The kids we grew up with.
Jimmy.
My mom.
You...
I see your mom every once in a while, but she doesn't look like she wants to talk to me, so I don't approach her.

I know she's angry with me for sending you away like I did. I also know she's hurting because her best friend is gone, though they weren't very good friends near the end, were they?

You won't see this, but I thought I'd write one anyway. Seems fitting.

Here's to 19, I guess.

Raven

CHAPTER TWENTY-SEVEN

phoenix

I wake up with an aching heart, and I know it's because I chose to sleep alone. I left the other three to cuddle in the large bed in the master bedroom, and I came down to sleep alone on the couch again.

It's like I've betrayed my family by not mourning them, and spending the first Thanksgiving without them with another family of sorts.

A found family, but a family nonetheless.

My heart is full for the first time in forever, and yet I'm full of guilt as well.

Like a damn traitor.

Once I manage to get my ass up, I meander around the kitchen and finish cleaning up what the other two doofuses didn't. I busy myself by making a breakfast scramble with what was left of the turkey last night, some eggs and veggies. It's a lonely task, sure, but I like to be alone with my thoughts more than the others do, though I remember Raven telling me at some point she enjoyed time alone just as much.

Not that she knew she was telling *me* that, but I know it anyway.

Half an hour after I've been down in the kitchen, the food is ready and I hear her soft footsteps. The guys could never be as quiet, even if they tried. I look up and watch as Raven makes her way into the kitchen, bright purple fuzzy socks on her feet, and her frame covered in one of River's hoodies. I smile for her as she makes her way around the counter toward the plates of food, and hold the one for her above her head.

She raises a brow at me and yawns, reaching up for the plate, which I hold higher.

I move my free hand to my lips and press a finger to them, grinning when she rolls her eyes.

She moves up onto her toes and steadies herself with her hands on my shoulders in order to place a soft kiss to my lips.

Wrapping my free arm around her waist, I place the plate down and pull her in with the other, anchoring her head in the position I want her as I deepen our kiss. Our lips ply each other with such gentle commands and I melt into her. A soft groan leaves me when her fingers dig in more. My tongue darts out to lick the seam of her lips and when they part for me, my heart soars at her open trust.

We simply stand there in the middle of the kitchen, exploring each other with our tongues, softly asking each other to open up in this moment.

Nothing has to be said when we can read the body language of the other, and right now? We're both relaxed and luxuriating in the silence provided to us.

Mine by choice. Hers...not so much.

I pull away, a little breathless, and grin at her, placing a soft parting kiss to her lips before placing one on the end of her nose. "Okay, now you can eat," I tell her gently, gesturing to the plate.

She nods and smiles bashfully, pulling herself away from me and grabbing her food. She plants herself on a stool at the island and begins to dig into her food. I commend myself on the taste when she closes her eyes and tilts her head back in silent pleasure.

My dick may or may not grow at the sight, and I may or may not have to adjust it to keep from having to take action on it.

Not the time.

Once I've finished my own plate, the other two come bounding down like a hoard of fucking elephants and I plant myself on the living room couch, making it my personal mission to finish going through the boxes in Raven's house today. We have two days left here, and we can't waste them.

Maxwell is going to murder someone if we don't find this recipe, and I don't want to be the lucky one chosen for the task.

Eventually, Raven joins me, and we spend the next couple of hours going through a dozen or so boxes in silence. River and Pierce join at some point and we simply push ourselves to keep going.

The silence would be unnerving, but the tension in the room could burst if we were to speak even once. Which River finds absolutely necessary to do when he stands up, stretching his lithe body and groaning loudly when he pops his neck.

"We aren't going to find this shit, guys. Let's take a break," he pleads, looking around the room and not finding any sympathy at this point. "We need to talk about Christmas, anyway. What're we gonna do? I don't wanna go home."

"Riv," Pierce tries to say, but River continues on.

"Y'know they'd put me in a monkey suit just to sit next to him, so let's like...stay here. It's not too much of a hardship for us to hang like this again, yeah, RaeRae? It's so quiet."

I grunt and stand up, tossing the last paper from the last box in my general vicinity. Stretching, I look around, trying to find an excuse to get me out of this fucking house for a moment to myself.

"See, even Nixy boy is getting up. This is p–" River says, but he's interrupted by Pierce.

"Riv, shut the fuck up, you insensitive airhead."

"Shutting up," River says, looking wide eyed at me when I glare at him.

Raven is staring at all of us in confusion, and I realize she doesn't know my story. I was less involved in therapy than she was, at least in a group setting, so she knows nothing.

Well, she knows some things...

I stop that thought and make it toward the front door, putting my boots and coat on before walking outside. Without another destination, I make it up the walkway of Pierce's mom's house.

It's so destitute over here, but the stench went with the trash when Pierce cleaned the house obsessively. The door's unlocked, so I head inside and make my way toward the fridge, grabbing the last beer which was stashed here from who knows when.

Popping the top, I take a swig as I remove my coat and toss it on the counter.

I'm so epically lonely at the moment, and it seems like being here with those I consider my best friends, and our girl, are able to ostracize me sometimes. Though River means nothing by it, he easily forgets the fact that we're all effectively orphans, aside from Pierce whose mom shouldn't be allowed in his life at this point.

Finishing the beer, I lean against the counter and look out of the window above the sink, trying to wrack my brain for where someone would keep a fucking drug recipe that was stolen nearly twenty years ago. Or why someone would steal it in the first place.

Surely running a drug trade isn't a childhood dream of many people, if any at all.

Maxwell Langston aside, that is.

Shaking my head, I kick my leg at a cabinet, roaring out in anger and punching the counter top with both of my fists. I hiss at the pain, shaking my hand out and twisting to find a towel to cover the blood from the new split in my knuckles.

It's as I'm holding a paper towel to my hand that I see it.

It's so inconspicuous, you wouldn't know it was there if you weren't looking as hard as I have been.

I lean forward toward the papers on the fridge and snatch up a full blown scientific report from behind an innocent looking recipe.

Now, I'm no science major or anything–thank god–but I do believe not a single soul uses ecstasy in their day to day food items. Nor do I think people need a full tox-screen for their recipes, either.

I toss the paper towel in the trash and grab my coat as I book it out of there, practically falling on my ass to get across the road toward the group.

Raven jumps out of her skin when the door slams against the wall, a picture frame falling. I make a mental note to pick it up later. Pierce and River look up with wide eyes and already defensive stances.

I hold the paper up with a wild look in my eye, I'm sure.

My heart is pounding in my chest and I nearly double over to try and catch my breath.

"I," I huff out, inhaling deeply before continuing. "I found it. I found Rapture."

"SO, is anyone going to point out the fact that Pierce's mom had it?" River says, although none of us needed to point it out. We were all thinking about it for the last three hours as we poured over the paperwork.

Again, not a science major, none of us are. I look up and meet his gray eyes, raising my brow at him as if to ask why he needed to voice the obvious.

"I'm just saying," he says, lifting his hands in surrender, "it's suspicious. Is Maxwell hiding more shit? Like, we thought he only wanted R–"

"Shut it," Pierce says, glaring at him.

All three of us agreed to keep that a complete secret from Raven for now, not wanting to overwhelm her more than she already is. So for now, we go with the fact Maxwell knew Everlyn from a while back, but we don't tell her their true connection. Though none of us know the full story anyway, so it's not like we're hiding too much from Raven.

River flops back against the couch and runs a hand across his face, groaning before yawning. It's nearly midnight and we've been trying to understand what's on this lab report.

"My contact in the city can figure this out. I'll bring a copy to him once we get back into town," Pierce says, placing the paper down onto the coffee table and leaning back against the couch as well. "For now, what do we do about Raven and

Maxwell? He wants to talk to her, but honestly, I don't want her around him."

Raven shoots up out of her seat and grabs her notepad from the table, glaring at Pierce before furiously writing something.

River laughs, pointing at Pierce. "Bro, you really need to stop trying to dictate her."

"She ran me around our whole fuckin' lives, dickhead! I'm allowed to protect her right now!" Pierce shouts, glaring between River and the furiously writing Raven.

Rae shoves the paper at me and plants her hands on her hips, glaring at Pierce as she waits for me to read her note out loud.

I grin and shake my head, looking at the paper. I laugh before reading it aloud. "Look here, you shithead, I don't care what you want. I care what works for the group. If I'm to be a part of it–your words by the way," I grin when I meet her eyes. Looking down, I start to read the rest of it, "I get a fucking say so. If you want your dick sucked by me ever again, you'll let me make my own choices. And I *choose*," I put emphasis on what she underlined, "to be a part of this, too."

When I finish, I look up to find Raven nodding as she wipes tears from her eyes. The tears are my undoing. I grab her around the waist and pull her into my lap, wrapping her up in my arms protectively. "We get it, Red. We just want to keep you safe, even if the dickhead is a dictator about it."

"Who came up with the word dictator, and was it a literal translation?" River says, catching us all off guard for a second.

Raven's shoulders shake in silent laughter and I grin, placing a kiss to the crown of her head.

Pierce is silent, looking between us all before his eyes soften when they meet Raven's pretty blues. He bobs his head and runs a hand over his face before he leans forward, elbows on his knees and hands clasped together. "If you want to help us run things, I guess you'll need to do the actual secretary job for Alpha Mu. Yes," he holds his hands up when Raven shoots a glare his way, "I know I created this bullshit situation so you were demeaned, and I'm trying to make up for it. When we get back to CU on Sunday, we'll spend more time at Junk. I don't like the idea of you being out at the frat house anymore. Too much bullshit going on that I don't want you around."

When I dip my head in agreement with him, Raven chews her nails for a moment, leaning back on me while she thinks.

Eventually, she nods.

"How will we explain that shit to Maxwell, though?" River asks.

"I'll tell him we're keeping his d–" Pierce clears his throat, "I'll let him know shit's going missing or something. I dunno. We keep most of our shit at junk anyway, so we'll make up some bullshit."

"We could," I interject, "just tell him some frat boys are fucking up and we don't want to go down like the previous prez."

"We'd need to name names for that to work," Pierce says, although he does look as if he likes the idea.

Raven reaches for her notepad and writes a few words down, handing the pad to Pierce.

He looks it over and nods, meeting her eyes for a few seconds.

"She said we have plenty of people to send to the gallows."

I get chills along my arms. I didn't know how absolutely ruthless Raven could be. She seems so meek all of the time–and not only because she can't speak. Her entire demeanor is enough to make anyone pause, but no one is threatened by her.

Until now.

"Fuck yeah, RaeRae," River says, holding out a fist to fist bump her with. He hoots in excitement when she meets his fist with her own. "Brutal. I like it."

"Well it's settled," I say, brushing hair away from Raven's neck so I can place a soft kiss to the back of it. "She'll take up her mantle as the Alpha Mu Secretary, and we'll appease Maxwell with how *involved* we get with this process."

"We can't let Rapture out," Pierce murmurs, grabbing the paper to look it over again. "Just a feeling."

"No shit, Sherlock," I mutter, earning a glare from him and flipping him off in response. I stand, helping Raven sit down on the couch when I vacate it. "Listen, I'm going to get our shit packed up so we can leave early on Sunday. Finals prep begins next week, so we gotta focus on that. Failing is not an option," I grit out, shooting a pointed look to a protesting River.

"Alright. I'll shoot a text to my contact and set up a meet with him sometime next week." Pierce says, placing the recipe down on the coffee table and pulling out his phone.

"What do you want Rae and me to do?" River says, looking from her to Pierce to me in question.

"You can help me pack. I'm not doing it alone. C'mon, you two." I wave them up, and Raven looks at a serious Pierce before nodding and shuffling to her feet, though I only just sat her back down.

THE NEXT AFTERNOON, we're lounging around watching movies and playing games. Simply existing, because fuck we deserve to do that sometimes.

We're all mentally exhausted from this trip.

I'm pretty sure River is asleep with his eyes open as he watches Pierce and Raven battle it out in Mario Kart for the hundredth time.

He wasn't lying. He can't win against her, much to my own amusement as I watch him lose time and time again.

At first, I thought he was letting her win, but he sucks and won't admit it.

"Oh come the fuck on!" He bellows, tossing the controller and glaring at Raven before snatching her up and pulling her to straddle him. "You're a fuckin' cheat, Blue. Admit it!"

She shakes her head, her eyes alight with laughter as her shoulders shake. She grins wide when he goes to grab her shirt, lifting it so he can tickle her. Squirming, Raven reaches for me and I hold my hands up in surrender, shaking my head as she throws a pout my way.

"No one will help you now, Rae," Pierce grunts out, cupping his junk with one hand as he tickles her side with the other. Her knee nearly came into full contact with his balls, and though I would have paid tons of money to see it, I don't want him bitching about it for years, either.

Quick as a damn snake, River reaches out and grabs her, pulling her onto his body and wrapping himself around her like a cocoon.

"I've got you, RaeRae," he says, grinning at Pierce, "I won't let the big bad wolf get you!"

"The fuck you call me?" Pierce barks out, readying himself to lunge at them both.

Before this can turn into a threesome—or moresome—Pierce's phone rings. It's so loud it's blaring through my skull more than my ears at this point, and I reach out to grab it before he can, my brows furrowing and my stomach sinking at the name flashing on the screen. I hold it out to Pierce, who has become somber at the ringtone alone. He must have set a special one for Maxwell.

He stands up and answers with a gruff, "Yeah?" before he disappears up the basement stairs.

"Buzz kill," River mutters, placing a kiss on Raven's cheek. Her eyes are on the stairs, though, her own brow furrowed in concern.

She doesn't get it yet.

I lean down over both of them, brushing hair from her face as I meet her gaze. "Go to him," I whisper, helping to untangle her from River's hold.

When my eyes meet his, he nods in agreement, helping her up and patting her on the ass as she walks away. She looks back and shoots a playful smile his way, but it quickly disappears when she sees that even River has grown serious.

Riv and I watch her ascend the stairs, and once she makes it to the top he turns to me and runs a hand along his jaw.

"Shit's about to hit the fan, isn't it?"

I smile ruefully. No words needed when the obvious is staring us in the face.

CHAPTER TWENTY-EIGHT

raven

Walking toward Pierce seems like a death sentence right now. I don't know what the hell is going on with Maxwell or why the head of the school is more interested in two kids from this small town than anyone else. He could have picked anyone from that school or the legacy kids from the frat.

What the hell do Pierce and I have to do with Maxwell Langston?

I keep my feet light, trying to catch on to the conversation he's having with Maxwell in the downstairs office.

"She doesn't know yet, Langston," Pierce mutters, and my hackles rise.

He's talking about me. What don't I know?

"She doesn't *need* to know yet. It's better for me if she doesn't know," Pierce grits out, and I hear him shuffle some papers before I hear a thud on the desk. He must have punched it. "I only just got her to trust me again, so why the fuck would I let her know you're her fucking father? She thinks her father died when she was five years old!" He bellows the last part.

The entire world falls off of its axis again.

I push my way into the room, my arms crossed and tears already falling down my cheeks as I glare at Pierce, his entire body stiffening when he sees it's me that's entered after him.

Our eyes meet, and he swallows hard, his face visibly paling. "Maxwell, I have an emergency, I have to go. I'll see you next weekend. Friday afternoon, yep. Got it. Bye." Pierce hangs up and slowly sets his phone down on the desk, pushing up from it in what seems like slow motion. He's panicking, as he should be.

I hold my shaking hand up, blinking back more tears and failing as I meet his green eyes.

"Raven, listen–" he says, but I shake my head quickly, taking a deep breath to steady my beating heart.

"Rae, please," he moves toward me, but I back up, my back pressing into the wall behind me, "listen, babe."

I glare at him when he uses the pet name, and he stops in his movements again, holding his hands up in surrender when I point at him, followed by the floor, demanding he stay the fuck put. I might murder this man right now, seriously.

"Please listen," he says after a few moments of silence, and his voice breaks on the words, shaky with the fear he rightfully should possess right now.

I shake my head and look at the floor, my breathing so hard I may pass out. After a few moments of the tears falling and me realizing I'm losing the battle, I shoulder past him and grab a piece of paper and a pen. I furiously write on it, but it's one word. It's the only word I need to write.

Explain.

When he reads it, Pierce dips his head and sits down behind the desk once more, and I curl up on the corner of the couch, as far from him as I can manage without leaving the room. I fold my arms under my chest and keep my eyes down, not wanting to watch him. I don't want to watch him break my heart.

"When I was fifteen," he says, and I can hear him swallow before he begins to tap his foot nervously, "when I was fifteen, I found my mom overdosed at the kitchen table. Some stan was sitting next to her eating my fuckin' cocoa puffs, and she was near death. He was too high to notice...but he never was there for her anyway."

Pierce inhales a deep breath and lets it out before continuing. "I knew mom was on some shit. Started noticing it when I was twelve, when she kept leaving me alone more and more. Well, that guy purposely injected ma with more than she could handle so he could have a *conversation* with me." Pierce puts the word conversation in air quotations.

I nod, looking back down and examining my fingernails. I don't want to pick at them, but that's what I do to keep my mind focused.

"Well, that conversation was to let me know that I was officially on Maxwell Langston's payroll. He'd keep my ma nice and happy and doped up to her content, so long as I kept watch on someone for him. That someone, Raven, was you."

My gaze snaps to his, and I tilt my head, my brows furrowed in confusion. I gesture with my hand for him to go on, bringing my thumbnail to my lips and biting down on it nervously as I await whatever fate Pierce is about to seal me into.

"You see, nearly twenty years ago...he and his wife were having problems with their families. They'd caught on to

Maxwell running drugs around the school, but instead of stopping, Maxwell took his *very* pregnant wife away from them. When it was time for them to deliver the baby," Pierce inhales once more, and tries to get me to meet his eyes. I won't. My stomach is fucking swirling with fear right now. "Well... Maxwell's sister took the baby from the hospital, as well as the recipe for a drug he'd been working on for so long to perfect."

I nod along while he talks, trying to wrap my head around where this is going. When it goes silent, I look up to see Pierce staring me down in absolute pity, which I hate, so I gesture for him to keep going again, uncaring of the tears falling down my cheeks now.

"Raven, that baby was *you*," he says in an almost whisper.

I'm shaking my head halfway through the sentence. My entire life changes with those words, and I refuse.

I refuse, I refuse, I refuse!

I stand up and shake my head, going to exit the office to escape this information, but Pierce is there in an instant, grabbing me and pulling my shaking form into him. My head rests in the center of his chest, and he places a hand on my head, massaging my scalp as I let the tears flow.

"Maxwell Langston is your father, Raven. You're his heir. You are the one who inherits his bullshit kingdom and all that's inside of it. Something that I," he pulls back, holding my wet cheeks in his hands as his eyes flit between mine, "refuse to let happen. You don't deserve this, Raven, and I've been trying to protect you from it."

He leads us to the couch when my legs shake like they might buckle on me, sitting down and then cradling me in his lap. He rubs my arm while he continues to talk. "I can't talk for the other guys, because they came on for their own reasons, but when Maxwell saw how close we were, he demanded I provide him with information on you. He wanted to know you, so that when you came to CU this fall he'd be able to manipulate you into his life, and throw you into the fold so you could take over for him eventually.

"You weren't supposed to know this until you graduated college. If nothing else, he did want the best for you," Pierce whispers this last part. Funny. It seems to me like Maxwell is mostly concerned with his drug empire over anything else. "Rapture was supposed to be his big break. The one drug that would continue to make him money. It was new and extremely effective. Highly addictive, too. Everlyn, his sister and your aunt, stole it from under him, not wanting anyone else to get hurt. The trials of that drug, in the beginning, were so badly done that five people died in one night. Maxwell didn't care. He got to work making a new batch without any real research being done. He simply chalked it up to idiot college kids and made a new batch.

"Everlyn destroyed the new batch, stole the recipe, and took you from the hospital in the dead of night. Priscilla, your biological mother, was high as a kite in the hospital and Maxwell was in the lab creating another deadly batch of Rapture. Everlyn and her husband David made it out unscathed with you, and Maxwell lost track of them for five years. He was furious, by the way. Hired guns and everything along the way. There's so much more to that than I know from the time I've spent with him...," Pierce leans down and presses a soft kiss to my forehead, breathing me in as he tries to calm both of us down. His breath along my skin calms me, and I press my palm to his chest so I can try and regulate my heartbeat with his.

"It's so much better that you grew up with Everlyn, I promise. Priscilla Langston is a bitch from hell and the Devil is glad to be rid of her, too." His joke falls flat for me, but I lean into him, realizing he's trying to save us both from the pain that's involved with this.

My entire world has crumbled in on me, and to learn that my biological father only wanted information on me for the drug itself? That's some absolute bullshit.

I wasn't important at all. Being made an orphan didn't get him to come out and get me. Though I guess the scholarship now seems like his way of fixing the situation.

"We have a meeting with him on Friday. I don't know what he wants, but it didn't sound good. I didn't let him know we had the recipe yet," he says, pausing as he thinks. "I want to see his hand before I show him my own cards, y'know?"

I nod, looking up to find his eyes on mine. I chew my lip for a moment before leaning up and pressing my lips to his in a soft kiss; a promise that I'm here with him. It only lasts for a few seconds, and I slide from his lap, fixing my clothes and wiping my eyes as I walk out of the room.

My brain is scrambled, and I know Pierce wants me to forgive him for the secrets, but it's not only him that had hidden this from me. All three guys hid this information and kept me close anyway. It's going to take a lot more groveling for them to get my full forgiveness.

I head toward my room, beginning to pack my own stuff up as I let my brain wander toward all of the things in my life that jarred me out of blissful happiness with my parents.

My dad dying in a car accident when I was five.

My mom—I guess aunt, actually—moving us soon after.

Three years later, Pierce and his mom entering our lives.

Pierce's mom ignoring him more and more when we turned twelve.

Pierce showing up with bruises and more and more anger in his eyes after he turned fifteen.

My mom getting sick–no. That was a shitty coincidence. Cancer is a beast and it doesn't care about personal relationships.

I toss the last of my clothes into my bag, leaving a comfortable outfit out for tomorrow. Tossing myself onto the bed and looking up at the ceiling, I lull myself into a long and fitful sleep that spans the rest of the afternoon until early morning when we're leaving to head back to school.

While in the car, it becomes so quiet that I find myself drifting off there, too.

It's as if my brain is trying to process all of this information so hard that my body can do nothing but the basics.

So I sleep, and sleep...and sleep.

"YOU'RE FUCKING KIDDING ME!" Pierce yells out, tossing books and notes everywhere. "I can't focus on this shit with Maxwell breathing down my damn neck, Phoenix. Break in or something to fix my grades. I don't care. Right now, I have to fucking go." He races past me, placing a kiss to my cheek–something he's done every single time he's exited or entered a room for the past three days.

We got back to CU late Sunday night, and now it's Wednesday–two days from the meeting with Maxwell. Finals begin next week, so we're all holed up in the loft with books and notes practically everywhere.

Surprisingly, River's notes are the best out of all of ours, and Pierce has none. Phoenix and I are about the same with how meticulous we are. We take so many that the main points are easily missed. So River's notes are the ones we've been studying for the past few days. He has the main points down and we're all able to study without re-reading the entirety of our textbooks.

"Well, alrighty then," River says, looking up from his notebook as we watch Pierce leave the loft. We listen as he starts his bike up, and watch on in silence as he leaves. The gate closes behind him and River speaks up again. "You think he'll bring back pizza?"

I huff out a laugh and shake my head, tossing a pen at River. I look down to my notes in exasperation. I'm so incredibly tired and fried and emotionally just...done.

"I think the Princess needs a break, Riv," Phoenix says, gathering my notes and placing them in a neat pile on the table before lording over me with his body.

My heart may have been shattered with the information I learned last weekend, but my body reacts instantly when both of the guys' eyes shadow with lust and prowl toward me like hungry wolves.

"Ya know, Nixy boy, I think she needs to take the edge off," River remarks. He traces his finger from my ankle up my bare leg until he reaches the hem of my shorts. I shiver at his touch, throwing my head back when Phoenix's hand joins River on the other leg. Both of them mirroring each others' movements.

"Up on the couch, princess, and strip on the way." Phoenix presses a kiss to my cheek, and pats my thigh when I don't move fast enough for him.

I practically scramble my way up to the couch, biting my lip as I strip like I'm in a 'how fast can you strip' competition. River laughs, and I can hear him attempt to strip, but when I look back, Phoenix is shaking his head.

Apparently, this is going to be solely about me.

A rarity around here with three dicks to please.

As soon as I'm naked and sitting on the couch, Phoenix orders River to grab one of my legs and he grabs the other. Meeting my eyes, both guys lower themselves to the floor at my feet. They begin the slowest torture of worship I've ever experienced or imagined. Their fingers trace lines along my skin, and their tongues and mouths lead that path. Though my body is heated, the air hits the now wet parts of my skin and I shiver, throwing my head back on a long exhale.

I'm fucking soaking, and by the way Phoenix lets out a dirty chuckle, he knows exactly what he's done to me in seconds.

"Oh, Red, what should we do to you, hm?" he muses.

"I think we should destroy her in the best way, Nixy boy," River says, his voice louder since he's moved closer. His lips land on my inner thigh as he plants himself between my legs, and I nearly combust when his breath ghosts across my wet folds. My eyes fly to his, and Phoenix makes it harder to breathe when he pushes my other leg wider, splaying me open for both of them. I'd be embarrassed, but when he leans in and presses a kiss to my inner thigh, I forget all reasoning.

"Who owns this pussy, Red?" Phoenix growls out, placing a finger right at my entrance but not moving an inch. My hips buck, seeking friction from one or both of them, and the tiny smirk which graces his lips is so frustrating. I point at Phoenix, my breathing becoming more labored the longer they stare at me. "And?" He prompts. When I roll my eyes, he lands a soft smack to my thigh. I point at River to appease them both. "Good fucking girl."

"Shit," River curses, joining me in watching Phoenix as he shoves two fingers inside of me so quickly I'm pushed against the couch with the force and shock of it. His thumb circles my clit and I throw my head back again, biting my lip when he adds a third finger.

"Fuck, you're so wet," Phoenix mutters, licking and nipping at my upper thigh before he bites down. My eyes fly open once more and meet his darkened chocolate eyes. "Such a good fucking slut, letting us please you like this," he growls out. He bites down on my thigh harder this time, and my hands fly to each of the guys' hair.

River grunts out, moving in to place his lips on my thigh, mirroring the same bite on that side as the other. I try to close my legs, seeking friction again, but they're both stronger than me, so they're able to hold my legs open with ease.

"Do you want to come on my fingers and River's tongue, Red?" Phoenix says, our eyes locking for a moment until I dip my head, letting out a stuttering breath when River's tongue finally meets my center. He circles my clit and enters me right alongside Phoenix's thrusting fingers.

River growls when I hold him steady at my aching center, the wetness creating an obscene sound when Phoenix thrusts his fingers in and out of me, holding me down on the couch with his free arm. Neither man cares that I'm pulling their hair. My hips can't buck up against their movements at this point, and River's free hand goes to his pants, freeing his erection so he can stroke it in time with his exploring tongue.

My eyes roll to the back of my head when he flicks my clit with his tongue in quick succession, and my entire body is alight when Phoenix strokes my g-spot at the same time. My eyes are wide as they meet his gaze, and he leans down to my cunt and slides his tongue right alongside River's. I'm about to combust. River reaches up with his free hand and squeezes my breasts, pinching my hardened nipples between his fingers.

Phoenix strokes my g-spot at the same time River bites

down gently on my clit, sucking it between his lips. I'm a goddamn goner.

I hear River's grunts as he finishes himself, but I am so far gone in my orgasm that it seems like the world itself has faded away into the white spots that invade my vision. My body is rolling on the couch, and I'm rigid otherwise.

I can't see or hear or feel anything but the overwhelming pleasure the boys are now guiding me down from, stroking me inside and out as they ride it out with me.

My breathing is labored when Phoenix climbs to the couch and enters my hazy vision, a grin on his face as he looks at how flushed I am. I try to lean up to get a kiss from him, but he leans down so I can stay there, aftershock wrecking me when River places kisses along my inner thigh before he climbs to the couch as well. I turn my head to smile at him, kissing his lips as effortlessly as I kissed Phoenix, and when I break from them both, I lean my head back on the couch and shut my eyes, letting out a long exhale both guys chuckle at.

"C'mon, Red," Phoenix says, pulling me from the couch a few minutes later. "Let's clean you up. We have a surprise for you tomorrow."

Letter from Pierce

Age 19

Dear Mom,

I've tried to write this a million times to you, and I don't really know how to say this any nicer than I am at this point...

You haven't chosen me since I was too young to notice that you even stopped.

I'm sure there was a last time, but I don't remember it.

So this is my last time.

This is the last time that I provide you with an answer, an excuse, my forgiveness.

The moment that you stopped choosing me, I decided to choose her.

So this is me telling you that I'm done.

I choose her, mom, because she's the only person that's ever truly chosen me.

Goodbye,

Pierce

pierce

As I return home from my solo meeting, I instantly smell sex all over this fucking loft and hate the luck that had me leaving Raven today. My dick is hard, and I have to adjust myself as I enter the kitchen, heading toward the fridge to grab a beer. Once I have it opened, I lean against the counter and look out into the green space the guys and I spent hours slaving over this past spring and summer.

"How'd it go?" River says, sliding up next to me, his bare shoulder pressing against my leather jacket.

I bob my head slightly a few times but then I start to shake it. "We may not be able to get it in time. Hell, the properties of Rapture are so intricate, we may have to travel to get what we need, and I'm not sure we're prepared for that shit right now." I take another long pull from my beer and let my head fall back as I look at the ceiling, praying the answers are there.

"Hmm," River grabs the beer from my hand and takes a sip from it. I raise a brow and glare at him. He places it on the counter in front of me. "Sounds like a road trip to me, Piercey Jackson."

I sigh and shake my head. "I dunno. For now, we have to figure out how to keep that shit from hurting other people on New Year's. Maxwell wants us to throw a party, and I know for a fact we have to be in attendance, too."

"Shit, he's a psychopath," River mutters, spinning and sitting on the kitchen island. My eyes instantly go to his abs and I groan out loud, and his gray eyes meet mine. "One day you'll give in, you know."

"Shut up," I grunt, reaching forward to grab my beer only for my wrist to get snatched by River's hand, his grip so tight his knuckles turn white.

"So we get each other's dicks hard? So the fuck what?" He grits out, his jaw ticking in frustration.

I don't say a word, meeting his fiery gaze with fire of my own.

"Stubborn asshole," he growls out, reaching forward and grabbing me by the scruff of my shirt, pulling me in until we're nose to nose.

"River," I warn.

He doesn't give me more time than that, pressing his lips to mine in a furious kiss that I should push away from. For what reason? I'm not sure. The stubble on his cheeks is intoxicating under my hands, and the forcefulness of his lips against mine make my dick so achingly hard that I forget why I ever stopped this shit.

His tongue darts between my lips without preamble, and our tongues begin dueling for dominance. I don't really care who wins this battle. Unlike with Raven where I want to take, take, take, I relax into River and allow myself to give. I give him my pain, my worries, and all of the vulnerabilities I hide from Rae.

I give him the hurts that I have.

I press myself in between his legs, our growing erections grinding against each other, eliciting a long groan from us at the same time. I move my hands to bracket River's hips, my hands precariously close to his ass as I lean in further to him. It's intoxicating, and he tastes and smells of the ocean. Suddenly, I'm warm all over and using him to quench the thirst he creates in me.

He groans when I rock my dick against his again, pushing his hands into my hair roughly before trailing them down until his hands are at my belt buckle. He doesn't wait for permission, simply undoing my belt buckle and reaching in to grip at my dick.

I release from the kiss and groan, loud, my eyes flying wide in hopes that I didn't wake up the other two. I'm struggling as it is with what's happening, so for them to come in right now would make it ten times worse and–

"Stop fucking thinking, dumb ass," River grits out, pulling my hair and forcing my lips to meet his. The bite of pain from his tight grip on my cock has me jutting forward each time he reaches my tip. The pre-cum leaking out works as lube, making it easier and easier for him to slide his palm along my length. I bite my lip and stare at where he's stroking me, my hands balling into fists at the side.

"Riv," I warn, but he tugs my hair again, my head tilting upwards so I'm looking up at his face.

"Listen here, Pierce," he grits out, his voice low and angry, but the deepness of his voice makes my dick throb. "You," he pulls me forward a bit more by my dick and I'm helpless at his touch, "will let me jerk you off and make you come until you see stars. After we're done, you'll get your happy ass in bed next to our girl and sleep like a good boy."

"Fuck," I groan out, my hands finally finding purchase in

his hips as I thrust forward with his movements, praying I'll last a little longer. I want to savor this in my dreams later.

"Got it?" River says, his eyes meeting mine. I nod, and the grin stretching his lips is so goofy in comparison to the dominance in his voice. "Fuck, your cock feels so good in my hand," he grunts, and I look down between us to see the strain in his sweatpants from his dick. My eyes meet his, and he shakes his head. "Leave it."

I go to object, but he slams his lips against mine again. He starts fisting my cock like it's his full-time fucking job. Within seconds of him rolling his thumb along the tip, I let out a long, low moan into River's mouth. He continues to pump me for all I'm worth as my cum begins to coat his sweatpants. It's such a dirty fucking mess, and I nearly get hard all over again.

We don't say a word as I catch my breath. After a moment, he lifts his sticky hand to his lips and licks all of the cum from it. My heart skips a beat at the action.

"Next time," he says, patting my cheek, "I'll suck your dick. We'll work up to the other shit. Go to bed and sleep your thoughts off, Pierce. We have a big day tomorrow." He gets off of the counter and I simply sit and stare at where he was sitting for who knows how fucking long.

Dunno what just happened, but I can at least confirm that my dick liked it.

I'll keep ignoring my heart for now, though.

EARLY THE NEXT MORNING, I'm already breaking out in a sweat, though it's the first week of December and cold as shit out. I've been working on Raven's surprise for the better part of this week, hoping this will get her to forgive me for the manhandling at the bank.

Small steps, I guess.

I stand up, wiping my brow with my shirt, and am met with those pretty blues when she exits the loft with the other two. Everyone is ready for this meeting to be over with, but we can't rush it, so we've all been on edge.

I glare at the other two. We had a plan to reveal her surprise after lunch today, and I'm met with a shrug from Phoenix and a sly grin from River.

He doesn't want me overthinking last night, so he's distracting me with the one other person who can fill my thoughts.

"Well, now that the cat's out of the bag," I grit out, moving toward Raven and holding my hand out. I smile a little when she grabs it, tugging her toward me and placing a soft kiss to her lips. Spinning her in my arms, I bring her back to my front and place my hands on her hips to rest my head on top of hers.

"This," I point to the newly restored motorcycle–all black, like ours, with purple accents, her favorite color–and walk her close to it, "Is yours."

Her head snaps around and she looks up at me as best she can from the side. She shakes it, glaring at me in the way she normally does.

I roll my eyes, nudging her toward it. "We'll teach you to ride it. If you're going to be part of the crew, Rae, you'll need to learn to ride one of these so you can make a speedy exit like the rest of us." I pat her on the ass to get her to walk forward, laughing when she flips me off for the action.

"Shit," River says when she straddles the back, sans hesitation.

Shit is right.

The guys made sure she dressed properly for bike riding; tight black jeans, her shit kickers, a long sleeve shirt, and the red leather jacket Phoenix found for her a while back. I quickly make my way toward the wall and grab her black helmet, placing it over her head and strapping it on. I flip the visor down and place the key in the ignition, lighting the baby up and stepping back with my arms folded across my chest.

"She can't ride this for a few days," I tell the boys as we watch Raven get used to the weight of the beast between her legs.

I don't hear what River or Phoenix say to my comment, since I'm imagining her naked, splayed out across the seat as I rail her. The sight of River with his dick in her mouth makes the vision more appealing and I have to clear my throat and adjust my dick before I turn to the guys. "What?" I ask, hoping they'll let me in on whatever they were talking about.

"Jesus Christ," Phoenix mutters, running a hand along his face. "I said I'll ride bitch for her for a while. But for tomorrow's meeting, she can ride with you."

"Got it," I mutter, watching as Raven frantically tries to turn the bike off.

River rushes over to turn it off for her, laughing while he takes off her helmet. He grins and helps her off, bringing her in for a quick hug. We all take a moment, looking around the garage.

"Think we have time to teach her today?" he asks, his eyes meeting mine. My heart skips a few beats as I dip my head incoherently. I'm like a bumbling idiot today.

"Alright. Pierce, get dressed properly. We'll take the bikes out for a ride. Should be alright to get her out on the tar, versus the dirt out here." Phoenix points to the door for me to go through, and I follow his orders.

Once I'm changed and back outside, Raven is on her bike, but she's riding behind Phoenix, wrapped around him like a little koala, and I pat her on the hip as I pass by, heading toward my own bike. River walks his bike toward mine, lining us up at the garage door right as it opens and I get mine going. I strap my helmet on and he meets my gaze before I flip my visor down.

"Hey," River says, leaning in to me and trying to keep his voice low, "We good?"

I nod once, gripping the handles of my bike and taking the fuck off. I'm leaving all of them in my dust as I fly through the now open gates of our little paradise and lead them along the dirt tracks.

In about ten minutes, we're in a remote stretch of straight road heading nowhere, and I break off to the side, watching in my mirror as Phoenix gets down and helps Raven get herself situated on the front of the bike.

This is going to be as much of a disaster as the day I taught her to drive a car...

And I'm fucking right. The amount of times she nearly burns the fucking engine out over the next few hours would be hilarious if I hadn't just fixed the fucking thing.

"KEEP. YOUR. FUCKING. FEET. UP. AND. YOUR. HANDS. OFF. OF. THE. FUCKING. BRAKE!" I throw my hands up, growling and kicking at the dirt on the side of the road in full-blown anger at this point. It's not even cute anymore. "Jesus Christ, I don't know how the hell she got her license in the first place, and now I'm trying to teach her to do this shit?"

"Bro, chill, you were probably shit your first time on a bike, too," River says from his perch on top of a guard rail. He's snacking on some sunflower seeds, spitting them in an ever-growing pile at his feet.

I flip him off and look at Raven as she stumbles off of the bike once more, throwing her hands up and glaring back at me.

"YOU GONNA FIGHT ME, PRINCESS?!" I yell across the road, since she's on the opposite side.

She shakes her head and flips me off, and I bark out a laugh.

"PUSSY!" I yell again, and River pelts me with a sunflower seed. "Dick," I tell him.

"Calm the fuck down or Nixy boy will nix you, boy," River winks when my face flushes with arousal and anger at the term of endearment he used last night. I roll my eyes and flip him off, out of words for the moment, which only makes him laugh and pop another fucking seed in his mouth.

"Alright," Phoenix says, "Your fuckin' attitude isn't helping a damn thing. I'll bring her out here some other time. For now, let's get going. We need to be on our toes tomorrow. I don't like what the hell Maxwell has planned."

"We should stop by Alpha Mu for a bit. We haven't been there since Monday and I don't feel right about leaving it this long." I tell him, hopping on my bike and putting my helmet back on my head. River gets a fucking clue, probably the first one in his life, and hops on his own bike.

Phoenix sits his happy ass on Rae's bike and she climbs on behind him, hugging herself close to him, her head resting in the center of his back. He grabs her hands in one of his and shoots me a wink before shooting down the road toward the frat house.

I have a nasty feeling in my gut...

"YOOOO, THE PREZ IS HERE!" Is shouted down the driveway as we pull in. Phoenix knows to pull in after me, and once we're all parked and off of our bikes, we stand in our typical formation, only with Raven between us now.

We shield her as we walk in. She's our precious cargo and we are in agreement that we keep her safest.

I make my way into the house, noting it's fucking trashed to shit, and groan. "Someone clean this shit up," I grit out, looking around at the filthy fucking pigs that are part of this frat.

I'm stopped short with a hand to my shoulder, snapping my head to see the culprit, only to find Phoenix looking at me, tilting his head to his left. My eyes find a goddamn nightmare in the den, looking like he's holding church for a motorcycle club. I fold my arms as I cross the room, raising a brow and tensing my body, ready for a fucking fight.

"All hail the prez and his two stooges!" Jimmy bellows through the room, clearly drunk and high out of his mind.

"Jimmy," I bark out, glaring at him.

Raven stiffens behind me, her hand clutching at my shirt. She's scared of this fuck, and I know what he did to her that last week of school, too. He hasn't gotten off easy since.

"Ahh, PJ! Do you have Raven here, too? I figured she could suck my dick. She was always so eager to try new shit, y'know?" He grins wide, a challenge in his eyes, and fuck if I'm not ready to meet the challenge with my fucking fists.

I don't think on it, I simply barrel forward, my fist slamming hard into his face, and my knuckles splitting when they meet the hard planes of his cheek bone. I grit my teeth in pain but throw my left fist out to hit his other cheek, and I keep fucking going.

A knee to his nuts, a fist to his rib, a foot to his shin, another fist to his nose.

He's so bruised and bloodied–again–by the time I'm done with him. I know he'll look like a walking billboard for the color purple tomorrow. I grin, spitting on his face as he lays curled up on the ground.

"Keep her name out of your mouth, you sick fuck," I tell him, wiping my bloodied hands off on his torn shirt before turning back and grabbing my girl around the shoulder and escorting her out of the house.

Before I exit, I turn around and meet the eyes of every fucker in the room. "That goes for all of you assholes. Hands to your damn selves, and don't look at her. She's ours, and we'll fuck you up worse than him in the future."

River grunts as he shoves me through the front door, holding my shoulders in a tight grip until I'm at my bike. He sets Rae on behind me, and she holds onto me, probably to keep me grounded.

Phoenix places her helmet on her head and meets my eyes, nodding in approval of the ass kicking I gave Jimmy. I nod back, and once he makes it onto his bike, all four of us take off toward Junk once more.

Tomorrow's a new fucking day, and there's not much Maxwell can surprise us with, honestly.

raven

We make it back to the loft right as snow begins to fall, and the flakes are large, angry, and mixed with some hail. I haven't ever been truly grateful for my red leather jacket until now, when all I can feel are little taps to my body rather than the full-on pelting sensation you get when you're walking unprotected through hail.

Once I slide off the back of Pierce's bike, I remove the helmet and set it on the back, turning to walk inside. All three guys let me be, giving me some silence as I walk inside of the loft and go to change. I put on one of Pierce's shirts, using his mahogany smell to ground me.

I don't want to see Jimmy ever again, but he keeps popping up, and I quite honestly don't understand why. I thought he was off to Harvard or Yale or somewhere *not here*. My brain is a cluster fuck, and though I'm starving, I curl up on the bed and hope like hell I can keep myself calm as the memories invade my brain at a steady pace...

"THERE YOU GO, MISS HILL," *the school counselor says, handing me the last of my school records I had asked for. I need to send in my transcripts to Cobalt University by the end of this week, and graduation is only a few days away on Sunday.*

Not that anyone will be there for me, anyway.

I dip my head in thanks, and turn to leave, only to stop short when I see Jimmy Perkins out in the waiting room. He's been hounding me for random bullshit for the last month since I came back from therapy. He knows I don't want to deal with him. I know he went to prom with Patty Gardner, and I don't particularly want a friendship or relationship with him.

I grit my teeth as I exit the room, sighing loudly when he steps up to me anyway, wrapping an arm around my shoulder to escort me out of the room.

"Milkshake, sugar?" he asks, trying to be as kind as possible to me.

I shake my head and pull from his arm, heading toward the front entrance of the school. I want to leave and go home, though home doesn't feel like anything but a wasteland as of late. No one is there, and no one visits me other than doctors who think they can cure my mutism. I'd rather be left alone than deal with anymore 'miracle cure' people.

Once I make it to my car, Jimmy stops me short by holding my door open, though I attempt to slam it closed before he manages to get his annoying as hell fingers involved. I glare through the space between us, even as he's making it shrink.

"C'mon Rae, come have a milkshake with me and we can talk this out. I want you, girl, and Patty's fuckin' off anyway." He pleads with me, pouting like a starving puppy. I roll my eyes

before I nod, hoping this is the last thing I'll ever do with Jimmy Perkins. He smacks an annoyingly wet kiss to my cheek and closes my door right as I turn on my engine.

Now, here's where I realize I could have gone home and not met up with him, but, in true people pleaser fashion...I drive to the diner and wait for him to meet me.

I even sit and enjoy the milkshake he buys me.

What I don't intend to do by spending this short amount of time with him...is to lead him on or give him any indication I want something more with him again.

Later that night, when I'm laying in bed and letting the tears flow for the silence that is now my life, I don't think anything of the rustling or the creaks and groans in the house.

I don't think anything of it when it sounds like the wind is rustling through the leaves outside, or that this house is a tad spooky while I'm all alone.

I do go on high alert, however, when my bedroom door creaks open and a shadow appears. The stench of some sort of smoke and alcohol combination enters the room with the shadow, and I scramble up the bed, trying to find something to fight this beast off with.

"Oh, well hi there, sugar, I'd hoped you'd be asleep for this but..."

I WAKE with my body covered in a cold sweat, warm arms wrapped around me. Tears have fallen but dried on my cheeks, and I cringe at the feel of them on my skin.

I scramble out of the bed as quietly as possible, heading toward the bathroom to splash my face with cold water. A few deep breaths, and I meet my own fiery gaze in the mirror. I stand up straighter, pulling my shoulders back.

I am in control here.

I am safe.

I am consenting to the things happening around me.

I am...happy?

The last one is confirmed when Phoenix enters the bathroom, wrapping his arms around my waist and placing a kiss on my exposed shoulder. "You okay, Red?"

I dip my head and he sighs, knowing I'm not telling the full truth but not wanting to fight in the middle of the night.

"Let's get you a drink. You can go back to bed after, 'kay?" His chocolate eyes meet mine and I nod, following him out of the bathroom.

I notice the bed is occupied by both Pierce and River and grin, rushing to grab my phone and snag a picture of their cuddling forms, Pierce's head resting on River's shoulder, and River's arm wrapped around Pierce's shoulder tightly. Their legs are intertwined and I swear it's the sweetest thing I've ever seen.

I jump when Phoenix grabs me gently by the hand, meeting his eyes as he grins at his friends.

"You'll get your ass handed to you if Pierce finds that picture, so you may want to make copies, sweetheart." Phoenix smiles softly as he leads me down the stairs. I slide onto the bar stool at the kitchen island, watching as he makes me a glass of bourbon mixed with water, raising a brow in question at his choice.

"It'll put you right to sleep. Calms your nerves and all that," he mutters. Once he slides the drink across the counter, he leans his elbows on it and looks at me, tilting his head as he thinks.

"Want to talk about it?" He taps the pad near my shoulder, something we've left there for my own convenience.

I shake my head and look down, sipping the drink and enjoying the fact it doesn't burn as much as usual. I smile a little, pointing at the drink before giving a thumbs up. Phoenix grins and shakes his head.

"PTSD is a bitch, and I feel like mine's getting worse the closer to Christmas we get," he states, his voice so plain and void of pain it makes me furrow my brow at him, wondering what the hell happened.

He shrugs when I stare at him, expecting an answer. He doesn't, grabbing my now empty glass. Coming around the counter, he lifts me away from the stool and brings me toward the couch. We plop down and, when I'm cradled in his arms, he grabs a blanket and wraps it around us both.

I rest my head on his shoulder, sighing wistfully when his hand makes its way into my hair, massaging my scalp in such a way that I'm put into a full state of comfort.

"Sleep, sweet Raven, I have a hunch that our day tomorrow will be a tough one," he says, and then sighs, leaning his head back on the couch.

Even though I try my damnedest to stay awake so the shadowed beast stays away from me, the drink, mixed with Phoenix's warm body, lulls me into a restful sleep.

The monsters can wait another night.

"ALRIGHT, we have an hour, is there anything else we need to get before we head to the damn lion's den?" Pierce asks, looking toward Phoenix as he cleans a damn gun on the kitchen counter.

Please tell me how I haven't thrown a fit yet about the fact that the guys all keep guns so close. They've kept them concealed so damn well it didn't cross my mind to worry about them.

Today, however?

Today they've brought out a damn box full of shit. It's been locked, of course, but there are all sorts of guns in here, and I'm not educated on firearms enough to pick out anything.

I do know each of them now have a handgun in their possession, and Pierce is currently looking at a longer gun with what can only be described as a longing expression. I glare at him when he goes to stroke it like it's a lover.

Like he strokes my skin when we're in bed.

He grins and places a placating kiss to my forehead, breathing me in before he backs away and looks at the other guys, waiting for an answer to his question.

"We got what we need," Phoenix says, doing some magic voodoo shit with his hands to piece the gun back together.

I at least know the safety gets flicked on, so I guess that's a good thing to know. He meets my eyes and winks at me, a dirty chuckle leaving him when I blush afterward.

Him holding me last night after my flashback was the best thing he could have done. Though I'm glad Pierce and River are working on...whatever it is they are...without someone holding me...all of the memories are becoming more and more prominent in my brain, which is normal as it's coming up on the anniversary of my mother's death.

I bite my lip and Pierce leans into me, turning my chin so I face him. He pulls my lip free and nips at it himself, grinning when he pulls back.

"Alright," he booms, "get our shit ready boys. I gotta tell the little bird something before we go."

I furrow my brows and my heart picks up. That nickname hasn't been used as casually before, with a smile on his face. So either he's about to turn on me or turn me on. Not sure which I want right now.

River places a kiss to my cheek as he passes by, and Phoenix squeezes my shoulder gently. Once they're both gone, I'm left alone with the boy I grew to love and hate and love again.

The sincerity in his eyes as he places himself between my legs is intense, and my heart begins to thunder so hard in my chest I can hear it. Pierce draws his hands up my arms, and brackets my face with them. The rough calluses on his fingers rub a steady friction on my cheeks as his forest green eyes meet my deep blue eyes. He swallows hard, and I don't know what he's about to say but I wish he'd get it over with. I see the shimmering of tears well up in those eyes, and I know that's so rare for him.

I watch as he nods to himself, his brows furrowing for a second in the cutest moment of confusion before he stands taller and throws his shoulders back in confidence. He keeps his hands on my face for a second before he reaches down and grabs my hands, placing them between his.

"Raven," he says, looking down at our hands, then back up to me, "I know shit's been bad. For you, for me, for all of us, honestly. I know I've treated you like shit and I ran the second you sent me running, but I don't want to run anymore, Blue." He swallows, nodding to himself before meeting my gaze again. He tracks the tear that falls down my cheek, and swipes it away quickly before grabbing my hands. "I've caused a lot of pain since you've been here, baby girl, and so this is me apologizing. I'm so fucking sorry," he chokes out, his voice breaking on the last word.

"I'm so incredibly fucking sorry. I'll fall at your feet and worship you until the end of time if you let me. I know they're just words and I need to show you with actions, but let me start with the declaration that I, Pierce Jackson, am still so head over heels in love with you, Raven Hill. I'll go to the ends of the universe and back for you and know it won't be enough."

He inhales once more and breathes out a long breath before he speaks again, his eyes searching mine for something, I'm not sure. He seems to find something to keep him going, though.

"Please, for the love of everything, tell me you are still in love with me and that the little backyard wedding we planned for those two kids can still be a possibility one day? I want you forever, little bird, please allow me to make all of this past year up to you."

The world is silent following his confession, except for the pounding of my heart and the rushing of blood through my ears. My hands are shaking, and my chest is heaving with the breaths I'm struggling to take. My eyes meet his and flit between them. I'm sure I look panicked, because he leans in closer to me, holding my hands tighter to keep me from flying away from this moment.

I may have broken us, and he may have crushed us further into oblivion, but I know in the end, we're on the same journey back to us.

I look up at the boy—no, the man—who stole my heart. The one who has owned it since the moment we met. The way he's looking at me? It makes me realize he's been waiting for this moment much longer than he's aware of.

Inhale.

Exhale.

"Pierce..."

To be continued in Phoenix Flames.

acknowledgments

This book was an absolute BEAST to write, edit, etcetera. Chapter 9? Yeah, that put me in a 3 month writing slump that I hope I never get put into again. Raven is much like me, and goes through a lot of the things I've gone through, just with a little bit more pizzazz, I suppose. I cannot wait to continue her story in the next installment of A Conspiracy of Ravens. I know the cliffy was brutal, and I'll probably do it again (oops?) but know that I will give all characters their justice, and our main cast will have a fabulous HEA! Now...on to thanking all of the wonderful people in my life who really helped this book sing!

My husband...the original dedication didn't make the book, so here's where I'll say thank you for being my very own group of guys all wrapped up in one–minus the extra dicks, fortunately or unfortunately. We'll never figure that out. This book would not have gotten done without you. Not even just monetarily. You are the absolute light to my life, and you have encouraged me and picked me up when I was feeling like shit. Thank you so much. I love you.

My kids...who should not have read this book until they're well above the age to do so. You guys helped me to write this whole thing with all of your creativity and your support over this summer. I appreciate you cheering me on, and I can't wait to work with you both on more stuff! Love you, bugs. <3

MiMi...you and I have been through a very short journey together this past year, but it's felt like a lifetime. I'll continue to push you just as much as you push me. We're in this forever together, and I hope you know that I'm just as proud of your journey as you are of mine. This is now a sisterhood, and you can't get rid of me. :)

Becca...your journey pushed me to do this. From writing my own story, to getting months of writers block over Chapter 9, to BETA reading for the Progeny Duet... I wouldn't have done this without being able to see *you* do it. Thank you for letting me in on your journey. And as I said above to MiMi, this is a sisterhood, and you're stuck with me!

P.S.: Go buy Progeny & Retribution by Rebecca Rathe!

Jenny...I don't know what number book attempt this is since we've known each other, but you have been the ultimate kick in the pants hype woman each and every time. Thank you for being you and helping me to be better throughout the last 10 years.

Alayna...you came from out of flippin' nowhere, and I feel like the BookTok gods gave us this friendship. You have been awesome at helping me with things, even if it's just a shoulder to lean on! I cannot wait to see where this friendship goes. *This is your cue to write your book, now!* ;)

My BETA Team...y'all were absolutely incredible and I am so freaking grateful for your time and energy. You have hyped me up and given me the final push to get through this amazing journey.

My ARC & Street Team... I absolutely enjoyed your feedback, even if it did have me editing/formatting up until that final bell rang to get this uploaded on time. You helped make this book shine, and you've been singing about it from the rooftops!

*My readers...*you don't know me that well, unless you've seen me on TikTok, and I am so eternally grateful that you decided to give these characters a shot. Thank you for your time and energy. The cast of Pierce Me will return in December, so you won't be hanging on that cliff for *too* long.

Sincerely, Shelby Lee

P.S.: If you could be so kind as to leave a review for Pierce Me, it would make my dark and twisted heart soar to new heights! Reviews are indie authors' bread and butter!

P.P.S.: Join my reader group on Facebook: Shelby Lee's Dark and Twisted Readers as well as Shelby Lee's Spoiler Room.

We'll be waiting for you...

also by shelby lee

A Conspiracy of Ravens

Pierce Me

Phoenix Flames

ACoR 3 (Early 2023)

ACoR 4 (Mid 2023)

Novellas

Overnight: An ACoR Spin-off Novella

about the author

Shelby Lee is a dark romance author specializing in the act of trauma dumping into her own stories in the hopes of eventually healing herself, and possibly others, along the way. She resides in a semi-small town in Nebraska with her husband, two kids, and guinea pigs.

When she's not writing, she's mentoring youth in the community on the off chance she just might leave the world a better place than she found it.

Other than that, you can probably find her on TikTok.

Find me on linktr.ee/authorshelbylee

facebook.com/authorshelbylee

instagram.com/@authorshelbylee

tiktok.com/@authorshelbylee

patreon.com/AuthorShelbyLee